DOING BIZNESS

A NUCLEAR THRILLER

By Mary Mycio

KIPLING GLOBAL MEDIA
WEST CHESTER, PA

On the cover: photograph of intercontinental nuclear
missile silo in Ukraine, by Mary Mycio.
Graphic design by Amy Ackerman

About the Book

This book is based on real events, beginning with a Ukrainian nuclear official offering 100 kilograms of highly enriched uranium to two American military contractors in the early 1990s. The events reported by the fictional Faxnews-Ukraine actually took place although many were only revealed years later. All of the characters are fictional. But the story told in *Doing Bizness* really could have happened. To experts on the design of the Soviet ZBV3 nuclear artillery shells, the scenario will be entirely plausible.

About the Author

A pioneering American journalist who first visited Kiev in still-Soviet 1989 to do a clandestine interview about Chernobyl for *OMNI* magazine, Mary Mycio reported on the nuclear disarmament of Ukraine for the *Los Angeles Times* and was the first American journalist to visit a strategic nuclear bomber base after the Soviet Union's collapse. The author of *Wormwood Forest: A Natural History of Chernobyl,* she is also a lawyer and works as a media development consultant in transitional countries.

TABLE OF CONTENTS

CHAPTER 1:

FISSION

FAXNEWS-UKRAINE

<u>December 25, 1991 (Kiev, Ukraine)</u>. The Soviet Union's breakup left Ukraine with a first class force package including: 700,000 ground, air, and air defense forces; the Black Sea Fleet; 500,000 paramilitary troops and 4,000 strategic and tactical nuclear weapons. The Ukrainian President rejected Russia's proposal to create joint armed forces for the Commonwealth of Independent States (CIS). "Ukraine will nationalize the conventional forces on its territory and personnel will take an oath of loyalty to Ukraine." He agreed to put the nuclear weapons under joint CIS command and to abide by the Strategic Arms Reduction Treaty.
END

Faxnews- Ukraine – Your source of English-language news about Ukraine

---

*S*weat trickled down the colonel's spine as he paced the frigid tarmac in front of four loaded AK-47s. The moonless heavens blazed with stars.

"He has clearance from Kiev. He's coming." A mechanical voice crackled over the walkie-talkie he gripped in his gloved hand together with the crumpled midnight cable from the Commander of the Long-Range Air Forces:

GEN. MIKHAIL SMIRNOV AWOL STOP ARREST UPON ARRIVAL AT 0500 ETA UZIN STRATEGIC BOMBER BASE STOP ILYUSHIN-78 TAIL NO. 86659 ORDERED TO LRAF MOSCOW STOP.

Moscow: now the capital of a separate country.

Colonel Pavlo Demiuk stuffed the walkie-talkie into the pocket of his rough wool coat. The handcuffs grew heavier when the Ilyushin's headlights appeared on the southern horizon.

"Ready!" he ordered and the officers snapped to attention as the Il-78 approached the runway with a distant roar of engines.

"We're arresting our commanding officer?" piped an alarmed voice.

"He stole a plane," responded an angry one. "The bastard."

Demiuk glared at the young lieutenant from Sochi. He had scowled in silent fury since the cable arrived. Next to him, three other junior officers shivered on the tarmac in the frozen February night.

"I'm your commanding officer," Demiuk grunted with little enthusiasm as the fat, heavy Ilyushin taxied on the tarmac, the numbers 86659 painted on its tail.

The tankers acted as flying gas stations, built for the in-air refueling of nuclear bombers during their long, grim -- and now hypothetical -- missions to American cities.

Demiuk squinted into the clouds of steam and exhaust glowing in the headlights. *He can see us*, he thought when the plane screamed to a halt in from of them. Gas fumes permeated the air.

The cockpit door opened.

"Aim!" barked Demiuk as Smirnov climbed out of the plane to face the subordinates ordered to arrest him. The general flicked his chin at the colonel.

"So, my old friend, this unpleasant task has fallen to you," he said. The backlighting from the tanker's headlights hid his eyes but exhaustion tugged at the patrician features under the silver fur officers hat.

Demiuk swallowed what felt like a dry rock. "The Commander of the Long-Range Air Forces of the Commonwealth of Independent States has ordered me to put you under arrest for violations of military and criminal codes."

Smirnov glanced at the circle of AK-47s.

"At ease, boys," he said, shouting when they hesitated: "Put down those fucking guns!"

Three of them lowered their weapons at the command. But the lieutenant from Sochi didn't move.

"God damn it, I ordered you to aim!" Demiuk boomed as the wavering group raised their guns, their eyes darting back and forth from the general to the colonel. They had rotten attitudes. All the Soviet officers did after the USSR's collapse left them ex-Soviet but still officers in armies belonging to no one.

Demiuk spoke as calmly as he could. "General, you are charged with insubordination and stealing state property and are relieved of your command pending the investigation."

While flying the Ilyushin from Russia's Far East to Moscow, Smirnov reported engine trouble and requested permission to land at his home base in newly independent Ukraine. When Moscow denied it, Smirnov, scion of a military dynasty that led Russia's 19th century conquest of the Caucasus, disobeyed and flew the Ilyushin to Uzin.

"I can't steal from a state that no longer exists," said Smirnov.

Demiuk stabbed a gloved finger at the tanker. "By disobeying orders, you stole that plane. Your duty as an officer is to surrender."

"Listen to me, Colonel," said Smirnov and Demiuk heard the entreaty in his voice. "If I surrender, it will be your turn tomorrow and after that, all of you." Smirnov directed a level gaze at the young officers. "Moscow wants to close us. As we stand here freezing our asses off, they're cabling orders to fly six more Ilyushins to Russia."

Demiuk blanched and the light sweat froze on his face, like sharp daggers. "A whole regiment?"

"The second regiment will follow in March. General Konstantinov is arriving at 1300 hours to make the announcement."

Gen. Sergei Konstantinov, the Commander of the Long-Range Air Forces, last visited Uzin to inaugurate the Tu-95 strategic nuclear bombers that the Americans called "Bears". Demiuk had just been transferred.

"How about us?" Demiuk asked with alarm. *The Ilyushins are our future.*

Smirnov's dropped his shoulders and sighed. "Because of the special circumstances following the Soviet Union's collapse, each officer will have a choice to transfer with the planes to…" The general's voice trailed as if for greater impact. "Vladivostok."

Demiuk's involuntary groan conveyed his distaste for Russia's frigid Pacific coast. But his only skill was commanding junior security officers at strategic nuclear bases.

"That's something to look forward to, isn't it, Comrade?" Smirnov eyes glinted. "They're already bursting with all the poor bastards withdrawn from East Germany. That means no more *shashliki* roasts with vegetables from Maria's garden."

Demiuk's wife would be heartbroken over the move. She was never happier than with her hands deep in the black earth of their backyard. They long ago tired of base-hopping. Komsomolsk, Mishelevka, Riga. The USSR had made up one sixth of the world's land mass, with military bases in 11 time zones. But somehow the army always stationed him too close to the Arctic – until Smirnov helped him transfer to his native Ukraine. He and Maria eagerly returned home.

"And the bombers, Misha?" In his alarm, Demiuk called his friend by his nickname. They maintained strict formality in public. "Do they go, too?"

"Right now, no," said Smirnov. "No one needs them."

The bombers were good for nothing but bombing. The Ilyushin-78 tankers, though, were good for plenty. Their capacity for carrying aviation fuel made them militarily dangerous during the Cold War. Their dual capacity for carrying dry cargo made them commercially valuable during peace.

"What happens if we stay?" asked Demiuk,

"We will receive honorable discharges, or…"

"Vladivostok or an honorable discharge just three years from my pension? Are you kidding me? That's not a fucking choice."

The junior officers lowered their guns and stared as Demiuk absorbed the blow about to hit them all. Even the lieutenant from Sochi appeared shocked. The Ilyushin's headlights glinted off the handcuffs he still clutched along with the cable and Moscow's impossible orders.

Smirnov's voice snapped him back. "Pavlo!" he said sharply. "Listen to me!"

His friend rose into his epaulets. "I have a plan to keep the planes – and us – in Uzin without any discharges. But we don't have much time. I want the officers in the mess hall at 0600."

Demiuk saw the blank spot left on Smirnov's coat. They both snipped the SA patches off their uniforms that snowy December evening when the last General Secretary announced on television that the Soviet Union was no more. It was darker than the surrounding fabric that faded with time.

SA. Soviet Army. Not anymore.

He snapped to attention and saluted.

"Comrade General."

Moscow be damned.

*A*nton Zvezda sat in the back of the mess hall, apart from the other engineers, his arms crossed. Rumors had ricocheted across the base when news of the midnight cable spread and the officers expected to hear exciting details about Smirnov's arrest. Their loud chatter punctuated by clinking dishes muted when the obviously free General strode inside at 0600, followed by Colonel Demiuk. Surprised murmuring rose above the assembly but most of the officers snapped to attention.

Zvezda scanned the room. All three divisions were there: the tankers, bombers and nuclear warhead custodians. Most of the bomber pilots stayed seated in the back, along with Zvezda's fellow 12th Directorate officers who kept exclusive charge of the nuclear weaponry. The 12th Directorate didn't take orders from Smirnov. Like Zvezda, they came out of curiosity.

"At ease," said Smirnov, ignoring the insubordination. He laid a sky-blue folder with a yellow stripe next to a tray of Georgian mineral water on the head table.

"Comrades," he began, "I know that many of you are surprised to see me but I will be brief." After recapping Moscow's orders to transfer the tanker regiment to Vladivostok, Smirnov waited for the eruption of shock in the mess hall to subside before continuing: "But we are not going to obey those orders. They are illegal."

Zvezda stiffened. *Illegal?*

"Bullshit."

The challenge came from the back of the room. Yuri Aivazian, a bomber pilot, stood up and pointed at the general. Like 12th Directory officers, bomber pilots had been selected for ideological fidelity and obedience. Aivazian's passport identified him as Armenian but he hailed from the Donetsk region in the eastern part of the Ukrainian S.S.R. He considered himself a Soviet. For most of his own life, Zvezda had, too.

Smirnov ignored the pilot. "The orders are illegal. I am going to disobey them and order you to do the same."

"Those orders came from the highest commander of the Long-Range Air Forces!"

The swarthy pilot marched to the front of the hall and crossed his arms in defiance, his worn leather jacket cracked at the elbows. The mess hall buzzed over the confrontation.

Smirnov raised his hands for quiet. "Since the USSR collapsed, the strategic nuclear weapons in Ukraine, Belarus and Kazakhstan are now under the joint command of the Commonwealth of Independent States. And that includes Uzin."

The officers murmured agreement. They didn't know what the CIS was, but they knew that they answered to it. So did Aivazian, who said nothing.

"Under that command structure, the Russian president has sole authority…"

Aivazian interrupted: "…to order the Ilyushins to leave Uzin."

Smirnov poured a steady stream of mineral water into a glass. "The Russian President has the sole authority to launch a nuclear attack. That is the only authority he has."

Zvezda's head pounded in mute rage and disgust over the disloyalty. The USSR had collapsed into a surreal nightmare in which everything appeared the same but monstrously malformed. Ukraine couldn't be independent. It was a plot to destroy Russia. For weeks, he tried to ignore it, sticking to the 12th Directorate's precise procedures.

And now, the general of an elite strategic nuclear bomber base had the audacity to disobey orders? He barely contained himself when Smirnov said: "Under Ukrainian law, those tankers are Ukrainian property."

Zvezda bit his lip and tasted blood.

"Russia has no authority to order them to leave this territory without the Ukrainian President's permission," the traitorous general continued. "And he did not allow the Ilyushins to leave. He understands their value as cargo planes."

Aivazian paced in front the head table. "You call that turncoat a president?" he asked with a sneer that Zvezda felt on his own face. "We are a strategic nuclear bomber base. Ukrainian law means shit here. So do Ukrainian presidents."

Once a Communist Party propagandist, the President had wrapped himself in the blue and yellow flag of Ukrainian bourgeois nationalism. The same colors decorated the folder that Smirnov picked up while he waited for the assembly to absorb his last statement.

"Maybe that's true," Smirnov's voice grew louder. "But given the circumstances, we have a choice. Obey Russia's orders, in violation of Ukrainian law and, I might add, our own self-interest. Or disobey, put ourselves under Ukraine's protection and start building our future."

"You mean your future," Aivazian shouted. "You just want to keep your ass out of jail."

Zvezda watched the general stand at attention and open the folder. *The cynical piece of shit.*

"Comrades, I have made my choice and order you to follow me." Smirnov began reading from a sheet of paper that the new Ukrainian Ministry of Defense cabled to every military unit in the country.

"I, Mikhail Smirnov, hereby join the military service of Ukraine…"

The words punctured Zvezda's stomach and he started in slight relief when Aivazian spun on his heels to face the head table.

"This is mutiny!" he cried, pointing his finger impudently at Smirnov. A handful of pilots murmured agreement but the tanker officers leaned forward, engrossed by the drama.

"Shut the fuck up, Aivazian!" shouted a tanker pilot at the front of the room.

"Yeah," said the engineer next to him. "We've had enough of Moscow giving the orders."

Smirnov continued the oath: "I swear to the people of Ukraine to be faithful and committed, to execute my military obligations, the orders of commanders and to unswervingly adhere to the Constitution and laws of Ukraine. I will never betray the people of Ukraine."

Smirnov saluted Demiuk and handed him the folder. "We must hurry. General Konstantinov will arrive in a few hours."

Aivazian turned around as Demiuk recited the infuriating oath, his rage dissolving into disbelief when he saw the officers' nodding heads. "You're traitors if you go along with this," he shouted. But the din of shocked and hurried voices drowned out his words.

When Demiuk finished, men began clustering around the head table. "Now, we'll do this alphabetically," he said, glancing at his watch before reading the first name on the roster. "Capt. Aivazian, Yuri."

The bomber pilot stormed out of the mess hall, shouting: "You know what they do to fucking traitors!"

Demiuk watched the rest of the bomber pilots follow him before calling out the next name.

Despite his disgust, Zvezda sat riveted to his seat, imagining Konstantinov arresting them all – and the penalty for mutiny was death.

But by the time the treacherous colonel reached the "Ts", the tally became clear. Both tanker regiments followed Smirnov to the man and left the mess hall to drive trucks onto the runway. No Il-78s could take off and General Konstantinov couldn't land without Smirnov's permission.

The bomber pilots and 12th Directorate boycotted entirely. They could stay in Uzin so long as the warheads remained and didn't need to take risky oaths to save their hides.

Zvezda stormed out of the mess hall. The sun had risen to a crystalline February morning and he squinted at the glare reflecting off the snow. He walked from the mess hall to his quarters near the depots, his breath steaming with every stride. His heart left Uzin months ago. Smirnov's treason supplied just the push the rest of him needed to follow.

When he reached the interior control point, the guard waved him in and he passed through the first perimeter of the 12th Directorate zone. The officers and their families lived there, in low-slung white buildings nestled against the second perimeter fence. The deceptively peaceful hillocks beyond it contained the reinforced concrete bunkers.

Though inside the base, the nuclear weapons that they held were under the exclusive jurisdiction of the 12th Directorate, which bypassed Smirnov and reported to the Ministry of Defense in Moscow. The chain of command remained the same even if it now answered to the Commonwealth of Independent States.

Zvezda spat at the idea. He answered only to Russia.

Silent forklifts herded under the guard tower. Since Moscow and Washington agreed to lower alert levels, they worked overtime to put the nuclear warheads from the cruise missiles into storage. But they had too many warheads and too few bunkers. The transfer of tactical warheads to Russia added to their headaches. Uzin had many dozens of them, ZBV3s for 152-mm howitzers that delivered a 1 kiloton punch – the smallest nuclear munitions in the world. But storing them took up a lot of space. The planners planned for everything except peace, so the overflow weapons were in field storage near the bomber hangars.

Zvezda trudged up the concrete stairwell to his room in building No. 7. He hadn't been at Uzin long after transferring from the Black Sea Fleet in the Crimea. The extra work meant Uzin needed extra hands.

He enjoyed Sevastopol, a jewel of a city, exclusively for the elite Navy and closed to the public. The fleet's commander refused to administer the traitorous Ukrainian oath. Separatists demanding the peninsula secede and join Russia filled television reports.

The crucifix that greeted Zvezda on the wall above his bed did little to quiet his anger.

He walked over to a shelf to pick out the Bible and retrieve his tool kit. When he first started talking about the Church, the others laughed. Then they stopped talking to him altogether, except when one of them paired with Zvezda as 12th Directorate regulations demanded whenever they touched a warhead.

The tool kit unzipped silently from the lubricants accumulated over many years and the instruments inside conjured memories of playing with similar tools at his father's feet. His old man designed the special wrench used for removing hydrogen filters. The chemical reaction of plutonium with the conventional explosives produced volatile hydrogen gas inside the warheads. The filters collected it and needed regular replacing.

He used the wrench's metal arch to flip the Bible open to the dog-eared, annotated and underlined pages of the Revelations. Raised by stalwart Communist atheists, he knew nothing of such prophecies until the monastery priest in neighboring Dikanka told him. But when he read of God's wrath in the fiery Armageddon, he remembered his father's stories from the early atomic tests in Semipalatinsk and imagined the staggering force of the unleashed atom in nuclear war.

For most of his 35 years, Zvezda's creed had been Communism and the nuclear force had been Nature. But St. John the Divine revealed that Lenin was a liar and the nuclear force was of God. Zvezda understood that his work had become God's work.

He leafed past his notes penciling "Russia is the Third Rome" next to a reference to the Whore of Babylon and found his favorite passage in Chapter 8:

> *And the third angel sounded, and*
> *There fell a great star from*
> *Heaven, burning as it were a*
> *Lamp, and it fell upon the third*
> *Part of the rivers, and upon the*
> *Fountains of water;*
> *And the name of the star is Wormwood;*
> *And the third part of the waters*
> *Became Wormwood, and many men*
> *Died of the waters,*
> *For they were made bitter.*

The monastery priest told Zvezda that the Ukrainian word *chernobyl* meant wormwood.

Zvezda shuddered with distaste. Ukrainian was a demented Polish mockery of Russian, spoken by peasants and bourgeois nationalists. But the Chernobyl nuclear reactor that exploded in 1986 burned many lamps and its radioactive fallout made the waters bitter, indeed.

He slammed the Bible closed. The signs of the Apocalypse were starting just as Russia repented the sin of Communism. For centuries, Moscow protected the one true Orthodox Christian Church. Now, Orthodoxy had to protect Russia in her time of weakness, holding her far-flung fragments together so that the Third Rome could again resurrect.

He stuffed the Bible into a pocket of his overalls. The tool kit on his bed belonged to the state.

But that state no longer existed.

He closed the zipper.

He would go to Kiev, the birthplace of Russia and her Church.

CHAPTER 2

PROBLEMS IN ACCOUNTING

FAXNEWS-UKRAINE

<u>April 6, 1992 (Kiev, Ukraine).</u> The Ukrainian President halted the transfer of tactical nuclear weapons to Russia. "We need guarantees that they are not falling into the wrong hands." Ukraine now has 2300 tactical weapons and 176 land-based intercontinental ballistic missiles. "As for the strategic bombers, we don't know," said a member of parliament.

<u>April 15, 1992 (Sevastopol, Ukraine).</u> The Russian Vice President told a cheering hall filled with naval officers: "Crimea is covered in Russian blood and it must be Russian." Three hours later, the President of Ukraine issued a decree taking control over all strategic forces in Ukraine, including the Black Sea Fleet.

<u>April 30, 1992 (Kiev, Ukraine).</u> Ukraine and Russia agreed on a procedure for removing the remaining tactical nuclear weapons. Representatives of each side will authenticate each warhead and check serial numbers against the logs kept at the 12th Directorate in Moscow. "Our accounting and verification procedure will be more reliable than what is being used to remove tactical weapons from other republics," said an anonymous source.
END

Faxnews-Ukraine – Your source of English-language news about Ukraine

*D*an Kruger pulled two quart-sized cartons from under a tray of marinating steaks and carried them to the kitchen island where his wife sliced carrots with expert speed. He picked a yellow dish out of the ceramics stacked on the island in utilitarian decoration.

"Perfect. With the blue salad bowl, we'll have the color of their flag," he said, shaking the potato salad out of the *Culinary Corner* carton with growing dismay. "This isn't right. It needs more mayonnaise."

"There isn't any mayonnaise," Jean said without interrupting her carrot chopping. "It's balsamic vinaigrette."

The *Culinary Corner* was the only take-out place in Golden Springs, Virginia, that cooked to Jean Kruger's exacting standards.

"It needs mayonnaise," Dan declared and marched to the refrigerator, searching the contents until he found the unopened jar of Hellman's behind chilling bottles of Heineken.

"You said that they drowned stuff in mayonnaise," Kruger said, spooning quivery globs onto the potatoes. He didn't want to blow it over a delicate yuppie dressing.

Jean tore leaves off a head of romaine. "That's over there, Dan. I'm sure Rozpad wants to try new things. He's in the U.S. for the first time."

"He's been in Washington, which isn't the same thing. I want him to feel at home, among friends."

Dan tossed the potatoes until they resembled lumpy glue. "I owe you for this one, honey," he said. His job depended on it.

"We can stipulate to that, Kruger."

Jean called him "Kruger" when staking out a tough negotiating position. He could always tell his wife's moods by what she called him.

"You owe my mother, too," she added.

Kruger winced. His mother-in-law clung to her disapproval of him even after 18 years. Not only did she sniff at his mongrel American lineage but also at his failure to prolong it by fathering a grandchild. She'd never let him forget a favor, even if it benefitted her daughter, whose Americanized name she refused to acknowledge.

"What do you want me to do?" he asked, knowing her answer.

"I'll call Dr. Jensen next week."

"Next week?" His voice croaked. He didn't mind coming into a cup. But he hated the clinic's smell of antiseptic sex and Jensen's fake sympathy for Kruger's sluggish sperm. If everyone bred like bunnies, the good fertility doctor would be quietly practicing proctology instead of mugging for TIME magazine.

"This isn't the best time to pour our finances into Jensen's bank account," he added.

Jean gave a final toss to the salad. "We've talked about this, Dan. My fertility window is closing fast. Even if…"

Don't say it out loud.

Jean continued: "Whatever happens, billions of the world's babies are born into families surviving on a dollar a day."

Kruger pointed at the stack of bills in the enamel tray that served as their inbox. "They don't have 1200 dollar mortgages to pay."

Jean tilted her head in an affectionate gaze at her husband. Beer had started to win over tennis in the contest for his 43-year-old gut and silver etched the curly black hair. But he still looked like the tie-dyed grad student she met as a freshman at Cornell and married, after his army stint.

"In the meantime, Daniel." Jean washed her hands and wiped them with a dish towel. She glanced at the digital clock on the microwave. "I think we have enough time."

The corner of Kruger's mouth turned up in a grin.

"For the old fashioned way?"

*W*hen Kruger opened the front door an hour later, he found Spike and Chopper, the Springer spaniels, rolling over in happy submission while a familiar figure crouched to scratch at their bellies.

"Hey, boss. Glad you made it on short notice. Where's Annette?" he asked. Neil Neilson, Ph.D. had parked his red MG behind Kruger's Toyota in the driveway but his voluptuous, young, second wife wasn't in it.

The dogs pawed at the guest's buff chinos, whimpering for more attention. "Oh, Susie felt feverish this morning. Nothing serious, but Annette doesn't want to leave her with a sitter. She sends her apologies."

Two-year-old Susie came down with "nothing serious" whenever her father had a business dinner, so Kruger hadn't seen Annette for months. Too bad, he thought, following Neilson and the dogs in the kitchen. He liked seeing her expensive new breasts.

Neilson kissed Jean on the cheek she offered over the salad bowl. "Beautiful as usual, Esquire."

"Thanks, Doc," Jean said. "I'd say the same for you. But you look tired."

Kruger popped the cork out of a California Chardonnay and handed Neilson a beer. "Yeah, it's amazing how no work can exhaust you."

Once funded lavishly for the Defense of the Free World, military contractors like their employer, Defense Systems Analysis, were reeling from their sudden redundancy. Free World taxpayers decided they felt safe after the other superpower imploded and slashed military budgets.

Neilson poured Heineken into a glass. "So, Dan, tell me why I had to cancel my tennis game with Sam Goldman. He has a lead on coal exports from Uzbekistan or Kazakhstan or one of those 'stan' countries."

Jean carried the tray of steaks to the island and turned them over in the marinade, releasing a waft of soy sauce and garlic. "Aren't we Mr. Cultural Sensitivity today?"

Neil grinned. "Sorry Jean. I didn't mean to offend your Slavic solidarity."

"The 'stan countries', as you call them, aren't Slavic. The people speak Turkic languages and they're Muslims."

Neilson raised his hands in mock defense. "Hey, counselor, I'm just a lowly physicist and a lowlier businessman. I can't keep up with all the details of the new world order."

Kruger reached for the manila folder that had kept him busy that morning with microfilm at the library. "The chairman of the Ukrainian Committee for Nuclear Safety and Security is coming for dinner tonight," he announced.

Neilson raised an eyebrow. "And this interests me how?"

"Ukraine now has the world's third largest nuclear arsenal on its territory." Kruger held up a newspaper article he had found in the *Washington Post*. "Remember, last fall, Congress passed the Nunn-Lugar Amendment to finance the safety of the ex-USSR's nuclear weapons? If that includes the weapons in Ukraine, it could mean contracts for us. This guy can put our foot in the door."

"He's in D.C. for a seminar on nuclear non-proliferation," said Jean. "My mother met him at a Ukrainian-American reception."

She pursed her lips. "I can show you where Ukraine is on the map, Neil."

"Nah, I know it's in Africa. The long lost Uke tribe of Lake Tanganyika. I read about them in Scientific American."

Jean narrowed her eyes but Kruger interrupted a doubtlessly witty comeback by handing Neilson the brand new almanac he bought on the way home from the library.

"Neil, why don't you brush up on the new world order while I start up the grill?"

Neilson scanned the Countries of the World entry for Ukraine. "So, 52-million people," he read. "Big tribe."

"And the world never noticed them all these years," said Jean Kruger, born Yevhenia Beniuk on a ship of displaced persons heading for Ellis Island in 1950.

Mesquite and cherry wood smoke drifted across the patio, mixing with Kruger's cigar for a pungent combination that made the man next to him cough harshly.

The same age as Kruger, Roman Rozpad appeared ten years older. But the blue eyes peering behind clunky Soviet eyeglasses reflected a sharp intelligence.

"Trying to kill him with secondhand smoke, Dan?" Neilson composed his face back into the false cheer he directed at the chairman of the Ukrainian State Committee for Nuclear Safety and Security.

"Now, Mr. Rozpad, the American government is very concerned -- which is diplomatic for shitting a brick -- over the nuclear weapons left in the Ukraine when the Soviet Union collapsed."

Next to Rozpad, Jean scribbled on a notepad wedged between baskets of chips and nuts. But before translating, she said: "It's Ukraine, Neil."

"That's what I said: the You-craine."

"You shouldn't use the "the"," Kruger explained, adding air quotes. "They consider it belittling, like a reference to a region rather than a country. It's just Ukraine; no the's."

"After reading that almanac, I can tell you how much pig iron, coal and manganese they have along with all those nukes. And you're bugging me about a "the"? Beside, how can he feel belittled if he doesn't understand me?"

"Easy boss, just keep it in mind," Kruger called over his shoulder as he headed for the kitchen. Lilacs bloomed over the psychedelic shades of green in Jean's moss garden. She called it her Zen corner and spent hours cleaning it, picking out the tiniest debris, while mulling over litigation strategies.

Rozpad swallowed the last of the wine in his glass and murmured something to Jean.

"He likes this wine" she told Neilson as Kruger came out of the French doors carrying the blue and yellow bowls to a small table by the grill. The dogs, waiting in the shade underneath, thumped their stumpy tails in anticipation of the rewards that followed human activity by the big smoke maker.

Jean picked up the wine bottle and poured the guest of honor another glass while they chatted in Ukrainian.

"What's he saying?" Neil asked.

"Mr. Rozpad's parents have a wine business."

"I didn't know that Ukraine produces wine," said Kruger.

"In Crimea and Transcarpathia," Jean translated. "The Mossandra dessert wines are well regarded."

"By Commies, maybe," Neil muttered. "Let's go back to the subject, please?"

Rozpad nodded upon hearing Jean's translation.

"In my meetings with government officials this week, they asked what we are planning to do with our nuclear weapons."

"Well, what *are* you planning to do with them?" Neilson asked the guest.

Rozpad reached for a potato chip. "We will dispose of them. Last week, our president announced that Ukraine will become a party to the START treaty together with Belarus and Kazakhstan. But our parliament must ratify it."

The Strategic Arms Reduction Treaty cutting U.S. and Soviet arsenals was signed in the U.S.S.R.'s waning days and orphaned by its demise. Washington desperately wanted its nuclear heirs to adopt it.

"Do you know when?" asked Neilson.

Rozpad examined the cheese plate while Jean translated the question.

"That's a political question, Neil," she added. "Roman used to work as a research physicist like you and, from what he's told me, you'll be interested in hearing about his current job."

Neilson drank from his second bottle of beer while Jean translated.

"My job is just beginning. Before, Moscow did the accounting of our nuclear materials. Some of the log books remained in Ukraine after independence. But Russia took many of them so we must create our own inventory."

Kruger jerked back in his chair. "You mean you don't know what you have?"

Rozpad displayed little concern and Jean translated his response. "The nuclear materials are in many locations: nuclear power plants, research institutes, factories."

"Well guarded, I hope," said Kruger.

Rozpad responded: "Guarded?" Jean stressed the question mark. "These are not weapons. The institutions keep them on their premises, in sealed rooms. But they are not guarded."

Disturbed by that bit of intelligence, Kruger returned to what made it alarming. "Mr. Rozpad, you mentioned log books? Did you mean books made of paper?"

Rozpad nodded when Jean asked for clarification.

"Tell us how that works," said Neilson, launching the guest on a long monologue.

"And this kind of accounting is used for the nuclear weapons?" Kruger asked when Jean finished translating.

Rozpad munched on salted peanuts while Jean took notes.

"I heard about America's computerized nuclear accounting system. But it costs millions of dollars my country can't afford."

Kruger mulled in silence. "This is not good," he whispered to Neilson. "They don't know what nuclear materials they have, plus their accounting is primitive." He watched Rozpad chew on a pickle spear while chatting with Jean. "Imagine if Iraq, or Iran or North Korea found any of this shit."

21

"Or terrorists," added Neilson with disquiet.

"But it's perfect for Nunn-Lugar." Kruger turned to the guest. "Mr. Rozpad, we believe it's possible to give Ukraine that computerized inventory system, if you're interested in our help."

When Rozpad said yes, Kruger continued. "The Nunn-Lugar amendment to the Pentagon budget sets aside 400 million dollars to help finance the safety and security of the former Soviet Union's nuclear weapons."

The Ukrainian brushed peanut crumbs sprinkled on his cuff. "But your government officials said my country cannot have this money."

"That's not exactly true," said Kruger, though he was sure Beltway bureaucrats had told Rozpad precisely that. He downed the last of his beer.

"Mr. Rozpad, we think Ukraine is eligible for Nunn-Lugar assistance now and we want to help you get it. But we need your help to meet with other officials in your government. Can you do that?"

"Tomorrow, I have a meeting at your State Department with Mr. George Hedgepeth. Our new Ambassador will be there, too. I will ask him to help you arrange meetings in Kiev."

Neilson leaned back in his chair and stretched out his long legs, displaying tasseled black loafers. "I'm sold, Dan. We're going for it."

Kruger relaxed visibly. "The creditors are safe for another month."

Rozpad displayed a gold incisor as he chatted, gazing past the Krugers into the kitchen.

"He says we have the biggest house he's ever seen," Jean translated.

"That's nice. If he helps us pay our mortgage, we'll invite him back."

Jean rolled her eyes. "C'mon Dan: Time for the 25 cent tour." She turned to Neilson. "Neil, the grill's ready for the steaks. Will you do the honors?"

Roman Rozpad walked to the French doors, placed his wine glass by the threshold and crouched.

"He's taking off his shoes," Kruger observed in surprise.

"It's the Ukrainian custom," Jean explained. "Like the Japanese."

"Then I say we take off ours, too," said Kruger, stooping to untie his Adidas.

Neilson's good humor overflowed from his place at the grill. "Hell, I'll take off my pants if Roz helps us win a contract."

Rozpad turned full circle in the spacious kitchen and pointed at the stained glass lampshade hanging over the kitchen table.

"He thinks it's a Tiffany lamp," she said.

Kruger laughed with little cheer. "Tell him it's a copy but thanks to him, we might be able to keep it."

Jean stared at her husband. "Desperation is a bad tactic, Kruger."

Rozpad launched into a long discourse. "He's only seen such big kitchens in magazines," Jean explained. "Their kitchens are tiny, especially in cities."

"Next, we should show him an efficiency apartment in Georgetown," Kruger interrupted.

"Khrushchev decreed Soviet women equal to men and said that their lives did not revolve around kitchen," Jean continued with a skeptical snort. "Damn Communist propaganda. The women I saw last summer worked harder *and* spent more time in the kitchen than we do. Christ, they have to do their own canning!"

Jean turned to usher the group into the dining room, talking to Rozpad.

"He agrees with me," she told Kruger. "They wanted to save space. But they still inherited the kitchens."

"Along with 6000 thermonuclear warheads," said Kruger while Rozpad admired the china and crystal in the credenza.

"For a long time they didn't know how many weapons they had. It's been chaotic since Moscow started shipping the tactical weapons to Russia last fall," Jean said after translating Kruger's comment. "The President of Ukraine suspended the shipments this month, to work with Russia to set up accounting procedures."

"Accounting with log books?" asked Kruger, though he knew the answer.

"He thinks so, but isn't sure."

Rozpad continued speaking and Jean leaned on the dining room table to take notes, pressing her hand to her forehead when he finished. "No wonder translators get paid so much," she said, picking up the notebook.

"Our Committee is charged with the safety and security of civilian nuclear fuel and other nuclear materials," she read. "Nuclear weapons are not within our jurisdiction." Seeing Kruger open his mouth to speak, she held up her hand and continued.

"In Soviet times, the 12th Directorate of the Ministry of Defense in Moscow handled everything to do with nuclear weapons – maintenance, transportation, inventory. When the USSR collapsed, the 12th Directorate in Ukraine remained there. At first, its personnel swore loyalty to the Commonwealth of Independent States. But now that our president has taken administrative control of the strategic forces, including the 12th Directorate, we are beginning to learn what exactly is on our territory."

Astounded that disciplined warhead custodians switched loyalty to Ukraine, Kruger wanted to ask more when Jean interrupted. "Dan, dear, I'm sure we'll be more comfortable discussing nuclear weapons on the patio."

"Dear" was a dead giveaway for sarcasm.

"Um, shall we move on?" he said.

Kruger led the group into the living room, flipped on the halogen ceiling lamps, and heard the guest of honor exclaim before dashing across the room, knocking an end table with his hip in an awkward maneuver around the sofas.

"What's he doing?" asked Kruger, sprinting behind him to steady a lavender lamp.

"He sees the Prymachenko," said Jean.

Rozpad spoke excitedly, leaning over an armchair to examine the large painting. The tempera primitive depicted a fanciful lion in bold primary colors.

"Well, he appreciates good Ukrainian art," she said. "Knows what it costs, too."

The guest launched into a long monologue that lasted through his inspection of the Kruger's bedroom, guest room, the second guest room that still hadn't become a nursery, and Jean's office. He found the bathroom fascinating.

While he used it, Kruger refreshed their drinks in the kitchen. "What's he been saying?"

"He dreams of owning an original Prymachenko. But he can't afford one on his salary." Jean took the wine spritzer her husband offered. "He makes 75 dollars a month, and that's the top of the government pay scale."

Low pay plus nuclear materials equaled a very bad combination.

"Hey Neil, ready for a refill?" Kruger called out of the French doors.

His face red from working the grill, Neilson leaned away from the heat and held up an empty green bottle. "The meat is ready, too."

Neil Neilson pierced a steak with the meat fork and relished the fragrant steam from the juices trickling on the embers. There had been no barbecue and no red meat at the Neilson's since Annette gave birth to Susie.

"The steroids they feed cattle cause aggression," she had explained, biting into a peach while reading a *Cosmopolitan* article entitled: "Are Your Breasts the Best?" So, he ate steaks on the sly, sometimes missing dinner at home, making Annette think he was cheating and prompting her to get the breast implants.

"They're for my self esteem," is what she said when Neilson balked at the 3,000 dollar price tag. He had to pay Ted and Tim's tuition at Princeton. The twins he had with Nancy didn't approve of their widower father's choice of a bride.

Neilson poured the last of the marinade on the steaks when Rozpad walked out, holding a full glass of wine. He smiled at the Ukrainian, who smiled back and walked over to the grill. Still smiling, though his face hurt after being frozen for an hour in the universal expression of good will, he pointed to the steaks and patted his belly. "I hope you're hungry," he said, feeling foolish and hoping that Jean would come out to translate.

Rozpad shook his head but then, as if rethinking, nodded. "In my country, is rude to say "yes" first time that host invites to eat. But I learn in America, no one ask a second time."

"You speak English?" Taken aback, Neilson rewound the day's conversations in a mental search for embarrassments.

Rozpad took a large gulp from his drink before answering: "A little bit," drawing out the vowels to sound like "leetl beet".

"So, why the translator?"

"Your American English is fast, pushed together. To comprehension hurts my head."

Flames threatened to engulf a steak and Neilson sprayed them with a water bottle. "Yeah, especially when you're dealing with our government."

"You not agree with your government?" Rozpad looked over his shoulder.

"Only under contract." Neilson waved away the aromatic clouds of steam from the sizzling juices.

The guest downed the last of his wine. "I have question."

"Shoot," said Neilson, hoping he wouldn't need to explain why he sounded like an insensitive, ugly American ass earlier in the afternoon.

When the Ukrainian didn't respond, Neilson noticed his confusion and realized he had taken him literally. "It is an expression that means I am listening," he said, enunciating every word.

Rozpad spoke so quietly, Neilson strained to hear.

"We, uh, I find 100 kilos of highly enriched uranium that is not in inventory logs." He lowered his voice even more. "What should we do with it?"

Neilson hoped the heat from the barbecue concealed the blood draining from his face. "Uranium 235?" he asked dumbly.

"What else could 90 percent pure HEU be," said Rozpad, using the English abbreviation. His language skills improved with every sentence.

It could be ten dirty nuclear bombs. It could give wet dreams to the Dictator in Iraq and Iranian mullahs. It could also be worth a pile of money and Neilson briefly speculated how much. Ninety percent pure, high-octane uranium was weapons grade, the stuff of Armageddon. The most tightly controlled and clandestinely coveted commodity on earth traded only on the blackest of markets to the scummiest of buyers from pariahs like Iran, Libya and North Korea.

Even if countries had uranium deposits of their own, they needed 200 kilos of natural uranium-238 to cull one kilo of the rare uranium-235 atoms that pack the Bomb's nuclear punch. And the "enrichment" process to collect that kilo was complicated, expensive and hard to hide from spy satellites, nuclear inspectors and cruise missiles.

But 100 kilos of the ready-made stuff could fit in a closet.

Neilson considered his fellow scientist. Now, his livelihood depended on the good will of a wannabee nuclear smuggler.

"Let me discuss this with Dan," he whispered when the Krugers walked out of the house.

"Another one, Neil?" asked Dan, pointing at his empty beer bottle.

Neilson swiped his brow with the back of his hand. "Let's break out the Stolichnaya."

After half a bottle of vodka and an hour of polite dinner conversation about the Krugers' Prymachenko masterpiece, they put Rozpad in a cab and Jean went to her home office to prepare arguments for a Monday morning motion in court.

Kruger tossed a piece of grilled fat to Chopper and the dog wriggled with joy. "That went well, huh?" he said, scraping mayonnaise into a plastic garbage bag. A lot remained on the plates.

Instead of answering, Neilson carried the vodka, an untouched bottle of Chivas and empty glasses on a tray into the kitchen. Kruger followed him in with dirty dishes and started stacking them in the dishwasher.

"What's up, boss? You looked off for the last hour, though I don't blame you after listening to Rozpad."

"How would you look if someone offered you 100 kilos of HEU?"

Kruger spun around. "What!?"

Neilson leaned against the island, sipping a scotch. "Our polite and cultured guest not only knows English. He has a side business in 90 percent enriched uranium," he said.

"You're sure you understood him?"

Neilson recounted the conversation. "Why ask me what 'we' should do with it unless he wants help to do something he's not supposed to do. Namely, sell it."

"Christ. What'd you tell him?"

"I'd talk to you and we'd meet tomorrow."

Kruger squinted in mock suspicion. The banter came no matter how black the subject, and the subjects among nuclear weapons specialists were black, indeed.

"So, why'd he offer it to you?"

"Because you look too dumb to know what it is."

Neilson's humor dissolved. "I'll bet he took my usual sarcasm about the government seriously. And I guess our comments, which we didn't think he understood, made him think that we're desperate for money."

Kruger started the dishwasher and began wrapping two leftover steaks in plastic wrap. In the old gravy-train days, Spike and Chopper got them as treats. Not anymore. The dogs whimpered in protest.

"We are desperate. At least I am," he said. "Fred is on our asses to bring in defense contracts that don't exist. The only way Jean can carry our mortgage is if we don't eat. And you have the new house with Annette and two kids in college."

And two at home, thought Neilson. After the surgery, Annette esteemed herself for six months before tiring of men (and a few women) talking to her nipples. When she joined a feminist support group, her implants ended up being the fault of men in general and Neil in particular.

"There's Nunn-Lugar," he said.

"Here's hoping," responded Kruger.

"Well, we can't tell Fred about the HEU," said Neilson. "He'll use it as the excuse he's needed to fire us. And if we get Rozpad into trouble, that means no contacts, no contracts and no jobs, too."

"But 100 kilos of loose HEU are knocking around. We can't keep it our little secret. Imagine if Rozpad tries to peddle it to someone else," Dan argued. "We have to report it."

Neilson sipped his drink.

"To whom does one report such things, anyway?" Kruger carried the leftovers to the refrigerator.

"CIA, FBI, DOD, State? Hell, no one ever offered me the chance to become my own nuclear mini-state before," Neilson said when the doorbell rang.

"Can you see who that is?" called Kruger from behind the refrigerator door.

"You expecting anyone?" Neilson walked out of the kitchen while the dogs raced ahead to perform their barking at doorbells trick.

"Not unless Rozpad is coming back to sweeten the offer with plutonium," Kruger called.

Neilson chuckled despite himself when he opened the door to find a gum-chewing brunette in a Hard Rock Café t-shirt.

"A delivery for Neil Neilson," she said, blowing a bubble.

"That's me," he said. "How'd you find…"

Before he finished, the bubble popped and the brunette said: "For you," handing him a blue-backed stack of paper. In a box on the upper left side he read the words: Annette Neilson, Plaintiff against Neil Neilson, Defendant.

ACTION FOR DIVORCE, from the law offices of Kate Olman, the bank account devouring shark known among impoverished ex-husbands for miles around as "Hate All Men".

"You serving in the armed forces?"

At Neilson's dazed stare, the process server cracked her gum. "Hey, I need to ask."

"No," said Neilson, slamming the door and walking towards Kruger, who appeared at the other end of the hallway. He leafed through the complaint until he reached the back pages listing Annette's demands: the house, alimony while she raised Susie, and 4,000 dollars a month in child support.

He held out the papers. "The nuclear state of Neil has a separatist crisis. Mind if I take asylum in your guest room?"

CHAPTER 3

RED MERCURY

FAXNEWS-UKRAINE

May 1992 Roundup

May 1: The 12th Directorate officers serving at the special warhead maintenance facilities known as S-Objects have taken the oath of loyalty to Ukraine.

May 5: While the President of Ukraine paid a working visit to Washington, D.C. the Crimean parliament declared independence.

May 7: The last shipment of tactical nuclear weapons from Ukraine arrived in Russia 25 days ahead of schedule.

May 21: The Crimean parliament rescinded its declaration of independence.

May 23: In Portugal, the presidents of the United States, Belarus, Kazakhstan, Ukraine and Russia signed the Lisbon Protocol, making all five states parties to the START treaty.
END

Faxnews-Ukraine – Your source of English-language news about Ukraine

---

*T*ariq abu Bakr splashed Johnny Walker Black Label into his glass and stared at the blank paper that refused to become his progress report to Baghdad. That's because he had no progress to report.

He swallowed his scotch, not enjoying the flavor. But after his terrifying stint as the taster at a Babil safe house, just surviving a sip of His Excellency, the Victorious, Glorious Iraqi Dictator's favorite drink filled him with a familiar elation even now, when the risk of poisoning was distant.

Tariq took another sip and went into the bathroom. A life-sized picture of the Dictator's thick moustache dangled from a string alongside the mirror. Tariq had cut it out from a cache of posters in the safe house basement, drawing in the measurements of its distance from nose, mouth and cheeks. He examined his face and painfully plucked out a tuft of nose hair threatening the perfection of the upper line. Tariq had performed the exercise every single day for years, ever since a thug from Tikrit drunkenly confided that the moustache held the key to the Dictator's favor.

Soon after, the double got poisoned. But his advice worked. The Dictator recognized the perfect replica of his moustache. When He learned of Tariq's excellent Russian and English, and his smattering of Ukrainian, He transferred him to the prestigious Petrochemical 3 – or what remained of it after the war against the American imperialists and UN inspectors.

There, under the Sultan's ruthless eye, Tariq memorized the list in English and Russian: ballistic missiles; beryllium; cruise missiles; deuterium; engineers; gas centrifuge; graphite, ultrapure; nuclear fuel rods; plutonium; triggers; trigger designs; tritium; uranium, reactor grade; uranium, weapons grade; warhead, designs; warhead, engineers; warhead, nuclear; warhead, parts; along with 87 other items he had had no success in finding since arriving in Kiev months earlier.

Tariq spun the diagram to face the bathroom tiles and returned to the blank page on the desk. The Sultan's main operations were in Russia. Ukraine was an afterthought. Petrochemical 3 wasn't sure what to make of the new country. But as a student at Patrice Lumumba University in Moscow, Tariq spent a summer on a collective farm in the Ukrainian Soviet Socialist Republic, where he picked up enough of the language to pick up the pretty peasant girls. He also learned that the "Dnipro" in the Dnipro Hotel referred to the Ukrainian name for the Dnieper River that sliced through Kiev like the Tigris in Baghdad.

They dispatched Tariq to Kiev with a fake passport identifying him as Mohammed Ali, a pile of glossy modem brochures for his legend, as well as precise instructions on finding a Bomb or the makings for one.

The ICBM missile fields and nuclear bomber bases housed warheads, but no one seriously expected Tariq to gain access to them. He was more likely to find parts. The Chernobyl nuclear plant in the north produced plutonium as well as the tritium used for "boosting" fission explosions. The heavy water production reactor somewhere in the south made deuterium. Ballistic missiles were too big to divert but the Ukrainian Missile Factory in Dnipropetrovsk had their blueprints and the Khartron institute in Kharkiv designed their guidance systems.

The Sultan ordered Tariq to buy in bulk and forbade him from even negotiating. *Just find the items, whatever it costs.*

But Tariq hadn't found anything, except the East German middleman who had yet to produce results.

So, what if I say there's a lead to gas centrifuges, who'll know, he thought, pulling up the chair when the ringing phone interrupted.

"Allah Akbar!" declared the voice on the other end. "We must meet."

Tariq sipped his scotch and listened.

"It's me, Ahmed," said the insistent voice with a southern Iraqi accent.

"Yes?" Tariq responded, cleaning his thumbnail with a calling card reading: SVETA, FOUR YOR PLESUR and a three digit hotel phone number that Tariq had memorized. Sveta pleasured him for lunch and he anticipated more for dinner.

"The usual, in 15 minutes," Ahmed commanded.

Tariq pulled on his purple silk suit and Hugo Boss loafers, smoothed a dollop of wax on his moustache and stuffed a thick wad of counterfeit 100 dollar bills into his pocket. The door to room 416 locked automatically when he walked out. Natasha, the hotel floor matron, did not interrupt her study of a Venezuelan soap opera when he deposited his key on her desk and walked through the lobby to the elevator.

Tariq took his time. A mere five-minute walk down the Khreshchatyk Boulevard would take him to the central post office.

Outside the Dnipro Hotel, the setting sun glinted off a metal arch rising above the horizon. It reminded him of the Victory-over-the-Fire-Worshipping-Persians Arch in downtown Baghdad, celebrating the Iran-Iraq War. But giant-sized bronze replicas of the Dictator's hands weren't brandishing it. Tariq had looked to make sure. It turned out to be the Friendship Arch, dedicated to Russian and Ukrainian fraternity.

Rebuilt after the devastation of World War II, Kiev had an intimacy that Moscow lacked and an ancient history still preserved in monuments like the twelfth century St. Sophia Cathedral. A chronic gasoline shortage fueled few cars on the Khreshchatyk's empty six lane expanse. The occasional Soviet model Ladas, Zhigulis and boxy Volga sedans, painted in bright primary colors, contrasted with the city's Soviet grey palate.

A similar stretch of road outside Tariq's apartment in Dictator City had four Dictators, including a giant mural of Him puffing on a cigar in dark glasses and facing Nebuchadnezzar against a backdrop of ancient Babylon. And that didn't count all the Dictators spying out of every newspaper and television channel, even wristwatches. The Kiev views were blissfully Dictator-free.

Here, the only watcher is Ahmed, Tariq thought, passing an empty granite pedestal from which a four-story Lenin once gazed into the shining future of Communism. Tariq first saw it in the days when Kiev's main square was called October Revolution. Now, they called it Independence Square and stored hunks of the long-gone Lenin in a graveyard for Soviet statuary behind the History Museum.

He weaved his way through the people enjoying the warm spring evening by the square's many fountains. He would have ignored them but too many of the young women wore tiny skirts with legs as long as Scud missiles. Tariq stopped to look when one bent over her bag.

"And that is Satan tempting you," an American voice announced. Tariq turned to see a young man in a white shirt surrounded by a curious crowd. "And we of the Missionary Evangelical Church have come here all the way from the You-nited States of America to tell you the good news. Your only hope of salvation is to give yourself up to Christ, our Savior," he declared in English. The Russian translator next to him conveyed little of the missionary's meaning and still less of his passion. Kiev crawled with American Christians on missions to convert the godless after Communism.

Tariq turned to leave, only to bump into the hard chest of a flak-jacketed policeman.

"*Bud laska, predstavte vashi dokumenti,*" his shorter but equally armored partner ordered in what Tariq recognized as Ukrainian. His heart pounded with the fear familiar from encounters with Iraqi police, but Petrochemical 3 had given him rudimentary training. Carefully, he reached into his pocket for his fake Mohammed Ali passport when the tall policeman grabbed his wrist.

"*Stiy, suka,*" he said, drawing back Tariq's lapel with his night stick and reaching into his pocket for whatever dangerous implement he suspected Tariq had concealed in there.

A *suka* was a bitch, though the expletive didn't carry the gender connotations that it did in English. "I'm sorry," Tariq said in Russian with a smile that he hoped concealed how insulted he felt. "My Ukrainian is poor."

The tall policeman leafed through the passport. "Iraq, eh?" he said, launching into a short discourse about his Iraqi brother-in-law.

"How nice," Tariq said.

"Nice?!" the officer shouted. "He's an asshole! Took off for the God damn Canary Islands and left her here with three kids I have to help support!"

Tariq held his hands out helplessly.

"What are you doing in Kiev?" asked the short policeman.

"Selling modems."

"Modems. What the fuck is a modem?"

Tariq held out his hand and slowly reached into another pocket for the brochure, slipping a counterfeit hundred inside before taking it out. The tall policeman snatched it away, unfolded it and studied the pictures. "You're selling computers?"

Tariq had learned never to make a policeman feel stupid. "Well, it's a part of a computer," he explained briefly, waiting to see what more they wanted.

"Are you familiar with the citrus market in Kiev?" The next question carried a friendlier tone. "Lemons, oranges."

"Pomegranates?" added the short policeman.

"Pomegranates aren't citrus," said the tall one.

His partner squared his shoulders in a challenge. "What the hell are they then?"

"Fucked if I know. Berries?"

"Whatever. They come from the Caucuses."

Tariq interrupted with his best imitation of outrage. "I have nothing to do with produce of any kind. I am in the high technology business."

"Are you familiar with traders from Georgia?"

"No, I'm not." Georgia didn't even have a nuclear reactor to scavenge for fuel rods. But the wines and women were said to be excellent.

The policemen backed off in unison. "Mind if we keep this?" asked the tall one, holding up the brochure with the counterfeit inside.

Tariq hesitated. He didn't have that many copies of the brochure. But he nodded and headed to the post office, where Ahmed stood in line at the International Telephone Calling Point, one of the few places in Kiev to make an international call. Even the lucky few with home phones had to order them through Moscow, days in advance.

"Allah Akbar," he hissed, fingering his tasseled, amber worry beads. "You're late! And why didn't you show up for the Finger of God meeting this morning?"

Because you were the only one there and I was getting laid…

Tariq restrained a chuckle and instead said: "I had an important meeting with a potential client." He whispered, though needlessly. The Ethiopian, Mongolian, North Korean and Cuban students in the queue loudly ordered calls to their families to find a way home after their fraternally socialist exchange program scholarships disappeared with the Soviet Union.

Ahmed snorted contemptuously. "You stink of intoxicants!"

So does our Great Leader, thought Tariq, surprising himself. The part of his mind chastising him felt miniscule compared to the dam of disloyalty unleashed by the giddy freedom of the Dictator-free environment. "So," he said smoothly, "this is why you made me delay a meeting with that client tonight?"

Ahmed handed him a folded note with his mutilated left hand, his pinky lost in a torture session during the 1980s crackdown on the Shiites. He emerged from it praising the Dictator as the worthy descendant of Ali, the fourth caliph and the original Shiite martyr. Once won, the Shiite's loyalty grew fanatic. His reputation as an informer and assassin was rivaled only by the whispers about his mental stability. Ahmed fancied himself the founder of a new sect that he called the Finger of God and spent all of his free time scouring the Koran for evidence proving the Dictator's destiny to command a nuclear arsenal.

Tariq wasn't sure if Ahmed was delusional or executing an elaborate and clever ruse. But he had to tolerate him. A bad word from Ahmed could mean getting sent home. By Tariq's calculation, the less Ahmed saw of him, the less he could report.

"I'm going to need more money," he whispered to distract Ahmed from the trembling of his hands when he took the note.

Ahmed clicked his worry beads. "You wouldn't if you didn't waste it all on whores and whiskey."

Tariq opened the paper which simply read: "Progress report?" No threats yet. His chest sagged in relief and he briefly wondered which delay tactic he should use to slip away when he heard Ahmed order a three-minute phone call to Baghdad in his halting Russian. Tariq recognized the number as Petrochemical 3. After the phone clerk calculated the price on a wooden abacus, Ahmed took his receipt indicating the booth he should use for his call and led Tariq to a vinyl bench where two students chattered happily in Russian about delaying their return to North Korea.

"I have a lead on windmills," he whispered, using the code word for gas centrifuges.

"Parts or whole machines?" asked Ahmed.

"Whole ones." If Tariq actually found any centrifuges, they would cost more than his 20,000 dollar spending limit. Ahmed would have to close the deal. For especially sensitive matters, he used a series of shell companies set up in Jordan, Switzerland, France and Malaysia for commercial camouflage.

Ahmed traced his moustache, which lacked several cubic centimeters of Dictator density. "Allah be praised! How much?"

Tariq held up his watch to fix his lie in real time. "Maybe I'll know tonight, maybe in a few days. Call me Monday," he said and left before

Ahmed could invite him to the next Finger of God meeting. Tariq would rather kiss The Dog, and Tariq hated dogs.

Sveta and another woman drank coffee in the otherwise empty Dnipro Hotel Night Bar. The whore's tilted eyes crinkled and a gold molar glinted from the back of her smile as she lifted her cup with a jangling of bracelets. "Darling! Here we were so lonely and just waiting for you," she said, pulling Tariq by the arm to sit on the couch next to her. A warm cloud of perfume enveloped him when Sveta pulled her long black hair across her shoulder and leaned back against the cushions.

"This is Irina. She's new," she said, indicating the other woman, though Sveta's sumptuous cleavage partially concealed her face. "I'm sponsoring her and wanted her to meet you first." Tariq leaned forward for a better view of Irina's blond hair and slim figure, such an intriguing contrast with Sveta's voluptuous darkness.

Sveta had an angel's face, iron legs and an advanced degree in mechanical engineering that proved useless when the institute she worked for ran out of money. It was all he knew and all he needed to know. But sometimes, when he collapsed into an exhausted heap from her expert erotic ministrations, she entertained him with her dream of opening a private business school for retired prostitutes.

"How about both of you for the price of one – as an introductory offer?" he suggested. Sveta enjoyed haggling. She whispered to Irina, who giggled and whispered back, glancing at Tariq shyly.

"Taking turns?" asked Sveta.

"Together," said Tariq.

The whore laughed. "For that, darling, you must pay double," she said. "In half an hour. I want to make introductions."

The Dog padded into the bar, followed by the tall German and the silent woman who carried the phone. A swarthy stranger with a hooked nose followed them. Claus Hesse glanced at Tariq with his good eye when the bartender sped up to them with uncommunist speed to take orders. The German tipped well.

"Half-an-hour," Tariq told Sveta and left in time to see the stranger order gin. Tariq took a seat by Claus and ordered scotch. "What is this?" he asked in English.

"You will see, my friend." The response came in a guttural German accent.

Tariq tried to avoid Claus's milky blue eye, blinded by the same sword that ripped through his cheek during an illegal duel at university. But the German's good eye focused on The Dog.

The Great Dane lifted its sledgehammer head framed by the spiked collar and rumbled at Tariq for subconsciously ejecting fear pheromones.

"Siegfried, *Main Schatz*, you remember our Iraqi friend," Claus murmured to the dog. "Let him sniff your hand, Ali."

No one in Kiev knew Tariq's real name except Ahmed. He forced himself to reach out his hand so the loathsome scavenger could smell him. But a droplet of dog spit splashed on his thumb and he jerked as though touched by fire. "Ekhh!" he sputtered.

The woman plugged in the telephone behind the bar with a long cord. Tariq knew neither her name nor whether she was East German, like Claus, or a local. He never heard her speak. The phone never rang either.

"Mohammed Ali," Claus said quietly in Russian, "meet Capt. Yuri Aivazian. Yuri is a bomber pilot at the Uzin nuclear bomber base and a private businessman. He has access to an extraordinary materiél."

Aivazian lit one of those *papirosy* cigarettes that stunk like roasting camel dung. "Red mercury," he whispered smugly. His eyes bored into Tariq's, like the Dictator's did that horrible night when He poisoned a traitor. With the wretched man writhing under the table, the Dictator dined on breaded calf brains and watched CNN. With a shudder at the memory, Tariq recalled "red mercury" from the Petrochemical 3 list while the waiter served their drinks. When he left, they huddled around the small table.

"Ali, you know about red mercury, *Ja*? The emphatic punctuation of Claus's question hung above the whisper. But before Tariq could respond, Aivazian explained: "Red mercury is an antimony mercury oxide that doesn't exist in nature. Our scientists developed it in the 1970s to make a simpler, more efficient trigger for tactical nuclear weapons."

Triggers were tricky, Tariq knew. The Bomb's conventional explosives had to be precisely shaped so that their explosion uniformly compressed the plutonium core into a critical mass, setting off the chain reaction. But after ten years of research, Petrochemical 3 still couldn't achieve the needed precision.

Aivazian continued. "Because of red mercury's unique hydrodynamic flow properties, it is easily shaped and can compress the smallest amounts of nuclear materiél into a critical mass. You can build nuclear bombs the size of a small grenade."

"And obviously, you need less nuclear materiél," Claus added, tracing a finger along his dueling scar.

"How much," asked Tariq.

"A kilo," said Claus.

Tariq spoke to Aivazian. "How much?"

"For a good friend of the late, great Soviet Union, 30,000 dollars," Aivazian said, swirling the gin in his glass.

Claus's scar twitched. "We agreed, Yuri. I will negotiate prices, *Nichtwar?*" The swarthy pilot tossed back his drink and chucked The Dog under the chin in return for a slobbering canine grin.

"I'll be in contact," he said before leaving the bar.

The Night Bar began filling up and a mini-Babel chattered in the background. The only bar in Kiev with Western alcohol exerted a gravitational pull on foreigners. Claus ordered another round of drinks, including a mineral water for the silent woman, who spent the meeting reading a German book with a Kiev cityscape on the cover.

"North Koreans." Claus gestured at the students Tariq had seen at the post office huddled with older Asians on a couch near Sveta, who looked at Tariq and tapped her watch.

"About the money," he asked Claus. He would have to involve Ahmed.

"He is offering you an excellent price. Aivazian has many contacts in the government and military. Red mercury is extremely rare. It can go for five times as much. But first, there is the question of expenses."

"Expenses" meant Claus's fee. Tariq would have disputed the need for it until they closed the deal but then he saw Sveta whisper something in Irina's ear.

"How much?"

"Two thousand dollars."

He had that much in his pocket. Tariq reached for the roll of counterfeits and slipped it under the table to count 20 bills only to feel The Dog's cold, slimy nose.

"Ugh!" he exclaimed, dropping the money.

"What?"

"The money, I dropped it."

Claus retrieved the wad and slipped it into his pocket. "*Scheisse*! You clumsy amateur: Never, *ever*, make a money drop in public again." Claus clipped his words in anger. The Dog detected the emotion and whined at its master hopefully. *For the command to rip out my throat*, thought Tariq. The German seemed to control the beast invisibly.

"Tomorrow afternoon, you must give me half the price up front, so think. We need a secluded place, dark, where you will not attract attention."

"Like a cave," Tariq mused. He had 15,000 dollars in his hotel room, but needed more counterfeits from Ahmed if he used it. Not relishing another meeting with the Shiite, he winked at Sveta, who languidly ran her finger up Irina's thigh.

"*Ja*, perfect!" Claus exclaimed. "The Kiev Cave Monastery."

Tariq forehead beaded with sweat. The North Koreans were approaching Sveta.

Claus explained the directions briefly. "In the Near Caves, find Nestor the Chronicler. He is in an isolated corner but he is very famous. Just ask. There is a space behind the coffin where you can drop the money."

The silent woman opened her notebook to a schedule written in German and showed it to Claus, who continued: "At four o'clock."

Tariq started to rise when he saw the North Koreans talking to Sveta. "Wait," said Claus. "If it goes as planned, you can pick up the package on Sunday night at ten o'clock. You will find it in a briefcase in the trunk of a blue BMW parked behind the Golden Gates."

He kept talking but Tariq verged on panic when he saw Sveta introducing Irina.

"Here is the license number," said Claus, handing him a small piece of paper.

Tariq took it and leaped to his feet, ignoring The Dog's annoyed rumble. "Nestor the Chronicler. Right," he said and rushed to Sveta's side.

CHAPTER 4

NONSTARTERS

Faxnews-Ukraine

June 7, 1992

<u>KIEV, Ukraine.</u> The ministry of defense is removing strategic warheads from ICBMs for the routine replacement of their hydrogen gas filters. But the Russian military is blocking 12th Directorate officers loyal to Ukraine from gaining access to the S-objects. It is also refusing to supply Ukraine with replacement filters. S-objects are equipped for partially dismantling the warheads but works on the nuclear explosives are only performed at the factories that built them and all of those are in Russia.

END

Faxnews-Ukraine – Your source of English-language news about Ukraine

---

Neil Neilson drove at his customary high speed past the sprawl of malls on Route 43 while Dan Kruger sat tightly buckled in the death seat, reading the Monday morning *Washington Post*. His Honda had a gas leak.

"Looks like the Candidate is going to win the Democratic nomination," he observed only to find a Chevy bumper fast approaching his face before Neilson swerved into the left lane to pass it.

"Slow down, Neil," he muttered. Kruger didn't like speed, not unless he did the driving, not since a group of American soldiers in Germany hijacked him for a white-knuckle cruise on the Autobahn.

Neilson downshifted for a curve and glided the MG back into the right lane to join the sedate commuters not rushing towards the Beltway and their government jobs.

"You mean the guy who avoided Vietnam, snorting and any number of venereal diseases," asked Neilson, who always voted Republican, including for Richard Nixon – twice.

The brewing scandal over the Candidate's presence at a cocaine party while draft-dodging in Canada competed for headlines with rumors of his Kennedy-esque liberalism on marital fidelity. His stockbroker wife was a stand-alone scandal, forced to bake broccoli soufflés to prove she didn't hide Y chromosomes under her power suits. Jean Kruger loved her.

Dan Kruger, who volunteered in 1970 after the Cornell ROTC recruiter swore he'd never see a rice paddy, didn't love either of them. But he loved Republicans even less.

"At least he hasn't avoided uttering a comprehensible sentence in the last four years," he retorted in a dig at the Republican Incumbent. The World War II fighter pilot, Ivy League, Eastern Establishment, Texas oil, master of the gentleman's C mangled syntax like a Cuisinart.

The partisan jabbing passed the time until the MG rolled into Neilson's space in DSA's empty parking lot.

Peggy, the matronly receptionist who replaced Annette, greeted them when they walked through the secured doors. "Message for you both."

Neilson took the pink While You Were Out slip. "George Hedgepeth wants us to call him at State," he told Kruger as they walked down the dark corridor to their neighboring offices. To save money, all electricity in areas not occupied by a working human had to be shut off. Even Mr. Coffee got taken off automatic.

Forced to reorganize, DSA's owner Fred Wexler demoted Neilson from Senior Scientist in a company of more than 100 employees to chief of the new International Operations unit. Kruger acted as the chief subordinate and only other member. Given their lack of any International Operations whatsoever, Neilson told Kruger to start working on his resume. If Kruger went, Neilson would be next.

Kruger flipped the light switch in his office, threw the newspaper on his beautifully carved and distressingly empty walnut desk, and walked next door where Neilson shuffled through his Rolodex.

"I guess Rozpad spilled our names during his meeting with Hedgepeth last month," he said. Though DSA was a frequent guest at the Pentagon, the State Department never called.

Slipping out the card he needed, Neilson laid some new papers from his divorce on the desk and picked up the phone to punch numbers.

"Why don't you call State and see what they want. I need to call Rape, Pillage and Slaughter," he said, taking a digital stopwatch out of his top drawer with his free hand.

He bought the stopwatch when selling the old house – a Victorian confection of turrets, gables and stained glass holding Nancy's memory in every corner – when he learned that Rossner, Pringle and Siebert billed in eighth-of-an-hour units. Even a simple: "Hi Neil, Dave Rossner here. We opened the escrow today" cost Neilson the full seven-and-a-half minute price of 15 dollars and 60 cents.

Kruger followed the smell of fresh coffee down the deserted hallway, past the old Theater Ballistic Missile Defense section, home to 15 analysts until the program ended in 1990. ACLM Security Ops followed in 1991. Administrative Logistical Support still hung on, catering Pentagon meetings with what Kruger thought of as "tea and crumpets". The Operations Analysis Group were also still breathing with life-support from CIA contracts on the other side of the building and usually kept to themselves. Back at his desk with his personal Dilbert mug full of coffee, Kruger took the message slip. But when he reached for the phone receiver, Mike Beedle from Op-Ans appeared in the doorway, his puffy features curled into a sneer.

"Fred still lets you guys work here?"

Fred hired Beedle even when he was firing everyone else.

"What's your covert mission, Beedle, to make us miserable enough to quit?" Kruger didn't hide his distaste.

Neither did Beedle. "That is the wussiest little desk I've ever seen, Kruger," he said, jerking his chin at the antique walnut.

"Guys with big dicks don't need big desks," Kruger retorted, enjoying the angry red flush that crept up Beedle's thick neck to his crew cut before he stormed off.

Kruger called Hedgepeth, chatted briefly with his secretary while scratching notes, and walked back into the neighboring office where Neilson cradled the phone receiver on his shoulder while staring at a stopwatch.

"Yeah, I'll fax you a copy right away," he said, then listened to his lawyer's response. "Not so fast, Dave. We've been talking for nine-and-a-half minutes and I know you're going to bill me for 15, so you have five minutes to go."

Silence.

"Talk about the weather for all I care."

Neilson studied the stopwatch.

"No, what's ridiculous is how you guys even manage to manipulate Einstein's theory of relativity.

Neilson listened.

"That's when we regular earthlings think one minute has passed while in the lawyer universe it expands to an hour."

The stopwatch displayed 14:30. Another 30 seconds and Rossner's third billing unit would kick in. Neilson coughed to interrupt. "OK, Dave. I know you're suffering from double billing withdrawal. Talk to you soon," he said and hung up right on the dot of 14:59 with a satisfied smirk.

Kruger sat down in one of the two upholstered armchairs facing the desk. The Ph.D. from Johns Hopkins hung prominently on the wall behind it, along with photos of Neilson in a cyclotron, Neilson with Nixon and Neilson against a backdrop of Pershing II missiles. A formal portrait of Annette and Susie graced the filing cabinet next to a photo of Nancy romping with Ted and Tim, the twins, dressed in identical toddler overalls.

"You don't seem too upset, boss," Kruger said. The subject hadn't come up since Neilson announced the divorce and went to sleep in the guest room. He moved into a furnished apartment the following day.

Neil leaned his elbows on the desk. "I'm sorry about Susie. Rossner said I should forget about challenging custody unless Annette is unfit, which she isn't. If I knew we had money coming in, I'd feel relieved. I can't remember now what possessed me to marry her."

"How about nubile flesh and hot sex," suggested Kruger, who covered for both of them during the early months of prodigiously long lunchtime trysts. He had been happy his friend found solace after Nancy's death.

Neilson grinned but changed the subject. "So, what did Hedgepeth want?"

"He wants to talk about, I quote: 'Ukrainian officials you've had meetings with'."

"What'd you say?"

"I said: 'Of course, sir'. What else am I going to say? You have anything in your appointment book?"

Neilson smoothed the blank pages of his desk calendar. "Not much, except figuring out what to do about our friend, Roman Rozpad, and his HEU."

"Neil Neilson and Dan Kruger are here to see you, Mr. Ambassador."

"Send them in, Kathleen," said the voice on the intercom.

When they entered the room, George "Hedge" Hedgepeth was standing at a conference table under a wall map of the world, his pink paisley tie an obvious sartorial tribute to the Secretary of State's pastel neckwear. He probably had a drawer full of obsolete, Reagan-era reds, thought Kruger.

Hedge's welcome didn't reach his eyes when they all shook hands. Most diplomats viewed arms contractors as necessary but distasteful, like garbage collectors, and loved making them less necessary than they used to be.

"Thank you for coming on such short notice, gentlemen. I'm George Hedgepeth, Deputy Assistant Secretary of State for Disarmament Affairs," he said leading them over to the conference table,

"This is Walter Duranty, my assistant," he said, indicating a balding blond sporting a chartreuse tie.

"Please, sit," said Hedge, taking his place behind a yellow legal pad at the head of the table, under a Currier & Ives fox hunting scene.

"I'll get right to the point," he said, tapping his pen on the pad. "We've learned that you've had meetings with Ukrainian government officials."

"We have, sir," said Neilson.

Hedge leaned towards them abruptly. "And who authorized you to deal with these people?"

Taken aback, Neilson blurted: "The free enterprise system, which is still legal in this country." Kruger kicked him lightly under the table.

Hedge leaned back in his chair but continued tapping. "Perhaps you better explain that, Mr. Neilson," he said. He must have seen their Top Secret security clearances in the files after talking to Rozpad. TS people did not say "no" to their government – not if they wanted those clearances renewed.

Neilson clutched the edge of the conference table. "Mr. Ambassador, our employer Defense Systems Analysis, wants to bid for a Nunn-Lugar contract. So, we need to gather information."

Hedge frowned at the wall map, printed in 1990 and already obsolete as cartography had yet to catch up with the New World Order. At the Pentagon, Kruger had seen many such maps with the new post-Soviet states drawn in with felt tip markers. But Hedge hadn't changed his map. "Information about the Ukraine," he asked dubiously.

"That rat shit little country won't even last out the year," said Duranty.

Kruger's contemptuous stare made Duranty squirm slightly. He was political appointee on sabbatical from teaching the newly irrelevant field of Soviet studies. If experts like him failed to predict that the object of their expertise would disappear, how could anyone consider them experts in anything? Kruger wished he could ask Duranty that.

Instead, Neilson said: "Ukraine is not little, Ambassador Hedgepeth. It's bigger than France. It's independent. And it has 176 ballistic missile silos, 1240 ICBM warheads, and around 600 nuclear-armed cruise missiles. That's more nuclear weaponry than England, France and China put together. It's also a party to the START treaty and, according to my reading of the Nunn-Lugar amendment, it's entitled to that assistance."

Hedge doodled the word START in bold capitals on his notepad. "But Russia is bigger than all them. It's the Soviet Union's sole legitimate nuclear successor and it's claiming all of the disarmament assistance for itself."

DSA could never compete in the Russian market against the giants of defense contracting like Hughes and Martin Marietta, so Kruger broke in. "Excuse me, sir. But if Ukraine isn't also one of the Soviet Union's nuclear successors – as well as Belarus and Kazakhstan – why did they become parties to START? Doesn't that muddy the waters?"

Duranty's nose wrinkled as though a dog turd plopped on the table. "The Ukraine wouldn't let Russia sign for it. They loved the idea of signing a treaty with the United States of America. And when the Ukraine insisted on signing the treaty, Belarus and Kazakhstan went along, too."

Kruger pressed the point. "But if the Ukrainians insist on joining START, independently of Russia, don't you think they'll want an independent share of aid, too?"

The diplomats hadn't thought about that at all and Hedgepeth's scowl signaled his disinclination to begin. "What they want doesn't matter. And even if they are theoretically eligible for Nunn-Lugar aid, we won't give them any until that parliament of theirs ratifies START," he said, adding an exclamation point to his legal pad.

Kruger hoped he had the right tone of obsequious astonishment when he asked: "Mr. Ambassador, are you saying that START's ratification is a precondition to Ukraine and Russia receiving disarmament aid?"

"For the Ukraine it is."

"Perhaps I'm misunderstanding something, but why?" Kruger tried to mask the desperation in his question, but if DSA had to wait for START to submit a contract bid, it could take too long for Fred to keep paying their salaries. He continued despite Hedge's obvious dislike. "Russia is going to remain a nuclear power but we're going to give it disarmament aid. While Ukraine wants to destroy its nuclear weapons and we won't give them any?"

Duranty interrupted. "Because it has never been established that the weapons belong to the Ukraine, it is incorrect to say "their nuclear weapons'."

Kruger wanted to choke the legal wonk and yell: who cares whose weapons they are if they're destroyed?! Instead, he said: "The Ukrainians say they want to destroy the nuclear weapons on their territory. Why not see if they're serious? The military can begin dismantling the weapons now and they'll be long gone before their parliament even gets around to ratifying START."

Hedge examined his fingernails with deliberate boredom but the last caught his attention. "Why did you say that?" he demanded. "Did they tell you they plan to take a long time?"

Kruger jerked in surprise. "Not at all, Mr. Ambassador. I just thought, it being a new country and all, that the parliament has other things on its agenda."

When the diplomats said nothing, Neilson spoke: "If I could change the subject, sir, can you tell us if a Nunn-Lugar funding agency has been designated yet?"

Funding agencies were really spending agencies through which the government gave money to contractors like DSA. But even six months after Nunn-Lugar became law, establishing a rapid-response emergency program to deal with the fragmentation of a deceased superpower's nuclear arsenal, no agency had been appointed.

Hedge raised an eyebrow. "What difference does it make? I said the Ukraine receives nothing until it ratifies START."

Neilson clasped his hands on the table for emphasis: "Mr. Ambassador, Ukraine does not have an adequate tracking system for the nuclear weapons and materials on its territory. This means both are very vulnerable…"

Duranty interrupted: "The Russians have assured us that they have that under control."

"Then they're lying," snapped Neilson.

Noting the Soviet expert's disbelief, Kruger tried to explain the intricacies of nuclear accounting. "Mr. Duranty, I'm sure you appreciate the need to accurately track the status and location of nuclear warheads and the special nuclear materials used in building them."

Duranty didn't seem happy about agreeing with merchants of death on anything.

"Well, the fact is that many modern weapons have a standard design. You can't tell just by looking at one whether it has a nuclear or conventional charge inside. So, you have to keep very precise records.

"Now, in our computerized system, if a weapon is touched, or moved, or accidentally spit on, the inventory officer enters that event into the computer, which immediately updates all the records up the chain of command."

"Surely, the Russians have that," said Duranty.

Kruger wanted to tell him about Rozpad's 100 kilos of high-octane uranium. But he and Neilson decided the diplomats didn't need to know and first rule of security was to tell people what they need to know, and no more.

"What they have are log books," said Kruger.

45

Hedge yawned. "You are talking about accounting? That's for clerks who obsess about minutiae. We think globally in this office. Besides, I imagine the Soviet system, which Russia inherited, was just like ours?"

"Like ours circa 1970," said Kruger. At the hint of interest in Hedge's expression, he continued. "Say in the course of the newest disarmament initiatives, a nuclear warhead is taken off a cruise missile and put into storage."

Hedge tapped his pen.

"In the log book system, the inventory officer will record in what is essentially a notebook that nuclear warhead, serial number XYZ, is located in depot number ZYX. Then, the inventory officer sends a cable with that information to whatever army commands that base. And the army makes a notation in its log book and sends a cable on to the next level, where they put it into their log book and send a cable, and so on."

Hedge's pen tapping grew more rapid. "And this means…?"

You're one stupid son of a bitch if you don't do something about it, is what Kruger thought.

"It means room for human error every step of the way," is what he said. "Serial numbers get mixed up. Inventory officers have dyslexic moments. Entries and cables are delayed. Before we computerized, Pentagon studies estimated the nuclear weapons' log books were 20 percent wrong about what we had and where."

Hedgepeth looked down his patrician nose. "A Pentagon study will prove the sky is falling if it means bigger budgets."

"In a year there won't even be a Ukraine," Duranty added. "It's in our interest for one country to control the ex-Soviet nuclear arsenal, and that's Russia."

Hedge tapped his pen again for quiet. "Must I keep repeating myself? No START, no aid."

Neilson made a last stab at logic. "But, sir, the system won't cost much, maybe ten million dollars. And given its importance to our national security, isn't it worth overlooking the treaty…"

The contempt in Hedge's voice rose above diplomatic decibels. "Overlook a treaty cutting the Soviet nuclear arsenal by a third?! That took three American presidents, four Soviet General Secretaries and twelve years to negotiate?! I hardly think so. Why, START is the crowning achievement of Cold War diplomacy!"

And Hedge's life. Since graduating Harvard Law in 1970, he missed the draft and smoothly climbed up from the Legal Advisor's office to become deputy to the chief negotiator in the START talks. Hedge famously formulated the penultimate phrasing of the silo destruction clauses.

Listing all the ways that START ill-suited the post-Cold War world would annoy Hedgepeth even more. But they had more than one way of tackling the hydra-headed U.S. government. Kruger tapped Neilson's foot to signal an end.

"It certainly is a great accomplishment, Mr. Ambassador," Neilson said smoothly. "And Mr. Kruger and I will stress the importance of ratifying it to Ukrainian officials on our next trip to Kiev."

"That's right," said Hedge. "We'll teach those nuclear proliferators some discipline."

Kruger couldn't let that go. "Proliferators? It's kind of an accident that they ended up with a nuclear arsenal after the Soviet Union's collapse."

"Doesn't matter. Fragmentation is still proliferation," Hedge responded. "Gentlemen, it's been…"

Neilson interrupted the epilogue. "Out of curiosity, sir, has a funding agency been appointed for Nunn-Luger?"

"The Defense Nuclear Agency," Hedge said curtly. "They decided on Friday."

DNA used to run nuclear weapons testing. It had nothing to do with disarmament. "And who's in charge of it?" Neilson asked.

"General Joe Hawkins," said Hedge, rising from the table to end the interview.

Kruger exchanged glances with Neilson. Joe "Hawker" Hawkins?

*A*ctually, Lt. Gen. Joseph Stanhope Hawkins thought of himself as Stalkin' Hawkins, the name a West Point classmate bestowed upon him in Vietnam after witnessing his skill in hunting down Viet Cong.

Wouldn't even come out and fight like real soldiers. He glanced at the framed *Life* magazine photo of him with his foot on the chest of some murderous little gook that tried to ambush him on the road to Chu Lai. Sweat and dirt and blood smeared his gaunt face, gazing wearily somewhere behind the camera.

The Viet Cong's face was turned away, obliterated.

Never did see it, he recalled. But he did recall the two faces seated before him across the broad expanse of his oak desk.

"So, boys, how do you like the world since the USSR kicked the bucket and we called off the Cold War," he said, attempting a smile through his soldierly scowl.

"Well, General, thank you for seeing us on such short notice," said Neil Neilson. "But I'm afraid that more misunderstandings between our two parts of the world are yet to come."

Instead of responding, Hawkins reached over his desk to pick up a detailed model of a Pershing II missile on its mobile truck launcher. "This sucker's a beaut'. And that was one ass-kicking party in Heidelberg when they gave it to me," he reminisced.

Hawkins still remembered the American officers' raucous relief when he got promoted to a desk job in the Pentagon. Appointed Deputy Commander for the Pershing missile forces in 1986, Hawkins spent three years in a despondent rage after the U.S. and the U.S.S.R. signed the Intermediate Nuclear Forces treaty that slated them for destruction.

"It was a great party, General. But there are two urgent matters we need to discuss with you," Kruger said. "The first is highly sensitive and we ask that you handle it carefully. But we want to do the right thing. And since you are now in a position to actually do something about it, we've decided to tell you."

While Kruger talked, Hawkins fiddled with the tiny ball lock pin on the Pershing model and pulled it out so that the little launcher popped off the back of the truck.

He made a gagging sound intended as a chuckle. "I forget," he said, interrupting Kruger in mid-sentence. "Which one of you guys was hiding the missiles, and which one was finding 'em?"

Kruger squeezed the top of his nose and rubbed something out of his eye. "Um, that was me hiding them," he said.

The general pressed the launcher back down. "Both of you, working for the same company, on opposite sides of the same contract and not even knowing each other," he said, shaking his head. "Tell me again how that happened?"

Both men looked at each other and seemed to deflate until Neilson finally spoke up: "Well, sir, when Defense Systems Analysis won the Theater Missile Survivability contract in the mid 1980s, about a third of the company's employees, including Dan, moved to Germany."

"And you..." Hawkins gestured at Neilson, "only joined the company after that. Didn't you used to work on Star Wars ray guns or something?"

"I did pure research, General, with proton beams," Neilson corrected. "In any case, when DSA won the Pentagon contract to design a NATO exercise in 1986, Dan was the Camouflage, Cover and Deception expert on the contract. His job was to hide the missiles while I designed the attack force simulation at DSA's office here."

The exercise simulated a band of Soviet Spetznaz supermen waging an attack on the Pershings.

"Yeah, and then I introduced you at the Yankee Doodle Bar in Heidelberg!" The general chortled, slamming his free hand on the desk while the other one held down the mini-Pershing's missile launcher.

"It was ironic, indeed, General," Neilson said and Kruger picked up on whatever he had been talking about.

While Kruger's voice droned in the background, Hawkins removed his hand from the Pershing model, and his gaze drifted from the popped up launcher to the window. His rank and decorations entitled him to a view of the Pentagon's inner courtyard, a prime Soviet target during the bad old days. Or were they the good old days? Hawkins loved hating the Commies. Not like that pissant Iraqi. He cost a lot to fight and it was fun watching the Patriot missiles on CNN, even if they missed most of the Dictator's Scuds. But the ease of beating him left little to hate and even less to spend money on.

It was nothing like the Cold War. The Commies proved the perfect enemy for bloating budgets. The apocalyptic risks of all out war made them impossible to fight, but the need to win that fight if it happened meant big programs and big bucks. He aimed the model Pershing and the wee warhead inside toward Congress. When he pressed the well-oiled lever on the truck's back bumper, the missile shot across his desk and landed at Kruger's feet.

Kruger picked it up, admiring the miniature's fine craftsmanship and focusing Hawkins attention while he repeated his last sentence.

"Did you say *undocumented* HEU?" the general responded, flashing his painful grin. "What's that boys, some kind of new illegal alien? Heh, heh, heh."

Kruger smiled. "In a way it is, General. But if we let this stuff wade across the Rio Grande, the crops won't get picked. They'll glow."

"Huh?" said Hawkins, confused. "What do you mean, glow?"

Neilson jumped in to explain. "They used highly enriched uranium to make those first nuclear weapons with the really dirty fallout. A hundred kilos of HEU equals enough bombs to wipe out the eastern seaboard."

Hawkins nodded sagely, though he didn't need to know how a bomb blew up, so long as it did when and where he wanted. Geeks took care of the details.

Leaning over to put the little Pershing back on Hawkins' desk, Kruger added: "Sir, I'm sure you appreciate the dangers of this material being on the loose. Even spreading a small amount of HEU on the ground could cause an environmental disaster. I hate to think what a terrorist could do with it."

Hawkins inserted the model missile back into its model launcher and pushed it away.

"Gentlemen, you've come to the right man," he said, squaring his shoulders. "Those fairies at Foggy Bottom can't prevent the spread of nukes from the new Russia…"

"Not Russia, sir. Ukraine," said Neilson.

Hawkins ignored him. "There is a failure of leadership here. Someone has to form up and enforce a new nuclear non-proliferation program and that someone should be the military. Hell, we invented the damn things."

The general interrupted himself for a breath, allowing Kruger to interject: "But the uranium..."

"I'll take it under my personal control," he assured them. "That Rasputin character won't..."

"Rozpad," Neilson corrected.

"... find out you reported it. I'll ask the spooks over at the CIA to use one of their resources to uncover it independently. You tell whatshisname that it's not your kind of business and wish him luck," Hawkins' advised. "We'll make sure he won't have any. No one will see even a ripple."

Neilson cleared his throat. "Thank you, General. Now, if we could take up just a few minutes of your time, we understand you've been put in charge of Nunn-Lugar spending."

The general moved the dummy hand grenade weighing down a thin stack of papers and picked them up, showing his guests the pink sticky slip marked "Nunn Lugar" in his bold penmanship.

"You call this spending?! This is some pinko plot to destroy the United States' military!" he exclaimed, tossing the papers back on his desk. "You guys know how they keep cutting our budget since the Cold War?"

A few months earlier, the Republican President announced a 50 billion dollar cut to the defense budget.

"Well, this legal mumbo jumbo cuts it even more. Instead of giving us new money for disarmament, this makes us take money away from existing programs!" Hawkins swiveled on his leather armchair, spitting in anger. "Why the hell should we spend our money to destroy the God damn Russkies' old missiles if they're just going to spend their money on new ones? If Congress wants us to do that, it has to give us a separate line item and not this budgetary voodoo bullshit."

Neilson wiped off some spit that fell on his wrist. "General, we share your suspicions of the Russians," he said. "That's why we'd like to submit a proposal for a very small part of the Nunn-Lugar budget to help Ukraine..."

Hawkins stopped swiveling and squinted. "The Ukraine, you say?"

The Secretary of Defense thought the Ukraine had some importance, but he didn't remember why. Instead of admitting his ignorance, he picked up the grenade and held it up. "I took this one in Dak To in 1967. Some slanty-eyed gook threw it two inches from my foot. Soviet piece of shit never went off," he said and turned to Kruger.

"You never did go to 'Nam, did you Kruger? You one of those Democratic draft dodgers?"

Dan shifted in his seat. "Um, no sir. I volunteered. They assigned me to Army security in Germany."

Hawkins shut up. What Kruger did for Army Security needed to stay between him and the people who needed to know, and Hawkins didn't.

Kruger continued. "General Hawkins, we want to bid for a contract to provide Ukraine with a computerized tracking system for nuclear materials. The fact that someone could offer us 100 kilos of HEU means that this system is very necessary."

Kruger went on about some paper log books and tracking special nuclear materials like enriched uranium and plutonium.

Hawkins tossed the grenade from hand to hand. "So, wait. Are you telling me that the Russkies don't know what nuclear stuff the Ukies have?"

Neilson answered: "General, the Russians don't even know what's in Russia, much less Ukraine. They all use the same primitive log book system."

Hawkins stopped tossing the grenade. "Hold on guys. Won't this computer system help the Ukraine grab the nukes? I remember reading in the paper that they now have some kind of administrative control, whatever the hell that is."

"We're not sure what it is either, General," said Neilson. "But the way the system is set up now, if they had a secret plan to rig themselves some kind of launch control, they'd have an easier time of it."

"How so?" Hawkins tossed the grenade with one hand, his eyes fixed on Kruger, who responded: "The Russians have a monopoly on warhead servicing, so they must have access to the weapons and I'm sure they'd raise holy hell if they suspected anything. But the log book system increases the risk of someone misplacing warheads without anyone knowing. It could even happen on a local level. Things are chaotic there. It's why the computerized system is so important."

"I getcha," said the general, placing his hands on his desk to stand up and end the meeting. "Lemme have the eggheads study this and I'll get back to you." That would delay things for a while.

Neilson stuck to his chair. "General Hawkins, we understand if you need to think about it but there's no need for more study. We've told you everything."

Hawkins didn't need to think about it. He didn't want to spend any of the Pentagon's money on a bunch Commie missiles. But before he could speak, Kruger suggested: "What if we brought a letter from the Ukrainian defense minister saying that they need it?"

The general put down the grenade and pulled the Pershing model closer, caressing the missile's nose peering out of the launcher. It would take them forever to bring him anything. "OK guys. For old times' sake, bring me a letter."

Neilson and Kruger thanked him quickly and when they left, the general picked up the phone to call his old friend and Cold War soul mate at the CIA. William Kensington III picked up after two rings.

"K3? Joe Hawkins here."

After the preliminary niceties, Hawkins lowered his voice: "We should have a drink this afternoon. There's news."

*T*he Japanese soldier's head, transformed into a misshapen lump of silicon in the Hiroshima blast, shared the glass display with a photo of the Enola Gay flying away from the mushroom cloud under a sign reading: "The Atomic Era".

"Passing on the left," a voice called out behind Neilson and Kruger right before a messenger sped past them on a bicycle.

"You think Hawkins will keep his mouth shut about us," Neilson asked quietly as they walked down a bustling corridor that sliced through the Pentagon's concentric rings.

"We'll know he didn't if we end up stored away with Roz's uranium cache," Kruger said. He hated humoring military brass. But for years his excellent pay for doing precisely that made up for it. Now, whether he would have any pay at all depended on it. Hawkins had a bad attitude for a funding agency. But it wasn't surprising given the lunatic decision to put the Pentagon in charge of a program that took money away from the Pentagon.

"Actually, I think we're safe for a while," said Neil once they were in the car turning out of the parking lot. "We did our patriotic duty and reported a potential security threat. But Hawkins hasn't caught anything except a cold since Vietnam, so I doubt if he'll catch Rozpad too soon. As for the CIA, the Agency depends on the information it gets and if Hawkins is giving it, they'll spend months going nowhere. He hardly listened to us." Neilson shifted into fifth and settled back in the leather seat, his eyes hidden by the prescription sunglasses he used for driving.

"But the HEU will still be knocking around," Kruger noted.

"That's what I've been thinking about. When we see Rozpad, we're going to give him a spiel about how important it is for him to log all the nuclear materials he finds."

The Ukrainian official had returned to D.C. for another seminar on nuclear safety that required equipment and training that Ukraine didn't have. They had invited him to dinner.

"And why should he listen to us?" said Kruger.

"Because we're going to offer him a job," Neilson responded. Leafy suburban trees reflected in his sunglasses.

"Actually, we'll just dangle a job at him. Say, a consultancy if we win the contract and we'll pay him – what's a lot to them and not to us, 2,000 dollars a month?"

Kruger approved. "That'll definitely give him an interest in helping us."

Neilson recalled Rozpad's nervousness at the barbecue, and his obvious poverty. "If we give him a chance to make honest money, it should put him off offering the HEU to someone else."

"For a while, at least," said Kruger, remembering the Ukrainian's expensive taste.

That taste expressed itself on the DSA expense account when Rozpad ordered Maine lobster a few hours later, full of excitement over his possible job offer with the company.

"I talk to our Ambassador," Rozpad said, cracking a claw. "He said foreign ministry will help you. I will give you his coordinates."

After wiping his hands, Rozpad took a vinyl bound notepad out of his jacket pocket and jotted the phone number with a pencil.

"He will get you visas and meetings," he said, handing Neilson the sheet and then giving his full attention to the meal.

TOP SECRET – PURPLE

Subject: Project Rasputin Initiation.

The Director of the Central Intelligence Agency directs the initiation of Project Rasputin. The Project is to report on nuclear-related issues in the Ukraine and conduct surveillance of American defense contractors Neil Neilson and Dan Kruger. The subjects are connected with a nuclear black market element named Rowan Rasputin.

For the DCIA, William Kensington III

CHAPTER 5:

NIGHT BAR

Date: July 29, 1992
To: K3
From: Chief of Station Kiev
Subject: SITREP Rasputin
(S)   1. Neilson and Kruger arrived via Air Ukraine at Borispil Airport in Kiev. They were met by Kostya Beniuk who escorted them to white Volga taxi. They checked in to the Dnipro Hotel at 17:45, room 411 and 412.

(TS) 2. Unable to identify nuclear-related or other officials named Rowan Rasputin. There is no such thing as a directory of the Ukrainian government.

(TS) 3. Request increase in entertainment budget by 500 dollars. END

---

*K*ostya Beniuk's knee bounced nervously while Dan Kruger rummaged through his duffle bag, packed for minimalist survival with what Jean called K – for Kiev – rations.

When he balked at smuggling a mini-market in his luggage, his wife warned him that few restaurants had food, room service didn't exist and store were empty after the Soviet distribution system collapsed. She lost five pounds the first and only time she visited her country of birth, in still-Soviet 1991. She said not to bother bringing his tennis racket.

Dan placed cans of tuna and soup, a jar of peanut butter, instant coffee, Ramen noodles, tea bags and packets of sugar on the desk in his room. Finally, he dug out a crumpled envelope and handed it to the cousin

Jean recommended as their translator and fixer. "This is for your mother, Kostya," he explained. Inside, Jean's letter instructed her aunt to buy black market blood pressure medicine and enclosed a crisp new 100 dollar bill.

Kostya slipped the envelope in his pocket without opening it while Kruger opened his Filofax to a photocopied page of phone numbers. They had tucked back-up copies into various pieces of their luggage, along with a list of churches and monuments that Jean said Kruger must see to survive debriefing by her mother.

It took weeks to organize the trip, getting their visas and travel arrangements, collecting contacts. Despite promises of help, the new Ukrainian Embassy in Washington only selectively answered its phone.

"Why did Yevhenia, um, Jean, not come with you?" Kostya asked.

"She has to work," Kruger explained. *One of us does.* "I'll tell you more later, but right now we want you to make a phone call for us."

Kostya smiled. Though gold, silver and steel mined every mouth they saw from the airport to the hotel, Kostya's teeth belonged in a toothpaste commercial.

When Kruger started reading from the phone list, he noticed the translator's discomforted eyes searching the room. On a guess, he picked through his suitcase until he found an extra wire bound notebook under a box of crackers. Kostya took it and slipped a pen out of his pocket. "Thank you," he said. "We have notebook deficit now because Russia has paper monopoly."

Kruger told him the phone number. "We need to speak to Yuri Holub. He's the foreign ministry's advisor on American affairs and he speaks English. But whoever answers the phone might not. So, call Holub and tell him that Neil Neilson wants to speak to him. He should be expecting us."

Kostya picked up the receiver of the plastic orange telephone on the desk but the flimsy rotary dialer weighed less than a toy, and the entire phone lifted and swung from the cord, tapping a can of Hungry Man beef stew. Anchoring the phone down with one hand, he dialed nine for an outside line.

"It is engaged," he said, tapping the button to disconnect. After dialing nine a few more times, he hung up the phone. "Phone system is old, hard to get connection sometimes."

"Well, keep trying," said Kruger.

Kostya bent over the phone to dial nine every few seconds. After a few minutes, he paused and dialed the seven digit main number.

"No one answer," he announced and hung up.

"Try it every few minutes. I'm going to Neil's room next door. We'll leave the doors open so shout if you get through."

Kostya hunched over the phone again to dial nine for an outside line.

Neil Neilson's room was a twin to Kruger's. A drab box crammed with a single bed, desk, easy chair and coffee table done up in shabby shades of brown. With Neilson's two suitcases on the floor, they had little room to move. And the travel agent promised the best hotel in Kiev.

Neilson opened the chintz drapes to let in the evening light. A small pendant lamp dimly lit the room. "When I tried to plug in my laptop, I only found one electrical outlet and it's for the TV set."

Kruger unscrewed the mouthpiece from the telephone.

"Seems clean," said Dan, replacing the mouthpiece. He lifted the mottled brown shade on the desk lamp. He saw nothing obvious, but was certain that the walls concealed bugs left over from Soviet times, like the hideous décor and the lobby matrons on each floor. When telling Dan what to expect, Jean called them "floor dragons". They didn't know who might eavesdrop on them in independent Ukraine or why, but old habits died hard.

"You are such an honest man, Dan Kruger, and committed to the cause of peace," said Neil.

"Thank you, Dr. Neil Neilson. That is a great compliment coming from a distinguished, peace loving physicist like you."

Neilson talked at the ceiling lamp. They scripted their lines on the plane. "I hope the peace loving Ukrainians will listen to our advice about the nuclear weapons they inherited from the evil Soviet empire."

Kruger felt foolish but responded to the plastic radio on the wall. It had one channel and no dial. "There is much new technology that we can offer them." But before they could read the good part, about the expensive computer tracking system that Ukraine could have courtesy of the U.S. taxpayer, a young woman in a trench coat walked through the open door.

"Hello. Excuse please. My name is Sveta. You want good time?" she asked, opening the coat to display her wares packaged into two slivers of black lace. "Cheap," she said. "Fifty bucks. Excellent, good sex. You will like."

The prostitute was gorgeous, with tilted eyes and golden skin but Kruger thought of the body part Jean swore she'd deprive him of if he used it in the wrong place. And the lovely lady at the door defined the wrong place. But he noticed Neilson's frank appreciation. He probably hadn't seen so much females flesh in the months since Annette filed for divorce. Nor had he seen Annette. She communicated with him only through her lawyer who communicated only with his lawyer whose communications with Neilson were too costly and too depressing. Some angry implant victim Annette befriended at her support group mediated the weekend visits with Susie. But he was proud of never having paid for sex.

"Sorry, not interested," said Neilson.

The prostitute pouted and turned with provocative indifference, her glossy black hair bouncing behind her as she walked out on red spike heels. "We better go rescue Kostya from her charms," Neilson said, following her out. "Or the other way around," said Kruger.

But after a glance at Kostya, still hunched over the telephone, the prostitute kept going down the hallway. "He not have 50 bucks," she said over her soldier. Kostya's pin striped jacket from half a suit crumpled in threadbare wrinkles at the elbows.

"Any luck, Kostya?" asked Kruger.

The translator rested his head on his hand. "I am sorry but no. It is sometimes engaged or when not engaged, no one answer. One time when someone answer, they hang up."

Neilson checked his travel clock. "It's almost six. Try it again."

"But it is end of work day, people are gone."

"The people who don't answer the phone are gone. Maybe the people who are still there will answer them," said Neilson. They learned that trick trying to call the Ukrainian Embassy.

"That is Soviet logic," Kostya said as he dialed.

"An oxymoron if I heard one," said Kruger while putting his suits on two of the three theft-proof hangers in the closet.

"Yeah, but like military intelligence, sometimes it works." Neilson motioned at Kostya talking to someone and waving his hand. He held the phone out. "It is Mr. Holub!"

Neilson took the receiver, which assaulted his ear with a series of loud clicks and static. But the noise cleared and he quickly made an appointment with the diplomat. "Ten o'clock tomorrow," he said after hanging up. Kruger scooped through packages of trail mix in his suitcase.

"Dan, let's see if this place has real food before we start hitting the strategic reserves."

The floor dragon belched a cloud of smoke, heaved her size 16 out the chair in her lobby lair and roared at the threesome waiting by the elevator.

"What's the problem?" asked Kruger.

"The keys," said Kostya. "You must give her keys so she can give you guest card."

The receptionist gave them the guest card when they checked in. Only after surrendering the cards to the lobby matron did they receive their keys, and that was after much huffing and puffing.

"We're just going to the restaurant downstairs,' said Neilson.

After an exchange of words, Kostya reported: "You must give her keys. This is procedure. You may only have key if you are in room."

"The better for the KGB to know when you're out so they can go through your luggage," said Neilson, producing his key and putting it on the floor dragon's desk.

"Give her five bucks," said the translator. "She be nice."

The key guardian's bouffant hair was an alien shade of lavender and the smoke from her cigarette had drifted into her face, twisting it into a grimace.

"Yeah, I'm afraid of that," said Neilson, but handed a five to Kostya, who maneuvered around the abundant flowers and ferns that made the lobby a surprisingly inviting little jungle. When he slipped the contents of his hand into the floor matron's open palm, her hostility melted. After checking the two corridors that stretched from either direction from her desk, she unfolded the crumpled bill while Kostya murmured something to her. She responded in a whisper, displaying a dental keyboard of silver and gold.

"Her name is Natasha," Kostya announced after returning their keys. "She likes Americans."

The elevator seemed to take forever, so they walked two flights down a dark staircase. "We have light bulb deficit," Kostya explained after Kruger complained about having to feel for each step. "You can only buy on black market, but expensive, 50 *kupons*."

A temporary currency introduced after Russia stopped supplying Ukraine with ruble notes, *kupons* looked and felt like Monopoly money and, at an exchange rate of 200 to the dollar, had about the same buying power. "At 90 dollars a night from each of us, this dump can afford 25 cent light bulbs," Neilson grumbled when they stepped into the brightly lit lobby on the second floor.

"No one care," said Kostya. "There is no competition."

As soon as they walked through the restaurant's double doors, a four-piece band launched into a familiar tune. A singer in pink spandex wiggled her ample bottom, belting: "Lambada, lambada, lambada…" for a bride and groom shimmying on the dance floor in a circle of swarthy men.

Neilson held up three fingers to the black-haired woman sitting at a floor dragon desk near one of the speakers. She counted a row of figures on an abacus with practiced speed.

They have nuclear weapons and count on abacuses, Kruger thought with disquiet, following Neilson and the hostess to one of many empty tables. The collection of ceramic plates decorating an entire wall of the restaurant resembled much of the folk art stored in his mother-in-law's credenza.

Kruger took his seat while more "Lambada, lambada, lambada…" blasted in the background. "Are those the only lyrics she knows?"

Neilson picked up the one menu the hostess left on the table. "Appetizers," he read loudly over the music. "Meat assortments. Fish assortments. Tongue under Mayonnaise. Shrimps under Mayonnaise. House Salad with Mayonnaise. Red Caviar. Black Caviar."

"What are the entrees?" Kruger shouted.

"Cutlet Kiev Style. Beefsteak. Fried Pork Pieces."

The band lambada'd into a break and they could speak normally.

"They're all cheap, too, just 30 kupons," said Neilson. "That's, what, 15 cents?"

Kruger turned to the translator. "What sounds good to you Kostya?"

The young man pointed at the menu. "Is there *salo*?"

"What's *salo*?" asked Kruger.

"It is pig part but I know not the word in English. It is great Ukrainian delicacy."

Neilson searched the menu. "There's no *salo* here," he said when the waiter approached their table.

"How about drinks? Is there any beer?" Kruger asked.

"No beer. Vodka," Kostya translated.

"How about champagne?" said Kruger. "Jean said the local champagne is pretty good. Cheap, too. Ninety kupons is less than fifty cents."

After the translation, the waiter spoke to Kostya, who told his companions: "Restaurant has no champagne but waiter has private supply and can sell you bottle for two bucks."

"Fine," said Kruger. Waiters with private supplies of missing items on the menu didn't surprise him at all. "I'd like a Coke, too."

The waiter didn't need translation. "No Coke. Pepsi."

"OK, Pepsi," said Kruger, recalling the classic Saturday Night Live skit, except there were no cheeseburgers, either.

"Ask him what's in the Fish Assortments, Kostya," Neilson said. But the question turned out theoretical anyway. Nothing on the menu actually existed except for the pork pieces, which they all had little choice but to order. The waiter brought a bottle of mineral water to the table and poured some into their glass goblets. Kostya picked up the bottle and showed them the label, covered with unfamiliar lettering.

"*Borjomi*," he said, pointing to the name on the label. "This is Georgian mineral water."

Kruger took a sip, and almost gagged. "It's salty," he said, "and warm, too."

"These are minerals. Good for health," said Kostya and happily took a drink.

Kruger refrained and waited for the Pepsi. "Warm, salty water," he said to Neilson. "Wonderful." But before Neilson could respond, the band again made conversation impossible, so they watched the swarthy men dance, in a manly display of drumming feet on the floorboards.

"This is Georgian," Kostya explained above the blasting music, which stopped when a trio of militiamen marched into the restaurant. The foot drumming also stopped and Kostya lowered his voice to a whisper in the suddenly quiet room where the Georgians had gathered into a defensive crowd on the dance floor. "They control citrus market in Kiev and our mayor trying to recapture market so militia stop people of Caucasian nationality to check their documents," Kostya explained.

Kruger leaned back in his straight backed chair to watch the drama. "According to the U.S. Census, Caucasian is a race, not a nationality."

"That's because the Census Bureau is nowhere near the Caucasus." Neilson had read up on all the former Soviet republics, now newly independent states, on the plane to Kiev.

The Georgians outnumbered the militia three to one but they showed their passports and motioned at the bride and groom seated at a long table laden with food and drink. "They probably gave bribes," said Kostya, turning to see the militiamen leave the room just as the waiter showed up with their food, reassuringly bored by what had just transpired.

Kruger examined his plate. A brown sauce covered the meat and spilled into boiled potatoes and canned peas. "It's like chipped meat, but I guess that chips count as pieces," he said, taking a nibble. "Seems edible, though." He had eaten plenty of Meals Ready to Eat during military exercises in Germany. Anyone who spent weeks on MRE diets learned to both appreciate fine food and be less than picky about metabolic energy sources when necessary. Neilson took a taste, too. Kostya wolfed his down without a word.

The band started up again and they ate to "Lady in Red" followed by an encore rendition of "Lambada" that ended with the bottle of champagne. Neilson motioned for the waiter, who came over immediately.

"He asks if we want more champagne. He has more in private supply," Kostya said.

"Just the check," said Neilson. The entire meal, including the champagne, cost less than three dollars. Fred Wexler at DSA would be thrilled.

"Kostya, judging by our conversation on the phone, Holub's English is excellent but we need your help to go to his office. Can you come to our rooms tomorrow at 9:30?"

The translator flashed his ultra-brights and bobbed his head: "Oh yes, thank you!"

*N*eilson's watch said 9:43 and Kostya still hadn't arrived. "Holub said the foreign ministry is less than a mile away, but this is cutting it too close," he said. Stout women in embroidered blouses and flowered kerchiefs warbled in a field of sunflowers on the TV.

"We'll have to go without him," Kruger said. "We have the address. The door dragons downstairs can hail us a cab." The hotel's doormen were the males of the floor dragon species. They probably breed bureaucrats when everyone's asleep, Kruger thought, passing Natasha's empty desk.

When the elevator door opened in the main lobby, dozens of eerily neat young Americans with "MY NAME IS" tags on their shirts surrounded a small mountain of suitcases.

"Now Brother Jim and Sister Alice go first," chirped a wiry woman with a clipboard.

Kruger followed Neilson around a group of boisterous Germans breakfasting on beer in the day bar, and across the worn marble floor to the exit where a diminutive man with a mouthful of steel stood guard.

"Ta-xi?" asked Neilson, exaggerating each syllable and pointing to himself and Kruger. But when he turned to point at the street, he saw Kostya outside the glass doors, waving his arms and shouting at another doorman. Kruger noticed him, too, and pushed open the ancient Plexiglas door into the warm, midsummer morning.

Kostya ran up the cobblestone boulevard in front of the hotel. "I am sorry Mr. Dan, but this communoid not let me into hotel because I am not guest."

"Communoid?" asked Kruger.

Kostya looked surprised. "Communist Party illegal, but communoids are still here."

He clutched the red document he had shown to the doorman.

"He wanted to see my passport," he complained, pointing at the Soviet hammer and sickle embossed in the fabric. "They still treat us like Soviet times when locals not allowed in hotels for foreigners. And we still have these stupid internal passports." He opened it to show them a stamp inside. "This says I am now Ukrainian citizen. But it is same stupid Stalinist document. Just so communoids can keep spying on everyone."

Kruger should have known this would happen. Jean had to meet with her family outside the hotel because of the restrictions. But that was when the USSR still existed. That little had changed in independent Ukraine wasn't reassuring. "Don't' worry, Kostya," he said. "We'll make it clear that you're with us when we come back. Right now, we need a cab to the foreign ministry on Karl Liebknecht Street."

A few battered Soviet cars huddled in the parking lot, along with an incongruously sleek line of identical navy blue BMWs. Kostya trotted over to a beige Volga with a checkered bubble on the roof and negotiated with the driver. "Two bucks," he reported when he returned. "All hotel taxis expensive. I find cheaper..."

Neilson stopped him. "We'll pay it Kostya. We have five minutes."

In less time than that, the cab lumbered up the steep hill from the hotel at a leisurely speed that even lulled Kruger and deposited them at a graceful yellow building nestled between grey apartment blocks.

Kostya read the brass sign next to an arched window. "Press Center," he announced, pulling open the heavy wood door for them.

"Wait outside for us," said Kruger and the translator stepped aside to let them pass into the paneled lobby, where a tall man in a double breasted suit awaited their arrival.

"Ah, that American punctuality," he said, his hand extended in welcome. "Good morning, gentlemen. I am Yuri Holub." After the introductions, Holub ushered them up the stairs into a conference room brightly lit with chandeliers. *So this must be where all the light bulbs live,* thought Kruger. He took a seat at the long oak conference table next to Neilson, who opened up his Filofax to a handwritten page of issues they needed to cover.

"Thank you for taking the time to meet with us, Mr. Holub," Neilson said to open the meeting. Kruger had to take notes and interrupt if Neilson missed anything.

Holub opened an embossed leather portfolio to an empty notepad and pushed up his wireframe glasses. "Our Ambassador in Washington told me you are interested in helping us with nuclear disarmament."

"We are, sir," said Neilson. "The company we work for, Defense Systems Analysis, has a good deal of experience with nuclear weapons systems. Mr. Kruger, for example, spent five years working with the Pershing intermediate range missiles in Germany. We came here to find out what kind of disarmament assistance you need."

Holub adjusted his glasses. "When you find out, please tell us."

Kruger scribbled the word "Shit" in his notepad and surrounded it with bold exclamation points.

"Frankly, we don't know the answers and are only beginning to think about the questions," Holub continued, pouring *Borjomi* water into a glass. He raised the bottle and lowered it amiably when his guests declined.

"That is not only the case when it comes to disarmament, but a host of other issues as well. But we know that nuclear weapons, and the START treaty in particular, are very important to your government."

Holub waited for a response, while Neilson and Kruger tried to think of one. They couldn't tell Holub their low opinion of Foggy Bottom's

START fixation because private citizens weren't supposed to meddle in U.S. foreign policy, especially if they wanted to keep their security clearances.

Neilson cleared his throat. "Well, some circles of the government want Ukraine to ratify START as soon as poss –."

Holub interrupted. "The ministry of foreign affairs is studying the treaty and when we are done, we will submit it to parliament with our recommendations."

Kruger wrote "Timeframe?" in his notes and tapped Neilson to look. "How long do you think that will take?" asked Neilson.

Holub's shoulders dropped wearily. "I'm sorry. But START is not a top priority right now. Your government should realize that the biggest problem is Russia insisting that it has the sole right to control all of the former Soviet Union's nuclear weapons." The diplomat's eyes were sad. "I don't know how familiar you are with Ukrainian history. But if that happens, neither Russia nor the weapons will leave our territory for a long time. That is why the President of Ukraine took administrative control over the strategic forces."

"Administrative control" topped their issue list.

"We heard," said Neilson. "We hoped you could explain what administrative control means."

Holub stared at the ceiling as if searching for patience. "It means that the military personnel who deal with the nuclear weapons are our draftees and officers who have taken an oath of loyalty to Ukraine."

"How many officers have taken the oath," asked Neilson.

"Enough," replied the diplomat. "The point is, the nuclear troops must belong to someone. If they are not Ukrainian, they will be Russian and that is unacceptable." Holub punctuated his conclusion by banging his glass on the table. "Russia is demanding that we give up administrative control, or allow them to remove the nuclear warheads. We have taken some of the warheads on the ICBMs off of deployment for servicing. But I'm sure you know, these are complex delivery systems."

When the Americans nodded, Holub continued. "If the warheads are removed, inert MIRVs – or dummies, if you will – must replace them for the missile's electronics to function. But Russia is refusing to provide us with enough dummies to remove all the warheads."

Neilson assembled an expression that looked like sympathy. "Mr. Holub, we think Ukraine's position is understandable and that's why we want to help you. Now, you are familiar with the Nunn-Lugar legislation?'

"This is the money we will not receive until START is ratified," Holub said without concealing his sarcasm.

"There are American officials who take that point of view," Neilson said. They had to tread carefully between not interfering in US foreign policy and letting Holub know that Washington was not a monolith.

"All the officials we talk to do."

"Actually," said Neilson, "we have a commitment from the Pentagon to fund certain new technologies now, even without START. But we need your cooperation."

Holub leaned forward in frank interest while Neilson described the computerized nuclear tracking system and added an edited summary of their meetings with General Joe Hawkins on the American side and Roman Rozpad on Ukraine's. He left out the part about the 100 kilos of highly enriched uranium unless and until Holub proved difficult to persuade.

He didn't. After jotting Cyrillic notes on his pad, he said: "And what you need is…"

"A letter from your defense minister to General Hawkins, requesting the system," Neilson responded.

Holub tapped the wooden arm rests of his chair. "Let me propose this:" he said finally: "You will meet the defense minister and anyone else you wish to talk to. But because our resources are too limited to do it ourselves, would you prepare a report for our government on what you think Ukraine's disarmament needs are?"

Inside access would put them way ahead of any other defense contractors considering the Ukrainian disarmament market. "Actually, aside from the computerized tracking system, we already have some ideas," Neilson said and would have told Holub about them except the latter held up his hand to interrupt.

"It will be much easier to work from a written report after you have met with more people," he said, with a pointed glance at the wall clock. "I'm sorry, but I have phone conference in 15 minutes," he said and stood up to end the meeting. "I will call you this afternoon or tomorrow."

"Just out of curiosity, Mr. Holub, where did you study English?" Neilson asked as they followed him down the stairs.

"Here in Kiev, at our International Relations Institute," Holub replied. "But I learned it well during the eight years I served with the Soviet mission to the United Nations in New York. It's strange. Ukrainian émigrés would hold big demonstrations at the mission, calling for independence. We would watch them from the roof and the windows. Independence, of all things. We called them "bourgeois nationalists" and dismissed them as crazy and dangerous. Some of them worked with your CIA."

"Bourgeois nationalists?" repeated Neilson.

For a moment, Holub seemed lost in the memory. "It was a code. Anyone who talked of Ukrainian independence was labeled a "bourgeois nationalist" – like an enemy of the people – and sent them to prison for anti-Soviet agitation and propaganda. The Soviets spied on them in the West, sent in occasional agent provocateurs, even murdered a few."

He shook his head, as though still in disbelief. "Who would have thought," he concluded. "But thank you for an illuminating meeting."

"We'll be waiting for your call," said Neilson.

Outside, Kostya suggested walking back to the hotel so that he could give them a tour. The road was empty of cars anyway.

"Well, Holub is either a mind reader, or he really did bug our rooms," Neilson commented while they strolled under a canopy of chestnut trees. "He's impressive, though. I hope everyone we talk to is like him."

"He is KGB." Kostya swept out both hands at the government buildings around them while leading them around an elderly couple, each lugging a handle on a coach bag bulging with potatoes. "They are all KGB, communoids here. They agreed to independence only when Russian President banned Communist Party after failed Moscow coup. They support independence only to protect themselves. Party made illegal here, too, but two days later – long enough for them to destroy evidence and steal Party money."

When they reached the main road that led down the hill to the hotel, Kostya pointed to a large white building topped with a glass cupola. "Our parliament. After independence we should have elected new MPs but same old communoids in there, like at hotel."

A flock of protesters holding placards gathered in front. All the men had long beards and a few wore colorful vestments and robes. Old women in faded print dresses and flowered kerchiefs surrounded the clergy along with nuns and monks scattered in the colorful crowd like black polka dots. A very tall monk with a straggly beard shook his fist and shouted at the building.

"What's all this?" Kruger asked.

The translator squinted at the placards. "They say: No IUOC."

"Catchy slogan," said Neilson, turning to walk to the hotel.

Kostya followed. "IUOC is Independent Ukrainian Orthodox Church. In Soviet Union, only one church for all Christians: Russian Orthodox Church. But Ukrainian branch of ROC declared independence and elected Kiev Metropolitan of the ROC as the new church's Patriarch. Patriarch is like Pope for Catholics. Those protesters are Russian Orthodox but they rename their church Ukrainian Orthodox Church (Moscow Patriarch) to confuse people." The translator went on to explain the schism, befittingly full of Byzantine complexity.

Neilson barely listened. Orthodoxy, of whatever flavor, wasn't their business. Instead, he gazed at the massive granite walls of a grey building across the street from the parliament, looming over the road like a canyon wall. "This High-Stalinist architecture is amazing."

"Amazingly oppressive," responded Kruger.

"This is government, cabinet of ministers," said Kostya, tapping the pavement with his heel and adding: "There is maze of secret tunnels here, very deep. They go to parliament and to KGB prison that is now International Palace of Culture, and to Central Committee of Communist Party, which is President's building now."

"Got that Dan? There's going to be a quiz," said Neilson and they all headed back to the hotel.

Grease bubbled out of Kruger's Cutlet Kiev Style when he sliced it in half and examined the interior. "I think they took pork chips and pressed them into a hollow ball." But he also had a plate of excellent summer tomatoes, sliced and sprinkled with coarse salt.

The hotel restaurant band had Lambada'd into a break, making it possible to talk without shouting.

Neilson took a bite. "It's not pork. It's Chicken Kiev. Pretty good, too."

"Then they must've put the chicken through the pork chipper, because the meat looks the same," Kruger surmised and dug in.

Neilson cleaned his plate, too. "Why not? If everything is chipped, you can shape the chips into anything and pretend to vary the menu."

Kruger speared a glistening white slab of smoked fish onto a slice of fresh black bread. "At least they have fish tonight. And the bread is great!" he said, washing down a bite with the last of his champagne. Though they had a different waiter, he too had a private supply.

"A beer would taste great right now," he said. "I saw some in that bar in the lobby this morning."

But the beer was gone when they reached the lobby. So was the bar, except for the tables and chairs stacked into a corner. Kruger called across to the dour doorman who reluctantly tore himself away from an issue of *Pravda*. "Bar?" he asked, pointing to the empty space.

The doorman responded by pointing to one of the many signs instructing guests what they could not, should not, and must not under any circumstances do. The DSA team had ignored them.

"NITEBAR FOUR YOU'RE ENJOYMENT OPEN 20:00 TO 01:00. SECOND FLORE" read one sign and they followed the arrow down a short corridor leading to a staircase and another sign.

"Thataway," Kruger said and started up the stairs when a shout came from somewhere nearby. "Help! Please! If you're normal people, please help!" yelled a distinctly American sounding female.

66

"Hey, we're normal," said Neilson, walking through another corridor into a small vestibule, where a slim young woman in a Yale t-shirt peeked from behind the doorman blocking her way into the building.

"Hi there, I'm Cristina Smythe," she said with a toothy smile.

Neilson smiled back. "And I'm Neil Neilson."

"Now that we're acquainted, can you tell Lurch here that I'm with you? He won't let me in otherwise."

The doorman looked over his shoulder to see Neilson point to Cristina, then to himself. With the reluctance that seemed a job requirement, he let her pass.

"Thanks Neil," said Cristina, offering a firm handshake and a level gaze of pewter eyes. "I'm already late for a meeting at the Night Bar."

Neilson introduced Kruger, who said: "Sounds like this Night Bar is a happening place."

Cristina led the way up the stairs. "You guys must be new here. It's the *only* place."

It was an almost empty place when they walked in, except for the attractive young woman sitting strategically alone at some of the tables. "It's still early. It really starts hopping when the restaurant closes," said Cristina, searching the room. "There he is," she said, striding with athletic grace across the maroon carpet to a short, bald man sipping a Heineken at the bar.

"Joe Marchetti, this is Neil Neilson and Dan Kruger," said Cristina. "They kindly escorted me into this dump."

Marchetti shook hands and ordered a round of beers.

"Thanks," said Kruger when the bartender set the cans on the counter.

"Thank Tambrands," Marchetti responded.

"Tambrands?" Neilson repeated, popping his beer.

"Tampons," said Cristina, tossing back a mane of curly black hair. "Women here give new meaning to being on the rag. Do you know they use cheesecloth? I'm trying to figure out how but they all just giggle when I ask. They're pretty puritanical here. But it's God damn medieval and a huge potential market. Tambrands is a pioneer. They set up one of the first joint ventures in Ukraine, back when it was still an S.S.R. Joe's here to do quality control."

"And Cristina is doing a story about us," said Marchetti, leading the way to an empty table.

"Except right now it's like writing about a cadaver," she said, taking a seat and popping open her beer.

"How about you guys?" asked Marchetti.

Neilson and Kruger exchanged glances. "We're military contractors," said Kruger.

"Yeah, we're exploring ways of helping Ukraine with nuclear disarmament," added Neilson, telling the truth but not telling too much.

Marchetti lit a Marlboro, prompting Kruger to unwrap a cigar. Cristina waved the smoke away. "Whoever sells cigarettes here is going to make a fortune. They never heard of Surgeon General's warnings."

"A journalist?" asked Kruger. "Who do you write for?"

"Usually the *Journal*, though I write for some British papers, too. There aren't many foreign reporters here, so I can sell my stuff to a lot of places," she said.

"Is that what brought you here?" asked Kruger.

Cristina leaned back in her chair and considered the question. "Let's just say that my mom is Ukrainian. My dad's a WASP. But he let her torture me with the whole Ukrainian thing growing up."

"Yeah," said Kruger. "My wife, too."

Cristina counted on her fingers. She wore no rings. "Ukrainian dancing on Monday. Ukrainian choir practice on Tuesdays. I forget what we did on Wednesdays, Ukrainian scouts or something. Then Ukrainian school on Saturdays. Church on Sundays. It took a lot of practice to be Ukrainian. I had to miss all the best cartoons growing up."

"I'm surprised you didn't get sick of it, like my wife," said Kruger. Jean had rebelled by becoming a hippie, something her mother still blamed him for.

"I did, for a long time. In my spare time in college, all I did were martial arts: about the most non-Ukrainian girl thing I could imagine," said Cristina. "But I decided to try journalism and a good way to start is to go somewhere with few foreigners – like Kiev. That's what I'm doing."

"Knowing Ukrainian probably helps," said Neilson.

"Not as much as you think," said Kruger.

"Yeah," said Cristina. "They passed a law that government business has to be in Ukrainian. But the Soviets did a pretty good job of pushing Russian on everyone. Most people in the cities speak Russian, while they speak Ukrainian in the villages, except in western Ukraine where they speak Ukrainian in cities, too. A lot of officials only speak Russian. But I took it in college, so I'm OK."

Cristina motioned with her can at Marchetti. "Anyway, I'm doing a story for the *L.A. Times* and using Tambrands as a case study of what companies should do here."

"Which is?" Neilson wondered about other business opportunities.

She replied briefly: "Go home."

"That's too harsh, Cristina," said Marchetti.

Cristina slapped the table. "Harsh? Tambrands has been here for nearly three years and women are still wearing rags. The only places you can buy tampons in Kiev are the hard currency stores and a little kiosk on the grounds of the St. Sophia Cathedral. I know because that's where I have to go. Do you know how weird that is, to buy tampons at a medieval cathedral?"

Neilson tried to think of a witty comeback but Cristina spared him the effort when she suddenly lowered her voice. "Look," she said and they all did to see a gaunt man walk a black Great Dane into the bar. A long scar slashed the man's pasty white cheek. Behind him, a woman with flaming red hair carried a telephone which she placed on a table, jerking her head to indicate that the single lady occupying it should find another place for her business.

"Aren't the prostitutes here amazing?" Cristina said to no one in particular.

"'Smoking hot' is how I'd put it." Marchetti surveyed the room.

"There isn't any other job for women to cash in on their beauty here, except prostitution." Cristina looked at Neilson who, in turn, wondered why. "There's no advertising, so no models. There's not much on TV, so no actresses. Pretty much everyone is poor, so they can't marry rich."

Cristina tilted her head towards the gaunt man. "He's some German, almost like a cartoon with that dog in a spiked collar. But I see him here every time. He must stay in the hotel. I just don't see how he's allowed to bring a giant dog in here when a nice person like me has to beg and plead just to get past the doormen."

The dog circled and sniffed the carpet before settling into a heap.

"I'm sure that ten bucks to the doorman would help you with that," said Marchetti, blowing smoke idly.

"Yeah, I still haven't mastered the art of giving bribes," said Cristina, watching a stocky man dressed in a purple suit join the couple with the dog. "And that guy, the Iraqi Dictator's clone. I've seen him here before, too, but I've never seen them together."

She turned her attention back to the table. "When I first came here last year, all the foreigners could fit at one table. What are all these people doing here?"

CHAPTER 6:

BABYLON RISING

Date: August 15, 1992
To: K3
From: Chief of Station Kiev
Subject: SITREP Rasputin

(S) 1. Neilson and Kruger claim that they have been touring Kiev churches and monasteries with Kostya Beniuk. He is the cousin of Kruger's wife, Jean Beniuk Kruger.

(S) 2. They tell interlocutors that they are in Ukraine to help it with nuclear disarmament. They have not mentioned a Rasputin.

(TS) 3. Repeat requested increase in entertainment budget.
END

---

*T*he Kiev Cave Monastery enclosed a sprawling complex of white stucco topped with green domes and golden cupolas. Baroque plasterwork and faded icons of saints and angels with gold leaf halos embellished the main gate. But Tariq abu Bakr walked swiftly past it, heading instead along the tall stone wall that surrounded the ancient Orthodox cloister. He'd save tourism for a different day.

When he entered the Near Caves, tourists crowded the vestibule. A guide pointed to the lower corner of a Dictator-sized mural depicting a crowd of people gathered around a man in bed.

"This man has died," the guide explained in English, "and here are different angels testifying about his sins." The dead man had many, judging by the dozens of angels in the procession up to the aged patriarch that the Christians considered their God. The Woman gazed down from beside him, too. Tariq never understood her role but it seemed vaguely pagan. Not that he was against pagans. He enjoyed the Dictator's Tammuz festivals, especially the Ishtar actresses.

Tariq purchased a skinny beeswax candle from a bearded monk, lit it from a burning lamp, and obeyed the diagram showing how to hold it upright in his cupped hand.

The stairs descending into the catacombs were steep and uneven, but the temperature dropped steadily from the summer heat outside. When the tour group caught up with him, their candles blazed so brightly they heated the air and sucked all the oxygen in the narrow corridor. Tariq pressed himself into an alcove to let the tourists pass and followed them at a less claustrophobic distance, listening to the guide.

"The Kiev Cave Monastery is one of the greatest Orthodox shrines, founded around 1050 by St. Antony of the Caves," she said, leading the group past a bearded pilgrim standing in front of a heavy wooden door. "Monks first used the caves as shelters, cells, where they could forget worldly life and become closer to God. When they died, this became a catacomb, an underground cemetery for monks," the guide continued. "The Near Caves contain the remains of 75 monks and Orthodox saints, among them Antony, Nikon, Nestor the Chronicler...."

The guide's next words got drowned out by a loud complaint. "Hey Marge, ain't these puny compared to them Roman catacombs?"

"But the beeswax smells nice, doesn't it, dear?"

"Near Caves are 228 meters long," said the guide. "The Church maintains that the monks were holy and that is why their bodies remained uncorrupted. But scientists say that the constant temperatures and qualities of the soil caused natural mummification." The guide pointed to a glass covered coffin encasing a figure clad in embroidered brocade. "Here, you can see their mummified hands."

"Cool!" A boy in an oversized Terminator t-shirt smeared the glass with chocolate stained fingers. "They're kinda' like monkey hands..." he exclaimed before receiving a whack on the rump. "I told you. This is a holy place. Shut up or God will punish you," said a harried woman fanning her face with a map of the sprawling monastery.

Tariq glanced at the desiccated fingers sticking out of a blue brocade sleeve but focused on reading the Old Church Slavonic nameplates above each of the coffins. Anastasi Diakon. Alipi the Artist. Simon.

No Nestor the Chronicler.

He followed the tourists up a steep flight of stairs into a sunlit hall. A young monk with long golden hair and a black skullcap held a basket for collecting candle stumps and a slotted box for donations.

Tariq dropped a counterfeit into the collection box and whispered: "Where is Nestor the Chronicler?"

The monk's jaw dropped at the donation and still more when he saw the familiar moustache of the Iraqi Dictator making it. "An infidel!" he gasped, dropping his basket.

Pagan, not infidel, thought Tariq, remembering the previous night's rites with Sveta and Irina, and himself in the role of the ithyphallic fertility god. But he crossed himself as he had seen his Dictator City neighbors, the clan of Lebanese clothing wholesalers, do many times.

The monk relaxed visibly. "You are a believer?"

Tariq nodded with feigned piety.

"The Soviets made the monastery into a museum. But to celebrate 1,000 years of Christianity in Rus' in 1988, they gave parts of it to the Russian Orthodox Church," the monk explained, crouching to collect the candle stumps that had spilled out of the basket. "We are renewing the monastery in parts, but we still have to let tourists in. So, we limit them to that one corridor, the one you were in. But believers, pilgrims, can go wherever they want in the caves."

Tariq crossed himself again, asking: "And Nestor?"

The monk placed the box and basket on a table of prayer cards. "Come with me, brother," he said, leading Tariq out into the courtyard. Not tall himself, Tariq towered over the monk, whose delicate frame made him look frail.

"You are from Iraq?" he asked.

Tariq bowed in acquiescence.

"You must know of Babylon? The Biblical Babylon?"

"I have been there many times," Tariq lied, though he had seen it on TV. "It is beautiful after the restoration." The Dictator liked appealing to the mantle of Nebuchadnezzar.

The monk's innocent blue eyes opened wide in surprise as they walked back into the caves. "My name is Brother Boris," he said, handing Tariq a beeswax candle.

Tariq lied easily. "My parents named me Ali. But I called myself Alipi when I found the true faith," he said, thinking the monk would assume that the true faith was his own. Luckily, he didn't ask any more questions as they proceeded down the stairwell into the catacombs. Tariq had exhausted his knowledge of Christianity.

Instead of following the newest group of tourists, they turned in the opposite direction, passing the pilgrim that guarded the heavy door, chanting an unintelligible prayer. Tariq's candle illuminated little in the dark corridor. Shadowy figures bowed in front of coffins and a young woman in a kerchief pressed her baby against a tiny pane of glass. Tariq lifted his candle to light the bricks behind it.

Brother Boris whispered: "Our holy fathers lived in these cells, with just these openings for food, until they died and their brethren bricked up the holes. But come."

Tariq wondered where the crazy hermits went to the toilet when the monk stopped in front of a small coffin resting on an alcove. He crossed himself, genuflected and prostrated.

"A child?" asked Tariq with exaggerated reverence when the ritual appeared over.

Brother Boris rose from the floor and braided a strand of his beard. "No, John the Long Suffering agonized so much from the temptations of the flesh that he buried himself to his waist until the sinful parts rotted off."

"His legs were sinful?" Tariq blurted, following the monk past alcoves and antechambers and candlelit chapels, descending deeper into the caves.

"There are many relics here," said Boris as they maneuvered the narrow passageways in the dim light. "The skull of St. Clements is somewhere but I still haven't seen it."

The monk turned a corner and stopped. "Nestor the Chronicler!" he whispered, his breath steaming in the cool, dry air.

The coffin rested on an alcove surrounded by icons and a bronze plaque embossed with an Old Church Slavonic exegesis about the learned monk who chronicled the grand history of medieval Kiev. Boris kissed the glass over the brocade-clad figure with colorful little slippers, crossed himself and genuflected several times.

It's like the Finger of God, Tariq thought with annoyance. Ahmed always genuflected.

When Boris sank to his knees in prayer, Tariq imagined his hotel bed with Sveta cleaving to Irina on the sheets. "A holy man of the Book!" he whispered vehemently and threw himself on the glass top. Murmuring an Arabic children's counting rhyme, he stretched out his arms and reached behind the coffin for the empty ledge.

Boris's candle cast grotesque shadows in the small chamber. But its illumination didn't reach Tariq, who reached into the pocket of his purple silk jacket for the pack of counterfeits wrapped in a black bag. He had almost taken it out when a wild-haired monk swept through, kissing every relic along the way. Tariq's penitential spread across Nestor the Chronicler left little room, but the monk found a spot on the coffin to kiss and bowed before descending deeper into the caves. Brother Boris had closed his eyes in prayer.

Tariq waited a few moments before stuffing the money into the dark ledge and dropping to his knees to contemplate Sveta and Irina's esthetic duality until the monk decided to leave. It didn't take long. Boris rose, placed his hand on Tariq's shoulder. "Your presence in our sacred caves has meaning that I must contemplate. Go with God," he said and disappeared into the dark.

When the sound of his footsteps faded, Tariq retraced the pathway out of the caves, passing Claus's red-haired woman by John the Long-Suffering, and hurried out into the bright light of the courtyard milling with tourists, monks and pilgrims.

Excellent, he thought, climbing the cobblestone hill out of the monastery. A barefoot gypsy boy with a dirty infant tied to his back begged for alms, reaching with filthy hands and jumping back before Tariq could push him away. The game continued until they reached the top of the hill where the boy saw something behind Tariq and scampered into the bushes.

Tariq turned to see dark figures climbing over the monastery walls and dropping expertly to the ground ten feet below.

They wore camouflage.

They were commandos.

And they were running for the caves!

Tariq bolted in the opposite direction.

*I*sn't that the guy from the Night Bar?" Neil Neilson asked.

Dan Kruger looked up from the packet of postcards he had just purchased when a purple blur passed them on the cobblestone street. "Didn't catch his face," he said.

"I'd recognize that moustache anywhere," Neil said. "Where's he rushing to?"

"Maybe that prostitute he's always with. She offered her charming services our first day here."

Kostya Beniuk reddened. "This is holy place. You should not speak of sinful things."

"Where else do people talk about sin these days?" Kruger asked. If Jean's cousin had a sense of humor, he kept it hidden during their tour of every monument and monastery on Kruger's mother-in-law list. Churches, chapels, cathedrals, cloisters. His head spun with saints. The cave monastery, judging by the postcards, was the mega-saint tour. He couldn't imagine how many religious monuments Kiev would have if the Communists hadn't brutally demolished churches and repressed religion.

Kostya stuffed his fists in his pockets as they walked down the cobblestone hill to the caves. "I could give you Communist tour of Revolutionary Kiev. We can go where Lenin's brother slept."

"Nah," said Neilson amiably. "I'm in a spiritually grateful mood after that meeting with Zymnyj this morning."

After weeks of delay, while the entire government went on summer vacation, the defense minister finally agreed to draft a letter to General

74

Hawkins and, for good measure, the U.S. Secretary of Defense. They had to pick it up Monday.

"Except that he didn't have much to tell us," said Kruger. "We knew more about nukes than he did." Shouts and screams interrupted and they turned a corner to see dozens of bearded monks surrounded by commandos dressed in camouflage.

"What are they doing? Arresting monks?" asked Neilson.

Kostya peered at the troops' insignia. "That is not police. It is UNSO. They are paramilitary. Very extreme."

One monk shouted and charged his captors only to hit a wall of muscle whose owner firmly returned him to the fold.

A commando spoke calmly through a megaphone. "He is telling them not to be afraid," the translator explained. "That no one will be harmed. That UNSO come today to claim Cave Monastery for the Independent Ukrainian Orthodox Church."

The monks started shouting and Kostya opened his mouth to continue explaining when Kruger stopped him. "Nuclear weapons are much easier to understand than Ukrainian church politics. Here," he said, handing him Jean's idiot-proof Minolta. "Take a picture of Neil and me by that tall bell tower over there."

That should make his mother-in-law happy.

*B*rother Boris clutched his crucifix in alarm when the uniformed intruder lifted his megaphone to speak. "You may stay only if you accept the jurisdiction of the Independent Ukrainian Orthodox Church and the new Patriarch as its blessed, anointed head. You have five minutes to decide."

Boris had to crane his neck to see his tall companion. In height and breadth, Anton towered a head above the other monks and two heads above Boris. "Again," he murmured. But before Boris could ask him what he meant, a question rose from the crowd.

"Where will we go if we refuse?" asked the fat monk who cleaned the brocade on the Cave's mummified relics every two months.

"Ask your patron, the Russian Patriarch." The commando had an impossibly thick moustache that covered his upper lip. The ends twisted into commas on his cheeks.

"Now I see. It was a sign of evil," Boris whispered, crossing himself. His sweat chilled him.

Anton rubbed his straggly, uneven beard, his brow furrowed in anger. "What sign?"

"An Arabian pilgrim, Brother Anton, from Babylon –" he began to say before the other monks interrupted with chatter about what to do.

Anton exploded in righteous rage. "You fools," he shouted from his lofty height. "If you go along with this, you will destroy the Third Rome. Who but Russia can defend Orthodoxy against the Papist Poles and Muslim infidels?"

"What Third Rome? That's czarist claptrap," said Brother Ivan, the baker, raising his hand for the commandos to notice him when he uttered the blasphemous words.

"Vile and corrupt traitors," Anton muttered.

Boris chewed his lip in dismay as the monks took turns betraying their Mother Church and returning to the cloister. But his companion's vehemence surprised him. Anton expressed little interest in the ecclesiastical and doctrinal nuances of their religion. All he knew of the Bible was the Book of Revelations.

Most of the monks had little education. Few had attended university, including Boris, and priestly education under the Soviets had been rote since their main role had been spying on believers.

"And you two?" asked the commando with the megaphone when everyone else had left. "Do you recognize the Independent Ukrainian Orthodox Church and its blessed Patriarch?"

"You bourgeois nationalists will burn in hell!" Anton shouted.

The gaze above the commando's moustache hardened as he rocked on his heels. "Well, now, that isn't up to you, is it?" he said coolly and then turned his hard gaze on Boris. "And you?"

Fear filled Boris's throat. He had found a home at the monastery. But he shook his head. These had to be Agents of Satan. He had read of their guile and duplicity.

The commando showed them his watch. "It is 1400 hours. You have half an hour to pack up your things. If you're not back by then, we'll find you and won't act so charitably Christian."

A few minutes later, Anton appeared at the door to Boris's tiny room with a brown canvas duffle bag slung over his shoulder. "You're packed?" Boris asked.

"I leave with what I brought," Anton said enigmatically. The monks said little about the secular lives they had abandoned, especially if they were tied with the atheist system of the past. Boris threw his extra robe into a vinyl shoulder bag and stacked his books on top.

Anton reached for an English-language volume. "You know English?"

"A little, with a dictionary."

Anton leafed through the book. "What's this?"

Boris recognized the cover. "It's about the Miracle of Fatima. I haven't read the whole thing, but it says that the Virgin Mary appeared to some children in Portugal in 1917 and gave them secret messages for the Pope."

Anton waved his hand. "The hell with the Pope. The Catholic Church is the Whore of Babylon. Tell me about the Arab."

Boris threw his toothbrush into the bag and crossed himself. "He asked me to show him Nestor the Chronicler and told me that Babylon has been restored."

"Babylon?" The tall monk slammed the book shut and threw it back into Boris's bag. "It's this damned schism. Now that our Church is weak and divided, that Whore of Babylon is going to try to rampage over our holy Orthodox land!"

"You mean the Catholic Church?" asked Boris.

"The Catholics, the Muslims." Anton spat with a disgusted sneer. "You'll see. If our Orthodox Church is dismembered, they'll crawl over us like maggots."

Boris braided the tip of his beard in concern. His confessor, Father Feodosi, told him that the Catholic Church was the Whore of Babylon. He dug his concordance out of the shoulder bag and leafed through the long entry next to Babylon. "There's a lot about Babylon in Isaiah," he said, replacing the concordance and taking out his Bible. With his bag tossed over his shoulder, he followed Anton to the courtyard, where the demon commando leader still stood.

"Now, please find another place for your salvation," he said, extending his arm towards the white stucco gate that led out of the courtyard.

While they climbed up the steep, cobblestone hill out of the monastery, Boris leafed through the pages of Isaiah. "And Babylon…will be like Sodom and Gomorrah when God overthrew them. It will never be inhabited or dwelt in for all generations," he read aloud. "You're right, Brother Anton. If Babylon has a new life, a new evil must be afoot. This schism is a part of it."

The tall monk said nothing until they reached the stop for the No. 20 trolleybus.

"Where will we go?" Boris asked.

Anton sounded resigned. "I know of a place."

*R*oman Rozpad nodded with enthusiasm at the good news about the defense minister.

"We're confident that this letter will help us win the contract," said Dan Kruger over drinks in the Night Bar.

"With a generous consultancy for you," Neil Neilson added. "So, you appreciate how important it is to keep the logs fully updated?"

The Ukrainian didn't hesitate. "Absolutely," he said and stood up. "This is very, very good, my friends. Thank You. I will correct the logs immediately,

Joe Marchetti walked into the bar a few moments after Rozpad left. "Hey, guys! How many churches today?" he asked, waving his hand at the bartender to bring a round of drinks before taking a seat at their table.

"None," said Dan, irritated that Marchetti didn't ask if he could join them. "Tried seeing that Cave Monastery but I think God's tired of Neil's face and intervened with a little revolution."

The Tambrands inspector ignored the remark and glanced around the bar. "Here comes that guy with the dog."

Neilson watched the German, the Great Dane and the red haired woman carrying the telephone. "The Red Valkyrie. Still haven't heard her say a single word."

"So, how's business?" asked Marchetti.

"Pretty good," said Neil.

"Yeah? I want to hear something good after this week."

"Problems with tampons?"

"The problem is no tampons. Our cotton supplier is Uzbekistan, which is a separate God damn country now. So, we have to negotiate totally new contracts. The phones are a complete mess." Marchetti blew smoke towards the ceiling. "And besides, their cotton sucks," he concluded before changing the subject. "And you guys? Had a good day?"

"Had a good meeting," Kruger said cryptically. When they called Fred with news about the letter, he told them that the Hughes Corporation also planned to sniff around the Ukrainian disarmament market. But if Hughes found out that DSA was in the game, they might do more than sniff.

Luckily, the bartender interrupted, placing Heinekens and two empty mugs in front of Kruger and Marchetti. "Chivas on rocks," he said, placing the glass in front of Neilson who lifted it, sniffed and took a sip.

"Now this is the drink of civilized man"

Dan wiped the beer can with a cocktail napkin and popped the top. "Nothing is more civilized than beer, boss. Civilization wouldn't have even existed without beer."

Neilson covered his ears in mock suffering. "Not the beer theory, *again.*"

Marchetti looked confused. "Beer theory?"

"The beer theory of civilization," said Kruger.

The tampon inspector shifted in his chair. "You're kidding me, right?"

"I'm serious as hell," said Kruger. "Scientists with alphabets after their names thought it up." He pointed at Marchetti. "How much do you know about the Neolithic revolution, the invention of agriculture, that kind of stuff?"

78

Marchetti wore the same blank stare that Kruger encountered in bars when he got bored enough to mention the beer theory, though in this case he wanted to bore Marchetti so he would leave.

"Well, for hundreds of thousands of years, humans obtained food by hunting, fishing and gathering wild plants," he began. "Then, about ten-thousand years ago in what is now the Middle East, people started cultivating plants, grains mostly. It's called the Neolithic Revolution and it was the first step towards the rise of cities, the invention of writing and what we now call civilization."

Marchetti tapped his beer can. "This sounds like a long story."

Neilson chuckled. "This is the condensed version. It's almost over."

"Anyway," Kruger continued, "the big mystery is: why? It turns out that hunter-gatherer tribes in Africa, South America and a few other places are pretty efficient. They spend less time getting their food than subsistence farmers spend cultivating their fields. So, why did these Neolithic people decide to work harder to grow grain that they could get more easily by gathering it in the wild?"

"No idea," said Marchetti.

"Because they didn't plant it for food," said Kruger. "They had plenty of food. But they needed extra grain for something else. And what might that something have been?"

"Beer?" Marchetti ventured.

"You win the prize," said Kruger. "From beer to the Bomb: civilization in a nutshell."

Marchetti sounded dubious. "This is a joke, right?"

"He never jokes about beer," said Neilson, stirring his whiskey.

The table fell silent. "So, who'd you guys meet with?" Marchetti asked. "Anyone interesting?"

"No one you know, I'm sure," said Neilson.

Marchetti scanned the small tables occupied by the usual prostitutes. A stout woman wearing a stained apron mopped up a spill by the door. "How is it that the young women here – not just at the hotel, but on the streets, everywhere – are so ass-kicking hot, but the older women are so absolutely not?"

"Life is tough," said Kruger. "It wears them down. The men aren't Adonises either."

The tampon inspector yawned. "Sorry, guys. It's been a long week. All I plan to do this weekend is sleep. How about you?"

"We're going to a genuine, authentic Ukrainian village," said Kruger.

"Where?"

"A place called Dikanka. My wife's family is from there. It's a few hours south of Kiev."

Marchetti stood up and stretched back his shoulders. "Well, enjoy your cultural experience. How long are you still in town?"

"We'll see. It depends on the rest of our meetings," said Neilson. "Thanks for the beer."

"Thank Tambrands," Marchetti replied and left.

Dan turned to watch him go. "Nosey fellow, isn't he?"

"He's alright, probably just bored. I mean, he actually sat through your beer theory."

Kruger lowered his voice. "So, you think Rozpad is telling the truth?"

"If he hasn't logged the HEU yet, he might not," said Neilson.

Both of them studied their drinks, so they didn't notice Claus Hesse picking up the receiver on his telephone, dialing a single number and listening from the tiny microphone planted in each bar table since the KGB used them to eavesdrop.

"Think he might offer it to someone else?" asked one of the Americans.

"Hope not," said the other one. "I suspect there are plenty of buyers for a 100 kilos of HEU."

Claus's pulse quickened, imagining the riches that 100 kilos of HEU could bring him. He'd never have to work again, or spend time among the smelly Slavs and ex-Soviet stink holes. He replaced the receiver and bent down to Siegfried, who perked up at his master's attention. "*Mein kliener Hund*," he said, stroking the dog's head. "Now we can do some real business."

CHAPTER 7

MESSENGERS

FAXNEWS-UKRAINE

September 1, 1992 (Lviv, Ukraine). On a local television talk show, an MP who returned from Washington, D.C. said: "The Americans now understand the complex problems involved in Ukraine's disarmament." When asked what had changed, he said: "Until now, they received their information from Russian sources. Now, they are dealing with us."

September 15, 1992 (Sevastopol, Ukraine). The Crimean Tatar population has grown from zero percent in 1989 to twelve percent today. Most cannot return to their old homes, which house new occupants, and are squatting on open land to build housing. They are well organized and oppose Crimean separatism, leading to occasional fights with Black Sea Fleet personnel.

END

Faxnews-Ukraine – Your source of English-language news about Ukraine

---

TOP SECRET – PURPLE
Handle via Agent Channels Only
Date: **September 16, 1992**
To: **K3**
From: **Chief of Station Kiev**
Subject: SITREP Rasputin

(TS) 1. Neilson and Kruger are visiting the village of Dikanka, located outside the Uzin nuclear bomber base. Humintel reports compromised custody and control there.

(TS) 2. Neilson and Kruger spend every evening in close proximity to notorious East German arms trafficker Claus Hesse; a woman registered as Greta Nichtgeil, who might be the Neo-Nazi terrorist Helga; and an Iraqi registered as Mohammed Ali.

(TS) 3. There is no government official surnamed Rasputin.

(S)   4. Acknowledge increase in entertainment budget.

END

TOP SECRET – PURPLE

Exempt from Automatic Downgrade

---

*N*eil Neilson groaned in astonishment when his host gestured at a table covered with food. How can they be awake, much less hungry, he thought through the dense fog in which alcohol residue soaked his neurons. "Toilet?" he croaked. He needed to pee but the smells of frying animal fats made vomiting equally attractive.

The lanky bald man Neil remembered as Kostya's father flashed a display of metal teeth framed by leathery skin. "*Tak, toilet, toilet,*" exclaimed Mr. Beniuk, waving both hands in emphatic direction for Neilson to follow him into the kitchen. Mrs. Beniuk waved a welcoming spoon at the American guest stumbling towards the mud room.

Neilson couldn't remember where the bathroom was and followed his host, who opened the rough wooden door as if to step outside but then turned and squealed: "*Ni, ni,*" pointing at the floor. Neil's boozy brain lurched back violently against his skull when he looked down and he closed his eyes until the neural fog cleared enough to register a stained rug covered with shoes and slippers.

Where'd I get these slippers, he wondered when his vision focused on his feet and moved up his legs to see the wrinkled trousers in which he had obviously slept. They had arrived at night, he recalled, because the bus from Kiev kept stalling. Chaotic images of pork kabobs sizzling over a campfire and an endless series of toasts flitted in his memory.

Mr. Beniuk handed Neil his mud-caked Docksiders, tucked his own tweed trousers into rubber galoshes and escorted his guest into a medley of barnyard odors. Before Neil reached the bottom of the stairs, a quartet of geese attacked him with a jarring fugue of honks and flapping wings. But the host shooed them away and led Neil through the vegetable garden to a wooden outhouse he had no recollection of seeing and no desire to

82

enter. But he couldn't just water the cabbages with Mr. Beniuk standing there. Breathing through his mouth, he swung open the wooden door with trepidation only to find a plush toilet seat over a hole dropping into an empty zinc tub. It was cleaner than the toilets on most transatlantic flights.

Outside, Kruger had replaced Mr. Beniuk and leaned against a pear tree to urinate. Thick red lines creased his face from spending the night pressed heavily into crumpled sheets. He opened his eyes a crack, zipped his pants and trudged back to the house. "My aunt-in-law, if there is such a thing, is requesting our company for breakfast."

Neilson grimaced and Kruger clutched his temples. "Do you have to walk so loud?"

"Hey buddy, this was your brilliant idea. What happened last night, anyway?" Neil asked when they entered the yard. A rumbling tractor belching clouds of diesel exhaust had distracted the guard geese.

"They poisoned us," responded Kruger. "But since we foiled their plans by surviving, they're going to increase the dosage. That must've been my mother-in-law's idea in making me come here."

At the bottom of Kruger's obligatory tourism list, Jean had written her mother's native village with instruction to photograph every inch. More weeks had passed with empty promises of meetings. The government officials seemed only vaguely acquainted with the concepts of meetings, appointments and schedules. Fred Wexler, waiting for results back at DSA's Washington office, expressed daily unhappiness over the added expenses.

They changed from muddy shoes into slippers and walked back into the house, where all three Beniuks sat at the table expectantly. Furniture crammed the whitewashed room, its walls decorated with icons, embroideries and framed photo collages.

"Good afternoon! You sleep well?" said Kostya, as chipper as his parents.

"If a stupor can be called sleep. What time is it?" asked Kruger, heading back to the tiny bedroom Kostya had sacrificed for his guests, while he slept on a sofa.

Mrs. Beniuk leaned towards her son. "Mama says: food is hot," Kostya translated. "It is 12 o'clock, time to eat."

Neilson followed Dan to find his shaving kit. "Can I wash up first?" The fuzz on his teeth felt ready to sprout.

"Not now. I bring water from well after we eat."

Bile rose in Neilson's throat when he saw the table laden with mashed potatoes, a roast chicken, eggs, ham, cheese, tomatoes, pickles, bread, butter, salted white fish. "I can't," he groaned.

When her son translated, Mrs. Beniuk's cheer didn't fade as she gestured at the table and chattered. "But you must eat," Kostya insisted.

Kruger held out his palm in protest. "Really, we're not…"

"Not hungry." Neilson completed the sentence.

When Kostya translated their answer to his mother, the reddening of her face as she muttered at her son reminded Kruger about her high blood pressure. "But Mama kill chicken for you," Kostya explained.

Kruger slumped his shoulders in resignation and headed for the table. "Now, that's a guilt trip."

Mr. Beniuk poured from a ceramic carafe into their glasses, motioning at his guests to pick them up. Kruger took a sniff and grimaced. "See," he whispered to Neilson. "Poison."

Their host patted his wife's hand while he spoke and listened to his son translate: "Father says: 'Thank God I live to see the day when two Americans could visit Dikanka in an independent Ukrainian state free of Communism and Moscow."

Mr. Beniuk raised his glass in conclusion. "May we in Ukraine live as well as our family in America!"

Neilson clinked glasses with Mrs. Beniuk, whose hair faded from silver to blond and ended in a bun. Wrinkles at her eyes and mouth drew a tired but kind face. Her floral dress strained against the safety pin at her bosom.

"I sincerely hope you do," he said, clinking with Mr. Beniuk and taking a sip of the homemade brew that smelled like his chemistry lab in college. A fly buzzed into his face and he waved it away, returning his attention to Mrs. Beniuk, who leaned in to ask a question.

"She hear there are no flies in America," Kostya said, nodding with vigorous agreement.

"Of course there are flies," Neilson said. Kruger's dazed expression suggested that the boss should handle the brunch repartee with the kinfolks.

"No, no," said Kostya. "Our neighbor visit family in Chicago and he say he see no flies. I remember this."

Of all the American myths Neilson had heard in his foreign travels, this was one of the oddest. "Just because he didn't see any doesn't mean they don't exist. Whoever he visited probably had screens on the windows."

Kostya explained to his mother, who pointed out the open window next to an ancient television and jabbed her husband, speaking rapidly. While the hosts chattered, Neilson picked at the food Mrs. Beniuk had heaped on his plate. His stomach had settled and the throbbing in his head had fuzzier edges. He laid a thin slab of smoked fish on a piece of bread only to find the topping melt tastelessly in his mouth. "What kind of fish is this, Kostya?" he asked, pointing at the plate of glistening white slices.

"It is not fish. It is *salo*. I tell you in hotel when we first met. It is Ukrainian delicacy," the translator said, putting a double layer of the stuff on black bread with a slice of raw onion.

"But what is it?"

Kostya took a bite dreamily. "Mama makes the best *salo*. It is a narcotic."

Neilson's brain pounded at his eyeballs. "I'm sure it is. But what the hell is it made of?"

"It is from pig, but I not know English word." Kostya pointed with his fork to the golden edge. "This is skin," he said and then pointed to the white part. "And this is *salo*."

"Fat," said Kruger, momentarily roused from his hangover.

"What?" exclaimed Neilson, throwing the canapé on his plate.

"It's pig fat," said Kruger. "Looks raw, too."

Neilson's stomach pitched and he ran out of the house, stumbling in his slippers to patch of grass where he leaned over, closed his eyes and…

"Hwoonk!"

…found himself staring into the throat of a killer gander. Flapping its wings and honking to summon the rest of the gang, the goose reached out to snap at the intruder's nose, triggering a burst of adrenaline that neutralized Neilson's gastric juices. He waved the bird into a temporary retreat and returned to the house. Mrs. Beniuk cleared dishes from the table where Dan clutched his shaving kit.

"Where is everyone?" he asked.

"Preparing for church," Dan replied in a monotone.

Neilson held his head in his hands. "Another church?"

Kostya walked into the kitchen with a bucket of water. "Church is in historical monastery father wants to show. Here is water. I show where to wash."

Dan followed, scratching his ear and muttering: "Another monastery. What luck."

*W*hen their little group strolled down the road ten minutes later, neighbors shouted from their yards and joined them, chattering excitedly about the *Amerkanskis*.

"You are first Americans in Dikanka," Kostya explained. "Look," he said pointing with Kruger's Minolta at an endless expanse of golden wheat swaying under the pale summer sky. "This is Ukrainian flag: The blue and yellow. Except it still belongs to red collective farm where my family live like serfs. Village people grow more food in private gardens than in all collective farms."

The wheat was sparser than what Neilson had seen in the American Midwest, despite Ukraine's fertile black earth. "Why keep the collective? Your laws allow private farming now, don't they?"

Kostya waved back at his parents following in their growing entourage. "I try to tell them. But they say: without collective farm, they have no place to steal."

They entered a small yard cluttered with shabby wooden stalls and a large, shiny steel cage. "That is cage for poles," Kostya explained. The size of a corral, it had wide openings around its perimeter.

"Why keep poles in a cage?" asked Neilson, stopping to take a closer look.

"People steal," said Kostya.

The cage appeared too new and expensive, given the village's poverty. "I don't understand. Why do you need a fancy, new cage for poles? Why not just lock them in a barn?"

Kostya gaped as thought he had uttered a monstrosity. "You cannot lock poles in barn!"

"Why not? They're just poles," said Neilson. The circumstances imposed too much confusion on his hung-over head.

"Dr. Nick, you are a good man. How can you talk of locking people in barn?"

Neilson's head began to pound again. "People? But you said poles..."

"As in Polish people, evidently" interrupted Kruger with a chuckle that brought one hand to his temple. "Ooh, that hurts."

"I still don't get it," said Neil. "It's a jail for Polish people who steal?"

"Polish traders come on market days to Dikanka with baggages and luggages of clothes from Turkey." Kostya tugged on his checkered shirt. "I buy this from Poles. And they bring cage so they can stay inside with things they sell and people outside can see but not steal." Kostya pointed to the wooden sign affixed to the cage. "That sign says: Trade by Foreign Citizens. Since Poles come to Dikanka, many people from military base come to our market. This is good for village," said Kostya, leading them away from the cage and past a row of cottages.

Neil jolted. "What base?"

"I tell you last night. Next to Dikanka is nuclear bomber base. That is why Cousin Jean could not come here when she visited Ukraine. And that is why Poles come only recently. This area closed to foreigners till independence."

Neil turned to Dan. Dots of tissue studded his face after shaving in cold water. "Did we know there's a base here, Dan?"

"If we did, I forgot," Kruger said, wincing at the whoop of laughter that erupted behind them when they stopped in front of a stucco church with iron domes on top.

"Mary, Holy Protector Church," Kostya announced, with a sweep of his arm at the surrounding whitewashed buildings. "Those are Hero of Socialism collective farm administrative buildings. But for many centuries people took refuge in monastery from infidel Muslim Turks and Tatars."

He pointed at a shed roofed with corrugated metal. "Bell tower stood there. But in 1930, Bolsheviks come and take bells for melting and cut off tower to make roof. The monks were arrested and sent to Siberia. Dikanka collectivized three years later." Kostya looked at his father, who gazed at his guests with proprietary pride while chatting with his curious neighbors. "My father's whole family died in 1932-33 famine, when Bolsheviks take away food to force peasants to join collective farm. Almost everyone in Dikanka starve to death. Seven-million people in Ukraine. The Soviets denied it for decades."

"Now when Protector church reopen in 1991, collective farm give one house to open new monastery," Kostya continued, leading them to a tidy glade where two bearded monks kneeled at an elaborate tombstone enclosed by a wrought iron fence. Kostya whispered in Neilson's ear while the villagers crossed themselves and murmured prayers: "This is grave of Protector Monastery martyr, Monk Timothy, kidnapped by Turks and killed in Constantinople. His body brought back here in 1678."

Kruger leaned towards Neil, who was watching the monk with long blond hair rising from his knees. "I'm sure I'll be sorry for asking, but what did I miss?"

"A martyr monk killed by Turks in Constantinople," Neilson whispered just as a lament rose from the crowd.

Kruger turned away and started quietly singing his favorite shower song.

>*It's Istanbul, not Constantinople*
>*No, you can't go back to Constantinople*
>*Coz its Istanbul not Constantinople.*

*T*he Mary, Holy Protector Monastery greeted Boris and Anton with an uproar when they arrived on the bus from Kiev. The only monk ordained to conduct mass had just celebrated the liturgy and mentioned the imposter Patriarch.

"He's taking the side of that schismatic Independent Ukrainian Orthodox Church," explained Vlad, the fat novice ordered to house the guests after feeding them black bread, scallions and buttermilk. He waddled up a narrow staircase to the cloisters on the second floor, panting as he talked. "And the sacristan is taking his side! He has the keys to the church and can lock the rest of us out!"

The floorboards trembled as they passed through a corridor of tiny rooms, each outfitted with pressboard beds, desks and chairs of the Soviet cookie-cutter kind. It reminded Boris of the furniture in his bedroom when his father ran the stud farm – until the livestock feed system collapsed along with everything else. His father begged collective farms as far away as Odessa for hay and grain but found nothing. They slaughtered hundreds of horses for sausage except for a few prime Ukrainian Warmbloods sold for pennies to German dressage riders.

The family had to move in with Boris's uncle on the outskirts of Kiev. They didn't have beds but slept instead on unfolding armchairs with bedcovers extracted nightly from the cupboard where his uncle hid the Lenin bust when parliament banned the Communist Party.

Too broken to work, his father spent his days drinking, smoking and arguing with the no-longer Communist TV. He'd berate Boris with verbal abuse that never descended into violence but always left a mark. After one vicious attack, Boris stormed out, taking the bus to central Kiev where he wandered for weeks, sleeping on park benches in the outdoor World War II museum. He stumbled accidentally onto the Cave Monastery next door, but the monks recognized a lost soul and had welcomed him just as they had welcomed Anton a year later.

"And the hegumen? Where does he stand?" asked Anton, punching his palm. The hegumen headed the monastery and had a powerful, if not decisive, voice.

Vlad panted and crossed himself. "God help us, I'm not sure. They're downstairs discussing it. But I pray for unity. We can't let our Holy Russian Church fragment."

The novice motioned towards a freshly painted room. "Here, Anton. You helped paint this one. It is fitting that you should have it."

Anton acknowledged the recognition and entered the room

While the novice ushered Boris into the neighboring cell. Angry voices rose from the ground floor. "The Church is Christ's body and schism means its dismemberment," shouted one voice followed by a loud and deep response: "Open your eyes, Brother! This is no longer Russia. Ukraine is independent and should have an independent Church."

Vlad appeared in Anton's doorway, his beard drooping around a pudgy pout that deepened into dismay at the sound of scuffles, shouts and crashing below. "This is truly Satan's work!" he whispered, lumbering off towards the fray.

Anton walked into Boris's room. "Damn this schism. It's infecting everything. Is there nothing we can do to stop it?" he cried, slamming his hand against the doorframe. The sound startled Boris, who dropped the books he had lifted from his shoulder bag. His Bible fell to the floor and opened along its worn spine.

"Oh, no!" Boris exclaimed, stooping to pick up the book and kiss it to remove the defilement. But when he saw that the faint dampness of his lips had left a mark on Revelations 13:18, he felt a chill. "Jesus, Mary and the Saints! Anton! Listen!" he said, reading the passage.

This calls for wisdom. If anyone
has insight, let him calculate the number
of the beast, for it is man's number.
His number is 666."

Boris crossed himself and slumped into a chair, grasping the Bible with both hands. "The Bible opened to this page just when you asked how we can stop the schism."

Anton's rage dissipated at the sight of Boris's shock as he explored the implications. "The schism, the Babylonian pilgrim and now this, the number of the beast." Boris braided a strand of his blond beard. "Why is God giving *us* the signs? We are mere novices." He jumped up from his seat to check the corridor. "We can't tell anyone," he whispered when he returned. "We don't know whose side they're on.

His eyes returned to the Bible. "It says the number of the beast is man's number, but which man's?"

Anton picked crumbs out of his beard listening to shouts of "Heretic!" and "Muscovite lackey!" He snapped his fingers. "Reagan," he said. "I read that Ronald Wilson Reagan had the number of the beast. Reagan began the destruction of Holy Russia."

Boris counted the letters in the American president's name on his fingers. "Six, six, six," he said. 'But Reagan is no longer president. Why would God give us a message about a person with no power? It makes no sense," Boris protested.

"It doesn't have to make sense to be true," insisted Anton. "It's like faith." But as he spoke, another thought coalesced and his eyes ignited. "The Ukrainian President!" He spat and began pacing the room. "He came up with this scheme to destroy the Third Rome. I saw him on TV saying Ukraine needs an independent Orthodox Church, the hypocrite. He calls himself an atheist, too."

Anton gaped at Boris. "His name is six times six letters."

Boris counted off the Cyrillic letters of the Ukrainian President's familiar name. "Six, six, six. Good God! Our president has the number of the beast!"

"Your president, not mine," said Anton. "The Anti-Christ! I knew this schism could only be hatched in the depths of hell!" Anton kept punching his palm with loud smacks while Boris bent his head over the Bible.

"The Beast himself is the Anti-Christ. Or maybe it's the other one, who does miracles?" Boris scratched his chin and read on. "A lot of people can have the number of the beast."

"Ah, so Reagan can still be one of them?"

"But the number lets them buy and sell. Why buy and sell?"

"Ca-pi-ta-lism," said Anton, punctuating each syllable with a punch. "Reagan always wanted to destroy Communism and now that the Soviet Union has collapsed, your Ukrainian President wants to let the capitalists run rampage here." The smacking stopped. "This schism is Satan's work. And by opposing it, we'll do God's work."

"How can we oppose it? There are only two of us." Boris closed the Bible and nervously braided a third strand of his beard while Anton paced. "We should pray for guidance, for the Lord to send us another message, explaining what we should do," he suggested, clasping his hands in the folds of his robe. "But the spirit of our faith is lacking in this place," he said, motioning with his chin at floor beneath them, where the monks continued their loud argument. "And I don't think they'll let us into the church."

Anton stopped pacing. "There's a martyr to Orthodoxy buried outside. St. Timothy. We can go there."

A few minutes later, they were kneeling in the mown grass surrounding the grave." Give us a sign, beloved Timothy, martyr to the faith. We humbly beseech thee," Boris prayed.

"A sign," said Anton, his head bowed over his clasped hands.

"Show us how to preserve the unity of our Lord's Incarnate body in the mystery of our apostolic church."

"Amen," said Anton.

Boris bent his head to pray, and then turned to his comrade. "Anything?"

"No. How long is it supposed to take?"

Boris wove the three braids anxiously. "I don't know," he said, leaning back to peer past Anton's shoulder at a large crowd following two men who approached the grave.

"Those two must be foreigners," he said, pointing his chin at the men whose clothes, though wrinkled, looked new. But their teeth were what betrayed them. A mouth without a multicolored collection of gold, silver and steel – or whatever the local dentist had available in the shortage ridden economy – had to be foreign.

"Foreigners?" asked Anton.

"Americans," said Boris after hearing them speak.

"Capitalists!" Anton spat the word.

"No wait," said Boris, patting his comrade's arm. "Not all Americans are capitalists. They have exploited workers, too. But if these are the first Americans here, maybe they are our messengers."

"Go talk to them."

Boris started to rise, then sank back to the grass. "But my English is poor, I could misunderstand."

"If they are God's messengers, you'll understand."

Boris crossed himself, murmured a short prayer and stood up to brush grass from his cassock. The Americans came closer, followed by a young man Boris's age describing the church and monastery. He had teeth as white as the Americans' but he spoke in accented English.

The crown sang a lament for the dead while the American with curly black hair stood with a dreamy face resembling Brother Varlaam back at the Cave Monastery when his Jesus prayer put him into a trance. He chanted quietly and Boris crept closer in time to hear him say: "Constantinople" when the singing suddenly stopped. A plump matron sidled up to his companion to offer him a jar of home-made pickled pig's feet.

The fair visitor's eyes glared like hot glass flashing in the midday sun as he gnashed his teeth at the legions surging around him with chattering questions.

"I have a brother in Chicago."

"An aunt in Arizona."

"Can you take a letter to them? They never write anymore…"

The monk moved closer. "What Constantinople?" he repeated in English when an old man sporting a toothless grin and rows of medals pinned to a faded grey jacket pushed him away to tap the translator on the arm. "Kostya, tell them I shook an American's hand in Berlin in 1945. Never thought I'd see one again. What brings them here?"

If God had sent the messengers, it had to be His will that the old man interrupted, thought Boris while trying to listen to the translation. He didn't recognize many of the words.

The fair visitor whispered to his companion, who had the groggy expression Varlaam displayed upon emerging from his mystical trances. Except Varlaam didn't shave and didn't have the unfortunate nicks and cuts afflicting the messenger. Boris tried not to stare.

"Nuclear weapons…" the dark visitor said, followed by a long discourse in which Boris only caught the word "destroy". He waited to listen to the translation. But when one of the schismatic monks showed up and offered to show the church, Boris retreated so that the adversary wouldn't suspect that the visitors had offered the One True Apostolic Church a message of salvation.

He trotted back to Anton, who flicked tiny ants off his robe. "Well?" he asked.

Boris sank to his knees. "They said: 'Constantinople, nuclear weapons, destroy.' What can it mean, Anton? If the Ukrainian President has the number of the beast, what does Constantinople have to do with it? And why nuclear weapons? It makes no sense."

Even kneeling, Anton's lanky frame came up to Boris's chin. His eyes lit again with strange fire.

"I told you. It doesn't have to make sense to be true," he said, clasping his hands. "We must pray more. We are righteous and all will become clear."

*D*an Kruger tucked his knees behind the front seat of the orange car weaving around a pothole obstacle course. "I actually preferred that rickety old bus we came here on," he said loudly over the squeaky suspension. "At least I didn't have to fold into a pretzel."

The translator turned from the front seat with a worried glance at his charges. "Sorry that bus cancel. Russia supply Ukraine with petrol and raise prices this year so there is deficit."

Neilson shifted uncomfortably. "You couldn't find a bigger car? Those Volgas looked roomy." Wires hung from under the steering wheel and the boxy interior stank of gasoline. "This damn thing makes a Yugo look good."

Kostya's head bounced from the bumpy ride. "No, no one else have petrol. Only Dima. He is driver for collective farm, so he takes petrol from garage," he said, gesturing at the driver, who studied the windshield with a concentrated scowl.

The car had just driven a few hundred feet from the Beniuk's house when the engine silenced and the car rolled to a quiet halt. Dima reached under his seat for a thick screwdriver and walked to the trunk. Dan turned to look through the grimy rear window. "What's going on?"

Kostya shrugged. "Fixing engine?"

"The engine's in the trunk?" Neilson checked the time. Six o'clock and Kostya said it was a two-hour drive. "Can you find out what the problem is?"

Kostya followed the driver and within a few minutes reported: "It is carburetor. He say it not take long to fix."

Kruger lifted the front seat and pushed it. Nothing but its own weight held it in place. "If we're stuck, I'd rather be stuck outside," he said, climbing out and walking a few feet to an old wooden bench outside one of the fenced yards. He watched a wagon clatter on the asphalt drawn by a dappled grey horse. A grizzled old man in the driver's seat held the reins in his one hand. The short sleeve of his missing left arm flapped in the warm breeze as he stopped the horse in front of a periwinkle blue cottage across the road. Two more doses of vodka after their church tour made him drowsy. The tranquil mooing of distant cows lulled him to sleep when Neilson's voice jerked him awake.

"Isn't that Roman Rozpad?" asked Neilson as a man in a baseball cap lifted a crate of tall green bottles from the back. "Roman," Neilson called across the road. But the man ignored him and carried the crate to a metal shed just when the car engine rattled to life. "We go now," called Kostya.

Kruger climbed into the back seat while Neilson kept studying the scene across the street. The man returned to the cart for another crate, but the cap hid much of his face. "That guy could be his twin," he said, climbing into the front seat. "Kostya," he asked, pointing out the window. "Who lives in that house, where the cart is?"

"That is Rozpad house." The car picked up speed and bounced over the potholes out of the village.

"Roman Rozpad's" Neilson asked in surprise.

"Roman is son. Nuclear official. You know him?" Kostya had never seen them with Rozpad, whose knowledge of English dispensed with the need for a translator.

"We do," said Kruger with a glance at Neilson: "But evidently we don't know him very well."

*K*ruger squeezed the vinyl cushion against his knees when Dima the driver passed a trailer spitting black smoke on the narrow road. "Tell him to slow down, Kostya!"

The translator leaned over to the driver, who chattered back, his eyes flickering in the rear view mirror in Kruger's direction. "He says not to worry. He is best driver in Dikanka," Kostya said.

"As far as we can tell, he's the only driver in Dikanka," Kruger muttered, keeping watch on the road. They had reached smoother asphalt but there were just two lanes and Dima sped up to tail a truck hauling dirty hogs. He zipped alongside and prepared to pass it when another truck appeared around the bend in the oncoming lane. Dima stomped on the gas peddle and the engine grinded, but without much added speed.

"Goddam it!" shouted Kruger. The driver was either an idiot or suicidal, trying to pass on a curving road, in a car with less pickup potential than most grandfathers.

Dima slid back into the right lane and the engine conked out to heed Kruger's command. When it rolled to a stop, the driver took his screwdriver from under the seat and went out to inspect the trunk.

"Again?" said Neilson. The car creaked and moaned with Dima's machinations.

"It is carburetor. It fill up with petrol," Kostya explained.

The driver carried a metal rim alongside the car and spilled its contents into a drainage ditch bordering a field of sunflowers.

"But if you have a shortage, why is he dumping perfectly good gasoline instead of saving it, or pouring it back into the gas tank?" asked Neilson.

Kostya translated the question for Dima.

"He says: 'Why? He has 40 liters in baggage and can always steal more.'"

"I thought you said the engine is in the trunk," said Kruger.

Kostya pointed to the hood of the car: "No, no. Baggage is there."

"Great," exclaimed Kruger, smacking the back of the driver's seat. "Tell that cretin that if I see the speedometer go above 60 kilometers or if he tries to pass so much as a wheelchair, I will pour those 40 liters over his head and light my fucking cigar off the flames."

The threat proved superfluous. Whenever the speedometer exceeded 45 kilometers, the engine died. They made eight stops to drain the carburetor and four hours passed before Kostya announced: "We are close to hotel."

Kruger woke with a start. After staring at the speedometer, the driver and the road for the first three hours, he had dozed off from boredom. The bus ride to Dikanka had been interesting, watching tired people trudging on and off at dusty stops carrying heavy bags of mysterious contents with taciturn fortitude. But at night in a car he saw nothing but an endless expanse of darkness without even a billboard to break the monotony. Outside his window, a restored gateway of medieval Kiev stood spotlighted above the chestnut trees. "The Golden Gate," he murmured, recalling his mother-in-law monument list.

Dima stopped the car. "Traffic police, checking documents," said Kostya. "No problem."

The traffic officer's uniformed pot belly, enclosed with a hammer and sickle belt buckle, almost concealed the stack of license plates he held under his arm. "What's with the license plates?" he asked Kostya.

"They park illegally."

"Don't they give them a ticket?"

"Fine is small. No one care. But license plates disappear for long time in traffic police bureaucracy. Then people care very much."

Kruger tried leaning back into the seat. It makes sense, he thought drowsily. The short narrow bed in his room began to seem inviting. His feet hung off the end, but at least he didn't have to squeeze his knees up to his chin.

"*S*tand back! The system is armed!" a metallic voice boomed in English followed by a trio of adolescent giggles. A dirty towheaded boy scampered up to the blue BMW to retrieve a sheet of cardboard and threw it at the windshield. "Stand back!" the car warned again, prompting another burst of merriment. "My turn," squealed the shortest of the three, jumping in excitement. Darkness had just fallen on the warm Sunday evening while Tariq abu Bakr sat on a bench near the Golden Gate, staring at three illegally parked blue BMWs with no license plates.

"Stand back! The system is armed!" the middle car pleaded to no avail after a third round of cardboard smacked it. "I never heard a car talk. What's it saying?" the small boy asked his friends.

"To stay the hell away from it," shouted a man from one of the balconies facing the historic monument, prompting the threesome to bolt across the street and disappear into the subway station.

Tariq crumpled the scrap of paper with the useless license plate number. The car with the red mercury had to be open, so it couldn't be the middle one with the shouting alarm. Of the remaining two, one stood under the sole streetlamp while the shadows of a chestnut tree hid the other. After studying the balconies to make sure that the man had gone back inside, he climbed the grassy hill to the shadowy car's trunk and clicked the lock.

"Stand back!" boomed the alarm. "The system is armed!"

"What the hell. I told you kids..." yelled the voice from the balcony.

Tariq jumped back against the middle car. "Stand back!" it boomed in response.

"Hey, Ivan, a Caucasian's messing with your car," the voice from the balcony shouted.

Tariq pushed himself from between the cars with both hands, launching another digital duet of "Stand back!" "Stand back!" that followed him through the park and across the main road to a waiting cab. "Back to the hotel," he ordered and worried the ends of his moustache while the taxi rumbled over the cobblestones to the Dnipro Hotel. He walked swiftly to the Night Bar where he found Claus Hesse writing in a notebook and sipping schnapps, alone, at a corner table. He turned his milky blue eye to the Iraqi. "Well, my friend," he asked in his accented English.

Tariq motioned at the bartender, who raced up to the table to take his order of 100 grams of Johnny Walker Black. "The delivery failed," he said, taking a seat. "We must arrange for another."

"No. There will be no other delivery. Aivazian told me he has many eager buyers." He jerked his finger at the North Koreans sitting at a neighboring table. "I told you on Friday when we made the arrangements."

Instead of admitting to his inattention, Tariq took the offensive. "Fine, but I just spent 17,000 dollars for a commodity that I don't have. I want it back."

The bills were only counterfeits. But smuggling replacement notes into Ukraine across the porous border with Russia involved a circuitous and dangerous route through Iraqi Kurdistan, Iranian Kurdistan, Azerbaijan, Georgia and the Caucuses. The bribes cost more than printing up the high quality contraband. Besides, he'd have to ask Ahmed for them and the fanatic Shiite was the last person he wanted to see.

Claus picked up his pen to write "$15,000" in his notebook.

"I said 17,000," Tariq whispered.

The German slowly sipped his drink. "You paid 15,000 for the commodity. If you did not receive it, I will return the price. But the other 2,000 is for my expenses."

Tariq waited for the bartender to serve his drink and swallowed half in one gulp. "Your expenses were contingent on completing the deal."

Claus lifted the tablecloth and peered at the Dog. "Seigfried, *Mein braver Hund*, perhaps you will persuade our comrade as to the necessity of expenses, whether a deal is done or not." The Dog rose from its haunches under the table and bared its teeth, dripping saliva on to Tariq's knee. "Ekh! Get it away from me," he exclaimed and turned to the German. "You're right. What's 2,000 dollars between friends?"

Claus waved at the bartender for another schnapps. "I'm glad you appreciate the circumstances. But do not worry. I have found us a much more valuable commodity."

Tariq saw Irina laughing with the North Koreans. A loud group of Americans walked in followed by a pair of subdued Persians. At Petrochemical 3 they had warned him that the Iranians also wanted a Bomb. He imagined the Dictator's murderous fury if the hated Persians got a Bomb before He did.

"I'm listening," he said to Claus after the waiter delivered his drink.

The German took a modest sip and leaned across the table, so close to Tariq that his dueling scar grazed Tariq's nose. "Red mercury requires highly enriched uranium, *Nichtwahr*? We both know that your leader has no HEU. I doubt if he even has any low enriched uranium diverted from the UN inspectors to enrich in those primitive centrifuges of his."

Petrochemical 3 had declined to tell Tariq how much low, high or medium enriched uranium it concealed in its bombed out bowels. After the war, the Western Imperialists forced the Dictator to destroy the Al Atheer Materials Center he had built to produce nuclear weapons. Without it, Tariq didn't know what the Great, Magnificent Dictator could do with HEU even if he found any. But it was not for him to question.

Claus leaned more closely and Tariq could smell the minty schnapps. "My friend, I have found two Americans with access to enough highly enriched uranium for your leader to bomb Tel Aviv, Cairo and Riyadh, with plenty left over for Washington, D.C."

CHAPTER 8

SCHISMS

FAXNEWS-UKRAINE

October 15, 1992

Moscow, Russia. An American Expert announced that the Khartron Institute in Kharkiv is developing launch codes for the missiles in Ukraine. Khartron used to be the Soviet Union's leading design bureau and production facility for missile guidance systems. Ukraine's National Security Advisor responded that the Expert misunderstood. "Khartron has that capacity. If we want it, they can do it. But we don't and they aren't."

Kiev, Ukraine. The parliament elected a new Prime Minister, the former Director of the Ukrainian Missile Factory – the world's largest – in the eastern city of Dnipropetrovsk. It built the SS-24 ICBMs deployed in Ukraine and the SS-18s deployed in Russia. It also services both types of missiles.

Bishkek, Kyrgyzstan. At the meeting of the Commonwealth of Independent States, Ukraine rejected Russian demands to take full control over the nuclear weapons in the former Soviet republics.
END

Faxnews-Ukraine – Your source of English-language news about Ukraine

---

TOP SECRET – PURPLE
Handle via Agent Channels Only

Date: **October 17, 1992**

---

*R*oman Rozpad stood up to crack his back and wiped the sweat off his forehead with the back of his wrist, trying not to dirty his face with his soil-caked hands.

"Tired Roman?" Petro Rozpad asked. His father, who had only one arm, worked faster than his dually armed son. The younger man crouched back down. "Not tired. But I'm not any good at this."

The senior Rozpad gazed with affection at his only child. Twin boys and later a girl had died within their first year during the post-War famine. "If you were good at this, it would mean you'd had a life like mine. Instead, you have an education. You've learned things that I've never dreamed of. And now you have an important position in the government."

"But I should help you more." Rozpad pointed at the wooden cottage of his birth and childhood until going off to school. "It's high time you bought a new roof and concrete steps." And a new arm, he thought. Petro's old prosthesis had broken in half at the elbow.

His father rubbed soil off a tiny red potato, too small to eat, and tossed it back into the rows. "Don't you worry. With the wines, your mother and I live much better than a lot of our neighbors."

"Except the Smetana's," Rozpad said. His childhood friend and lifelong rival, Yuri Smetana, had built his parents a brick house, complete with indoor plumbing, a paved driveway and a satellite dish.

The World War II medal that his father pinned to his chest every morning glinted in the sun as he tossed a potato into a plastic basin on the ground. "None of them have figured out how to work that plate on the roof. Yuri may have money from selling steel. But he has more bricks in his brain than in that house. He doesn't have your smarts."

Rozpad tried to hide his bitterness with a joke. "The Americans say: if you're so smart, why aren't you rich?"

Petro bent over his trowel. "Roman, envy is a terrible thing. If I had envied every man with two arms, or every man that spent the War behind the Urals instead of in the carnage that those German Fascist Invaders wrought here..." Petro used the official Soviet sobriquet for Nazi Germany when he talked about the War and would have continued, but his wife called from the cottage door.

"Roman, can you review the books?"

"Go on," Petro urged him. "We can do the potatoes ourselves but neither of us can do the accounts. We still can't get used to buying a bottle of wine from Ivan at the state price of 30 *kupons* and selling it for 10 times that!"

Uncle Ivan, a warehouse operator for the state-owned Transcarpathian Wine Factory, handled supply while Petro, with his central Ukrainian location, handled distribution to local black market middlemen. They split the profits fifty-fifty.

Rozpad straightened his back. "No wonder the state liquor shops in Kiev are empty."

Petro's squinted at the sky in an instinctive check on the time. "Soon we can expand into Snickers Bars. Ivan found us an excellent wholesale price in Hungary but the minimum order is 500 dollars and we have to come up with half."

Snickers Bars had become the Marlboro cigarettes of the former Soviet Union, a coveted commodity and symbol of the West. They even appeared on menus in restaurants.

The zeros bounced around Rozpad's mind when he checked the columns of numbers written in his mother's neat script. Since crates of Transcarpathian Riesling began falling off trucks into Uncle Ivan's car in February, the Rozpad brothers' business had earned total profits of 400 dollars, a handsome sum. But September had been expensive – buying a new horse harness, plus the conductor demanded a bigger fee for storing the wine crates in her sleeper on the Uzhorod-Kiev train. From Petro's share of the month's earnings, they cleared 32 dollars, squirreled away with the other 200 under a plank in the kitchen floor.

In the unheated summer kitchen, Anastasia watched over jars of apple preserves simmering in a pot, singing an old folk tune that carried far across the village during performances of Dikanka's amateur choir.

"It's not good news, Mama," said Rozpad, interrupting the song and handing her the ledger.

His mother wiped her hands on her stained apron and turned around to scan the figures. "But we still have a profit."

"But not as big as previous months," Rozpad said. He couldn't afford to give them the 18 dollars they needed for their share of Snickers.

Anastasia tucked a lock of faded brown hair under her paisley kerchief. "Oh, Roman. Your cup is always half empty. We'll have the Snickers money soon enough. Ivan says we can double our investment in just a month."

When she turned back to the apples, Rozpad said: "I'm going to the house for tea. Do you want any?"

She fished out a steaming jar with insulated gloves. "Not now. It's just time to take these out."

*R*ozpad carried his tea to the worn armchair in the parlor and placed it on the scarred end table, next to his precious Sotheby's catalogue. From the détente days of academic exchanges, it drifted into the Central Institute for Nuclear Research in a box of technical journals. No one noticed when he filched it, though such bourgeois interests could cause trouble with the KGB, and his study of English to read the listings remained a secret.

The paper had become brittle and creased, though he had memorized the listings: Chippendale armoire, matching Louis XV chairs, Venetian crystal goblets. But he was too poor to buy the humblest Roman coin. He couldn't even add to the rose paintings he collected in his one room apartment in *Akademistechko*, the scientists' and scholars' colony on the outskirts of Kiev. Not after tourists drove prices up to 20, 30, and sometimes 100 dollars for original oils.

Rozpad banged the teacup on the table in frustration but closed the catalogue gently, sifting the pages where they had broken off from the spine. He walked out of the house thinking of Ming vases, rose petals and Tanya, the lovely engineer at the Committee for Nuclear Safety and Security. Passion, she said, was one thing. But her five-year-old son needed a father to provide for them both.

The job the Americans had offered seemed promising. With 2,000 dollars a month, he'd be able to help his parents and support his own family with Tanya, too; buy the occasional rose painting; or even save up for an original Prymachenko. But he wasn't a good liar and tried to spend as little time with them as possible. Now he'd have to tell more lies explaining why Neilson saw him in Dikanka instead of back in Kiev adding 100 kilos of HEU to the nuclear material logs.

100

Rozpad snapped his fingers nervously as he walked through the courtyard. Lord, the Alsatian guard dog, rested his head on his paws and ignored him while Rosa, the terrier, ran alongside, whining in supplication. Every village house had at least two dogs, a big one with just enough chain to protect the yard and small one that patrolled the road, barking at passers by. Rozpad found Rosa's racket annoying and shoved her away with his foot.

Petro had left the garden. Later, Rozpad would help him carry the potatoes to the root cellar built two years earlier when the old one in back of the tool shed developed mildew. Dasha, the dappled grey mare, grazed in the pasture, picking up her head at the unfamiliar sound of the old cellar's battered iron door squeaking open. Grasping a flashlight in one hand and his Proton-4 in the other, Rozpad descended the wooden ladder into the dank chamber cluttered with old wagon wheels, rusty cans and burlap bags. His parents didn't own enough to throw things out.

The Proton-4 clicked with each step he took to the far corner of the cellar. Light reflected off clouds of dust that dimmed his view of the 20 pewter-colored bottles standing one meter apart to prevent a critical mass from forming.

He bent to one knee to check the Proton-4's reading near the stainless steel bottles, lined with lead. The liquid crystal displayed a gamma radiation level higher than normal but he expected that given the contents. Even the lead-lined bottles didn't block all the gamma rays. But the alpha, beta and neutron readings were normal. Nothing had leaked.

He had found them in a warehouse during an inventory around the Chernobyl nuclear power station. His escorts from the Administration of the Zone of Alienation had laughed when he went to inspect the empty building. "There's nothing there," they had insisted. "It's a waste of time." But they asked no questions when he returned, so he didn't tell them of his discovery in an underground antechamber, forgotten during the huge area's evacuation after the 1986 explosion. Taking the bottles past the checkpoint guards who screened vehicles for contamination posed no problem for a nuclear safety official.

Rozpad flickered the flashlight beam on the coded serial numbers that betrayed the bottles' contents, as did the weight of lead bottles, each filled with five kilograms of 90 percent enriched uranium. The heaviest natural element, five kilos of it amounted to only a cup. Two bottles cobbled into an atomic bomb would destroy a city. Twenty bottles would destroy a country.

He remembered his father's stories describing the devastation after the Great Fatherland War. The charred wasteland around Dikanka extended for miles around. But though millions had died and millions more suffered, even more millions survived. Few would survive the force inside the lead bottles but he blocked the vision from his mind. He had a valuable commodity, like the stainless steel ingots Yuri Smetana sold to any exporter with the right price. Steel could also be used to make weapons.

"If Smetana isn't responsible for what the exporter does with that commodity later, neither am I," he said aloud to the dark chamber and covered the crates with a burlap sack. If he sold the HEU, he could buy a bigger apartment in Kiev and one of those fancy computerized prosthetic arms for his father, maybe even bid at Sotheby's.

The Americans worried him. He had blundered, mentioning the HEU to Neilson. But he had no idea of how to find the type of people who might want to buy it.

*T*he monks filed slowly out of the church. All the brothers had joined in because the noon prayers, unlike the morning liturgy, didn't require mentions of competing patriarchs. Contrite after the scuffle that left one monk with a bruised lip and another with a sprained ankle, no one tried to lock anyone out.

Vlad the novice waddled alongside Anton and Boris, waving his arms like rudders that kept his bulk on the proper path. "The hegumen has summoned us to the refectory. It's unusual, to interrupt our regular chores," the novice whispered. "I take care of the horse." He glanced at his companions with pride and Boris brightened for a moment at the mention of a horse. "The collective farm gave her to us, along with a cart and I planned on repairing the reins this afternoon. But this schism is disrupting everything."

"Whose side is the hegumen on?" Boris whispered back.

Vlad watched the other monks murmuring in groups of two or three. "I don't know. He hasn't mentioned the scuffle, yet."

The newcomers said nothing. For weeks, Vlad had been their sole source of information but they shared nothing with him while they pondered the message from God. Boris braided the tip of his beard. If only they knew someone to help them interpret the meaning of "Constantinople, nuclear weapons, destroy", a person with knowledge and unquestioned loyalty. The fat novice seemed knowledgeable but too unfamiliar to trust.

Anton gestured at the other monks. "Did the hegumen attend the schismatic's morning mass?"

The novice's fat cheeks, flushed red from the exertion of stomping on the flagstones, quivered. "No, he just came back from Kiev an hour ago. I'm sure that's why he's calling this meeting."

When they entered the refectory, the head of the monastery occupied the end of the long table, under an icon of Mary the Protector. Many of the monks did not sit in their regular seats and the new arrangements revealed the loyalties of the monastery's office holders, and the power of each side. The cellarer – who controlled secular supplies – sat with the loyalists on the left. But on the right, the chamberlain had joined the sacristan. The monks charged with monastery finances and access to the church made for a potent alliance.

The hegumen spoke with the quiet, deceptively gentle voice he had cultivated as a KGB investigator charged with repressing religious dissidents. The Soviets banned all religions except Russian Orthodoxy and ferreting out their secret gatherings had been a big part of his job.

"My brothers. The Patriarch of the Independent Ukrainian Orthodox Church informed me in Kiev that he has written to the Ecumenical Patriarch in Constantinople, seeking recognition of the new church."

The head of the monastery raised his hand to quiet the murmuring. "Now, if Constantinople recognizes the new Church, the other Patriarchs will surely follow. So, instead of making rash decisions, I think we should wait to see what happens and pray for God's will to be done."

He surveyed the room. "Your thoughts?"

One of the loyalists grumbled. "The Russian Patriarch will not recognize it."

A monk on the other side of the table jumped to his feet. "If everyone else does, then he'll be the schismatic."

"How can one of the world's largest Orthodox Churches be schismatic?" the loyalist exclaimed.

"If the Ukrainian church is recognized, Russia will no longer be the world's largest Orthodox church. More than half of its parishes are in Ukraine," replied the monk.

"Calm, my brothers," said the hegumen. He rarely raised his voice even during his old sinful life of extracting confessions from the anti-Soviet faithful. Anger never moved them. But a desire to help him often did. "This is why we should wait and see how Constantinople reacts."

"Do you see, Boris?" Anton whispered. "Constantinople is a key to the schism."

The hegumen grasped the silver cross that hung at his waist. "Until the situation resolves, we will hold two masses. At nine o'clock, we will mention the Russian Patriarch," he said with a nod to the loyalists. Then he turned his attention to the powerful alliance on his right. "And at ten o'clock, we won't."

When Tariq abu Bakr rose naked from the floor in Room 416 to answer the phone, a burst of static and clicks greeted him, followed by a vehement "Allah Akbar!" Tariq turned and leaned against the desk to watch Sveta and Irina on the blanket he'd laid on the floor for his newest game with the whores.

"It's me, Ahmed," shouted the voice at the other end.

"Yes," said Tariq, taking the Johnny Walker off the TV set and splashing some into a glass. "What's that noise?" Clanks and groans blared in the background before another round of static drowned them out and the phone went dead. Even to Tariq's ear, accustomed to Soviet phone lines, the connection sounded particularly terrible. But he replaced the receiver and started dressing. Ahmed called only to set up meetings.

"I must go," he said. "But I want you two to wait for me. No matter what, I'll pay you for the whole night." He stepped over the blanket between Irina and Sveta to check the moustache diagram in the bathroom. The tips of his own facial hair had dipped a millimeter below the Dictator's standard. Two precise snips, plus the daily plucking of nose hair restored perfection.

When he returned to the room, the whores shared a pomegranate on the bed while a slim blond sang on television in a sea of blue and yellow flags. Sveta wrote in her leather-bound notebook and hummed along, tossing the succulent red seeds into her mouth one by one. "This is fine, darling. We'll wait."

Irina ripped a handful of seeds from the pomegranate's leathery skin. "This beats being at home with grandma and papa and mama and Stefan and his wife and the twins."

Irena and her eight-year-old daughter shared two rooms with seven other people. She took up whoring to save for her own apartment, a goal that would take two lifetimes at her official job as a mathematician in a research institute. Tariq considered asking her to do the complex calculations the Dictator needed for trigger geometries. Sveta, too, had many underemployed engineering friends. But he didn't want to offer the women alternative work until he had tired of them.

Good thing I said nothing to Ahmed about the red mercury, he thought, opening the drawer for his underwear, lying next to the Koran he needed for encrypting messages.

He had one leg in his underwear when the phone rang again. "God is great!" Ahmed repeated over the metallic clamor. "I'm in the metro. The Sultan is in town and demands that I report. What's with the windmills?"

Fear chilled Tariq's spine and the freedom he had felt in Kiev dissolved. He had forgotten his gas centrifuge lie. But that worried him less than the Sultan. The Petrochemical-3 case officer who ran operations in the former Soviet Union slipped in and out along the same route as the counterfeit 100 dollar bills. "This is a terrible line. Can you go to a different phone?" Tariq asked, pulling on his purple silk trousers and ignoring the stain left by his sweating palms. Ahmed shouted above the din. "There's no time. You must tell me now. I'm already late."

He shared the Shiite's panic. The Sultan had authority to kill both of them. According to Ahmed's Finger of God tenets, only those who succeed in providing the fourth caliph's descendant with a Bomb had a guaranteed place in paradise.

The phone clicked madly for a few moments while Tariq gulped his drink and collected his thoughts. "Forget the windmills," he shouted in Arabic, noting that Sveta was listening. "A fellow investor," he explained in Russian, holding his hand over the receiver. "He wants to introduce alternative energy sources but I think that exporting Ukraine's agricultural chemicals is more promising."

He shouted back into the phone in Russian: "Very strong fertilizer," but more static interrupted. When it stopped, he heard Ahmed's "What?" The Shiite spoke only a few words of Russian.

"Very strong fertilizer," he repeated in Arabic. "Two Americans have access to a supplier of very strong fertilizer."

"Fertilizer? What is this, you fool? I don't have time…" Ahmed managed to say when a cacophony of clicks broke up his voice.

Had he forgotten the code in his panic? Sveta and Irina were engrossed in a television soap opera from Brazil. Besides, they didn't understand Arabic.

"Highly enriched uranium," he whispered with studied calm into the abruptly clear line.

Ahmed's response resonated with relief. "Allah be praised. How much?"

"One hundred…" The clicking resumed but Tariq was able to add "kilos!" when it stopped and right before the line went dead.

He watched Irina lick pomegranate juice off her fingers. But even the unconsciously erotic picture she presented did nothing to distract him from his fear. "My plans have changed. I'm not going anywhere," he announced, though Sveta didn't even turn her head.

"That's wonderful, darling," she said, studying a diagram in her notebook.

The phone rang again. "How many kilos?" asked Ahmed.

"One…" Tariq repeated to more static.

"One what?"

"One zero, zero…" Tariq said, followed by more static. "Hallo!" he shouted, close to panic.

Ahmed repeated: "One zero zero…," when a subway train screamed into the station and snorted to a halt.

"Correct?" Ahmed shouted when the noise stopped.

"Correct!" Tariq affirmed.

And the line went dead.

*H*ammers and sickles decorated the iron railings and plaster moldings in the spacious gallery streaming low October light into the Ukrainian parliament. Bolshevik detailing, thought Neil Neilson, returning his attention to the two faces – one eager, the other wary and both curious – watching him from across a polished conference table after his introductory spiel.

After wasting weeks in Kiev, spending for too many evenings in the Night Bar with Cristina Smythe and Joe Marchetti, he and Dan Kruger had returned to the US to save money. They returned only after Kostya finally confirmed a date with the MPs and, they hoped, the defense minister. Despite many promises, their meetings with him never materialized.

The wary face belonged to Yuri Klimenko, an athletic type with boyish features who led a subcommittee of lawmakers studying the START treaty. He sat across from Neilson while Kruger's vis-à-vis was Dmytro Padlo, owner of the eager face and the head of the parliament's foreign relations commission.

"So, you come to pressure us about disarmament, too," Klimenko said in English, after Neilson finished speaking. "Tell me, why should Ukraine give weapons to Russia, to country that enslaved us for 350 years?"

Cristina had told them that Klimenko supported keeping Ukraine's nuclear arsenal.

"I didn't say to give the weapons to Russia," Neilson protested.

Padlo listened to Kostya's Ukrainian translation and opened his mouth to speak but Klimenko continued: "Russia demands control of our warheads and Washington says nothing. This means it agrees."

"Mr. Klimenko," said Neilson, "we do not represent the United States government. We're private businessmen."

Klimenko folded his arms. "United States is just waiting for Russia to renew control of USSR territory."

Remembering George Hedgepeth and his genius Soviet advisors, Neilson repeated: "We are private businessmen, who may criticize our government more than you do. But we're not going to do that here."

Padlo's bushy brows curled up at the ends as he spoke and Kostya translated: "Do not misunderstand. Ukraine is committed to nuclear disarmament. We want to set example, so that whole world give up these terrible weapons."

"Fat chance," whispered Kruger as he drew a dove next to a missile.

"But we do not want to give weapons to Russia because that is not disarmament," declared the head of the foreign relations committee, his eyebrows darting in dramatic punctuation. "It does nothing to reduce total number of nuclear weapons in world. Ukraine will disarm by destroying weapons on our territory."

Kostya translation skills were improving, though he still had trouble with "the" and "a". Slavic languages didn't use definite articles, and he often left them out or used them in the wrong places.

"We want to help you..." said Neilson.

Padlo ignored him. "Besides, Russia just wants warheads. They want to leave missiles in Ukraine. These are very dangerous and Ukraine not have money to deactivate them safely. Ukraine has 130 missiles, what Americans call SS-19." Kostya translated.

The DSA team nodded. The two-stage, liquid fueled SS-19 "Stiletto" carried six independently targetable 550 kiloton warheads. But they were old, too, and the U.S.S.R. had been replacing them with modern SS-24 "Scalpels": solid fueled hydras bristling with ten warheads. Ukraine had inherited 46 of them, accurate and powerful enough to take out missiles in fixed, hardened silos in a preemptive strike. They cold launched, too. A gas generator popped the missile out of the silo before the main booster engines fired, limiting damage to the shaft. In theory, this meant the silos could be reloaded. In practice, it meant that there might be spare SS-24s in the deployment zones. And in politics, it meant Washington worried more about the SS-24s than the SS-19s.

Padlo continued: "Liquid fuel in SS-19s is extremely toxic. Just one drop can kill whole city."

"That's not true," Neilson retorted in amazement. Though highly toxic, a single droplet of fuel would kill one person, not millions.

Padlo's brows underlined his certainty. "This *is* true," he insisted through the translator.

"Are you a chemist, sir?" Kruger broke in.

Kostya answered the question. "No, he is poet."

"The head of the foreign relations committee is a poet?" asked Neilson.

"He is famous. We study his poems in school."

"Can't beat those qualifications," muttered Kruger and hunched over his notes.

Klimenko whispered to Padlo, who blew out his cheeks in a huff.

"He told Padlo to stay out of technical discussions," Kostya whispered before Klimenko continued the conversation.

"Actually, I am a chemical engineer – plasma chemistry – or I used to be, before...." He waved his hand towards the massive oak doors to the parliament's chambers, already closed for the evening. "Politics."

He glanced at their business cards on the table, and picked up Neil's. "Dr. Neilson, you are correct. But you must admit that the fuel components, heptyl and amyl, are lethal. Each SS-19 holds 150 tons." He leaned forward for emphasis. "If Ukraine gives warheads to Russia, who will take care of those missiles? Or Ukraine? Our impression is Washington is interested in us only because of nuclear weapons."

Neilson shifted in his chair. "Help me out, Dan," he whispered.

Kruger sat up. "But interest can be positive and negative. Russia has an interest in making Ukraine a pariah, so you risk international isolation if you start playing political games with nuclear weapons."

Before Kostya translated, Padlo understood enough to mistake what Kruger had said. "START! START?!" he exclaimed and added, with annoyance demonstrated by his furrowed forehead: "That's all we ever hear is START!"

"But I..." stuttered Kruger. They hadn't mentioned the treaty until first testing the lawmakers' mood and Padlo, despite his friendliness, had a bad one on the subject.

"Big help you are, pal," Neilson whispered when both members of parliament spoke at once.

"START is a terrible treaty for Ukraine," said Klimenko.

"Terrible," said Padlo.

Klimenko tilted his head quizzically. "Why does United States want us to ratify treaty that destroys missile silos instead of warheads? And costs much money, too?"

Neilson and Kruger exchanged glances. It was a dirty little secret that the strategic arms reduction treaty didn't destroy nuclear warheads. During the Cold War, that would have been impossible to verify, anyway. Neither side let its adversary see its warheads, much less count them. Nuclear "design secrets" were the most tightly held secrets on the planet.

So, instead of destroying warheads, START destroyed the means for delivering them, since spy satellites could monitor the process. In the case of ICBMs, that meant missiles and silos. Full compliance with START would still leave Ukraine with its full arsenal of 1800 thermonuclear warheads.

"We want to destroy what's in the silos," said Padlo. "Why should we have to destroy the silos, too? They have economic uses."

Glad for the diversion – the treaty had little relevance to post-Soviet disarmament, regardless of Foggy Bottom's fixation – Neilson asked: "How?" He didn't know of any use for nuclear missile silos except to hold nuclear missiles.

Padlo's brows swept up in surprise at the silly question. "Silos are complex engineering structures, hermetically sealed with temperature controls and sensors. They will last centuries."

"But what can you do with them?" asked Neil.

Kostya translated Padlo's response: "It is American to throw out what you do not need. Here, we are poor and find uses for everything. For example, silos have uses for champignons."

"What," said Kruger, interrupting his doodling.

"Champignons," Kostya repeated.

"You mean mushrooms," Neilson asked, incredulous.

After clarifying with Padlo, Kostya said: "Champignon mushrooms."

"What can you do with mushrooms in a missile silo?"

"Grow them," said Padlo.

"That's crazy," said Neilson. But Kruger interrupted drawing a mushroom in a mushroom cloud to lightly kick him under the table.

"Well you should study that proposal closely," Neilson concluded with difficult diplomacy. Destroying silos would only waste time and money if Ukraine really planned to dispose of its warheads. But why bother cultivating mushrooms in a ten-storey deep silo contaminated with missile toxins?

"We have colleagues who say we should keep missiles, that SS-24s still have another 15 years of useful life and to hell with America," said Klimenko, studying their reaction.

Neilson thought carefully before answering. "How will nuclear weapons protect Ukraine if you can't launch them?"

"Who says we cannot launch them?" Klimenko asked.

Neilson raised his voice in alarm. "Everyone in your government and so does Russia, which I'm sure is watching closely." *Or as closely as its primitive inventory lets it*, he thought with disquiet.

Klimenko flicked the edge of Neilson's business card. "No, we do not have launch control now but that does not mean we cannot. We are not a naked, illiterate tribe that found these weapons by accident in the jungle. Ukrainians worked in Soviet nuclear weapons programs from the beginning. Our experts are able to change launch codes."

That's probably true, Neilson thought. Engineers and mechanics familiar with the weapons would have little trouble taking launch control.

"Gentlemen," Klimenko said affably, "Ukraine will not take launch control of these weapons. We have suffered enough from the atom after Chernobyl. But even without it, the weapons do give us certain strategic benefits."

"Such as," asked Neilson.

"For centuries, Russia attacked Ukraine and the world ignored us. But if Russia attacked now, the world would pay attention because of the weapons are here."

Neilson imagined Hedgepeth cheering the Russians on across his unchanged map of the U.S.S.R. "That's a risky tactic."

Klimenko stood up to end the interview. "Ukrainian independence is a great historical risk. The rest is detail."

*C*laus Hesse crouched next to the large suitcase on the floor. Underwear and socks draped over the sides, on the back of the room's sole chair, even on the lampshade. Sloppy Americans, he thought with distaste, reaching under crackling cellophane packets of dried fruits and nuts.

He froze at a noise from the corridor and listened to footsteps pass the door and continue further. He wasn't too concerned. He had paid Natasha, the lavender-haired floor matron, ten dollars to let him into the room and warn him when the Americans returned.

He rummaged under the packages and felt a roll of soft material with a hard edge. He pulled it out. Socks, with the visible outline of an object stuffed inside. Claus pulled out a folded paper and opened it to find a list: Golden Gates, Cave Monastery, St. Sophia Cathedral and a variety of other architectural monuments and churches that he skimmed with little interest until stopping at the last item. Dikanka.

The fictional village of Gogol's story had a real counterpart that neighbored the nuclear bomber base in Uzin, just two hours south of Kiev. Aivazian, the bomber pilot with the red mercury, was based there. Despite Claus's requests, he had refused to tell him anything about Uzin's nuclear warheads. *Does he want me to name a price first?* He needed to discuss it with Tariq.

Why would the Americans go to Dikanka, he wondered, refolding the paper and stuffing it back into the sock.

Reaching again into the suitcase, he found another soft object with a hard edge and took it out. The scrunched t-shirt fell open, dropping another folded sheet of paper on the cellophane packages. The contact list, with the name he needed. Roman Rozpad, chairman of the Ukrainian State Committee for Nuclear Safety and Security. Taking a pencil stub and notepad out of his pocket, he copied what he needed, his thoughts racing. He couldn't just call the official and ask if he had highly enriched uranium for sale. No, he had to handle it with care. Aivazian claimed extensive contacts in the government. He'd have to send him a telegram for a meeting.

Highly enriched uranium could sell for one-million, ten-million, even one-hundred-million dollars – depending on the buyer's desperation and wealth. No matter. He stood to make a lucrative commission.

It would please Helga, too. Losing her vocal cords in the Dusseldorf explosion had deepened her fanaticism. Nuclear weapons didn't interest her, not in Germany. Serious Neo-Nazis wouldn't risk scarring the Aryan homeland. But helping Claus find an Islamic Bomb to counter Israel fit her dogmas and raised cash for buying conventional explosives from the *Untermenschen* Slavs. As the Soviet war machine's storage depot for the European theater, Ukraine had mountains of ordnance.

Sexless and silent, she did everything efficiently, including kill.

A sharp rap on the door interrupted. "They just arrived by taxi," Natasha reported.

*D*an Kruger sank into the soft couch at the last empty table in the Night Bar. The sounds of Abba rose above the noisy din while Neil Neilson perused the notes from the meeting at parliament. "Dan, these are just scribbles and doodles."

"I don't need notes to tell you that START is a non-starter, at least with parliament and they're the ones that have to ratify it." Kruger blew out a smoke ring that drifted until Joe Marchetti's bald head appeared inside and, luckily, drifted away after a brief: "Catch'ya later guys." No thanks, thought Kruger, in no mood for the tampon inspector's pushy questions.

Neilson riffled through the papers in his briefcase for the letter they picked up at the defense ministry after leaving the parliament. Neilson read its two short paragraphs aloud:

"Most Esteemed Sir," he began. "Ukraine is firmly on the path of nuclear disarmament and intends to cooperate with the United States of America and the world community in achieving that worthy goal.

"If you grant Defense Systems Analysis, Inc. the role of disarmament program planning advisors, we will be grateful. We are especially interested in their proposal to advise us on computerized materials control and accounting."

"It's kind of wimpy," said Kruger. "And it doesn't mention money."

Neilson replaced the letter. "No one expects this stuff for free. Besides, it's all we have," he said when a squat, heavily tanned man with powerful arms approached the table with an amiable smile. "Is this chair taken?" he asked, resting his hand on one of the two empty chairs at their table.

"Nah, go ahead," said Kruger.

"Thank you," the man said, his accent reminiscent of the Mediterranean. "It is crowded tonight," he noted when a burly German bumped into him on his way to the bar. "I am Pannaioties Kookouvaios. My friends call me Coco."

After completing the group introductions, Coco called over the waiter. "The usual for me and please bring my friends here whatever they want." He leaned back with a satisfied stretch of his arms while they ordered. "You are Americans?" he asked when the waiter left. "I am Greek. Once I tried to become American. But taxes!" His nose wrinkled with distaste. "Lawyers say I cannot stay in American more than 182 days a year. I have a house in Malibu, in California. My wife is there with my children."

He pulled out a wallet photo of an attractive olive skinned woman surrounded by six girls of various sizes and caressed it while the waiter delivered the drinks.

"You must miss them," said Kruger.

"It is not too terrible. I have been a sailor my whole life, never lived in one place. And they summer at the house in Patmos, and sometimes London or Sydney. We ski at Grenoble for Christmas." Coco glanced at Kruger. "You are a kind man, compassionate." He pointed to the strong hook of his nose. "I smell out people immediately. Always act on instinct."

The Greek's global domiciliary claims sounded of barroom bravura, though he sported a beautifully cut suit and real gold on his stubby fingers.

"What is it you do, Coco?" asked Kruger

The Greek chortled. "It is so pleasant to meet people who don't know. I am in shipping."

Kruger almost gagged on his smoke. Coco the shipping tycoon! Richer than most countries and famously devoted to his family, he had a shadowy past. Kruger recalled arms shipments to Africa. "Good Lord, I saw your picture in Fortune magazine last month," he said. "What brings you here?"

Coco grinned. "Oh, I have been doing business here for many, many years. You don't think that the Soviets themselves shipped that grain they used to import from the West?"

Kruger knew that they didn't. Commodities traders used to keep tabs on Soviet shipping contracts to predict the big import orders that drove up futures prices for grain.

Coco sipped his drink and continued: "Now my company does exports, mostly steel to the Middle East. But I come here because it is a new country, in transition, very exciting and challenging. And I have a soft spot for Ukraine. The first ancestor in my family genealogy lived in Chersonesos when the Kievan Prince Vladimir got baptized."

Seeing Kruger's blank expression, the Greek explained: "Chersonesos. This is in Crimea, in Sevastopol, where the Black Sea Fleet is based. But 1,000 years ago, it was a Byzantine city. This is how Eastern Christianity came to the Kievan Rus' empire. And 2,000 years ago, ancient Greeks had a trading colony there, called Chersonesos."

"Crimea has Greek ruins?" asked Kruger with surprise. His interest in ancient history had led him to the beer theory of civilization.

Coco nodded. "Sevastopol is a closed city. Foreigners must have an entry permit. But if you ever have a chance, you must see the fascinating ruins of Chersonesos."

Twirling the amber liquid in his glass, Coco changed the subject. "And you, my new friends? What brings you here?"

Kruger saw Neilson signal his approval. They had nothing to lose with someone richer than God and who clearly liked Kruger. Dan slipped his business card across the table and explained their mission, confessing uncertainty about winning a contract and keeping their jobs.

"This is noble, nuclear disarmament," Coco said, tucking the card into his pocket. "It would be a shame if your hopes are not realized." Suddenly he brightened. "But if other industries interest you, Ukraine offers many business opportunities."

"Such as," asked Kruger.

"Coal!"

"Coal?"

"Turkey is in the market for a closer supplier. They import from South Africa, but shipping costs have grown too high. I don't do South African shipping, so this is good for me."

"I thought Greeks and Turks don't like each other," said Kruger.

"My business has no borders."

"But you must have many contacts here. Can't you find a coal supplier?"

"I have contacts in agriculture and steel. Many years ago, I worked with the coal people in Moscow. But here…." Coco adjusted a golden signet ring on his pinky. "You see, I do not need to work. I work because it is good for a man to work; for satisfaction, fun. I discuss the shipping industry, visit shipyards with ministers – Ukraine has a wonderful, powerful shipbuilding industry. But the coal industry…" His nose wrinkled disagreeably again. "For me, this is not fun."

His Rolex flashed the bar's low light into his eyes as he reached into his jacket. "I must go," he said, sliding his own card across the table. It was simple, with just his name and a phone number. "It is morning in Malibu and time to talk to my family. But if you decide you are interested, please call. If you find me coal, I will ship it."

CHAPTER 9

COUNTING

FAXNEWS-UKRAINE

November 15, 1992

Minsk, Belarus. An American senator (D-Ga) returning from a tour of five ex-Soviet republics raised alarms over nuclear smuggling. "Senior officials in Belarus told us of several cases in which they intercepted low-enriched uranium as smugglers tried to take it across the border into Poland," said the Senator. "This particular material wasn't useable for weapons. But it shows that the system is leaking."

Washington, D.C. Following the ratification of START by the U.S. Congress and the Russian parliament, the State Department called on Belarus, Kazakhstan and Ukraine to ratify the treaty. "The failure to ratify will prevent Ukraine's integration into the West and will damage its ability to get economic aid."

Kiev, Ukraine. The Ukrainian President responded: "Demands to ratify START would be more persuasive if they included proposals for providing Ukraine with security guarantees for giving up the weapons as well as financing for their environmentally safe destruction."

The President also announced that German technology has made it possible to dial directly from Ukraine to 167 countries instead of routing all calls through Moscow. But internal communications are still poor. "Now, it will be easier to call New York than a village outside Kiev," he said.

Washington, D.C. The Ukrainian Ambassador to the United States congratulated the Democratic Candidate on winning the American presidential race. "We anticipate fruitful relations with the new administration," he said.
END

TOP SECRET – PURPLE
Handle via Agent Channels Only

Date: December 1, 1992
To: K3
From: Chief of Station Kiev
Subject: SITREP Rasputin

(TS) 1. Neilson and Kruger are to see Ivan Yastrub, the Minister of Machine Building, which oversees all weapons production, conversion and demilitarization.

(TS) 2. Repeat, there is no nuclear official named Rasputin.

(S)   3. Humintel from the Uzin reports that ICBM warheads due for routine maintenance are being stored on the missile bases instead of S-Objects because Russia refuses to deliver replacement hydrogen gas filters.

(U) 4. In a newspaper interview, the Prime Minister complained that Ukraine has a cadre shortage. "Russia has all the experts."

(U) 5. In Moscow, police arrested more than 50 Russian scientists from a weapons design bureau at Sheremetyevo Airport on route to North Korea.

END

TOP SECRET – PURPLE

Exempt from automatic downgrade

---

*W*illiam Kensington III crumpled the dispatch and tossed it blind into the wastebasket he always had placed in the same position alongside his desk. It bounced on the carpet, rolling next to the cost-cutting memo that also missed its mark.

He made a note to order a special satellite sweep of the Uzin area and then reached for the secret Senate Intelligence Committee report that arrived on his desk that morning. An aide had flagged the highlights and Kensington opened the thick volume to an excerpt from a closed hearing with the Director of the Central Intelligence Agency.

SEN. CRISPIN: Mr. Portal, can you explain to me and my esteemed colleagues how you all there at the Agency, in which American taxpayers sunk billions of dollars to figure out the aims and acts of the Soviet Union, utterly failed to foresee the internal collapse of this great country's chief adversary for most of this century?

MR. PORTAL: [Unintelligible]

SEN. CRISPIN: Sir?

MR. PORTAL: Repeat the question, please?

Kensington flipped to the next yellow sticky paper and read the title: "Budgetary Proposals to Reduce Redundancy and Maximize Efficiency of U.S. Intelligence Capability in Post-Cold War Arena". He grabbed a Marlboro Light and lit it. It violated his schedule for cutting down but he hated the word "efficiency". That drove him into intelligence instead of banking as William Kensington II had demanded. While the secretive U.S.S.R. was still a going superpower, information of any kind – winter wheat yields, shipping contracts, venereal disease rates, airplane disasters – acquired at whatever cost, had value.

Unfortunately, while collecting it, the Agency missed signs of the Soviet Union's imminent demise. They missed Iraq's nuclear program, too. We'd still be in the dark if the Dictator hadn't stupidly invaded Kuwait and started a war he would lose, Kensington thought with a shudder when a knock interrupted the depressing thoughts.

His aide's bald pate appeared in the open door. "K3. There's a report from our Kiev listening post." Kensington crushed his cigarette. "Finally coming up with something, Petrie?" John Petrie had convinced him of the need to monitor all electronic comings and goings from Kiev's Dnipro Hotel.

"It's big," Petrie said, sliding a computer printout on Kensington's desk. "It's that Iraqi talking on the phone with a contact. We had it translated."

Kensington skimmed the highlighted excerpts. "Two Americans with access to very strong fertilizer?" He saw Petrie over the rims of his reading glasses. "What is this shit?"

"It's a code, boss. Keep reading."

Kensington did and exclaimed: "Highly enriched uranium?!"

Petrie pointed to the bottom of the page where the printout read: "One, zero, zero ... o"

"We missed a lot because of interference on the line, K3. The phones there are awful. But maybe that last 'o' was the end of the last 'zero', which means Neilson and Kruger might have access to a thousand kilos of the stuff."

Kensington tapped his fingers. "Those bastards told Hawkins about a hundred kilos and a Rasputin character that doesn't even exist just to throw us off while they go peddle ten times that much to Iraq or Iran?"

Petrie balled his hands in his pockets and paced in front of the desk. "But our guy at their company, Mike Beedle, said they're serious. They want Ukraine to have that computerized inventory system," he pointed out. "How does that fit in?"

"Stop pacing, Petrie, and sit."

Petrie sat.

Kensington made a note on his calendar. "If Neilson and Kruger are expert advisors on the Ukraine's nuclear materials, they'll find out where everything is." He squinted at his aide. "How much HEU do you need for a bomb?"

Petrie shrugged. "Nuclear warhead design secrets are the biggest secrets around, K3. The people who'll say anything, don't know. And the ones who know, won't say. The rule of thumb is that ten kilos of HEU is enough to make a simple fission device. And the more pure the HEU, the less you need. So, a thousand kilos is will make a hundred bombs. But with plutonium and good Russian engineers, you could build smaller bombs, and more of them."

Kensington opened a drawer to pull out a Cyrillic newspaper clipping with a translation stapled to the corner. "This says there's a super secret Soviet material that lets you make bombs as small as a hand grenade. Red mercury. Ever heard of it, Petrie?"

The aide laughed, a snorting sound that drove Kensington nuts. Good thing they didn't have much to laugh about. "As far as we can tell, it's a scam, boss. Soviet shysters dreamed it up to fleece wannabee nuclear powers. It can do whatever a buyer might want. The pitch goes: 'You want a short cut to making an atom bomb? You want the key to Soviet ballistic missile guidance systems or to the anti-radar paint on the stealth bomber? What you need is red mercury.' "

"You mean it doesn't exist?"

"Well, red mercury is like ghosts, K3. You can't prove it doesn't exist. But our scientists have never heard of it. The red mercury we've picked up has just been regular mercury mixed with red dye or dust."

"But HEU does exist," said Kensington. "We have to stop them."

"A wet job?" the aide asked eagerly.

"No, you idiot! Then how'd we find out where the uranium is?"

"Torture?"

For a guy who wore a plastic pocket protector, Petrie was bloodthirsty.

"No, no, no," said Kensington. "We need mileage out of this." He pointed at the Senate report. "You saw this damn thing. They want to cut our budget just because the Cold War is over – as if that means the Free World is safe. This proves it isn't safe at all, hell, might be even more dangerous than before."

"So, what should we do? Tell the Senate that two traitors want to help some tin pot dictator buy an arsenal of a hundred nuclear weapons?"

Kensington made a steeple with his fingers and tapped the cleft in his chin. "No. What we have now isn't proof. We have to catch them in the act."

"A sting?"

"Yeah, and then we'll trumpet it in the media."

"So, where's our mileage," asked Petrie.

"Are you kidding? After missing Iraq's nuke program, this'll make us heroes. When we announce a new program, call it counter-proliferation, the media will lobby for *us* to get more money for it." Kensington pulled a file marked *Neil Neilson, Ph.D.* from under a small, neat pile on his desk and leafed through it. "What else did Beedle say about Neilson and Kruger?"

"Nothing, except that DSA is going to fire them if they don't win a contract soon."

"How soon is soon?"

"A month, maybe. Beedle is already searching their offices to make sure they don't take any of the company's classified material."

"Good. Make them desperate enough to do something stupid." Kensington rubbed his forehead. "Do they have any intelligence training?"

"Not Neilson. Kruger might, but Army Security isn't talking."

Kensington glanced at his antique grandfather's clock. Not time for a cigarette yet. He studied Neilson's file. "Who's Purple?"

"A freelancer, works for Tambrands as an inspector. We pay him two grand a month to file those reports you keep throwing away."

"Tambrands?"

"It's a joint venture in the Ukraine, K3. They make tampons."

Kensington picked up the phone. "Keep him on, for now," he ordered and punched in a four digit internal number. "Is White still there?"

"Let me check to make sure, K3."

"Good, because this next job isn't for feminine hygiene inspectors."

*I*van Yastrub had a booming laugh that first rumbled deep in his barrel chest, scaled up his throat and burst out like the roar of a tank. Tears streamed down his cheeks when his mirth ended and he wiped them away, asking: "Give them up? For nothing? Are you mad?"

Neil Neilson shifted in his seat after listening to Kostya's translation and glanced at Dan Kruger, who raised his eyebrows in commiseration and continued taking notes. Their trip should have lasted a week but their promised meetings met delay after delay. The novelty of their first trip had dissipated and the hotel felt increasingly claustrophobic.'

"Well, sir, I don't see what choice you have," said Neilson. "No one is going to buy them from you unless you sell to one of the pariah countries and that would make Ukraine a pariah, too."

Yastrub clasped his hands over a Buddha-sized belly. Unbuttoned at the neck, his brown polyester shirt revealed a sprinkling of grey chest hairs. "Not to worry. We sell them to most respectable, civilized country on earth."

"Who," asked Neilson.

"You!"

"Us?"

"Yes!" Yastrub riffled through a collection of business cards in a small cardboard box and slid one of them across the desk.

"That is your compatriot," said Yastrub. Neilson recognized the name of an aging peacenik that always showed up on news shows about nuclear disarmament.

"He told me that uranium and plutonium in each nuclear warhead is worth 250,000 dollars. They should be worth more considering how Moscow impoverished us to build them," he said, slapping the desk. "But OK, we charge that price. With more than 1600 warheads in Ukraine, that equals 400 million dollars."

Neilson wondered why the peacenik told Yastrub to ask for the entire Nunn-Lugar budget, which had a lot to do besides dispose of Ukraine's nuclear weapons. "But what makes you think Washington will pay?" he asked.

"Why not?" asked Yastrub. "America is rich and this means 1600 fewer warheads pointed at your cities."

Kruger broke in. "But Mr. Yastrub, what you're proposing is blackmail."

Yastrub boomed again in laughter. "No, no. We have something your government wants us not to have. Why should you not pay us not to have it? This is business," he said, using the English word. But he pronounced it – as did everyone they had spoken to – as *bizness*. Kostya once explained that Ukrainians spelled the borrowed word in Cyrillic with an "i" that sounded like a long "e" in English.

Neilson held up his hand. "Mr. Yastrub, we are private businessmen. We do not make U.S. government policy. This is an interesting debate, but what concern us now are the *expenses* – and not the price – of helping Ukraine dispose of its nuclear weapons."

"A billion dollars."

"What!?" Neilson exclaimed.

"No? Two billion?" Yastrub amended.

"Two billion?!"

Seeing Neilson's astonishment, Yastrub ventured: "Five?"

"Take over, Kruger," Neilson whispered, "I'm tempted to wring his neck."

Kruger leaned towards the minister who cast bewildered winces at Neilson. "Sir, do you have any calculations to back your estimates?"

Yastrub tapped the peacenik's card on the edge of his desk. "Calculations?"

Neilson had recovered. "Mr. Yastrub, if buying Ukraine's weapons would cost 400-million, then why should it cost billions to dismantle them?"

Yastrub lifted a bushy brow. "Destroying nuclear weapons cost as much as building them. We must remove valuable metals from the missiles, utilize fuels, dismantle warheads, de-enrich uranium for nuclear reactor fuel. We must store plutonium, convert missile silos to peaceful uses..."

"If he mentions mushrooms, *I'll* wring his neck," Kruger whispered, while the minister rambled, disposing of every screw and wire.

"When he stops for breath, we're out of here."

Yastrub had powerful lungs and a long list, parts of which he repeated for good measure, so his guests had to wait ten minutes to make their polite good-byes. The minister led them out into his secretary's office, where a man in a Soviet air force uniform waited for him.

The minister boomed at Kostya, who translated: "This is Colonel Demiuk, from Uzin bomber base – by my parents' house, you remember? He is here to discuss plans to turn bomber base into air cargo airport. Minister Yastrub asked if rich Americans want to invest."

Neilson noticed the Ukrainian trident pinned to the colonel's lapel. "Kostya, tell him we'll let him know if we ever become rich Americans."

*T*he low winter sun dipped below the horizon when they left the building and headed toward the hotel. The inside of Kruger's nostrils froze in the bitter cold.

"That was a waste of time," he said when they descended into the warm underpass to the other side of the Khreshchatyk boulevard. "He didn't have a clue about what things cost."

"Except warheads," Neilson noted and shook his head at a toothless flower seller shoving a bouquet of dried pink carnations at him.

Kostya stopped at the entrance to the metro that took him to a dormitory on the edge of the city. "This way of thinking is from Soviet times."

"C'mon Kostya, even Commies had to count," said Kruger.

The translator ignored the two teenagers who stared at him and giggled while passing through the station's clouded glass doors. He seemed immune to the female attention he routinely attracted. "You will see," he insisted. "They count different from capitalists."

"We'll see if we come back here," said Kruger. "We enjoyed working with you, Kostya, and we'll send you a telegram when we decide what to do."

The young man brightened. They had paid him 200 dollars. "Please say hello to Cousin Jean."

"Will do," said Kruger, watching their almost constant companion disappear into the crowd of commuters. "He's a good kid. Gives me hope for this place."

Neilson nodded but had to shake his head emphatically when another flower seller in the crowded underpass took his assent for interest in her long stemmed roses. But two women with teased masses of hair pushed her aside.

"You Americans," said one of them, an attractive blond except for the wart on her cheek. Many people in Kiev had facial warts, moles and other minor but unsightly growths they couldn't afford to have removed.

"Good sex, 300 bucks," said the other, a petite brunette with dark, arching brows. But in a common Kiev fashion statement, her sheer pantyhose flattened the thick black hair on her legs into a web. Kruger had no problem with women not shaving. Back in their hippie days at Cornell, Jean got rather hirsute and Kruger found her incredibly hot. But the hippie Jean didn't wear pantyhose. And the lawyer Jean shaved her legs.

"No thanks," said Neilson as he followed Kruger past them.

The blond called out behind them. "Why no?"

"Too expensive," said Neilson. "The rate at the hotel is 50 bucks."

"Fucking capitalists," muttered the dark haired one.

"Americans rich," said the other.

"I wish," said Neilson.

"I wish I was home already," said Kruger.

*S*veta bit Tariq abu Bakr's ear, adding a fillip of pain to Irina's exquisite ministrations further down when a sharp knock on the door interrupted. "Don't stop," he groaned.

Irina didn't, but neither did the knocking. "It's me," called the last voice that Tariq wanted to hear. "I know you're in there, so open the door."

Tariq rose from the floor and pulled on his purple silk trousers. After a quick glance at his moustache in the bathroom mirror, he opened the door a crack to find an unshaved Ahmed, his eyes hard. "Allah Akbar," he announced vehemently.

Tariq slipped into the corridor and closed the door, glancing around the dim hallway to see no one. Natasha, the floor matron, had stepped away from her desk in the lobby.

"I tried calling. The Sultan is furious with you," Ahmed said with a whispered growl and then peered over Tariq's shoulder at the closed door. "Why are we standing here? Let's go into your room."

Though fear struck Tariq at the thought of the spy master's fury, he shot out his hand to block the way.

"You're fornicating in there, aren't you, you dog!"

As far as Tariq could tell, sex for Ahmed began and ended with dreams of the virgins he'd find in Paradise if he fulfilled the Finger of God's sole guiding tenet. "No," he said. "I'm talking to you. Tell me what happened."

Ahmed clicked his worry beads in his mutilated hand. "As soon as I arrived, he told me to tell you that he'll cut off your money if you don't start producing results."

"But the fertilizer?" asked Tariq, hoping that this time the Shiite would remember the code.

The beads' clicking slowed. "That calmed him down. He smiled. I've never seen him do that. But he said that you must avoid dealing with the Americans. Go directly to the source."

Tariq had no idea of the source's identity and neither, he suspected, did the German. But the Sultan wiles had enabled him to survive many of the Dictator's purges. They would have to double their efforts.

"He's giving us six months," Ahmed continued. "If we don't produce, he said that he'll make you His Excellency, the Victorious Glorious Iraqi President's taster again and send me to Kurd territory, to infiltrate the rebels." Ahmed swallowed. "Land mines are all over the place there, from the last war with the Persians."

Tariq shivered with fear at the thought of being anywhere close to Him and raised his hand for quiet when he heard the elevator stop. The Americans exited and he heard one of them say: "Five billion dollars. Can you imagine?" as they disappeared into the murky length of the hotel's other wing. That's the price, he wondered. How would it possible to bring that many counterfeit notes into the country?

But that wasn't Tariq's problem. His problem was avoiding the Dictator's dangerous safe houses – and Iraq – altogether. His archeologist neighbor disappeared after he criticized the army's use of a 4,000-year-old ziggurat to hide aircraft during the war against the American imperialists. Bullet holes pocked the combined temple-granary built by Ur-Nammu, founder of the third dynasty of Ur in 2,000 B.C.E. Four missiles missed the ancient temple tower itself but cratered the surrounding site.

After the neighbor disappeared, Tariq's father told him to leave Iraq and not return. But the Sultan could kidnap him, or kill him on the spot if he didn't perform, or even if he did. He already knew too much. He also had no place to hide and no real money.

When he heard the Americans close the doors to their rooms, he turned to Ahmed, who looked as frightened as Tariq felt. "You have to find the fertilizer, Tariq, or windmills, anything that's on that list. The Kurds will kill me and it won't even count as a jihad!"

"Alright, alright!" Tariq whispered. "I'm working on it. But you have to go now."

The television flickered in the corner when he returned to the room but Irina studied an accounting textbook while Sveta took notes from a management tome. "My business associate," he explained without being asked. "We have a small crisis with the fertilizers and I have to take care of it."

Sveta, the engineer, stretched out a lithe leg to massage her foot. "I told you, darling. You should invest in my school. You can't even imagine how demand for business training will grow in a few years."

Irina, the mathematician, made a note in the margin of her book. "Sveta's right. Soviet accounting was creative lying. No one here uses generally accepted accounting practices. They don't do basic inventory. They have no idea of how to calculate profit. They even put accounts receivable in with income. Can you imagine?"

Tariq didn't care. His own bookkeeping amounted to two columns: business and pleasure. He picked up the phone and dialed Claus's room. When no one answered, he hung up and pulled on a shirt. The German rarely left the hotel except to walk The Dog. "Here's my investment, then. Go buy more books," he said, throwing three counterfeit hundreds on the desk. "I have to go."

Sveta wagged a finger when Tariq grabbed his winter coat. "It's not an investment if you're paying what you already owe." Tariq paid the whores more in a day than they usually made in a week.

Tariq slammed the door and hurried down the dark stairwell to the restaurant. The business school might offer a good cover for the number-crunching that Petrochemical 3 needed to develop trigger designs, he thought, passing between the tables without seeing the German. Taking the back exit, he descended the short staircase to the Night Bar, surprised to find the crowd spill out into the vestibule. He squinted through the clouds of smoke but too many people blocked his view.

"Hey, buddy, looking for your friend with the dog?" asked an American voice and he turned to see a short, familiar man in a dark suit.

"Joe Marchetti," said the man, extending his hand. "I work for Tambrands. I've seen you here a few times."

Tariq shook his hand. "Call me Ali."

Marchetti waved towards the stairs. "Your friend just left, Ali. Guess it's too crowded for him. Can I buy you a drink?"

"No, no thank you." Tariq backed. "I must go."

The American lifted his beer. "Another time, maybe?"

Wondering what the man wanted from him, Tariq ran down to the lobby where a group of Christians were returning from their missionary work on Kiev's streets. They looked identical and their women were not attractive. "Have you seen the man with the Great Dane?" he asked the sour faced doorman with a little Lenin pinned close to his heart. When the doorman pointed outside, Tariq slipped on his coat and burst through the doors. For once he was relieved to see The Dog, lifting its leg on the side of a newspaper kiosk and prompting the grey haired matron inside to scream curses.

"Go to hell, *suka*," Claus growled in his guttural Russian. "What we didn't capture in World War II, we'll buy now."

"Fascist scum," yelled the woman. "I should've killed more of you at Stalingrad!"

The Dog barked at the potential threat to its master until Tariq called from a safe distance and Siegfried immediately obeyed the German's subtle signal to quiet down. "Ali, my friend, you have come to join Seggi and me on our evening stroll?" Since his university duel damaged a vital nerve, only half of Claus's face smiled and to sinister effect.

"We need to talk," Tariq whispered. "I'm under pressure to produce."

Claus motioned for The Dog to follow and led Tariq towards an underpass. We can walk and talk, *Nicht wahr*? Seggi enjoys chasing crows in that park up the hill."

Tariq didn't speak as he followed the German's swift pace, panting clouds of steam. "My father spent two months here in 1942 as a supply officer for the Wehrmacht. He told me stories about how beautiful the Ukrainian girls were."

"They still are," Tariq said between gulps of frigid air. His eyes watered.

"You should exercise caution with the hotel prostitutes." Claus turned his sightless eye at his companion. "In Soviet times, they worked for the KGB."

Tariq stared at the cobblestones that led up the steep and narrow street to the park. Sveta wasn't a spy. "The KGB is broken into 15 little pieces," is all he said when they reached the park and The Dog bounded off into an open field. Claus steered them to one of the benches lining a promenade. A few dog walkers braved the bitter cold.

"We can't deal with the Americans," Tariq whispered, watching a flock of crows fly away from The Dog, cawing frantically. He had grown used to the beast after so much time.

"I had no intention of doing so. I already have an independent lead to the person who is offering the materiél.

"You do? How?" asked Tariq, not much expecting an answer.

"I have my methods. That is why my services are valuable."

"I have six months to find something valuable. After that…"

Claus slipped a flask out of his pocket and took a sip. "After that, what?"

Tariq took the offered schnapps. "After that, nothing."

*V*lad the novice leaned his heavy bulk against the horse and lifted her back hoof to pick out caked mud and manure. "She's a good one, Dora is," he said, patting her chestnut rump when he finished. "Solid. Not much fazes her." He pointed the hoof pick at the monks assigned to help him during their stay. "Anton, grab the curry comb."

The tall monk scratched his sparse beard in confusion at the sundry implements on the stable floor and picked up a metal comb, but kept his distance.

"Afraid of horses, Brother Anton?" asked Boris, reaching for the hard rubber scrubber to clean dried mud off the mare's flank.

"I've never been this close to one," Anton admitted. "My parents lived in a city, though my father had a boat and we hunted a lot, too, especially boar."

Boris loosened the mud and swept it off with a soft brush. "My father worked at the Poltava Horse Factory. Then the farm collapsed. We had nothing to feed the horses and had to move to my uncle's apartment in Kiev," he said. He had just turned 15. Though his small frame meant little on the farm, where his equestrian skill won him local fame, it brought taunts and bullying in the city. None of the girls would speak to him.

Assured that Boris had the grooming under control, Vlad waddled into Dora's stall, announced that the horse needed a new salt lick and waddled off to the collective farm to ask for one.

When he left, Boris saw his companion sitting on a bale of hay, lost in thought. "Where did you grow up, Anton?" he asked, turning back to his grooming and trying not to sound too curious.

For a few moments, Dora munched her oats. Then, the quiet answer: "Arzamas-16."

Boris's back was turned so that only Dora saw his jaw drop and, true to reputation, barely flicked an ear. "The secret city?" he asked. "Where they built those Satanic nuclear weapons?" Boris had grown up terrified of a nuclear attack by the United States.

Anton picked up a twig and scraped a trefoil in the fresh sawdust covering the floor. "It wasn't secret to us. My father worked a physicist at the All Union Scientific Research Institute for Experimental Physics. He still does, though it's called the All-Russian Institute now."

Boris walked around Dora's bucket of oats to clean her other flank. Each brush stroke burst clouds of horse hair and dust that flickered in a stream of sunlight. "You came to the monastery from there?"

Instead of answering, the tall monk asked: "Why do you keep calling nuclear weapons Satanic? Are they more Satanic than other weapons? All weapons kill." He tossed the twig aside and leaned against a stall door. "Besides, the messengers mentioned nuclear weapons."

"But they said 'nuclear weapons, destroy'. I've prayed for guidance and I think it means that nuclear weapons should be destroyed because they *are* Satanic."

Anton picked a stalk of hay out of the bale and chewed the tip. "Our Church says that nuclear weapons are Satanic if they aren't blessed by Orthodox prayer."

"Our Church said that? When?"

"Not too long ago, at the Saint Daniel's monastery in Moscow. The Church held a hearing on national security. They said that two things will save Russia: nuclear weapons and Orthodoxy. And because they built Arzamas-16 on the site of the Hermitage of Sarov, Russia's nuclear weapons have the protection of St. Seraphim of Sarov. The imperialist Americans' weapons are Satanic. They used them to kill innocent Japanese. Ours are guardian angels."

Boris grasped Dora's tail to pick out the tangles and bits of straw, shaking his head in disbelief. "Weapons of mass destruction are guardian angels?"

Instead of answering, Anton pulled out his Bible, leafed to a worn page and read aloud.

And I will strike down upon thee with great vengeance and furious anger, those who attempt to poison and destroy my brothers. And you will know my name is the Lord when I lay my vengeance upon thee.

"Ezekiel 25:17," he concluded, closing the Book. "God's work isn't just creation, Boris. It's destruction. Sodom and Gomorrah, the Flood, and the destruction promised in the Revelations. Nuclear weapons are the most perfect means for God to show his power and his wrath."

Boris threw the grooming tools into a wooden box and stood up. "His wrath against evil, Anton."

"What brings more evil than the faithless hearts of men? See how that usurping, self-appointed Ukrainian Patriarch has been dismembering our church: pitting brother against brother and bringing violence to our monasteries."

Dora stretched in pleasure when Boris scratched her neck. "That's true. And if the Ecumenical Patriarch recognizes the Ukrainian Church, it will be even more divisive."

Anton brushed bits of horse hair off his robe. "Now that the Soviet Union is no more, the Church is what's holding the Eastern Slavs together. If it fragments, just imagine how the infidel Muslims will overrun us. The Turks already have a foothold in Crimea through the Crimean Tatars. I heard that they've funded military training for them, probably to prepare them for terrorism."

Boris led the mare into the stall, threw in a pile of hay and closed the gate. "Do you think the message is a warning about Istanbul and a Muslim threat?" he said with uncertainty. "But that doesn't make sense. We were praying to find out how to stop the fragmentation of our Church."

"Don't you see? They're related. The Ecumenical Patriarch is the patriarch of Constantinople, and that's the old name of Istanbul. The messengers appeared at the grave of Monk Timothy. The Turks executed him in Constantinople. Turks have always been the enemies of Orthodoxy."

"So, what are we supposed to do? Destroy nuclear weapons that Turkey doesn't have? It makes no sense."

Anton picked at his thumbnail with a pocket knife. "It does if you reverse the words a little."

Boris thought for a few moments, too shocked to speak. "You're not serious," he said. "Destroy Istanbul with nuclear weapons?!"

Anton flicked a speck of dirt off his knife and gave his companion a sidelong gaze.

Boris spoke more sharply than usual. "Aside from the fact that monks can't kill and this would mean killing millions of innocent people, I would point out here that we don't have nuclear weapons, Anton."

When his companion said nothing, Boris insisted: "That means it's impossible that the messengers meant we're supposed to bomb Istanbul."

"So, if we had a nuclear weapon, you would believe it?"

Boris turned to leave. "This is a ridiculous conversation!"

The squeaking door to the barn opened and Vlad lumbered in holding a salt lick in one hand and a sheet of paper in the other. "Here, hang this up in Dora's stall," he said, handing Boris the salt lick. "There's a letter from Inkerman and I have to go tell the Hegumen."

"From Crimea?" asked Anton, locking on Boris's eyes.

The fat novice's cheeks reddened from his unaccustomed exercise. "That cave monastery by Sevastopol, St. Clements, had a big influx of new monks. Seeing how they don't have a collective farm sponsoring them, they're sending letters to the monasteries asking for food. They want potatoes from us."

Dora didn't even lift her head from the hay when Boris entered her stall. "Whose side have they taken?" he asked, fitting the salt into its frame.

"It's Crimea, Brother Boris," said Vlad. "I can't imagine them backing the Ukrainians' schismatic church." Then his fat face sagged into a frown. "But that will make it hard to find anyone here to help them. The farm director promised to donate a wagonload of potatoes in the spring but we have to deliver them."

"We'll do it," said Anton.

"You will?" The novice's face brightened.

"We will?" Boris mouthed the words at Anton.

"We'll take Dora," said Anton.

"Dora?" Vlad's face sagged again at the prospect of losing his charge. The mare raised her head at the sound of her name.

"How else can we deliver it?" asked Anton. "The monastery doesn't have a truck even if it did, there's no petrol. We'll go in the spring, when it's warmer. It will take us a few weeks. That's a small sacrifice to help our cause, isn't it?"

The novice stroked the mare's nose. "No, it's a big sacrifice, but I'll go tell the hegumen. He's neutral right now, so if we have volunteers, he can't very well deny charity to our brethren."

After the novice waddled off, Anton didn't look at Boris when he said: "Let us see whose understanding of the message is right."

*G*eneral Joe Hawkins leaned back in his leather armchair and tossed his Viet Cong hand grenade while perusing the letter from the Ukrainian defense minister. "Good work, guys," he said, scanning the page. "I'll send a copy up to the Secretary first thing."

"Thank you, General," said Neil Neilson, leaning forward to slide a thick envelope onto Hawkins's desk. "Here's our proposal for the computerized inventory system." They had waited a long time for the meeting.

Hawkins pulled it closer and placed the grenade on top. "I'll see to it that you're the front runners in the bidding."

Neilson jolted. "But General, we're applying for a sole source award. There isn't any bidding."

Hawkins pushed the envelope away. "Waddaya mean, no bidding. Everything's bid on. That's democracy."

"But sir, I'm sure you realize that you can't open bidding in these situations," Neilson explained, trying to keep his voice patient. Most senior officers knew only enough about government procurements to tell an aide what they wanted, needed or wished for.

"Which situations?" asked Hawkins.

Dan Kruger broke in. "General Hawkins, since we came to you with the idea, it wouldn't be fair to let our competitors bid for it."

"Fair?" Hawkins sputtered, spraying the DSA proposal with a fine mist of spit. "What's fair got to do with it? I can't give you guys a contract just because you came up with the idea. We have to follow the law."

"That is the law, sir," said Neilson.

"What is?" the general asked suspiciously, reaching for the grenade.

Kruger explained. "The sole source award, General. If you decide to release Nunn-Lugar funding to give Ukraine a computerized inventory system, you have to offer the contract to us first, because it was our idea and we're uniquely qualified to do it. You can't open bidding on it unless we say 'no'."

"Yeah?" said Hawkins, rolling the grenade on his palm. "What makes you two so unique?"

"Aside from the qualifications we've set out in the proposal," Neilson said, motioning at the envelope, "there's also the letter. The Ukrainian military wants us, and no one else, to do this."

When Hawkins scowled and checked his watch, Kruger said: "We won't take up anymore of your time, sir. How soon can we expect an answer?"

Hawkins pushed his chair away from his desk. "It's not up to the Pentagon anymore. They handed the whole shebang over to the Interagency Group," said Hawkins.

Alarmed, Neilson asked: "When?"

"A few weeks ago, after Congress complained that we weren't spending money fast enough. They accused us of stalling," Hawkins said, standing up. "There's me, a guy named Hedgepeth from State, Bill Kensington from the CIA and a bunch of other wonks. I forget their names."

Hedgepeth, Neilson thought, squeezing his fists in frustration. Without START's ratification, they'd never get a contract. Besides, the Interagency Group had managed complex and very lengthy arms talks with the Soviet Union. It couldn't handle the rapid decision-making needed for post-Soviet nuclear disarmament. Neilson predicted that much of Nunn-Lugar's 400 million dollars would be spent on many, many plane tickets to Moscow.

Hawkins walked around the desk and held out his hand. "I'll put in a good word for you at our meeting in two weeks," he said. "For old times' sake."

*W*hen Neilson and Kruger left, Hawkins returned to his desk, and pulled the model of the Pershing missile closer. When the launcher popped up, he adjusted the trajectory with a tiny crank and pressed the lever, watching the missile shoot into the seat Neilson had occupied.

"What a pair of losers," he chortled, taking a cigar out of the mahogany humidor. After lighting it, he took the letter from the Ukrainian defense minister, crumpled it into a ball in the ashtray and lit it. When it collapsed into ashes, he picked up the phone and called an aide to check on a legal question and then punched the number for Langley.

"K3? The deed's done. They won't see a penny," he said. "And the sly bastards didn't mention that Rasputin guy once. But there's one thing. If they can't supply the inventory system, no one can."

"What the hell does that mean, no one can?" Kensington shouted. "The more I'm finding out, the more I think it's a good idea. I just don't want them to do it."

Hawkins let out a stream of smoke. "Well, if we give anyone else the contract, they can sue us."

"So, what if they do?"

"They'd win."

*T*he candles cast a golden sheen on Jean Kruger's hair when she took her seat at the dining table with the two pairs of expectant faces watching her reaction. She sampled the chicken on her plate. "Umm, picatta, my favorite."

"Try the asparagus, Esquire," urged Neil. "The hollandaise is from an old family recipe."

"Steaks, yes, but I never took you for a sauce man, Neil."

Dan poured his wife a glass of Chardonnay. "Particle beams, submarine launched ballistic missiles, hollandaise sauce: A snap for my partner here."

Neilson lifted his Heineken. "A regular Renaissance man, that's me."

Jean pushed aside the wine, poured herself a glass of water. "What's happening with Annette these days, Neil?"

"It's silly," he responded. "But she still refuses to talk to me. My lawyer says she's enrolled in evening courses for pottery making. It's a Mother Goddess thing. She says that soil is her creative outlet. And since she's counting on hefty child support from me, she figures she doesn't need a real job."

"You should know that raising a child is a job, Neil," Jean said shortly, cutting off a piece of asparagus and soaking it in the sauce. "And how's Susie?"

Neilson picked up a chicken thigh. "I'm going to pick her up after dinner. We're going to spend the weekend in Princeton with the twins."

Jean laid down her flatware, wiped her mouth with a paper napkin and took a large gulp of water. "O.K. guys, what's up? Dan only cooks me dinner on my birthday and you never do, Neil."

"I wanted to thank you for your hospitality, counselor." Neilson was still living in a furnished apartment that didn't have a washing machine, so he did his laundry at the Kruger's. A load was finishing up in the dryer.

Kruger placed his beer bottle on the table. "Jean…"

"I don't like pauses after you say my name, Kruger," Jean said. "They're always bad news."

Her expression persuaded Neil to leave the rest of the conversation to his partner. "Well, folks, I've had fun but a little lady is waiting for me. I'll go fold my laundry."

Neither Kruger argued. When he left, Dan took Jean's hand. "Jeannie, I'm going to lose my job."

"Oh?" she responded, her voice hollow.

He recounted the meeting with Hawkins. "There is no way that interagency committee's going to give us a contract. It'll take just a few weeks for us to receive the final rejections and get fired."

"Oh?" she repeated, ripping the paper napkin.

"We'll have four months severance pay, so that's a nice pillow. We also have an interesting offer in Kiev." He traced a question mark on the beer bottle. "When do my sperm have their next appointment with Dr. Jensen?"

"An offer in Kiev?"

"Ukrainian coal. If we export it, we can make millions."

"When?" Jean kept ripping the napkin into smaller pieces.

"A few months, I hope."

Jean picked up her fork and stared at her plate. A single tear glistened on her cheek. "I hope so, too, Kruger, because I'm pregnant."

CHAPTER 10:

ARMS

FAXNEWS-UKRAINE

Nuclear Roundup

February 1, 1993

December 3, 1992 (Moscow, Russia). The CIS Commander rejected Kiev's claims to "own" nuclear weapons, declaring that the weapons in Ukraine belong to no one. He also called for removing all multiple independently targetable reentry vehicles (MIRVs) from the ICBMs in Ukraine.

December 11, 1992 (Washington, D.C.). The American President offered Ukraine 176 million dollars in assistance if it ratifies START and the Non-Proliferation Treaty (NPT). The Secretary of State warned that continued delays will damage bilateral relations.

January 3, 1993 (Moscow, Russia). The Presidents of Russia and the United States signed the START II treaty, prohibiting the deployment of MIRVs on ICBMs and eliminating SS-18s, the ICBMs built by the Ukrainian Missile Factory and deployed in Russia.

January 18, 1993 (Kiev, Ukraine). Ukraine has created a center for the administrative control of the nuclear weapons and their facilities, including S-Objects.
END

Faxnews-Ukraine – Your source of English-language news about Ukraine

---

TOP SECRET – PURPLE
Handle via Agent Channels Only
Date: Feb 15, 1993
To: K3
From: Deputy Chief of Station Kiev
Subject: SITREP Rasputin

(TS) 1. Acknowledge demotion. Change direct deposit from Third Texas Bank joint account with Elaine Marchetti to Swiss Bank, account details to follow under Code Name: Irina.

(TS) 2. Nuclear warhead custodians in Uzin are concerned about Russia suspending deliveries of replacement hydrogen gas filters. Some warheads are as much as ten months overdue for filter replacements.

(S) 3. Ukrainian defense officials denied rumors that Russia is amassing troops on the border to capture Sevastopol. "This is a provocation, just more pressure to make us denuclearize."

(U) 4. The New Prime Minister said: "In the euphoria over independence in 1991, Ukraine was too hasty in declaring its nuclear free status. How can we declare ourselves nuclear free under the NPT if we have nuclear weapons?"

END
TOP SECRET – PURPLE
Exempt from automatic downgrade

TOP SECRET – WHITE
Handle via Agent Channels Only
Date: February 16, 1993
To: K3
From: Chief of Station Kiev
Subject: SITREP Fertilizer

(TS) 1. Activation orders received. Legend is intact.

(TS) 2. Neilson and Kruger returned to Kiev on February 10th. They now have their own company called "Neptune". They say it's "for doing business in Ukraine".

(TS) 3. International Atomic Energy Agency sources in Vienna identified Claus Hesse as the middleman in Iraq's purchase of maraging steel for gas centrifuge rotors used for uranium enrichment.

(S) 4. Many 100 dollar bills circulating in Kiev are counterfeits.

(U) 5. The Chief Nuclear Negotiator denied Russian media claims that the warheads in Ukraine are in dangerous ill-repair and that Ukrainian officials held secret meetings in Moscow to reach an agreement on servicing them.

END

---

*R*oman Rozpad laid his newspaper on the bench to watch a woman strolling under the bare chestnut trees with an Alsatian puppy whose large paws and deep bark promised a formidable, full-grown guardian. It was cool, but no longer cold in the park

The Armenian bomber pilot from Uzin, Yuri Aivazian, said that the German had a Great Dane. But even on a gloomy winter afternoon, dozens of dog owners were exercising their pets in the park. In half an hour, two Great Danes, five German Shepherds, three Dobermans, and a pug sprinkled the 19th century statue of St. Vladimir, the Grand Prince of medieval Kiev, gazing over the treetops at the Dnieper River.

He picked up the newspaper again and studied an advertisement for Italian furniture. Imported furniture was still a rarity but after selling off yet another shipment of stainless steel, Yuri Smetana bought himself an Italian bedroom set and invited Rozpad over for a half-liter of vodka to show it off.

"The babes won't resist this, buddy," Yuri had said, bouncing on the mattress and stretching his arms towards a white plastic headboard shaped like ocean waves. Rozpad imagined other crude embezzlers turning the country into an international dump for tacky furniture. Everything manmade in Soviet times was ugly. Beauty was considered bourgeois. As a result, millions of people had horrible taste. *And now some of them have money,* he though with a shudder.

Loud yelping interrupted his thoughts and he saw a pasty-faced man with a deeply scarred cheek standing near a large Great Dane that grasped the Alsatian puppy's exposed belly in his jaws. The man smiled as the puppy screamed in terror. "Control your dog!" shouted the woman, running to her pet. Before she reached him, the big dog obeyed the man's signal to release. Rozpad heard him apologize in German-accented Russian as he led the dog away. "Seggi was playing. He meant no harm." When they reached a safe distance, the puppy scampered to its owner.

Rozpad pulled his woolen cap around his ears and adjusted the big black sunglasses he had bought in America. For good measure, he had wrapped his throat in a thick scarf. Only his nose and upper lip were visible.

"Good day," said the German, sitting next to Rozpad on the wooden bench. "Yuri said the sun would be shining today."

It was the password. "But February can be cloudy." Rozpad responded guardedly. Tanya had introduced him to Aivazian, who claimed many contacts in the government. The Armenian said that the German businessman wanted to discuss nuclear energy, but when the meeting place turned out to be the park, he suspected that he really wanted to discuss the contents of a root cellar in Dikanka. How did the German find out? Not from the Americans. They wanted him to report the cache. Maybe he knew that strange Swedish man, the one with a plan to extort Western aid for Ukraine by planting a nuclear warhead in Stockholm. But Rozpad didn't think the Swede understood his subtle hints about the HEU. Besides, they arrested him.

Or maybe he's a spy, trying to catch me, he thought as the woman threw a stick for the puppy to chase. "Fetch, Icarus," she shouted.

The German spoke from behind a gloved hand: "You have the sensitive materiél? One hundred kilograms." His breath smelled of schnapps.

When Rozpad said nothing, the German continued. "Do not worry, our mutual acquaintance, Mr. Aivazian, knows nothing."

The puppy raced after the stick. Icarus flew on wax wings too close to the sun and plunged to his death. It wasn't a good omen.

"What is the purity?" asked the German

Rozpad turned to him but said nothing.

"Of the materiél. What's the level of enrichment?" the German insisted.

"I never mentioned materiél." Luckily his disguise concealed his face.

The German's mouth twisted into a lopsided expression that Rozpad couldn't decipher. "Very well. This materiél you haven't mentioned, is the enrichment greater than 20 percent?"

Taking Rozpad's silence as assent, the German asked: "More than 90 percent?"

With deliberate ambiguity, Rozpad lowered his head toward the Great Dane resting in front of them and then lifted his head again without saying a word.

"I'll pay you one million dollars for it," said the German.

A kaleidoscope of riches exploded before the Ukrainian and he started coughing from the shock. He never dreamed the HEU could be worth that much.

The German's good eye fixed on his companion until the coughing stopped. "Two-million," he said finally. "I have an impatient client who will top whatever price you are offered."

Anything would top zero. He didn't even have the job the Americans had promised.

When his companion said nothing, the German gestured towards the bare trees in the park. "Kiev is difficult in the winter. But the summertime! My father praised the wonderful weather."

"Your father?" said Rozpad, breaking his silence. "When?"

"1942."

"A Nazi?"

The German waved a dismissive hand. "Two generations have passed since then. Hitler and Stalin are long gone. And, now, so is the Soviet Union. But if we work together now, I'll make you a rich man."

Rozpad turned away to see the puppy tumble after a blue rubber ball. Tanya's son had begged for a dog. He imagined driving the boy and his mother in a Mercedes, or maybe a BMW – he couldn't tell foreign cars apart – to the grand apartment where they would make their new home. After showing off the elegant antiques from Sotheby's, he would open a door for a puppy to run out. Then, he'd place a diamond ring in a glass of champagne, like he'd seen in an old American movie, and ask Tanya to marry him.

"So, my friend, do we have an understanding? I can make payment however you want it: cash, Swiss bank account."

Rozpad adjusted his sunglasses and turned to look at the German. "What did your father do here during the war?"

"He was a supply officer, why?"

In the summer of 1942, a Nazi supply officer hunting for hidden stores of potatoes interrogated an 18-year-old Ukrainian soldier on leave in Dikanka. For each denial, the officer had shot him in the left arm with German precision, and continued long after he fainted. The barrage shattered every bone beyond repair.

Without another word, that soldier's only son stood up from the park bench in the shadow of St. Vladimir's statue.

"But wait!" The German protested. "We haven't worked out the details, yet."

Rozpad had taken a few steps away when he heard the German's vehement whisper: "Stop! Just name your price."

He stopped and slowly turned around. "An arm."

The German's scar twitched. "An arm? What the devil?"

Rozpad turned away and kept walking.

*Y*uri Holub pointed at the thick manila envelope on his desk with evident surprise. "You're no longer seeking a Nunn-Lugar contract but you completed the report I asked for anyway?" he asked, gesturing at his guest to take a seat.

Neil Neilson shook his head. "Sorry, my partner is waiting in a taxi. But you promised to set up meetings, and you did. It's not your fault that we got laid off." Fred Wexler had wasted no time. The day after they lost their bid, they arrived at the office to find Kruger's walnut desk in the corridor and two boxes of diplomas and personal photos on top. Severance notices were taped to their locked and sealed doors. Fred took none of their calls.

"Tell me," said the diplomat, pulling out the report to leaf through it. "Did they deny your proposal because of START?"

"We think so. The State Department now has a say in how the money is spent and they insist that START ratification is a precondition." The New Democratic President's election hadn't changed that.

Holub turned a page of the report. "Voluntary Denuclearization?" he read aloud, adding his own question mark to the heading.

"It's an idea we had, to counter the notion that Ukraine is delaying on START because it plans to take control of the nuclear weapons."

The diplomat pushed up his glasses and skimmed the page. "Demobilize and then destroy an ICBM?"

"Why not?" said Neilson. "It would be a gesture of good will and give you an idea of what disarmament will cost..." He motioned at the clock. "We can discuss it with you at another time, but we have a meeting soon at the Coal Ministry."

"The Coal Ministry? Whatever for?" asked Holub, rising from his seat to shake hands.

"For coal," said Neilson.

"You're going to the Coal Ministry for coal?"

"We're interested in exporting it."

"For coal? You're going to the Coal *Ministry* for coal?"

Neilson felt foolish. "It seems logical." He held out his hand. "But we'll keep in touch," he said and turned to leave while Holub quietly chuckled to himself, repeating: "The Coal Ministry for coal."

*F*our people waited in the reception room for the Coal Ministry's Director for Foreign Relations, but the only sound came from Dan Kruger's tapping foot.

"Cut it out, Dan," said Neilson. "It's annoying."

Zoya, the Director's translator, interrupted doing nothing at a desk covered with telephones. "Just a few minutes, he will see you soon," she said when one of the phones rang.

"Annoying?" Kruger whispered. "After five years of trying, my wife is finally pregnant and the doctor says to take it easy, I get fired and our one chance of making any money is not, according to Yuri Holub, in this stupid place where we've been waiting for half an hour."

"No, Mr. Dan, it is 45 minutes," said Kostya Beniuk.

Zoya hung up the phone and stood up, smoothing the skirt of her grey linen suit. Her eyes flashed knowingly when she announced that the director would see them. After tucking a blue pulp folder under her arm, she led them through the double doors into the Director's dreary office, decorated in proletarian brown down to the faded chintz patterns on the wallpaper. A bright square above the Director's head betrayed the spot from which a Soviet godlet had fallen.

After making the introductions, Zoya joined the Director at a broad desk scattered with thick stacks of paper and handed him the folder. Murmuring in his ear, she pointed out various details in the file's mysterious contents, which the Director studied, raising his eyes to squint suspiciously from under bushy Brezhnevite eyebrows. Five minutes of murmurs and squints ended when the Director leaned back in his chair, cleared his throat and started talking in a monotone that appeared directed at his shoes.

Kruger turned to Kostya, who fidgeted uncomfortably. "Kostya, you're here to translate, remember?"

"I am sorry, Mr. Dan. But I am waiting for him to say something important. He is talking about engineers."

The Director pointed into the air for emphasis as he continued his treatise.

"Engineers?" asked Neilson.

"Excellent coal mining engineers: Super engineers, excellently trained under severest conditions, perform great feats." Kostya stopped, listened to the Director and continued. "Engineers have high professional standards. Every day they face death in coal mines but dedicated super engineers have no fear."

Zoya winked at the Americans, titled her head at her boss and rolled her eyes while Kostya continued translating: "Equipment in Ukrainian coal industry is already old, rusty because we have no capital. But super engineers perform great feats to keep machines working."

Kruger pictured a muscle bound mining engineer with a billowing Communist-red cape and a big "E" embroidered on his shirt. His inadvertent snort halted the Director's drone. While Kruger coughed to cover for his disrespect, Neilson took the opportunity to leap in with their pitch. "Sir, my partner and I appreciate the extraordinary talents of your coal mining engineers. All they need to be supreme in the world of coal is capital."

138

When Zoya finished translating, Neilson continued. "Now, with modest exports of coal, you can raise the capital to support the efforts of your worthy engineers. And we want to help you do that."

After translating but without waiting for the Director to speak, Zoya twisted a lock of coppery hair and announced: "This is waste of your time."

Kruger's heartbeat quickened as he scribbled "waste of time" in his notes. Jean had begun spotting just days after they left for Kiev and the MD told her to lessen her caseload or risk losing the baby. *Less cases means less money*, he thought while doodling question marks and trying to remember how poor people kept infants in dresser drawers instead of cradles.

Neilson gestured at the blue pulp folder on the desk. "As we wrote in our letter, we are interested in exporting half-a-million tons of metallurgical coal and can offer 50 dollars per ton."

The Director sputtered at Zoya's translation. "But Ukrainian price is 64 per ton."

Kruger felt the blood drain from his face. "That's insane. The world market price is 54, and that's for better quality coal than Ukraine has."

"Government sets these prices. Everyone in Ukraine must pay this price."

Zoya folded her hands on the table and tilted her head at her boss. "This is not Director's job, to determine coal prices. His job is to find foreign customers for Ukrainian coal."

"But who is going to buy your coal if it costs 20 percent more than the world market price?" asked Neilson.

The Director leafed through the pulp folder. "Ukrainian customers."

"But why should they pay your price if they can import, say, Polish coal for less money?"

The Director eyes widened. "Metallurgical industries buy Ukrainian coal."

"Well, sir, they may use Ukrainian coal but do they pay for it?" Neilson asked, rummaging through his briefcase for a photocopied pamphlet from the Commerce Department. "This American anti-dumping case says that the government sets prices for Ukrainian steel well below world market prices – and your exporters are lining their pockets on that margin. Now, it's impossible to sell steel at such a low price if your metallurgical industries really pay 64 dollars for a ton of coal."

The Director responded but Zoya rolled her eyes again and said nothing.

"He says: Buy? Pay? What is the difference?" Kostya whispered.

Communism really did make people incapable of counting. Neilson changed tactics. "Mr. Director, how do the metallurgical industries pay for coal? Is it by check, or bank transfers, or just cash?"

The Director pulled another pulp folder off a stack on his desk, leafed through the loose sheets and closed the folder. "Credit: They give a promissory note, an IOU, and pay when they have money."

"And how soon after they've received the coal do they pay?"

The pulp folders produced no answer. Zoya ignored her boss and leaned on the desk, displaying a crack of cleavage. "Mr. Neilson, they do not pay," she said, directing a contemptuous glance at the Director, who continued examining the folder and scratching a hairy mole on his cheek. "Do not worry. He understands nothing that I say."

Zoya shifted her gaze with conspiratorial charm. "Old people here understand nothing. But I received my MBA in Pennsylvania on exchange program and my father is head of mining association in the Donbas. He first took me in coal mine when I was ten years old and asked why he always came home so dirty. I know coal, and I know capitalism," she said proudly before the Director interrupted her by pointing at the folder.

"He says: they don't pay," Kostya whispered.

Ignoring her befuddled boss, Zoya said: "Tell him you will consider his offer and say goodbye. You can buy me a drink and we can talk."

Neilson and Kruger cheerfully left the Director alone with his piles of pulp and soon found themselves sitting with Zoya at a table in the empty Dnipro Hotel Night Bar.

"You want coal, no?" she asked, twirling the swizzle stick in her vodka and soda. "Half-a-million tons at fifty bucks a ton for total of twenty-five-million bucks?"

"More if the first deal goes through with no problems," said Neilson.

"It is good that Director's usual translator is sick today. He is old, fat and just a translator but I am young and beautiful and translate to find customers to buy coal for real cash money."

Neilson nodded in polite appreciation. By any standard, Zoya was beautiful. "But how can you get cash money if your Ukrainian customers don't pay and your export prices are too high?"

Zoya pulled a thin binder out of her bag. "Regulations," she said.

"Seems as though regulations are your problem," said Kruger, intrigued by her brittle enthusiasm.

"Not if you know them," she said, laying the binder open on the table. "How will you pay?"

"The usual method," said Neilson. "Payment on delivery, after our bonded agent makes sure that the coal is of the quality we ordered."

"Payment where?"

"At whatever Ukrainian bank you designate."

"No Ukrainian banks: Cash."

Kruger groaned inside, silently promising Jean that he'd take care of the baby while she went to work to support them.

"Sorry, cash is impossible," said Neilson.

Unperturbed, Zoya offered: "Swiss bank?"

Kruger leaned forward in his chair, practically shouting: "Just give us the account number!"

"Wait a minute," said Neilson. "The official coal price is 64 dollars. Is this legal?"

"Perfectly." The young woman tapped her finger on the open page in front of her. "Regulations allow any mine or mining association to do what it wants with ten percent of production. My father is head of mining association and he can sell you half-million tons, or more, if you want."

Zoya scribbled on a slip of paper that she handed to Neilson. "This is where you must go," she said.

MYRON VICTOROVICH PLAVIUK

V.I. LENIN MINING ASSOCIATION NO. 134

40-YEARS-OF-OCTOBER REVOLUTION ST.

PRVOMAYSK, DONETSK OBLAST.

Neilson examined the address. "Prvomysk?" he asked, stumbling over the consecutive consonants.

Zoya put down her drink and took the slip of paper back. "Sorry, my written English is not the best. This was my difficulty in the MBA program," she said, writing PERVOMAYSK in large block letters on the back of the slip followed by: "(0622) 48 10 22" and, under it: "30 55 56".

"This is important. Ukraine has many, many Pervomaysks – this means First of May, International Labor Day. It was a popular Soviet name. There are *seven* Pervomaysks in Donetsk region. You must go to Pervomaysk that is closest to city of Donetske." After pointing out her father's work and home numbers, she slid the paper across the table along with her business card. "You should not need those numbers but I give them to you just in case. Call me at Coal Ministry when you have your plans. I tell my father and will meet you there."

When she left, Kruger asked Neilson: "So, you think she's legit?"

Neilson tapped the slip of paper. "She sounded serious; more serious than that bozo, the extoller of engineers. How does he expect to export coal that way?"

"I suspect he doesn't," said Kruger, blowing a smoke ring. "The system's set up so that it makes no sense to do things by the book."

Neilson leaned back in his chair. "We have to ask Kostya to buy us tickets," he said, noticing the tall, slim woman entering the bar with a young man wearing what looked like a pile of laundry. "Hey Cristina, no more trouble with the doorman?" he said when they approached the table.

Cristina Smythe slipped into the chair Zoya had just occupied. "Nah. I used to speak to them in Ukrainian. Now I just speak English and act like I belong here. If they try to stop me, I pretend I don't understand them and keep going. It's worked every time."

She turned to her companion, slumped next to her, and waved towards Neilson and Kruger. "Neil Neilson and Dan Kruger, this is my buddy Bob Baine. He's with the Washington Post. He's here to do a nuclear weapons story."

"Pleased to meet you," said Bob with a British accent, proceeding to ignore everyone at the table.

Cristina motioned to the bartender then turned to Neilson with a sidelong glance, resting her hand on the table near his. She didn't touch him but sat close enough for him to smell the fresh shampoo of her unruly curls. "The nuclear story is the sexy thing in the States and my editors keep bugging me to cover loose nukes and START and the Arabs sniffing around for weapons grade uranium. But it just doesn't excite me."

Cristina's last words reminded Neilson about Rozpad, who had dropped from their radar since they left DSA. They still hadn't told him that they no longer had a job to dangle at him. *He damn well better log that HEU.* But Cristina interrupted his disquieting thoughts. "I'd take a junk bond over a throw-weight any day." She turned to Bob and Neilson felt a surprising twinge of disappointment. Cristina had a fresh-faced athleticism that he did not usually find attractive.

"Bob, Neil and Dan here are into nuclear disarmament, Nunn-Lugar and all that..." Bob took a sudden interest in his barroom companions and whipped a wire bound notebook out of his back pocket.

"Not anymore," said Kruger.

"Not what," asked Cristina

"Not 'into', as you put it, disarmament. We lost our jobs."

Cristina's black eyebrows arched. "Oh, sorry to hear that. What brings you back here?"

The Neptune team exchanged glances behind the waiter delivering their beer. "We decided to ignore your advice and try to do business here. Exports," Kruger said. He agreed with Coco the Greek that coal was not fun, unless it produced profits, and it was certainly no fun to talk about at the end of a long day when coal was all that they had talked about. Besides, a contact like Zoya – if things worked out – should be kept to themselves.

Bob interrupted to ask for an interview. "I mean, you still know disarmament, even if you aren't doing it anymore, right?"

*T*he conscripts laid the first batch of artillery shells in uneven rows on the open-air bunker's concrete floor, separated just enough for Col. Pavlo Demiuk to pace alongside them. An inventory officer followed him, checking the serial numbers against the log book. Uzin's serial numbers

142

began at 600. But the inventories got mixed up during the chaotic withdrawal of the Soviets' vast Cold War military arsenals from Eastern Europe.

The shells had been in outdoor storage for a while and the markings had faded. "Repaint these, soldier," he commanded a scrawny private with red ears. The recruits were in terrible shape. Not a single part of what was once the mighty Soviet military had any money to feed them well.

Demiuk turned to the inventory officer, motioning at the shells. "Log these after they're painted and take the rest of the day off."

Demiuk left, passing bare birches and whispering pines on the shortcut through the woods to the gastronome to see if it had food. The base's stores had emptied and for weeks, the gastronome only had an ironic selection of brown bread and salt – the traditional Ukrainian symbols of welcome.

He found the street bustling when he emerged from the woods. On Soviet Officer Day, the men wanted to drink and celebrate – or mourn – what no longer existed. The Uzin strategic bomber base considered it a big holiday. But the base had become a political lightening rod since the mutiny. First, those foreign journalists visited right after the news reached Kiev. They just drove into the base in a mud encrusted Lada, saying that they wanted to see General Mikhail Smirnov. When they dropped the names of generals in Ukraine's new army, the confused conscripts guarding the gate had let them in. All day, they waited in a bare room with one chair and a dusty light bulb, laughing fitfully every time the poor junior lieutenant charged with guarding them told one lie or another about the general's doings.

What the general had done that day was tell the Commander of the Strategic Air Force of the Commonwealth of Independent States, in the most polite military terms possible, to go to hell.

Then came the members of parliament, the government commissions, the military brass. But they had no way to get rid of the officers that refused to take the Ukrainian oath. The base split into two almost equal parts, one loyal to Kiev and the other subordinated to the CIS, but in fact loyal to Moscow. Fistfights broke out regularly and to maintain order, Smirnov had ordered each camp to eat in shifts.

"Hey shithead." The familiar voice slurred heavily. Demiuk passed a small group of bomber pilots by the gastronome. A drunk Yuri Aivazian, the Armenian, sneered at him.

Demiuk ignored him. Not one of the strategic bomber pilots had flown for months. So, they wandered in and out of the base, answerable to no one. Aivazian travelled to Kiev frequently, showing up in Uzin with expensive Heineken beer and Dunhill cigarettes from the hard currency shops.

The more disciplined 12th Directorate officers kept to their strict routines regardless of loyalties and oaths – except for Anton Zvezda, who went AWOL after the mutiny.

The gastronome smelled of ancient milk and fresh bread when he took his place in a queue for kielbasa, a special treat for when he met with Smirnov for the traditional Officer's Day toasts.

*D*ora snorted when the wagon groaned to a halt and Brother Anton leaped out to inspect a hole in the barbed wire fence around the base. The mare swished her tail when Brother Boris led her to a clearing in a bare orchard shrouded with dirty snow. After tethering her to a tree, he loosened the bridle and locked the brakes. "We won't take long," he whispered, patting her neck.

Anton crouched near the ground by the hole. "We can fit," he said and waved for Boris to follow.

Boris crossed himself and whispered a short prayer to the sky for guidance. The full winter moon barely dimmed the stars and he wondered where heaven hid itself in that brilliance. He walked towards Anton, twisting his beard nervously. Was God behind the blackness that was behind the stars? The Bible said He made light. But that meant that the light was not Him. Was He the blackness then?

That can't be right, Boris thought, lowering himself through the hole in the fence. God wasn't the blackness. The thought troubled him even more. What was beyond the blackness?

He wished the Ukrainian schismatics hadn't taken over the Cave Monastery. He could have studied and prayed and tried to satisfy the yearning of his mind to fill the void in his soul. When his parents found out he had joined the monastery, his mother came to see him. She told him of his father's fury and pleaded for him to come home. Boris hadn't spoken to either of his parents since.

He slipped through the hole in the fence and into an empty field. Tall weeds poking through the snow testified to indifferent caretakers.

Anton rubbed muddy snow on his forehead and cheeks and told Boris to do the same. He obeyed reluctantly, recalling how he had agreed to Anton's crazy scheme never believing that he would succeed. But then, these days, nothing worked like it should.

When he finished dirtying his face, Anton inspected his appearance. "Your hair is a beacon. Pull your cowl up and tuck your beard inside your collar.

Though the black robe had been taken in to fit Boris's small frame, the cowl flopped over his face. "We'll get caught," he whispered after tripping over a clump of dried grass.

"If we do, it'll mean that I'm wrong. But we won't. It's Officers Day and everyone is drunk or getting there," said Anton, setting out with long confident strides that forced Boris to trot to keep up.

"They'll shoot us," he said.

"They're not going to shoot monks."

"How do you know?"

"I just do."

"How," Boris insisted.

They walked for a while through the field.

"I worked here," Anton finally answered, "in the 12th Directorate."

Boris let his cowl fall over his face to hide his shock. He had never heard of a 12th Directorate but if Anton used to work on the base, his plan could succeed.

Boris prayed fervently for Anton to change his mind. For a moment he believed that God had listened when they reached another fence topped with concertina wire, a sign reading "High Voltage" and no evident holes. Two-story buildings, painted white, lined the perimeter.

"I used to live there," said Anton, pointing to a low-slung apartment building. A bare bulb lit the entrance. "The storage depots are behind the buildings."

Boris peered through the chain link fence to see another fence and rolling hillocks beyond it. He thought he saw watchtowers in the distance.

"It seems well guarded," he said.

"It is," Anton responded.

Boris expected him to admit defeat but instead he said: "Follow me," and led him on a path through a copse of evergreens. Inebriated harmonies drifted from a distant campfire. Boris saw the firelight flickering on the faces of men and women too busy contemplating sin to hear his crashing through the underbrush.

"Where are we going," asked Boris.

"I want to see who's manning the checkpoint to the depots," said Anton. "It's Officer's Day, so they might just be conscripts."

Boris pulled out a lock of his beard and twisted it as he followed Anton out of the woods and onto a paved road, praying that they wouldn't find what Anton wanted. The tall monk stopped by a shed and wet the edge of his sleeve in a rusted bowl of water on the ground. "Clean your face," he commanded, wiping the dirt off his own with his sleeve.

"But why," asked Boris. "I thought…"

Anton squeezed the excess water from his robe. "Now we have to look as if we belong here."

Boris knelt by the bowl and had just finished washing in the icy water when he heard raucous voices and boots clumping unevenly on the pavement. His heart pumped wildly when he saw two drunken pilots staggering towards Anton, who fell to his knees and lowered his head in prayer.

"Eh, fuckin' monks. Waddfuck're goddam monks doin' 'ere?" said one pilot, swaying in a circle.

Anton didn't raise his head but spoke calmly. "The Order of St. Timothy sent us here to pray for your immortal souls."

"My fuckin' soul's just fine, monk," the officer snarled, making Boris glad that they didn't see him still crouching by the shed.

The other pilot burped and poked his buddy in the arm. "Fuckin' Smirnov must've let 'em in 'ere. That fuckin' traitor's gonna have fuckin' priests living here."

The first officer squinted at Anton, who kept his head piously lowered. "That piece of shit Smirnov sent you?" The pilot then twisted his head in confusion. "Doniknowyou?" he asked, slurring the question into a single word.

The other pilot answered with a mumbled: "You dunnno any fuckin' monks, Aivazian. Lesgo to'd fire 'fore they drink everythin'"

When the crunching of their boots on the pavement faded into the forest, Boris kept his crouch by the shed on shaky knees. "You see?" said Anton, holding out a hand to pull him to his feet. "The Lord is protecting us."

The two monks set off on the road again. It's as big as a town, thought Boris after they passed a huddle of brick buildings and a closed grocery store. A movie theater displayed a poster for "Chasing Two Rabbits", Boris's favorite movie, about a pompous but penniless barber in turn of the century Kiev. In his parallel pursuit of an ugly rich girl and a beautiful proletarian, he pretends to great wealth and stature only to be humiliated at the end.

Here and there, groups of people, some drunk, others less so, eyed them with curiosity but did nothing more. When he asked why one tried to stop them, Anton's face twisted bitterly. "Uzin is the same as our church. It's split and neither side has any idea of what the other is doing. Whoever sees us thinks that the other side let us in. Besides, we're monks. We're innocent."

No we aren't. But Boris kept that thought to himself.

Half a kilometer past the base's center, they entered a birch forest and climbed a hill overlooking a windowless concrete building with a flat roof. In the distance, enormous hangars cast shadows in the moonlight.

"The bombers," whispered Anton, following his companion's gaze. "Tu-95s: there are 21 of them. Each can carry 16 As-14 air-launched cruise missiles. The lot could destroy every large city in America."

"That's horrible," Boris murmured.

"They started it. Don't forget Hiroshima," Anton retorted and then pointed at a dark fixture on the guard tower that rose above the birches. "Dammit. That spotlight is still broken."

Torn between relief and despair to find no one else there, Boris lifted his robe off the ground to edge down the grassy slope and follow Anton to the front of the building.

A padlock hung on the metal door.

"It's locked," said Boris. "Let's go."

Anton turned to him curiously. "Of course, it's locked. What did you think?" he said, pulling a leather case out of voluminous robe pocket. He unzipped it to take out a thin instrument that he poked into the keyhole, probing the inner mechanism until the padlock clicked open. After removing it, he opened the door slowly so it wouldn't squeak and slipped inside, holding the heavy door open for Boris.

The door closed them in a pitch black interior. Anton fumbled with a match box. "I have a candle." he whispered. But Boris closed his eyes, afraid of seeing the destructive force that would decide his fate. The candle sputtered while Anton trod heavily on the concrete floor. Each time the footsteps stopped, Anton muttered angrily. After the fifth mutter, curiosity overcame fear and Boris turned to see Anton holding the candle over an empty bay.

"They're gone," Anton exclaimed. "They're God damn gone!"

"Gone?" whispered Boris, too happy to make a fuss over the curse -- not that Anton seemed monkish anymore, except for his robe. Back outside, Boris's pulse raced gleefully but he saw Anton snap his fingers in frustration and said nothing.

"There were 24 cruise missiles in here," he said, banging his fist. "They took them off the bombers a year ago when they lowered alert levels."

"Much has changed in that time, Anton." Boris tilted his head in the direction they came from. "We should go. Dora's been alone for over an hour."

"They must have taken them to the S-Objects for storage," Anton said to himself, leaving Boris mystified as to his meaning but pleased to see his companion's shoulders sag with disappointment. "We'll go back a quicker way," he said, setting out on a different path that emerged from the birches near an open-air bunker. Moonlight drifted under the corrugated metal roof to reveal stacks of crates.

"Conventional munitions," said Anton, trudging past them without a glance.

They came across another shelter, and then another. Anton navigated the dozens of bunkers separated by copses of birch and pine woods as easily as he had picked the lock on the empty building. Boris lagged, pulling his robe in with both hands when it caught on the bare bushes and shrubs. He kept his eyes on the ground, trying to follow Anton's footsteps in the dark and didn't see him stop.

"Shhh," Anton whispered when Boris bumped into his back.

For a few minutes, Anton listened but it was quiet except for an owl, hooting in the treetops. "What is it," asked Boris, trying to see around his companion's massive back.

Instead of answering, Anton couched and waved his hand for them to move forward before running into the moonlit field. Howitzers cluttered a low slung bunker. Boris had seen the heavy cannons dozens of times during the Kremlin military parades.

Anton darted past them with Boris struggling to keep up until they slipped back into the shadows. He panted heavily, having grown unused to exercise during his monastic life. "Can we slow down?" he asked and Anton obliged by stopping in front of a smaller bunker next to the howitzers. Wooden crates filled it to the ceiling.

"Artillery shells for the howitzers," Anton explained while Boris leaned against a crate to catch his breath. Again lighting his candle and cupping his hand to protect it from gusts of air, Anton walked into the bunker, holding the flame to a thin cylinder with a pointed blue tip.

"The blue tip means it's conventional," the tall monk said as though he expected it. "The howitzer can also fire one kiloton ZBV3 nuclear artillery shells. They have a blast radius of a little less than a kilometer. They look the same as the conventional shells, but they have red tips. They're the smallest nuclear explosives in the world."

Boris didn't respond, tired of the subject. Instead, he thanked the Lord for the twentieth time in the last half hour. "I'm better," he said, peering inside the bunker to see Anton shining his candle on the weapons. "We can go now," he said.

Anton grunted in response and held the candle flame to another cone with a blue tip. "These are all conventional. Russia withdrew the artillery shells along with the rest of the tactical nuclear weapons last year. We had dozens of them here at Uzin," he said when the shadows caught his attention and he crouched for a closer examination, holding up his candle.

Boris saw the red tip and his spirit plummeted.

"Nuclear!" Anton whispered, passing the yellow flame along the cone to light its serial number: UZ666.

The burning candle reflected in Anton's eyes when he leveled his gaze on Boris. "Behold, our sign from God!"

A dull weight descended on Boris's chest as he walked inside the bunker and fell to his knees, reaching out to touch the metal casing, its red tip piercing the darkness. "It even has the Number of the Beast," he said

148

with wonder. "Destroy Istanbul," he whispered, imagining the blinding fireball that would reduce the city to cinders.

"It won't destroy Istanbul," said Anton. "It's too small. But if we're in the right place, it'll do the job."

I'll die, too. An icy chill gripped Boris.

But if the Heavenly Father didn't spare his only begotten son an agonizing death on the cross to create the one true faith, why spare the son of an atheist Communist to preserve it?

He faced Anton, no longer afraid of getting caught, or shot. He felt only sadness when he finally asked: "What now?"

CHAPTER 11:

ALMS

FAXNEWS-UKRAINE

March 20, 1993, (Moscow, Russia). The Speaker of Parliament accused the Russian President of acting unconstitutionally. At an emergency session, lawmakers voted to amend the Constitution, stripping the President of many of his powers.

March 24, 1993 (New York, N.Y.). Experts here say that Ukraine could cut the communications "cable" with Moscow and then retarget the nuclear weapons without the Kremlin knowing. According to one Russian engineer who designed the nuclear command and control system: "We didn't build it for chaos."

March 24, 1993 (Washington, D.C.). The ratification of START had become more uncertain in light of the political tensions in Moscow. The Ukrainian government called for the creation of an international commission to monitor the safety of the nuclear weapons in Ukraine.
END

Faxnews-Ukraine – Your source of English-language news about Ukraine

---

TOP SECRET – PURPLE
Handle via Agent Channels Only
Date: **April 1, 1993**
To: **K3**
From: **Deputy Chief of Station Kiev**
Subject: **SITREP Rasputin**

(TS) 1. **Please verify bank transfer under code name Irina.**

(S)   2. Require increase in entertainment budget for the Iraqi, alias Mohammed Ali's consumption of Johnny Walker Black Label.

(S)   3. After five shots of scotch, Mohammed Ali mumbled of the Iraqi Dictator: "That bastard killed my neighbor the archaeologist because he complained about the zig rats."

(U)   4. My desktop encyclopedia has no entry for zig rats. Is this an Iraqi rodent species?

END

TOP SECRET – PURPLE

Exempt from automatic downgrade

TOP SECRET – WHITE

Handle via Agent Channels Only

Date: April 21, 1993
To: K3
From: Chief of Station Kiev
Subject: SITREP Fertilizer

(TS)   1. Neil Neilson and Dan Kruger leave today for Pervomaysk. Atlas shows a dozen Pervomaysks in Ukraine but coordinates 48 10 22 and 33 55 56 written on their notes point to Pervomaysk in Kirovohrad region, site of ICBM missile fields.

(S)   2. Before leaving Kiev, they will also meet with the Minister of Foreign Economic Relations, the agency which issues export licenses. Although Ukraine controls exports of sugar, wheat, coal, steel and other commodities, it has no mechanisms for controlling exports of weapons or weapons-related materials. It is possible to conceal canisters of nuclear materials, warheads, and entire weapons systems in innocuous appearing shipments of sugar or coal.

END

TOP SECRET – WHITE

Exempt from automatic downgrade

---

*V*ictor Vidkat smoothed his Hermes tie and brandished a Mont Blanc pen over a stack of bonded paper. While he calculated the license fee for exporting half-a-million tons of coal, Neil Neilson examined the incongruously luxurious office. Nothing in the unlit corridors and dreary reception room of the Ministry of Foreign Economic Relations prepared him for the gleaming teak desk, the sumptuous Asian carpets and crystal goblets from which they sipped Evian.

After drinking Pepsi and salty Georgian mineral water, designer water – even tepid – was a treat. *Where did he find it?* Cristina Smythe had raved over a new shop with imported foods as though Wal-Mart had come to Kiev. But they only found Vienna sausages, canned corn and long-life milk. No water.

The Mont Blanc's nib scratched when Vidkat circled the result of his calculations. "Fifty thousand dollars," he announced.

Neilson felt rather than saw Dan Kruger's apoplectic reaction and opened his mouth to protest when Vidkat raised his hand to stop him. "This is terrible big license fee," he said, shaking his head. "You are not first importers to come to my office." He lifted his glass and twirled it so that the crystal fractured the light into shards of color.

"It is terrible," he repeated, gazing at his guests from over the glass rim. "And I very much want to help you. But these regulations…" his voice trailed off with fake regret. "What can we do?"

Neilson saw Kruger raise an eyebrow. Cristina interviewed exporters for a story on Ukrainian wool coats and warned them that the minister in charge of export licenses spoke English and had greasy palms. They had agreed to sniff but not bite at what he offered.

"Well, Mr. Vidkat, can you find any exceptions to the licensing fee?" Neilson asked.

"Exceptions? There are many exceptions," Vidkat responded and took a sheet of paper from a shelf. "Did you work on the clean-up after the Chernobyl disaster?"

"No."

"Do you provide humanitarian aid?" Vidkat shook his head for them.

"Are you a church?" Vidkat smirked and without waiting for an answer, skimmed the rest of the list. "Other exceptions are for Ukrainian citizens," he said.

Kruger closed his notebook and slumped in disappointment.

"Except one." Vidkat leaned back in his cordovan leather chair, tapping the Mont Blanc. "The exception is for members of the Fund for the Improvement of the Architecture of Kiev."

When neither American responded, Vidkat displayed a gold incisor. "I am Fund president. Membership fee is 5,000 dollars – each."

Kruger pulled his seatbelt tighter and clutched the armrests of his seat on the groaning Tupelev twin-prop plane that lurched through turbulent skies. "God, this sucks," he muttered as the plane dropped and swooped, spilling the boiled potatoes that an army officer a few rows ahead had unwrapped from a worn newspaper. They rolled on the bare metal floor and stopped at Kruger's sneaker, leaving a tendril of dill on his left shoelace when the plane pitched again and the potato tumbled away.

A male monotone crackled in Slavic over the ancient loudspeakers and two flight attendants trotted through the smoke filled cabin, grasping the seatbacks to keep their balance as the plane sea-sawed and spasmed. Kruger elbowed Neilson, who was reading commodity prices in the *International Herald Tribune*. "This is wrong," he said, ending the word on a squeakier note than planned when another sudden drop left his throat at a higher altitude.

Neilson saw Kruger's clenched fists and looked out the window. "Nothing's wrong, we're descending."

The plane plunged and wobbled for a few seconds while the potatoes rolled back and forth on the aisle, collecting lint and grime.

"Not very smoothly, though," said Neilson. A loose object in the back of the jolting aircraft banged over the mechanical scream of the landing gear.

The male voice snapped and crackled through the speakers followed by the two flight attendants, who trotted back up the aisle. Kruger craned his neck to watch one of them strap herself into a seat by the lavatory.

"Put on seat belts," Kostya announced from the seat across the aisle, where he worked on a crossword puzzle. Neilson clipped his belt and picked up his newspaper.

"What's up, Dan?" he said, "You're not a fearful flier."

Kruger turned around again to see the flight attendants chatting. But they received special training to remain maniacally cheerful as the plane plunged them to a fiery death. Not that the stewardesses on Aeroflot Flight 301 to Donetsk displayed any cheer, at least at him. Nor did they serve food. They were just flying floor dragons.

"You've never seen me on a plane that belongs to a collapsing Soviet airline," he retorted. "Who the hell is maintaining these tin cans while Kiev and Moscow fight over each plane."

As if in agreement, the plane made three short plunges and then pitched to the left before leveling out. Kruger saw the treetops outside the window at eye level and closed his eyes when the airplane dropped suddenly. The wheels slammed on the runway with a jolt and the plane bounced back up to the treetops to descend again and land smoothly. Kruger sighed in relief when they trundled to a sudden stop for a final jostling.

"I'm taking the train back to Kiev," he announced, following Neilson onto the tarmac. Laden with bouquets, baskets, and bottles of champagne; a small crowd gazed up at the plane, cheering and applauding under a red banner with handwritten Cyrillic lettering. Off to the side, next to a stocky man in a faded corduroy suit, Zoya stood conspicuous and sleek in a moss green sheath that set off her coppery hair.

She rushed up to them in a light cloud of perfume and clacking of spike heels.

"Is this for us, Zoya?" asked Neilson, gesturing at the cheering crowd while Kruger used his carry on bag to fend off a basket of dried apricots. The cheerful throng streamed around them, popping champagne corks into the air.

Zoya pointed at the beaming young pilot who emerged from the plane clasping his hands victoriously over his head. "This was his first time landing," she said, watching the pilot take the glass of champagne offered by the older pilot next to him and raised it to a roar of cheers. A bald man ran up to encase them both in a bear hug and grizzled kiss.

"First time?" Neilson asked. Maybe a train didn't sound so bad.

Zoya greeted Neilson and Kruger warmly, but her expression cooled when she saw Kostya. "You did not have to bring him," she said. "I can translate. He is unnecessary business expense." Kostya's expression didn't change but he whispered something that brought an angry blush to Zoya's smooth cheeks. To stop the escalating duel, Kruger broke in with forced ease. "Oh, the first rule of doing business in a foreign country is: Always bring your own translator." Not the first rule, but a good one nonetheless.

Zoya's ebullience sputtered for a moment but she recovered her aplomb, taking Neilson's arm to lead him to the stocky man standing alone on the tarmac. "Now we must go meet my father, who will make us rich!"

Myron Viktorovich Plaviuk, Hero of the Great Fatherland War, three time Hero of Socialist Labor and director of the V.I. Lenin Mining Association for 15 years didn't look like he could make anyone rich. His greeting revealed stumpy stained teeth. Black crescents embedded under his fingernails.

It's probably coal, thought Kruger, *and we do need a guy who's swimming in it.*

After the introductions, Zoya swept them into a black Volga. While the driver packed their bags into the trunk, Zoya placed the Americans, her father and herself in the car, tucking her long legs in the front seat.

Kruger saw their translator outside. "You forgot Kostya."

Zoya tossed her head without turning. "You can see there is no room. He can follow us in taxi," she said, slipping round black sunglasses on her nose and pointing to a group of cabbies playing cards on an overturned wastebasket.

It was a half hour to drive to the coal mining town and they needed Kostya to watch Zoya's translation for her father. Her transparent efforts to exclude him were suspicious.

Kruger got out of the car. He was dispensable for this part of the journey.

"Where are you going?" Zoya asked with surprise.

154

"Oh, I'll be more comfortable traveling alone. I like the driver to take it more slowly than most people," he said. "Kostya will find me a cab and then he can go with you."

After the drivers discussed the destination and directions, Kruger settled into the worn vinyl back seat of the cab. Smokestacks, steel plants, cinderblock housing and mountains of coal flitted by his view as they drove at legal speed through the outskirts of Donetsk.

"You sell dollars?"

Brown eyes under a shaggy brow glanced at him through the rear view mirror.

"Beg your pardon?"

"You are American, *da*?" The driver turned around, displaying a checkerboard of iron, gold and ivory in his mouth. "I buy dollars. One thousand *kupons*, one dollar – excellent rate."

Kruger agreed, though Ukraine's ersatz currency didn't buy much. Anything worth having could be had for dollars. "I'll think about it," said Kruger, adding: "So, you speak English."

The driver hunched over the steering wheel and waved dismissively. "I am out of practice. That is why I drive this junk car. I am engineer, read many American journals. But my design bureau, it have no money since Soviet Union collapse. No one wants to be engineer. Young people, they want to work in business, banking, go to America."

"No one in America wants to be an engineer either," said Kruger. "We import them from Pakistan."

The driver's eyes reflected seriousness in the mirror. "Then you import me? I move to America like this," he said, snapping tapered fingers in the air. His fingernails were clean. Dental work did not reflect personal hygiene.

Kruger responded with exaggerated helplessness. "Sorry, but I don't need engineers in my business." *What business?* He wondered about the doings in the black Volga they tailed at a defensive driving distance.

The driver glanced over his shoulder and flashed his dental mosaic. "It is OK. I drive Iranian businessman last week, and German businessman yesterday. Pakistan, too. They very interested in my engineering." After a while, he added: "But I like America better."

"Yeah, me, too" said Kruger. "But there's more competition there."

The driver opened his window a crack and propped his elbows on the steering wheel to light a cigarette. "In my engineering, there is very little competition," he said, with little pleasure, "but big demand in some places."

"And what kind of engineering is that," Kruger asked politely.

A puff of smoke swirled around the car and streamed out of the window.

"Engineering guidance systems, for missiles."

*M*ining Association No.134 appeared just like what Neilson expected for anything named after V.I. Lenin. Battered and rusty, the buildings and machinery seemed held together with twine, chewing gum and a force that defied the laws of physics. Ukraine's coal mining engineers had to be exceptional to keep the decrepit industry working. It wasn't encouraging until the black Volga stopped at a squat brick building in a valley framed by anthracite Alps.

"This is it," Zoya announced and turned to her father in the back seat. During the entire trip, whenever Zoya spoke to him, he grunted or responded angrily. The first time Kostya leaned over to whisper a translation in Neilson's ear, Zoya's piercing stare from the front seat threatened to create too hostile a climate in the crowded car. So Neilson signaled his translator to keep quiet, glad that Kruger had his own cab for their escape in case the talks went sour.

When that cab trundled next to their Volga minutes later, Zoya muttered an admonition at her father who turned with obvious reluctance to disappear into the brick building. "Mr. Kruger, you have arrived. Now we can do business, yes?" she said brightly and turned to lead them into the building.

"Do I have a story for you," Kruger whispered as they followed a few steps behind. "How was your ride?"

"I don't know. But Kostya does."

The translator caught up with them. "He is Communist," he whispered. "He doesn't want to sell coal to bourgeois capitalist Americans. They fight about it."

"And who won?" whispered Neilson. As if in response, Zoya stopped at the door to the building and turned around, glittering like a diamond against the grimy windows and soot-stained bricks. She crossed her arms and her eyes, blazing with confidence, rested on her guests. "I will do the talking," she said. "You will sign the papers."

*Z*oya proved brilliant, browbeating her stubborn father into selling a small mountain of coal to the despised capitalists whose presence besmirched the proletarian purity of his coal mines. His daughter had already betrayed him by defecting to the bourgeoisie he so despised. He never should have let her go to America. But making him sell coal to the enemy was like a dagger through his heart. You young people don't care about moral values, just money.

That, at least, was the meaning Kruger ascribed to the emotional family drama they witnessed without the benefit of translation, since Zoya had admonished Kostya to say nothing. *Amerika, kapitalisti, buzhwazi:* those words he recognized. His imagination, and Myron Plaviuk's fierce glowering in their direction, filled in the rest.

Whatever father and daughter actually discussed, the resulting contract with Mining Association No. 134 for 500,000 tons of metallurgical coal at a total price of 25 million dollars was worth it. The ink on Neilson's signature smeared when Zoya grabbed his arm to whisk him away.

"Zoya, we didn't even shake hands," he protested as she propelled them out of the building.

"If you shake hands, he will say: 'we must drink to celebrate'," she explained. "If he drinks, he becomes very mad at America. Then, he can change his mind and I cannot stop him."

They emerged from the building into the courtyard, where the two cars awaited them. "Now, we must go back to Kiev to begin export procedures," said Zoya.

"Can we take the train?" Kruger asked hopefully.

"Tickets difficult to buy," said Kostya. "Many people traveling now. If we pay bribes…"

Zoya cut him off. "No bribes. Our mining association has a ticket quota."

"Excellent. Then, let's go to the train station," said Kruger. "Neil and I need to talk, so why don't you two go in the faster car and we'll meet there. You can buy our tickets."

Both translators froze in alarm. "But you will not find us," Kostya protested. "I must go with you."

"We'll be OK," said Kruger, feeling sorry for Kostya. The beautiful coal princess treated him like a serf. "Zoya, tell our driver a landmark at the train station where we can find you."

With the rendezvous settled, they parted into their respective cars. Watching the black Volga gain distance and speed, Kruger told Neilson about the taxi driver eager to peddle his knowledge of missile technologies to rogue states.

"And we thought we had a problem with Rozpad," he concluded.

"This is serious," said Neilson. "We have to report this when we're back stateside. And tell them about Rozpad, too."

"With pleasure," said Kruger. "But to whom? Washington is focused on the wrong stuff. If we tell Hedgepeth about missile technologies, he'll rant about START. If we tell General Hawkins, he'll just worry about the Pentagon budget and stab us in the back."

"The CIA?" asked Neilson. "We haven't gone there yet."

"Yeah, we'll tell the CIA just to make sure we did our patriotic duty. But it's not going to make a difference. They just don't know what

157

they're up against. I mean, even if Hawkins wasn't a double dealing piece of shit, he's incompetent when it comes to non-proliferation in this part of the world." He lit a cigar, a Cuban that proved easy to buy in Kiev. "You have high octane uranium, unemployed rocket scientists, and nuclear weapons whose custody still isn't clear to anyone. And that's just the stuff that you and I know about. Add those unsavory characters at the Night Bar, like that Iraqi fixture. I'm sure he isn't here just for the prostitutes."

"Yeah, and that German with the dog," said Neilson. "I just don't see what's to stop a catastrophe."

Kruger had no answers. They had to report the problem to the proper authorities, even if those authorities were too stupid or stubborn to understand the implications. Hesitantly he asked: "How about luck?"

*K*ruger stood next to Kostya at the train wagon's open window to see boxes, bags and suitcases piled on the platform. A woman sat on one of the boxes, nursing an infant from inside a discretely open blouse. Next to her, a boy bounced a rubber ball around an elderly man who had fallen asleep over a pile of pillows tied with twine.

"That's a lot of luggage for a train trip," said Kruger, watching the woman tuck a strand of hair under her faded kerchief. A bearded man in dusty clothes handed her a bruised apple, patted the baby and crouched on the platform to sip from a pale brown bottle.

The translator watched the vignette. "They are moving. Many people moving since Soviet Union collapse. Russians in Ukraine go to Russia. Ukrainians in Russia come to Ukraine." He pointed at the packages. "For a whole family, that is not very much."

The woman noticed the motion and squinted at them, pulling her blouse over her baby's face as the train rumbled and groaned on its slow way out of the station. Kruger turned away and leaned against the open door to their sleeper compartment, a square box with faux plywood walls and two sets of sleeping platforms stacked like bunk beds on either side. The overnight train would arrive in Kiev in the morning. He wanted to call Jean, now in her fourth month and still suffering with morning sickness.

Neilson studied Kruger's meager notes from the Vidkat meeting and leaned back against the red vinyl sideboard that cushioned the compartment wall. "And we thought the problem was buying coal."

Kruger dug a bottle of Pepsi out of a large plastic bag of groceries. Zoya had insisted that they buy food, as the trains had none, and bought a jar of pickled tomatoes, smoked sausage, cheese and black bread from weathered women in faded print dresses outside the train station.

"Nope," he said, popping open the bottle. "Now our problem is getting the coal out of here."

Kostya turned from watching the passing scenery and poked his head into the compartment. "But you have Mr. Coco who has ships."

"First we have to load the coal on the ships," said Kruger, "and to do that, we have to pay 50,000 dollars for an export license or a 10,000 dollar bribe to the suave Mr. Vidkat."

The door to Zoya's neighboring compartment slid open and she emerged, having changed into a blue velour gym suit and a loose ponytail that made her softer and younger than the angles and spikes of her business clothes.

"It's also illegal," said Neilson.

"What is illegal?" asked Zoya, pushing Kostya aside to enter the compartment.

"*Suka*," muttered Kostya to which Zoya retorted: "*Zhlob*".

Neilson ignored the exchange. The two had been bickering since they met up at the information booth at the train station. "Paying bribes is illegal."

Zoya waved her hand. "Everyone pays bribes. No one cares."

"The U.S. government does," said Kruger.

"But we are not in America," protested Zoya, pulling a slippered foot underneath her.

"It doesn't matter," explained Neilson. "There's a law called the Foreign Corrupt Practices Act that makes it illegal for American businesses to pay bribes in other countries. If we got caught doing that, we could be fined, or go to jail, or barred from bidding on U.S. government contracts."

Not to mention losing our security clearances, thought Kruger. Not that he wanted to do any government work ever again, but he still needed the option. The coal deal remained uncertain. Paying the bribe was risky. But paying the extortionate fee for the export license was impossible since neither of them had that kind of money. The Kruger home had a second mortgage and the Neilson's divorce proceedings had locked up his.

"Ah. I remember this from my studies," said Zoya. "But you will not get caught."

Kostya stabbed a finger at her. "Did you listen? What if they go to jail?"

"Do not point at me, *debil*," said Zoya.

"Do not call me *debil*! I am not stupid, you Soviet!"

Zoya's cheeks reddened with indignation. "Stop calling me Soviet. I have an MBA from Pennsylvania State University!"

"So, what are you?"

"What do you mean, what am I?"

"If you're not Soviet, what are you? We now live in independent Ukraine. Are you Ukrainian?"

Her eyes were wary. "What difference does it make?"

"I want to know."

"My father is Ukrainian but my mother is Russian. They were allowed to choose either as my nationality on my birth certificate, so they made me Russian."

Kostya swept his arm back in the direction they were leaving. "Donetsk is Soviet. There is nothing of Russian culture in Donetsk except the language most people speak. Communists made Donetsk the crucible for making Soviet Man. They ordered hundreds of thousands of people of different nationalities – but especially Russians – to settle there. Then they brainwashed them into believing they were models for humanity and superior – even though they had no education, no culture and no spirit. Donetsk is result of Soviet social experiments. It is a reservation for Communists, like your father."

At the mention of the Communist on whom his future business success depended, Kruger blew up at their constant arguing. "What the hell is wrong with you two?"

Zoya studied her manicured fingernails. "He keeps calling me Soviet," she said petulantly.

"It is true," exclaimed Kostya. "You think people had good life in U.S.S.R."

"Well, they did."

"They did not! It was terrible, like prison."

"Your family must have been bourgeois nationalists. People who stayed out of politics lived well."

Kostya slapped the corridor wall. "Bourgeois nationalist!?' That Soviet slur? You prove my point. For most people, life only felt good compared with horrible civil war, famine, purges, World War II. Millions and millions of people died…"

"Everyone had jobs, money."

"How can you say that? You will make money on coal."

"I am not talking about me. I am lucky. I am talking about other people," said Zoya, displaying a humility that caught the compartment's occupants by surprise. "Have you seen how coal miners live nowadays, how many of them die each year?"

She wiped at her eyes. "This is how I convinced Father to sell you coal, so that his mining association can make money to improve safety. Last year, 35 miners died in methane explosion at his mine. My uncle died."

"At least you had an uncle," Kostya retorted, though more in sadness than anger. "All my aunts and uncles died in Great Famine, except one aunt who went to America. This is thanks to the wonderful Soviet Union that you praise."

"Enough!" Kruger shouted them both into silence. "I do not want to listen to this crap anymore. Kostya, take this historical debate next door or in another wagon or anywhere I don't have to hear it? Neil and I have things to discuss privately."

Zoya didn't have to do his bidding, but she followed Kostya out of the compartment when the door to the neighboring wagon opened and the corridor filled with the clangs and wails of the lumbering train.

"Darlin'," said a young male voice with a Texas twang. "I think we're in the right wagon. You have the tickets. Remind me which compartment we're in."

"It doesn't say which compartment, just the seat number, Roy," said a woman's voice. She sounded young. "We're in numbers 15 and 16."

"Praise the Lord, here 'tis," said the man, followed by blunt and heavy sound of bags falling to the ground.

"Roy, the Bibles," cried the woman.

"Sorry, hon'. The door won't open and they fell."

Kruger leaned out to see a couple struggling to open their compartment, not realizing that they were contending with a sliding door. He saw no sign of Kostya or Zoya and her compartment was closed.

Neilson had tuned out during the Kostya vs. Zoya match to read a spy novel he brought along for such contingencies. "For Chrissakes, Dan, they're Bible thumpers. This place is lousy with them. But if *you* help them, *you* have to talk to them. I hate listening to evangelicals."

Kruger stood up. "Yeah, but if I don't, I'll feel like a shit."

When he returned, Roy and Barbara Connor came with him.

"Thank the Lord for your friend," said Barbara, after the introductions. "We'd still be tryin' to open that door."

"And it's real good to hear American voices," said Roy, leaning against the handrail in the corridor like a former football player, big on top and bigger around the middle. "We stayed in Donetsk for two weeks, preaching Christ, and we didn't understand nothin' except our translator."

"We understood enough to tell them that they're lost in sin," added Barbara, clenching her jaw with disapproval. "One person asked Christ into his heart. The other ones who said they were religious belonged to that Orthodox Church. They didn't believe us when we told them they'd burn in to hell for it."

"That was confusin', too," added Roy, "You see, there're two kinds of Orthodox churches, Russian and Ukrainian."

"There are more of those Ukrainian Orthodox Churches," said Barbara.

"But people we talked to weren't sure which one they belonged to," said Roy. "The priest decides, and the priests don't always tell the parishioners."

"Doesn't matter, Roy," said Barbara. "They're still goin' to hell."

Neilson said nothing while Kruger sat on his platform, sprawling in a way that didn't encourage company. Barbara jerked her chin in their direction. "Do you two know the Lord?"

Neilson raised his eyebrows pointedly at Kruger, who responded. "Uh, not personally and, I'm too tired for any introductions right now."

Barbara pursed her lips but Roy massaged his shoulder. "I'm too tired, too. There were no taxis and I had to carry the extra Bibles to the train station." He yawned. "It's been a long two weeks."

"Why, Roy, how can you complain about winning souls?" Barbara chided her husband. "We're blessed to do that."

"Darlin', I'm not complaining. I'm beat." Roy massaged his neck. "I think I sprained something."

"I am so saddened by this," Barbara exclaimed, on the verge of tears. "You had a light burden compared to my…"

Roy patted his wife's arm. "Barbara, you're tired, too. We had a hard mission."

"Do not patronize me, Roy Connor!" Barbara pushed his hand off her arm and, ignoring Kruger and Neilson, stomped away. The door to the Connor compartment slid into a loud slam.

Roy grasped his head and bent it back for an audible crack of his back. "Sorry. Barbara is a wonderful woman and I praise the Lord for every day she's in my life. But she took this trip rough."

When his interlocutors responded with silence, he chuckled. "Nope, I ain't gonna try to convert you. Barbara, yeah, if she'd have stayed, but not me. I'm willing to spread the Good Word, but you don't want to listen, I figure there's room for 144,000 souls in heaven after the Rapture. The more people who get saved, the more crowded it'll be."

Despite Neilson's misgivings, Roy's pragmatic approach to proselytizing disarmed him. "I don't share your religious outlook, Roy. And I guess that means more room for you in heaven," he said. "But this is a rough and frustrating place if you don't have your heart in what you're doing."

Roy leaned into their compartment and lodged his hands against the doorframe. "Aside from my wife, who needs me to protect her, I kept busy. You know how much steel they produce in Donetsk?"

Neilson remembered the steel dumping case against Ukraine in the US but he said nothing and Roy continued. "A lot. And it's cheap. Unbelievably cheap. It's all subsidized and, praise the Lord, we can make a bundle exporting it to the U.S."

"But the high export duties," said Neilson. "Don't they cut heavily into your profits?"

"God helps those who help themselves, Neil. Barbara and I represent the Church of Christ and churches don't have to pay export duties."

The train squealed to a stop and Roy turned to look at his compartment. "I better go check on Barbara." He reached out to shake hands. "Good to meet you, and thanks for your help, Dan."

When he left, Neilson closed the door and took out the Vidkat meeting notes, where Kruger had written: "Exemptions: Chernobyl, humanitarian, church" followed by "NOT!"

"We need to find a church that wants money and will do a joint venture with us," he said.

"Show me a church that doesn't want money," Kruger responded, slicing cheese with a pocketknife. "The Russian Orthodox Church has financial support from Moscow. But the Ukrainian church? I'll bet that flock doesn't have much for the collection plate. We need Kostya to set up a meeting with them."

"Where is Kostya? He's been gone for a …" Neilson stopped at the sound of Zoya's compartment door opening and then slamming shut. The low hum of voices followed by long silences and soft creaking penetrated the thin compartment walls.

Kruger took a bite of cheese. "I hope this means Kostya is losing his virginity."

Neilson broke off a piece of sausage. "So, back to this Church thing: What do *you* think?"

Kruger popped open a Ukrainian beer in a dark brown bottle. Outside, at a dreary train stop in the middle of the Ukrainian steppe, women hawked corn on the cob and bright red crayfish. Grilled chickens glistened in the setting sun. He didn't see a single car but two monks in a horse drawn cart piled high with potatoes trotted in and out of view.

That's a good enough sign for me. He turned to Neilson. "Praise the Lord!"

*D*ora's mane bounced in rhythm with her clip-clopping hooves as she pulled the cart through the dusty crumbling outskirts of a village. Boris had to drive the mare very slowly on vast stretches of cracked and cratered roadways to avoid falling into a hole or breaking a wheel. They had traveled for weeks, but had only made it less than 250 kilometers south of Kiev. Boris dreaded the long trip ahead.

"Where are we?" asked Anton, who roused himself after dozing away on the passenger side. Incapable of driving the wagon, he spent most of the days either reading his Bible or sleeping but not talking much except to give Boris directions. The wagon bumped too much for him to work on the thing they had taken from the Uzin bomber base. Anton had hidden it easily in his canvas duffle bag while they waited for warm weather to travel.

"We're in Kapitanka, about 20 kilometers from Pervomaysk," said Boris. They had passed the village sign just before Anton woke up.

He clucked to Dora out of habit rather than need. The mare was an honest worker and pulled her burden without as much as a snort. When a hare scampered out of a field in front of her, she just waggled her ears. Dogs she ignored, but not cars. Clearly she hadn't seen many in her life. But they encountered few on the road.

When he spied a public well snuggled against a vine-covered fence near the village store, Boris stopped the cart and set the brake. "We need water," he announced and clambered to the well, cranking the wooden bucket to fill it with water. After he poured it into the zinc pail the monastery gave them for their journey, the mare drank her fill and then rubbed her face against Boris's arm.

He pushed her away to see Anton swiveling his head furtively. "We must go, the store is still open and someone might see us."

"We're monks with a cart of potatoes. No one cares."

"Monks are still unusual after the atheist years. You've seen people stare at us. If we stop, they may try to talk to us, like that old woman outside Dikanka."

The woman had asked for guidance about her dying husband. Boris felt pity for her. "But let's fill the water bottle while we're here," he said, again dipping the wooden bucket into the well.

"Hurry," said Anton, taking the empty five liter jar from the large bin behind their seat and prying off the plastic cover. Once he filled it, Boris replaced the cover, lifted it to Anton and climbed back into the cart to gather up the reins and release the brake.

"It is growing dark," Anton observed. "We need to leave and make camp."

"Why make camp? St. Vladimir's monastery is in Pervomaysk. It's not far away and I thought we'd seek shelter there. It's the first monastery we've come across since we left Dikanka."

"I won't be able to work there. They might see."

Boris had wearied of camping. Their old canvas tent smelled and they had to sleep on the ground. He had so wearied of eating potatoes, too. If the Lord willed these to be his last days on earth, he hoped for at least one good meal. "It can wait a night, can't it?" he argued. He wanted to take a bath. They had been washing in cold streams and buckets of well-water.

"No, it, can't," Anton whispered, emphasizing each word. "You have no idea about how much time it takes to bypass the permissive action links,

164

hotwire the barometric fuse and build a new trigger. We'll make camp as soon as we find a good spot."

On a good stretch of road near the train station, Boris tapped Dora with the whip to pick up a brisk trot that carried them out of the village, past a patchwork of manicured vegetable gardens and vast fields overgrown with weeds. Finally, they reached a forest, just as the setting sun's long rays bathed the landscape in gold.

"It's so beautiful," he murmured. How he would miss such things.

Anton swept his arm out at the surrounding forest, draped in the bright green leaves of spring. "There's an intercontinental nuclear missile under every tree around here."

Since Anton sneaked them in and out of the bomber base, Boris tended to trust him on matters nuclear. "But how can you fit a missile under a tree? I saw them on TV during the May Day parades in Moscow. They're huge."

Anton smacked his forehead. "I'm exaggerating, Christ! But there is an ICBM missile silo in almost every village. There are about a hundred of them around here."

The road had worsened and Boris slowed Dora to a walk. "But how can you have a missile silo in a village? Aren't those things secret?"

"They're not in the village, but a kilometer or two outside it. But you wouldn't know it because it's surrounded by twin chain-link barbed wire fences and marked as a medical research institute."

When they came upon a dirt path into the woods, the cart bumped and creaked over the uneven surface. After crossing a ramp over a swift stream, they stopped in a clearing surrounded by birch and pine. Anton leaped to the ground and reached for the tent, setting it up with practiced ease while Boris removed Dora's harness to let her graze. After days of traveling, they had divided the rest of the evening labors. Boris built the fire, washed the potatoes in the stream, cooked them, served them, cleaned up and laid the bedding inside the tent.

Meanwhile, Anton lit the kerosene lamp and worked. Boris wasn't sure what "bypassing the permissive action links, hotwiring the barometric fuse and building a trigger" meant but he had his suspicions since it required taking the thing out of the canvas bag. It appeared so innocuous. But he couldn't bring himself to call it by its name. To escape from Anton and his project, he'd climb on Dora and ride her bareback in the cool evenings if he saw empty fields. But he had avoided forest trails since his grandmother frightened him with tales of *rysalky*, the evil water nymphs who tickled men to death in underwater crystal lairs.

Yet, his companion seemed untroubled each night when he removed the plate that protected the switches and numbers. While studying the displays and tinkering with implements from his large collection of tools,

Anton would lean against a tree and lay out the mysterious wires and bits of metal he had found in the monastery basement. After removing the back of the remote control from the monastery's broken TV set, he worked on taking it apart or putting it back together – Boris wasn't sure – rewiring it, removing parts, twisting and screwing in new ones, while muttering mysterious things like: "If I could open the physics package" and the occasional: "Aha!"

His chores done, Boris leaned against a gnarled oak by the fading embers of the fire, listening to the night choir of frogs and crickets. Darkness had fallen and the kerosene lamp illuminated Anton's disembodied face floating above his black robe. *These are my last days*, he thought and gazed at the heavens, though the forest canopy concealed the stars. He wanted to pray for the innocents who had to die. But he thought only of a warm bed, a good meal, and the woman's touch he would never know.

*S*veta touched Tariq in a place he didn't know he had and crooned. "Oh, my *mal'chik*, my little one. You like that. Now let me …"

The phone interrupted Sveta's exotic techniques. Groaning in frustration, Tariq wanted to ignore it. But he disentangled himself from the harness to pick up the receiver.

"*Salaam*," said Ahmed. "It has been a while. The Sultan wants news."

Tariq's bowels turned to liquid at the mention of the Sultan and sweat suddenly poured from his palms. The German told him about his unsuccessful meeting with the HEU source but now promised a rocket engineer willing to emigrate for the right price. A success like that would win him more time to be anywhere but Iraq. But it was taking too long and Tariq hid from his fear in sex games and whiskey.

"But we still have time," Tariq protested, his voice shaking. "Is he here?"

Ahmed sounded troubled. "He might be. But he sent a message saying *HE* wants to know more about the fertilizer."

The Great and Magnificent One's personal interest terrified Tariq as much as the Sultan's possible presence in Kiev. The Petrochemical-3 case officer could snatch him back to Iraq where he'd have to explain his failure to Him, right before getting shot, or hanged, or tortured to death. Tariq poured Johnny Walker Black into a glass with a shaky hand and gulped it, feeling it spread a warm wave throughout his body.

"Did you hear me?" exclaimed Ahmed.

"I did. Tell him I'll have a report in a few days."

Tariq hung up the phone and turned to Sveta, who had slipped into a tight silk dress and bent to zip up her black, thigh high boots. "Yes, darling, you have to go," she said. "You always have to go when the phone rings. So, I'm going home."

Unlike many other prostitutes, Sveta had no roommates and kept her two room apartment to herself, choosing to live in the inexpensive Left Bank bedroom district.

Sveta stood and reached out her hand as always when leaving. He slipped on his purple silk trousers and pulled three 100 dollar notes out of the pocket. Tariq didn't think she slept with any other clients anymore. She made plenty of money from him. Sometimes, he invited Irina – the blond whore – to join them, but more and more he wanted Sveta, alone. Irina started spending a lot of time with the American, Joe Marchetti.

"What's wrong with you," she asked, peering into his face. "You look worried."

"It's just the difficulties of doing business here," he said, leading her to the door.

"Wait until my business school opens," she said brightly. "Qualified people will make it easier."

Ten minutes later, Tariq was at the Night Bar, where he found the German sitting alone at a table with the Dog at his feet. Many people had to stand in the crowded bar, but the two made it clear they did not want uninvited company.

Tariq pulled out a chair next to him. The Dog lifted its head with a soft whine, awaiting orders, but lowered it again when none came.

"We must try again with the HEU," Tariq said, keeping his voice low out of habit though the din made it unnecessary.

"I have been thinking about that, as well. I suspect that the source has agreed to sell it to the Americans. If we eliminate them, he may become more cooperative, *Ja*?"

Eliminate them? Claus spoke as if it was the most normal thing in the world. But Tariq wasn't an assassin. He had a degree in Russian literature. But instead of saying so, he asked: "How?"

"We need to think about that," Claus said and rose from the table with the Dog following his every move. "But we must act."

Tariq shook his head. "Not yet."

Claus's good eye narrowed at Tariq. "There is no time for delay. We must act. This opportunity is too potentially lucrative for us both."

The German left without waiting for a response and Tariq motioned to the waiter to bring him the usual, pondering his dilemma while he waited for his drink. The Dictator or the Sultan wouldn't hesitate to kill him for failure. And Claus could have the Americans killed, for the right price. Contract killings were common in the capitol. Even foreigners, like that American who jumped from his balcony to his death under mysterious circumstances, were not immune. They were often the targets of mugging and robbery.

But Tariq couldn't kill, not even by proxy.

"Hey, Ali, how are you doing'" said a familiar voice. At first Tariq didn't respond, but then he saw Joe Marchetti and remembered that the tampon inspector knew him by his alias. Marchetti motioned at the glass of whiskey and said: "Let me buy you that one."

Tariq nodded and a happy realization dawned when Marchetti sat next to him. Just the other night, Irina told Sveta that Marchetti bragged to her about working for the CIA.

The Iraqi sipped his whiskey and considered his companion. There was more than one way to eliminate the competition.

CHAPTER 12:

FINDING OUT

FAXNEWS-UKRAINE

April 5, 1993 (Vancouver, Canada). During the summit with the Russian President, the new American President reportedly told his counterpart to increase the pressure on Ukraine to denuclearize.

April 5, 1993 (Moscow, Russia). Today, the government stated: "The nuclear weapons in Ukraine must come under Russian jurisdiction. The warheads must be removed and transported to Russia for destruction." Ukraine's Chief Nuclear Negotiator responded: "Removing the warheads without the parallel destruction of the missiles is dangerous. The missiles are explosive and toxic objects that will become less safe because no one will care about them if they are not armed with warheads."

April 7, 1993 (Moscow, Russia). Russian media report dangerous overloading of warhead storage depots in Ukraine. Ukraine's Chief Nuclear Negotiator asserted in response that Russian facilities are also exceeding their capacity with nuclear weapons from other ex-Soviet republics.

April 17, 1993 (Kiev, Ukraine). Russia's refusal to supply Ukraine with replacement filters for the warheads means that explosive hydrogen gas is building up inside them. The process is even more explosive on top of SS-24 ICBMs carrying 84 tons of rocket fuel. But Ukraine's chief missile designer ordered the unmaintained warheads placed back on the missiles because "it is less dangerous than keeping them stored in the depots".

<u>April 17, 1993 (Simferopol, Ukraine).</u> A Russian MP said that Moscow is ready to supervise a referendum on Crimean independence and include the republic as a separate entity in the Commonwealth of Independent States.

END

Faxnews-Ukraine –Your source of English-language news about Ukraine

---

TOP SECRET – PURPLE
Handle via Agent Channels Only
Date: **April 18, 1993**
To: **K3**
From: **Deputy Chief of Station Kiev**
Subject: SITREP Rasputin
(TS) 1. Iraqi, alias Mohammed Ali, reports that Neilson and Kruger are seeking to smuggle highly enriched uranium. He believes that 100 kilos are available and has not heard about 1,000. He is trying to learn the identity of their HEU source.
S)   2. Neilson and Kruger claim that they want to export raw materials. They also keep avoiding my company.
END
TOP SECRET – PURPLE
Exempt from automatic downgrade

TOP SECRET – WHITE
Handle via Agent Channels Only
Date: April 22, 1993
To: K3
From: Chief of Station Kiev
Subject: SITREP Fertilize
(TS)   1. Instead of flying to the Pervomaysk missile fields, Neilson, Kruger and translator Kostya Beniuk boarded a flight for Donetsk. It may have been a diversion. No time to prepare a disguise. Mission aborted.
(S)   2. Yesterday, the paramilitary UNSO organization held a pro-nuclear and anti-American demonstration in Kiev against the START treaty. They reportedly work for Ukrainian intelligence services.
END
TOP SECRET – WHITE
Exempt from automatic downgrade

The Independent Ukrainian Orthodox Patriarch had a white beard that flowed to the middle of his chest in stark contrast with his black cassock. Cottony locks peered from under an elaborate head dress, embroidered with crosses and inlaid with brocade and silk. While his American guests waited, he clasped his delicate fingers and raised them in joy at the news delivered by two burly fellows with shaved heads and camouflage clothes.

"They tell him UNSO has captured another church for Ukrainian Orthodoxy" whispered Kostya, who watched with anger. "They say most parishioners are old women who listen to their priest. UNSO have files on priests who collaborated with KGB and those priests willing to join Ukrainian Church."

"The Patriarch, he also collaborated with KGB," said Kostya. "All of Orthodox Church worked with KGB. Russian Patriarch, too."

"Wait a minute," said Kruger. "I thought you supported an independent Ukrainian church."

"Not with hypocrite KGB priests."

Dan Kruger marveled at the translator's brooding intensity. He had no evident sense of humor. When they all emerged from their train compartments upon arriving in Kiev, Kostya came out with embarrassed red cheeks and a downcast eyes, avoiding his employers'. Zoya, in contrast, acted matter-of-fact, as though she and Kostya had always spent their nights together instead of spitting like cats. Encased in her sleek business armor, she had again become cheerful, confident and sharp in planning their next moves.

While she negotiated the paperwork that the Coal Ministry demanded for a license to export coal at less than the state price, Neilson and Kruger waited for the Patriarch to take a break from listening to parish poaching reports. They set up the meeting easily. The break-away church's leader was eager for anyone to recognize him. But getting his attention proved more difficult. They had been waiting for almost an hour when the commandos bent their knees for a blessing and left.

"Patriarch said they are on mission from God," Kostya whispered, adding: "He is not about God. He is about property, money."

"So are we," Kruger whispered.

"But you do not pretend to be men of God."

"Well, you better pretend that he is one anyway," said Kruger, feeling a twinge of guilt about tempting a man of God with filthy lucre. Then he remembered that the Patriarch could help them avoid paying a 10,000 dollar bribe for an export license and his guilt dissolved in the desperate hope of finding the prelate on the same page. But when the Patriarch joined them, his eagerness suggested he wanted to be on any page, so long as that page included his church.

Sipping the tea that a wizened nun served with a china plate of sliced Snickers, the Patriarch listened to the combination of truth, toadying and white lies that the Neptune team had concocted for the presentation.

"Your Holiness, we understand the dire financial situation that the Church is enduring during this period of ecclesiastical uncertainty," said Neilson after the introductions.

The prelate spoke for a long time and then nibbled a Snickers while Kostya translated. "It is so difficult. We have heavy responsibility to our faithful, and it pains our hearts that we cannot properly minister them by gaining full autocephaly in spiritual communion with other Orthodox Churches. Russian church has help from their brethren in Moscow, and profits from contraband cigarettes. And we have nothing, except patriotism and faith of our people."

"Contraband cigarettes?" asked a surprised Neilson.

The Patriarch sighed. "Churches exempt from import duties. Russian Orthodox Church uses that exemption to import contraband cigarettes from Turkey and Bulgaria. They make very good profits."

"Is that true, Kostya?" Kruger whispered.

The translator nodded. "Everyone knows this."

A major church is involved in smuggling and no one stops it, Kruger thought. *And we're trying to do business here?* But then this was precisely the right place to be doing business. If priests could make money, why couldn't they – with a little help from the priest sitting across from them.

That priest continued, his eyes wistful. "Russians fly back and forth to the Ecumenical Patriarch of Constantinople, to pressure him not to accept spiritual communion with Ukrainian Orthodoxy. And we do not even have enough money for a plane ticket and hotel for me to present our case to him."

Their research prepared them to hear that and Neilson continued, hoping that he had the unfamiliar religious phraseology correct. "Your Holiness, we want to help you achieve full autocephaly in spiritual communion with your Orthodox brethren by making a financial contribution."

The Patriarch brightened until Neilson explained that they would donate the church's share of future profits from exporting coal.

"We propose forming a joint venture between our company, Neptune, and the Independent Ukrainian Orthodox Church, in which the church will earn two percent of the profits. Our first contract is for 500,000 tons of coal and we'll earn two million dollars. We expect more in the future." Upon returning to Kiev, they received a fax from Coco the Greek. The Turks wanted as much coal as they could offer and would pay for Coco to ship it.

The prelate's expression changed. "You want an export duty exemption? Is this the source of your proposed generosity?"

Neilson hesitated, debating whether to tell the truth. Finally, he said: "We do, your Holiness."

The Patriarch walked to his desk for a calculator, punched in numbers and then returned to the table, grasping the cross that hung from his waist.

"Four percent."

Neilson glanced at Kruger. They had discussed going as high as five.

"We can agree to four percent of the profits."

The Patriarch brushed a bit of lint off the cross that hung at his waist. "That is acceptable. But our Church may form joint ventures only if there is another Orthodox church in the venture. To register such an enterprise, I must have letter from an Orthodox parish in America, agreeing to this."

*I*ndependence Square crowded with people enjoying the spring evening when Neilson and Kruger left the Patriarch's residence. Teenagers flirted and bantered around the fountains, couples walked hand in hand, and stout women hawked sunflower seeds and pies. Passing a man selling wooden candlesticks and napkins embroidered with geometric flowers, Kruger noticed that he was seeing plenty of teenagers, but almost no infants, toddlers or small children. "Why aren't there more kids, Kostya?" he asked, imagining his own daughter revealed in the sonogram.

"It is because of Chernobyl. Many women afraid to have children because of radiation."

"But radiation levels in Kiev are normal, now" said Neilson. He had checked when planning their first trip. But levels were slightly higher on Independence Square because of the natural uranium in the plaza's granite stones.

"But now people have no money. Economic situation is very, very difficult."

"It sure is," said Neilson. "We need to go back to the US soon and find an Orthodox church that wants to do business with us."

After they sent Kostya off to find Zoya, Neilson followed Kruger around a small crowd gathered around a white-shirted missionary exhort them with an American twang. "So, where do we find an Orthodox Church?" he asked.

"My mother-in-law," said Kruger. "She belongs to a Ukrainian Orthodox Church near Bethesda. That's a good place to start…"

Before Kruger finished, he saw Cristina Smythe and her friend Bob Baine emerge from the crowd. The British journalist perused topographical maps stacked on a table next to Ukrainian flag pins and paperbacks with Cyrillic titles.

"Brilliant!" Bob exclaimed, unfolding one map. "The detail is excellent. Topographical maps cost 40 pounds in London and here they're just pennies."

Cristina stood with her arms crossed before she noticed Neil and her face lit up. Her tight white t-shirt showed off an inch of cleavage over slim jeans tucked into black suede cowboy boots.

"Hey guys!" she exclaimed. "We've been calling your rooms for days."

Bob poked his face out from behind the map and extended his hand to greet them. "What a brilliant day," he said. "Cristina brought me here to see these declassified maps."

"The Soviets kept them secret," Cristina added. "But now you can buy them anywhere."

"What luck running into the two of you," said Bob. "My editors have been on my ass because our competition scooped us on a nuclear weapons story. People in Washington think Ukraine may get launch control of the ICBMs. But no one here will talk to me."

Neilson pointed to at the detailed map. "Planning any reconnaissance missions with those?"

"Not exactly," said Bob. He was a wearing a different pile of laundry, all of it wrinkled. "But there are ICBM missile fields down south and I wanted to drive there for some local color. The regular road maps don't tell you much."

"I doubt going there will tell you much either," said Kruger.

"Why is that?"

"They don't keep ICBMs in open view. I doubt if you'll even know if you're close to one."

Cristina tucked her hands into her jeans' pockets and bumped Bob with her shoulder. "C'mon, buy the map and let's go to your place. Why don't you invite these guys for tea or whatever you Brits drink at this hour? I suspect they'll disappear again if you don't nail them down now."

Bob handed a note of Ukrainian ersatz currency to the vendor, slipped the map into a canvas backpack and turned to Neilson and Kruger as they set off towards their hotel. "Tea, beer, whiskey, vodka, water," he said, walking alongside them and waved his hands eagerly. "The Moscow bureau just sent me a supply of tins. I have minced meat, tuna fish, canned peas."

Flanking them from the other side, Cristina gave Neilson a sidelong glance. "Don't worry. I won't let him feed you canned minced meat." She stood close enough to Neilson that even Kruger smelled her perfume.

Kruger did not want to be interviewed. A German journalist reporting on the Pershing missiles once quoted him in a way that suggested the very opposite of what he had said. "Thank you very much for that generous offer, but I'm going back to my room to call my wife. She's going through a difficult pregnancy."

Pregnant women trump everything, he thought as he continued walking towards the hotel. And he did worry. Jean cut back her caseload but still had to pay the bills. She complained of cramps and had asked her mother to stay with her while he travelled to Kiev. Though she encouraged his business venture in her ancestral homeland, he felt too guilty to even socialize when he wasn't working.

Cristina stopped, forcing the rest of the group to do so, too, and brushed invisible lint off Neilson's shoulder. "But Neil can go with us. You two aren't joined at the hip." It was a statement, not a question.

*N*eilson parted ways with his partner and followed the journalists in the opposite direction on the Khreshchatyk Boulevard, its usual gloom enlivened by the setting sun. He had taken to carrying a small flashlight for the dark city streets at night.

Cristina brushed against him as they walked, but said little until they reached a beautiful but faded stucco building on a side street. Bob led them through a driveway arch into a courtyard, then around another building and down a short hill into another courtyard.

"I had no idea there were all these buildings behind buildings here," said Neilson, stumbling over rubble.

Cristina gazed at him quizzically. "Neil, what is it you do here for months at a time? You must not see much of Kiev. The city blocks are huge. There are entire towns inside them that you can't see from the street."

"Mostly we wait for meetings that get postponed." Neilson followed her and Bob into a low slung brick building with sagging balconies. The door lock was broken and the vestibule stank of rotting trash and urine. I'm not missing much, he thought, stepping through the darkness while fishing around his pocket for the flashlight.

"God, Bob, this is disgusting," said Cristina. "What happened?"

Bob fumbled for his keys to open another door that led into a dimly lit corridor. "Homeless people broke the lock and live there at night. I called my landlord to fix it but he's in Bulgaria, buying a truckload of black market cigarettes." He led them into the hall and up two flights of stairs to a black vinyl door that he opened with a skeleton key.

Though more brightly lit, the apartment wasn't much better than the vestibule. Clothing hung on furniture and covered the floors. Papers and notebooks littered the desk around a laptop computer spotted with dried stains. Opened cans of food, dishes and spilled cereal cluttered the kitchen counter.

"Yeah, Bob the Slob," said Cristina, following Neilson's gaze while their host tossed clothing off the kitchen table and used a slice of bread to sweep crumbs and debris into his hand. "He grows penicillin in that kitchen. But he's smart and a good reporter."

"Oh?" Neilson said doubtfully. Cristina leaned against him, her breast brushing against his arm. "Really," she murmured. "And when it's over, you can walk me home."

Bob pulled back the kitchen chairs and swept out his arm in invitation. "Sit, sit," he said. "I can offer you tea, whiskey, beer?"

"Tea is fine," said Neilson, taking a seat and laying his briefcase by his feet. It contained their coal contract and research he had done on shipping before the Turks offered to pay for it.

A large oil painting of a grizzled old man sitting next to a young woman dominated the kitchen. Evening shadows bathed the couple with a warm copper palette, so it took Neilson a moment to see that the man had his hand inside the woman's blouse.

The checkered tablecloth had streaks left from whatever Bob had wiped off, as well as crumbs that he had missed. A table lamp perched precariously on a loose stack of newspapers and magazines. Cristina pulled her chair close enough for him to feel the heat from her thigh. She slid a Marlboro from an open pack on the table and lit it with a box match, sending a stream of smoke towards the kitchen sink where Bob filled a cast iron kettle with water.

"I thought you didn't smoke," said Neilson.

She took a drag and then flicked the ash into a stained metal screw cap full of butts. "I didn't. But everyone smokes here," she responded, giving Neilson another sidelong glance. "Does it bother you?"

"Not a bit," said Neilson.

Bob set the kettle on a gas flame and reached into the mess on the counter for a stenographers notebook stained with ketchup or blood. Pulling a fountain pen out of the wire spiral, he flipped pages to an empty sheet. "So," he said. "Nuclear weapons: The Ukrainians want control. Can they do that?"

Neilson leveled a skeptical gaze on his interviewer. "That's a very complicated question. Can you be more specific?"

Bob rolled the pen between his fingers. "Well, the way I understand it, Ukraine can rig things to take control of the weapons from Moscow."

"Control of what?" asked Neilson, contemplating the enticing promise of walking Cristina home.

"Control of the weapons."

"Which weapons?"

"The nuclear weapons. I thought that that's what we're talking about."

Cristina leafed through a magazine but turned to Neilson and whispered: "Be nice."

"Which kind?" Neilson asked. "ICBMs, cruise missiles, gravity bombs? They have different authorizing systems and different enabling systems, so the answer depends on the type of weapon."

"What's the difference between authorizing and enabling?" asked Bob, holding the unlit cigarette in his right hand and scribbling furiously with his left, the fountain pen's nub scratching on the paper.

Neilson rested his elbows on the table. "No offense, Bob, but you need to do your homework for an interview. I should be giving you a quote, not teaching you the ABCs."

Bob stopped writing. "I apologize. But I can't just walk into a library in Kiev and do research. I asked the paper's researchers look into it in the States. But they only found background, nothing specific. No one dreamed that a former Soviet republic could take control of nuclear weapons."

"It's true, Neil," added Cristina. "He has tried, and chewed my ear off while he's at it." Then she looked at Bob. "Even though this stuff *bores* me," she said.

Bob clasped his hands and bowed his head in gratitude. "Cristina, sweetie, you're a gem."

She returned her attention to the magazine. "You owe me."

Neilson tried to assess their relationship. They bickered like an unhappy couple but he detected nothing physical between them while Cristina's thigh hovered invitingly close to his. "I'm going to simplify things," he said, relenting. "And this is off the record. But the authorizing system is what says you *may* launch a weapon. It's usually in the form of a numerical code from the commander in chief to fire away."

"That's what's in that briefcase they call 'the football' that always follows the American President?" asked Bob, rising to take the kettle off the fire.

"That's right," said Neilson. "It contains the authorization codes. Now, the enabling systems are different. If the authorization code controls whether you *may* launch a weapon, the enabling system is what controls whether you *can*. In the U.S., enabling systems can be simple mechanical locks or very complex digital electronics."

After bringing Neilson a steaming mug, Bob took up his notebook. "So, are the Ukrainians trying to rig the authorization systems or the enabling systems?"

"What makes you think they're trying to do either?"

The journalist leaped from his chair and shuffled through the papers on the desk, pulling out a crumpled fax of a newspaper article entitled: "Ukraine Seeks Control of Nukes". He handed it to Neilson, who skimmed it. "This is nothing more than sensationalist conjecture and surmise," he said, holding up the article. "All that it says is that Kiev is studying ways to get launch control of the weapons, not that they're actually doing it."

"But my editors want me to see if there's anything to it." Bob picked up his pen. "So, *is* there anything to it?"

Neilson shrugged. "It would be expensive. It seems to me that they don't want to control the weapons. They want to control their destruction. But if they wanted to, I'm sure that they have the technical capacity to take control of at least some of the weapons."

"You do?" asked Bob.

"Well, they don't have access to the physics package."

"The physics package?"

"It's the nuclear part of the bomb," Neilson explained. "I'm pretty sure that only the Russian factories that built the warheads can get inside the physics package. Those designs are the most top secret around. The Russians won't let anyone discover their design secrets if they can help it."

"Do the Ukrainians need do anything inside the physics package?"

"Eventually. It needs regular maintenance for the bomb to work properly, or to work at all for that matter."

"But you're saying that they have access to the other parts. The codes, right?"

"Bob, the West's mistake is overestimating Ukraine's desire to take control and underestimating its technical ability to do so."

Bob scribbled in his notebook. "Excellent! Can I quote you on that?" he asked. When Neilson agreed, Bob continued: "But let's say, hypothetically that Ukraine wanted to take control. Can they? How?"

Neilson glanced at Cristina, who read an old Time magazine featuring the Iraqi Dictator on the cover. Her leg still hovered close to his. "I don't know *how* to do it. I'm not a missile engineer. What I do know is that the weapons' security systems are designed to prevent unauthorized use by thieves, terrorists and hostile forces. They can buy time. But people with the right expertise could take control of them.

"Besides," he continued, "the weapons don't have the same authorization and security systems. ICBMs have the most robust, where you have separate authorization and enabling for the launcher and the warhead. At least, that's the way it is in the U.S."

Bob wrote for a few minutes. "And here?"

Neilson traced the top of his mug with his finger. "Rumor has it that the newer ICBMs can let Moscow bypass the local missile crews and launch the missiles directly. But that's just ICBMs. There are also cruise missiles here, too, and they can have different systems."

"They used to have tactical weapons, too, right?" asked Bob.

"Used to, but Moscow says that it withdrew them to Russia."

"Do you have any doubt?"

Neilson leaned back in his chair, inadvertently brushing his thigh against Cristina's. *She doesn't mind.* "I'm sure that they think they've accounted for them," he said to Bob, debating whether to tell him how using the antiquated Soviet inventory made it easy to divert a small, tactical bomb.

Cristina decided for him by standing up and wiping her hands. "Enough, Bob. I still have to call my editor in Brussels and it's late." She tilted her head towards Neilson. "And this fine gentleman is walking me home."

"Wait a minute," cried Bob, tapping his notebook. "I still have a lot of questions. There's no way I can write a story with just this."

When Neilson also stood up, Bob leaped out of his chair, jolting the table and knocking over Neilson's mug of tea. Ignoring the puddle dripping onto the floor, he grabbed his notebook. "Can we talk again? Please. Where can I reach you tomorrow?"

"I can't," said Neilson as Cristina took his briefcase and propelled him towards the door. "Dave and I are leaving for the US," he said, glad for the excuse. He wouldn't have even spoken to Bob if Cristina hadn't asked.

She said little during their short walk on a back street that Neilson didn't recognize and kept jerking her head, peering into dark corners.

"What's the matter?" asked Neilson.

Cristina slipped her hands into her back pockets and leaned in towards him, without touching. She smelled of soap, shampoo and smoke. "Nothing. Sorry. Force of habit. Being a foreigner and a woman, I tend to stick out." She glanced at him. "Lots can happen in the dark."

"I'm here," said Neilson as they stopped at an empty intersection. Cristina smiled. "That's one of the things I had in mind."

Before he could consider where such a flattering statement might lead, he felt a jab in his back and turned to see a thug with a shaved head pointing a gun.

"Dollars!" he demanded in accented English. "Or I kill."

Neilson raised his hands in the air. "Cristina, don't move…"

"Not this time, buddy," she shouted as she whirled instantly, kicked the gun out of the thug's hands and delivered a blow to the chest that sent him flying into the shadows.

Cristina landed on her feet to see Neilson's jaw drop and she lowered her head, as if embarrassed. "Please pretend that you didn't see that."

"How can I pretend? That was amazing! How did you learn to do that?"

"In college," she said. "I told you when we met. I had a radical feminist phase and studied martial arts to have no fear of men."

"I guess you're not afraid of men now."

179

Cristina tucked her arm in his elbow. "But I enjoy them a lot more," she said, leading him to a stucco building near the Conservatory and through a dark tunnel into an empty courtyard where they stopped. Cristina turned to him, her face unreadable in the dim light spilling from an apartment window.

"Come up for a nightcap?" she asked, tracing her finger down the front of his shirt. "After all, I saved your wallet."

Neilson moved in closer. It had been more than a year. "Is this a seduction?"

Cristina took his hand and placed it on her breast. Her nipple was hard under her light cotton t-shirt. "It is if you want it to be."

Sveta's breasts heaved in magnificent fury when she burst into Tariq's hotel room and stormed in without shutting the door. Tossing back her gleaming black hair and muttering angrily, she reached into a tattered plastic bag and pulled out a packed handful of crumpled 100 dollar bills and threw it at Tariq, who sprawled on the bed naked, awaiting a new sex game he had devised.

"You mother fucking, lying scum," she spat. Tears trickled on her cheeks as she threw more and more bills at him, covering the bed like a blanket of leaves. Tariq scrambled off the bed while Sveta threw more bills. "You dirty rotten prick. How could you do this? You paid me with fucking COUNTERFEITS? Goddamn you, you MOTHERFUCKER!" she shouted.

Tariq darted to close the door, desperation shaking in his voice as he pleaded: "Shh, Sveta, please. Please. People will hear you."

He had worried about Sveta discovering the counterfeits. He should have used different prostitutes to elude discovery instead of just one, who had only him as a client. But his abject terror of the Sultan and The Dictator had grown so massive, it eclipsed everything else.

Sveta spun on her spike heels and glared through her tears. "Oh, you bet people will hear, you fucking asshole. No whore in this hotel – no, no whore in this entire city will service you again – not even a lap dance."

No more whores? Sweat poured from his temples as he pulled on his underwear and came upon an unexpected and chilling thought. *No more Sveta?*

She stabbed her finger at him and then at the crumpled counterfeits. "I saved that for my SCHOOL, you filthy, rotten bastard," she growled. "I had 10,000 bucks to rent space and buy books and advertising and pay teachers AND finally stop having to service assholes like you and those fucking Pakistanis, and Iranians and North Koreans crawling around this fucking hotel for those oh-so-fucking-secret meetings."

Secret meetings. How much did Sveta know? Tariq slipped on his purple silk trousers, his hands shaking so hard he could barely work the zipper. If word of the counterfeits spread, no one would do business with him. He'd get arrested. Even if he didn't, the hotel would kick him out and he wouldn't have money for food. Claus might kill him. If he didn't, the Sultan would.

Tariq collapsed into the room's only chair, leaned on his knees and rested his head in his hands. He tried to think of a lie.

"That's all you're going to do, you big shit? You don't even have the balls to apologize?!" Sveta shouted and whirled to leave the room, scattering the crumpled counterfeits."

Tariq leaped from the chair. "Stop, Sveta," he begged, grabbing her arm. "I'm sorry. It's complicated but I'm very, very sorry. Please. You can't do this to me. Don't do this to me. You can't tell anyone."

"Take your filthy hands off of me!" she cried, her face hard with contempt. "I'll tell everyone, you shit! After what you did to me. You turned my life's savings into garbage!"

Tariq's panicked mind raced. *I have to kill her,* he thought and immediately recoiled. *No, I can't kill her. I can't kill anyone. I couldn't even cheat on the university exams.* Then, unbidden, another thought: *I can't kill Sveta. What will I do without her?*

Images flashed like a movie theater in his head. HEU. Red Mercury. The Americans. North Koreans. Pakistanis. Who else did he always see at the Night Bar with the other whores? "I need to think," he whispered. *I'm going to die. They're going to kill me.*

Sveta tried to push him aside. "You needed to do that before you started paying me with this green fucking toilet paper."

Tariq pleaded. "Stop, Sveta. Listen to me. I'll bring you your money: Real money. I promise. Give me a week. But don't tell anyone about the counterfeits."

Her voice softened. "Why the hell should I believe you?"

"If you don't, there's no chance that you'll see that money. I will be dead and your life will be in danger, too.'

"What?" she said sharply. "This is MY territory. I have protection here."

Protection; I need protection. And real money. Who could offer him that? Finding HEU for The Dictator might save his life, but it wouldn't give him the genuine US dollars he needed to pay Sveta. The German still hadn't produced and the Sultan's deadline loomed. But if he didn't pay her soon, it would be moot. He had to find real money, and a lot of it, fast.

"Your protection is no good against these people," he said. "They are very bad; with blood on their hands." The Sultan could take many baths in the blood he had spilled. "Your connection to me puts you in danger."

A demanding tone replaced the contempt in her voice. "Why?" she asked. "You trade in modems, windmills and fertilizers. Why should that put me in danger?"

Sveta surprised Tariq with her memory. He talked of his supposed doings in front of her only when forced to by Ahmed's few calls and visits. But she always read books and took notes when not having sex with him. He had no idea what she wrote in those notebooks. *Maybe Claus is right and she's working for the KGB.* But the KGB didn't exist anymore. The Ukrainian government inherited the personnel and property of the republic's branch of the KGB and renamed it the SBU. But it had been geared at fighting dissidents, not counterintelligence. Tariq once overheard journalists at the Night Bar interviewing Ukrainian-Americans who held a pierogi sale fundraiser on Long Island to buy the SBU its first two computers.

It seemed impossible that Sveta spied for them. She was who she said she was: an unemployed mechanical engineer who turned to prostitution to make enough money to open a business school. Suddenly, a wave of warmth coursed through him as he contemplated the beautiful, smart, ambitious, sexy woman before him, followed by a frisson of fear over losing her.

"Why?" she repeated. "Tell me why, Ali, or I'm leaving."

His eyes fixed on the floor, he whispered: "My real name isn't Ali. It's Tariq. Tariq abu Bakr."

When she didn't respond, he saw the steel still in her eyes. But she was listening.

Gingerly, he touched her arm. "Come and sit," he said, leading her to the bed and sitting on the chair himself. His hands trembled as he poured Johnny Walker Black into a glass and offered it to her. She took it but didn't drink while he poured a splash for himself. He tapped her glass with his. "To the truth," he said, and then proceeded to tell her precisely that. All of it.

Golden domes crowned St. Vladimir's Ukrainian Orthodox Church and faded strip malls and gas stations flanked its ornate stucco walls in the middle of a busy street outside Bethesda. After parallel parking the Toyota into a tight spot between two pickup trucks, Dan Kruger squeezed around the back of the car to open the passenger door for his mother-in-law, who waved away his outstretched hand to help her out of the car.

Slava Beniuk was a tiny woman who looked frail, but wasn't. She had stayed on to help Jean after Kruger returned from Kiev and spent his entire first day back muttering a monologue about Jean's difficult pregnancy, her workload, and her unemployed loser of a husband forcing her to support him and risking the life of her only grandchild.

Kruger felt too guilty to defend himself, but Jean told her mother to either leave or keep her opinions to herself. So, Slava bit her tongue, dutifully set up an appointment for Kruger with her Orthodox pastor and then insisted on attending the meeting, using the drive as an opportunity to harangue him out of Jean's earshot.

"If anything happens to that baby, Lord forbid, it will be your fault," she concluded with her heavy accent and crossed herself as they pulled in front of the church. After smoothing her skirt and patting her hair, Slava led him to the pastor's residence, a simple brick building in the back, where Ivan Pastukh greeted them.

The pastor looked happy to see Slava and they conversed in Ukrainian for quite a while, paying Kruger no attention until a lull in their conversation when Pastukh finally turned to him.

"Ivan Pastukh," he said, holding out his hand. "Mrs. Beniuk tells me you want to discuss a project of yours in Ukraine."

Kruger introduced himself, doubting that his mother-in-law had presented the situation with such neutrality. She must have pleaded with Pastukh to help save her daughter from a miserable life of penury.

Whatever works, he thought with no small degree of urgency. Jean put on a brave front, but the strain reflected in her pale face. She spent most of her days in bed, surrounded by laptops, phones and stacks of files, papers and casebooks that her secretary brought from the office. The dogs joined her, whining gentle alarms over the unusual circumstances.

Holding his arm out in welcome, the pastor led them into a sunny sitting room right off the entrance and took a leather armchair, motioning his guests towards the couches. Seeing children's toys scattered around the room, Kruger recalled that Orthodox parish priests could marry and have families.

"Now, tell me," said Pastukh, leaning back in his chair, a large cross hanging on a gold chain around his neck. "How can I help you?"

Kruger explained the situation. "In short," he concluded, "we're trying to find an Orthodox church in the U.S. to partner with the Independent Ukrainian Orthodox Church and our company, Neptune, in a joint venture to export Ukrainian coal to Turkey. Neptune will do the work, and your church, and the Ukrainian church, will each earn four percent of the profits. On this first shipment, that will be 80,000 dollars."

Pastukh tilted his head. "You mean the church led by that self-styled Patriarch?"

Kruger's heart sank. "Self-styled?"

Distaste flashed across the pastor's face. "The history is very complicated. But during Soviet times, the man was the Kiev Metropolitan in the Russian Orthodox Church, which was an arm of the KGB and worked to suppress independent Ukrainian Orthodoxy. He was notorious. Then, when Ukraine declared independence, he broke away from the Russian church and fixed himself an election as Patriarch. He has the Ukrainian President's full support.

"Please don't misunderstand me," Pastukh continued. "We welcome the resurrection of independent Ukrainian Orthodoxy. But not with such an odious figure at its head."

Kruger's stomach knotted in frustration. "Does this mean that the Ukrainian Orthodox Church in America doesn't recognize the Independent Ukrainian Orthodox Church in Ukraine?"

"Right now, no one recognizes it. It's not canonical. If the Ecumenical Patriarch of Constantinople does it, the other churches will follow, including ours. The Russian Orthodox Church won't recognize it, though. More than half of the ROC's parishes are in Ukraine. For the ROC, Ukraine plays a similar role to what it played in the Soviet Union. It makes the Moscow Patriarch the head of a religious superpower – the largest Orthodox church in the world."

It was an interesting and thoroughly depressing analogy. "The Ukrainian Patriarch told us he hoped for a meeting with the Ecumenical Patriarch but his church couldn't afford to even send him for a meeting," said Kruger. "That's why he agreed to this deal."

"With that man, I'm sure that isn't the reason he wants money. He got quite used to the good life in Soviet times," said Pastukh. "So, I'm sorry," he said, rising to his feet. "Though your proposal is very interesting, our church cannot take part in such a joint venture."

Kruger also rose, avoiding his mother-in-law's stern scowl. "Pastor Pastukh, I appreciate your condemnation of the Patriarch's past. But do I understand you correctly that no Orthodox Church in the U.S. will join such a joint venture if the Independent Ukrainian Orthodox Church in Ukraine is not recognized?"

Pastukh led them to the door. "You might find rogue parishes, that aren't canonical themselves. But I'm certain that no mainstream church will do it – at least not at this time."

*W*illiam Kensington III leaned against the edge of his desk and crossed his arms, tapping his fingers on his crisp blue shirt.

"How much?" he demanded.

"One hundred kilos, sir," said Neil Neilson, who had just finished telling him about Roman Rozpad. "At least that's what we know."

"And the man's name again? Rasputin?"

"Roz-pad," Neilson repeated. "R-O-Z-P-A-D."

"Make a note, Petrie," K3 ordered his aide, who wrote on a legal pad.

K3 exchanged glances with his aide. "This Rozpad character has been peddling 100 kilos of HEU for months and you're reporting it now?"

Neilson shifted in his chair. "We're not sure that he's still peddling it. But we told General Hawkins at the Pentagon. Unfortunately…" Neilson tried to formulate a diplomatic way of putting it. "He had different priorities. But this is a very dangerous situation and we wanted to inform the relevant agencies."

"What makes you think we're not informed?" K3 picked up a thick pile of computer printouts bristling with handwritten notes.

"Are you familiar with the Iraqi, Tariq abu Bakr? He frequents the Dnipro Hotel night bar, usually in the company of a Ukrainian prostitute, Sveta Shevchuk. Or an East German, Claus Hesse, with a Great Dane?"

So, the CIA *had* been doing something. "We have seen the Iraqi and the German."

K3 flipped through the pages of print out to a sheet marked with a yellow sticky note. "Well, Mr. Neilson, our sources in Kiev say that there are two Americans with access to 1,000 kilos of HEU."

He flipped the page closed and laid the printouts back on his desk. "Isn't it odd that two Americans in Kiev have access to 100 kilos of HEU, and another two Americans in Kiev to have access to 1,000 kilos – at the same time?"

Neilson didn't know what to do say, except the truth: "Sir, my partner and I have heard nothing about 1,000 kilos; only 100."

K3 reached over his desk to pick up another stack of paper stamped Top Secret.

"Your bid for the computerized inventory system was rejected. So, why did you return to the country and travel to Donetsk?"

They've been watching us. Neilson felt invaded but couldn't tell the CIA that his doings were none of its business. Kensington might be testing him. "My partner and I want to export Ukrainian coal to Turkey."

"Coal?" Kensington turned up a skeptical corner of his mouth. "You went to eastern Ukraine for coal?"

"They have a lot of it there," said Neilson.

"Now, the eastern part of the country is seething and wants to break away and join Russia."

"I'm sorry, what is it doing?"

"Seething. You must have seen evidence of it."

"I can assure you we saw no seething." The Donetsk he saw looked depressed.

K3 waved the report in his hand. "Our intelligence says that the Ukraine is seething and will split in two within a year."

"If it's true, and I saw no evidence that it is, it's important for the United State's to secure the country's nuclear materials," said Neilson. There was nothing more to do except make that plea. "And its nuclear expertise," he added, telling Kensington about the taxi-driving missile engineer talking to Pakistanis and Iranians in Donetsk.

Instead of responding when he finished, K3 stood to end the interview, but did not shake Neilson's hand. When Neilson turned to leave, he called out behind him: "Remember, we're watching you."

CHAPTER 13:

COUNTDOWN

FAXNEWS-UKRAINE

<u>May 10, 1993 (Kiev, Ukraine).</u> The American Envoy announced a "New Start" in bilateral relations. Washington will treat Ukraine with the dignity it deserves as the world's third ranking nuclear power and an important European country larger than France. The Envoy's gesture marked a turn-around from the New President's prior insistence that Ukraine's had to ratify the START treaty as "a precondition to a long-term successful relationship."

<u>May 11, 1993. (Kiev, Ukraine).</u> The Defense Minister said today that it will experimentally explode a missile silo. Under the START treaty, Ukraine must explode 36 percent of its silos.

<u>May 13, 1993 (Moscow, Russia).</u> At a meeting of the CIS Collective Security Council, Russia rejected joint CIS control over the former Soviet Union's strategic forces and declared itself the USSR's sole nuclear successor state.

<u>May 25, 1993 (Washington, D.C.).</u> The American Envoy met today with Ukrainian-Americans. "He pressured us to put pressure on Ukraine on denuclearization." said one Leader, who has criticized US policy as too sympathetic to Moscow. The US opposed the Polish idea of forming an Eastern European NATO II because it would exclude Russia.
END

Faxnews-Ukraine – Your source of English-language news about Ukraine

---

TOP SECRET – PURPLE
Handle via Agent Channels Only
Date: June 1, 1993

To: **K3**
From: **Deputy Chief of Station Kiev**
Subject: **SITREP Rasputin**

(TS) 1. Confirm 20,000 dollars cash paid to Tariq abu Bakr for his intelligence on nuclear black market. Deposit remaining 30,000 dollars in Swiss bank account code named SVETA.

(TS) 2. I need monthly cash payments of 3,000 dollars to pay Tariq abu Bakr for HUMINTEL on Claus Hesse's activities.

(TS) 3. Claus Hesse sold five kilos of red mercury to Iranian agents posing as citrus merchants at the Bessarabian produce market.

(TS) 4. Abu Bakr can't identify the Ukrainian source of the HEU to which Neilson and Kruger have access. Claus Hesse told him that the source has 100 kilos, not 1,000.

(TS) 5. Abu Bakr's co-conspirator, alias Ahmed, received their orders to return back to Iraq.

    END

TOP SECRET – PURPLE

Exempt from automatic downgrade

TOP SECRET – WHITE

Handle via Agent Channels Only

Date: June 15, 1993
To: K3
From: Chief of Station Kiev
Subject: SITREP Fertilizer

(TS)   1. Roman Rozpad, age 40, is chairman of the Ukrainian Committee for Nuclear Safety and Security. He used to be the director of Khartron, which builds guidance systems for SS-18 missiles. His parents live in Dikanka, a village next to the Uzin nuclear bomber base. His one-room apartment is in Akademistechko, a bedroom community for scholars and scientists and his office is at 10 Kostiolna Street, just one block from the Dnipro Hotel in Kiev.

(TS)   2. Neil Neilson and Dan Kruger are renting an apartment at 8 Kostiolna Street.

(U)   3. The Ukrainian President rejected Russia's proposal to remove the strategic nuclear warheads from Ukraine within one year and also demanded compensation for the enriched plutonium and uranium that the warheads contain.

    END

TOP SECRET – WHITE

Exempt from automatic downgrade

*R*oman Rozpad poured the last of the champagne into Tanya's glass and raised his own in a toast: "To my beloved," he began during a quiet moment while the band took a break. "I promise you that I will spend each day of my life making you feel loved, happy and well taken care of."

Tanya blushed, her blue eyes dewy with sentiment. They had just spent a magical hour at the Dnipro Hotel restaurant, dining on the Chicken Kiev that Rozpad had ensured would be on the menu by bribing a waiter. He also paid the band to play her favorite songs and made sure they had champagne, too.

After a large sale of Transcarpathian Riesling to Kazakhstan, his parents bought 1,000 dollars of wholesale Hungarian Snickers bars and exponentially increased their profits when Petro found a network of private kiosks that sold candy and bootleg Marlboros. At the same time, Petro's brother in Transcarpathia stopped stealing the wines and started paying bribes for more volume at the low state price.

In just a few weeks, Petro had a new prosthetic arm, their cottage had a new roof and they even had money to pay their son – in real US dollars – to do their difficult bookkeeping. They kept no inventories on their old Soviet collective farm and lost 37 dollars when Petro counted one box of Snickers, assuming that the rest contained the same number of candy bars. They didn't.

Together with his state salary, Rozpad earned 300 dollars a month. It wasn't as much as the Americans had offered, but that job no longer seemed promising. They last talked when Neilson called him in May. The American didn't mention seeing him in Dikanka and only informed him that they still had no news on their bid. But 300 was a princely sum for Kiev.

And finally, after waiting for years, Tanya had agreed to marry him.

Rozpad couldn't believe his good fortune and started planning for a larger apartment closer to his office on Kostiolna Street so he could spend more time at home. The big park nearby, where he had met with the German, was perfect for family walks with the puppy he would buy for Tanya's son. *He's going to be my son, too, now.*

He also had a plan to return the HEU to where he had found it at Chernobyl-2, but this time he would "discover" it and log it in the inventory books. He could arrange it easily. He often travelled to the Chernobyl exclusion zone.

Now that he had something to lose, his interest in trying to sell the HEU had waned. The German's ability to discover that he possessed the cache had frightened him and drove home the dangers of dealing with the black market. Back when he despaired of Tanya agreeing to marry him, he might have risked it. But now he would have a family.

"Let me order more champagne, sweetheart," he said to Tanya, rising from the table to find the waiter with the private supply. His face glowed with warmth as he maneuvered around the crowded restaurant. Each day, he saw more and more foreigners in Kiev. But all the hotels were like the Dnipro, an old Soviet Intourist, designed to corral foreigners into one place, wired for KGB eavesdropping. Independent Ukraine's security service inherited most of the old operatives and put a representative on Rozpad's nuclear committee but he didn't think they spied on the hotels anymore.

A man calling his name from behind interrupted his thoughts and he turned to see the two Americans at a table near the door.

"Roman, what a surprise to run into you here," said Neil Neilson, greeting him with an outstretched hand.

Rozpad returned the greeting and shook hands with Dan Kruger, too. "I am here with my fiancée to celebrate her birthday. Kiev does not have many restaurants."

"Fiancée!" Neilson exclaimed. "Why, congratulations!" He turned to his partner. "Hey Dan, our friend Roman is engaged. Why don't you offer him a drink to celebrate?"

Kruger poured beer into a glass and motioned for Rozpad to sit at their table. He wanted to return to Tanya, but accepted the glass. "You are back in Ukraine?" he asked. "Does this mean there is news on your bid?"

"I'm sorry Roman, but we lost our bid. We're here on other business now," said Neilson.

Rozpad shrugged. He expected little and wasn't disappointed. "Will you stay long?"

"A few more days," said Neilson, leaning across the table and dropping his voice. "I'm sorry that we couldn't offer you a job. But even without the computerized inventory system, it's critically important to account for all of the nuclear materials in Ukraine in your log books. Our government is very, very concerned. They are watching…"

The American's voice trailed off, leaving his meaning clear. Rozpad sipped his beer with a steady hand. He no longer had to lie and exuded a new confidence with the Americans. "Soon, I am going to marry the love of my life. I am not going to jeopardize that."

Rozpad finished his beer. "I am also sorry that you lost your bid. It is true that I entertained other ideas. But I am going to complete the inventory. You have my assurances on that," he said, standing up. "Thank you for the drink but I must not keep my fiancée waiting."

They wished him well and when he left, Kruger toyed with his glass. "He sounded sincere."

"Yeah, he did," Neilson agreed.

"Now I feel bad that we ratted on him to the CIA."

"Not me. The bastard barely knew us and he offered to sell me HEU."

"He may have wanted us to take it for safekeeping."

"I doubt it." Neilson frowned. "I wonder why Kensington thinks that Rozpad has 1,000 kilos of HEU. Maybe the son of bitch was hiding the total amount from us."

"Well, we're not angels, either," said Kruger.

"That's different," Neilson insisted. "We made up a white lie that doesn't threaten to anyone."

Kruger motioned at the waiter for their check. The menu changed since their last visit. Instead of pork pieces, they had mushrooms baked in sour cream and Chicken Kiev. Prices were higher, too.

"I think the technical term is forgery," he said quietly.

After the Orthodox pastor in Bethesda rejected their offer and it appeared that every other Orthodox parish in the U.S. would do the same, a desperate Neilson and Kruger found it easy to invent a breakaway St. Nicholas Orthodox Church with its own letterhead, official stamp and convenient location at a nonexistent address. In his effusive letter, its invented pastor expressed great joy in welcoming the Ukrainian Patriarch and his church into communion with the true Orthodox believers of St. Nicholas. He gave prayerful thanks and affirmation for the creation of a coal exporting joint venture with their Ukrainian brethren and the American company Neptune, L.L.C.

The letter delighted the Patriarch, who used it to register the joint venture and then added it to his lamentably thin file of other churches' letters of recognition. But soon he would have the money he needed to fly to Constantinople to make his case for recognition to the Ecumenical Patriarch. They went together to deliver their documents to Viktor Vidkat who didn't utter a hint of protest in approving their export duty exemption – at least not in front of the Ukrainian President's protégé Patriarch.

They told no one. Kruger didn't dare tell Jean in her condition. Her lawyer mind would conjure nothing but worst case scenarios. But Vidkat hadn't even read the letter. Neilson and Kruger each had the only copies.

"We're not going to get caught," Neilson said after a while.

"You said Kensington at the CIA is watching us," Kruger noted.

Neilson threw Ukrainian *kupon* currency on the table. "Kensington doesn't give a rat's ass about coal or Orthodox churches," he said with a certainty he didn't feel. "I just don't see how he could find out. I mean, the spooks have done more on loose nukes than I thought, but this is an opaque place."

"I wonder who they have here," said Kruger, surveying the restaurant as they walked out. The ubiquitous floor dragon had abandoned her post. "There are a lot more foreigners these days, but not that many Americans."

"It wouldn't necessarily be an American," said Neilson, thinking with disquiet about Cristina Smythe and her professional martial arts display on the night of her direct, effective and pleasurable seduction. He hadn't seen her since, except for the note on her kitchen table telling him she was going to a morning press conference. *Now THAT was fun*, she wrote. She could have looked in his briefcase in the course of the night, but that was before they wrote the incriminating letter.

"Well, it's a burden I can bear for a million dollars," Kruger said as they walked back to the spacious apartment Kostya found for 270 dollars a month – with maid service. They paid that much for three nights in a cramped double hotel room.

He reached for the door to leave the building but the Iraqi, Tariq abu Bakr, jolted him as he rushed past with a large suitcase, a bouquet of roses and desperate eyes.

*T*ariq cleaned out his room and packed his few belongings in minutes after Ahmed called him to say that they both had orders to return to Iraq. He left the Dictator moustache diagram hanging in the bathroom. It wouldn't do him any good anymore.

His heart thumped in his brain as the elevator slowly descended to the lobby where he checked out and paid his final bill with his dwindling supply of counterfeits. The lobby bustled with the arrival of elderly Japanese tourists and Tariq maneuvered around their piles of luggage to leave the building.

A light drizzle fell on the summer evening as Tariq rushed along the Khreshchatyk Boulevard, wheeling his suitcase behind him. In the labyrinthine underground passageways of Independence Square, he ignored the flower sellers waving bouquets at him as he slalomed through crowds of young people drinking strong coffee in clouds of cigarette smoke. He joined the line at the cashier to buy a token and tried to make himself as small and invisible as possible while he waited, his hands shaking in his pockets.

I'm going to die. I'm going to die. I'm going to die. Terror had looped endlessly in his brain since Ahmed told him their orders. *Find a safe house*, Joe Marchetti told him.

Through the turnstile and endless escalator, built when Metro stations served double duty as potential bomb shelters, Tariq didn't see the elaborate chandeliers, murals and statuary. When he made it to the subway platform he peered into the dark tunnel, feeling with relief the breeze of an oncoming train.

The Metro screamed to a halt and Tariq stepped inside, making sure to stay surrounded by people. He took a corner seat, burying his face in a newspaper for the five stops to his destination: a bedroom complex of the cinderblock buildings that rose outside every large Soviet city he visited as a student. Built to accommodate growing urban populations, the *spalniy raions* – or sleeping districts – were functional, fungible and ugly be they in Kiev or Kyrgyzstan.

It took Tariq a while to find No.33 in the falling darkness and drizzle. Finally, he found the building and raced inside, expecting the Sultan to slip out from the gloom to kill him right on the spot. But he saw no one except a young couple walking arm in arm. Sweat poured into his eyes. He lost the roses long before.

A handwritten sign on the elevator declared it broken, so he lugged his suitcase up the concrete stairs to the fourth floor landing, where he found four apartment doors, each padded with black vinyl. His head pounded when he rang the bell to No. 43.

He heard no other sound as he rocked on his heels and rang again, and again, and again. "Please," he whispered desperately at the door. "Please!"

Finally, he heard footsteps, the soft padding of slippers and felt the gaze on him through the peephole. He tried to compose himself but his voice still shook. "It's me, Tariq," he whispered. "Open the door, I beg you!"

The responding silence lasted for a lifetime. Then he heard the music of sliding chains and bolts. Praying thanks to any deity that might be listening, he grasped the suitcase handle.

The door swung open and Sveta peered from behind it, her black hair hanging in a braid over her shoulder. She wore a bathrobe, no makeup and more beauty than Tariq had ever seen in her.

She opened the door wider for him to come in and he wheeled the suitcase over the threshold, wiping his feet on a rag rug surrounded by her stilettos. After shutting and locking the door, Sveta turned to Tariq and crossed her arms.

When she opened her mouth to speak, Tariq stopped her by holding up the suitcase with both hands. "I did it," he said, his voice hollow. "I did it. I brought the money for you: Real money."

Sveta bit her lip skeptically. "Come here," she said and led him into the sitting room off the corridor. Faded wallpaper covered the walls and lace curtains framed the windows. Inspecting the large wall unit with glassware, rows of books and framed photographs; Tariq realized that he knew almost nothing about her. Her leather notebook lay on the coffee table.

"Show me," Sveta said, motioning at the suitcase. Tariq laid it on the floor, fished the key out of his pocket and snapped open the locks. A green vinyl bag lay atop his clothes and he unzipped it to show Sveta the fresh 100 dollar bills stacked inside. "This is for you," he said, handing her the bag. "Twenty thousand dollars."

Sveta took the bag, riffling through the money to pick out a random bill. She held it up to the light to see the telltale metallic security thread of authenticity and looked at Tariq. "My God," she said, her eyes wide. "Where did you get this?"

He saw no point in lying. He told Sveta the truth about his work. But there had been no sex since.

The story spilled out in a torrent of how he sold his inside information about the Dictator's nuclear shopping program to Joe Marchetti, the tampon inspector working for the CIA. Marchetti paid him a lump sum of 50,000 dollars -- 20,000 in cash, and 30,000 in a Swiss bank – and would pay him a monthly retainer of 3,000 dollars to continue to meet with the German and pretend that he still worked for the Dictator. He also promised Tariq protection against Iraqi retaliation, with a secret second agent to watch his back.

"I'm a traitor," he concluded, his head hanging. Then he straightened his shoulders. "But that doesn't matter. The Dictator is a tyrant and will burn in hell. But they'll kill me if they find me. They've ordered me back to Iraq, and they'll kill me there for failing in my mission. If they find me here, they'll kill me too," he said. "That's why I left the hotel to come here. You have to help me, Sveta. Please help me!"

Sveta counted the money. "This is twice what you owe me," she said. "Why?"

"Because you said that paying what I owe isn't an investment. The rest is my investment in your school."

He fished through his suitcase for the half empty bottle of Johnny Walker Black and placed it on the small coffee table in front of the couch. "Let's toast to our new partnership!"

With a glance that Tariq could not decipher, Sveta took two crystal goblets from the wall unit and placed them next to the bottle.

"This is not a partnership, Ali. I mean Tariq," she said, still unaccustomed to his real name. "You can be an investor, but I'm going to be in charge."

Tariq poured the scotch with sweating hands, raising a toast: "To the boss."

Sveta sipped her drink in silence and twisted the end of her braid. "So, Marchetti is going to pay you 3,000 a month?"

Tariq hadn't known how much to ask for but that was what he spent in counterfeits.

"And this is just to keep contact with the German?"

"He's the only source that I have here," said Tariq. "Claus says those two Americans are trying to buy HEU, but I've never spoken to them." Then he recalled the scene at the hotel elevator. "But their price keeps changing. A few months ago, I overheard them mention five billion dollars, and then this evening, one of them talked about a million. Or they might be prices for different things."

"I talked to them when they first arrived," said Sveta. "But they don't use prostitutes."

Her forehead creased in thought and she opened her notebook to a blank page, making notes with a sharp pencil. Tariq watched her as Johnny Walker's warm embrace quieted his clattering nerves.

Sveta flipped the notebook shut. "We can do better then that."

"We?" Tariq hid his thrill that Sveta thought of them as a "we".

"Yes, we," she said. "Those two Americans may not use prostitutes but, believe me, the other ones do."

"The other ones? What other ones?"

Sveta stood up to pace the small sitting room. "Did you know that Iran was one of the first countries to recognize Ukrainian independence? They opened their embassy in the National Hotel, by the parliament. A lot of countries did. I didn't work there. The Communist Party used the hotel for the *nomenklatura*, and the bribes to the doormen were too expensive for me. But friends of mine did."

She stopped pacing. "You'd be surprised at what men tell prostitutes, and the things we overhear. The Arabs are especially stupid about women. I guess most of them don't see many except in their families."

Tariq was guilty as charged, though most Iraqi women did not cover themselves. He had no idea that Sveta entertained any thoughts besides whoring and her business school.

"And you, too, Tariq" she said. "You thought you fooled me. But I figured it out. You just told me the details. I also didn't know about the counterfeits for a long time. But I figured that out, too."

Tariq wondered how she did figure it out, but didn't want to change the subject from whatever she and he could be a "we" for. "What do you have in mind?" he asked cautiously.

Sveta picked up her notebook and showed him what she had written in her precise Cyrillic handwriting. He saw a list of women's names – Maria, Tanya, Nadia, Oksana. Next to each, Sveta wrote a country: Pakistan, North Korea, Iran, Libya. "What do you think the Americans will pay for this?"

Tariq reached for the notebook, but Sveta held it. "These are the hotel whores?" he said, pointing at the women's names.

"And these are their regular clients," Sveta said, pointing at the next column. "They're using aliases, like you did. But the girls have a good idea of what they're doing here."

"You think that they're nuclear smugglers?"

Sveta snapped the book shut and shook her head. "That's the point, Tariq. Let the Americans pay us to find out."

Tariq had to admit, Sveta had a hard-nosed business sense – much harder than his own. But then, another thought. "Wait a minute. Shouldn't you inform your own government instead of the Americans?"

"Our government doesn't have the money and doesn't care. I know. I worked as a mechanical engineer at the Kharkiv Institute of Physics and Technology."

"What?" blurted Tariq in astonishment. At Petrochemical 3 they told him that the Kharkiv Institute was considered the "father" of Soviet nuclear physics. When he still worked for the Dictator, he planned on travelling there.

Sveta shrewdly assessed his expression. "That's right, Tariq; me, here, right under your nose. I quit when they ran out of money in 1990. Six-thousand people worked there when I did and only a few thousand were still there when I left. But I still have contacts there. They stored enriched uranium in three different places and never counted it. They still don't. The ledgers listed 75 kilos but Irina was right. Soviet accounting was creative lying, whether it was shoe production, wheat harvests or enriched uranium stockpiles. If it wasn't a weapon, it wasn't important.

"Our leaders inherited that attitude. They won't care unless the Americans make them care," Sveta concluded in a speech that astonished Tariq both in its length and its content. Those months he wasted on the German with no results, and here stood his whore (well, his former whore) matter-of-factly informing him that she was not just intelligent and well spoken, but also had access to exactly what he came to Ukraine to find. Marchetti would appreciate her as an asset.

"You're amazing," he said simply.

Sveta surprised him by caressing his hair. "I guess that you'll need a place to stay," she crooned in the soothing and familiar voice that Tariq hadn't heard in weeks.

He stood up to draw her into a gentle embrace. They were no longer client and whore, and he was glad.

*T*he road to Inkerman cut through vast fields of old grape arbors, hacked off at their roots during the misguided anti-alcohol campaign of the USSR's declining years. The remains of abandoned irrigation lines snaked around the vines' shriveled stumps, their metals sold as scrap for kopeks. Crimea was so arid, any agriculture demanded irrigation. Brother Boris never appreciated the peninsula's desert climate until he had to drive in a horse-drawn cart for miles at a time without water. He always lived amid the rolling forests and wetlands of northern Ukraine, never even travelling anywhere else.

For weeks, they drove through the parched steppe, on dusty back roads swept by harsh winds. He wiped grit off his face, burned brown by the sun, and noticed yet another stain on his robe. When they passed over the narrow Perekop Isthmus, barely tethering Crimea to Ukraine's Black Sea shore, the scenery didn't change: flat plains, scrub and not a stream or pond to be seen, though the occasional village wells provided welcome replenishment of their water jars. If they found a green patch of grass, Boris stopped the cart no matter what the time of day so that Dora could eat, ignoring Anton's complaints. He could see the mare's ribs.

Boris wanted it to end, and feared for the moment when it would. He and Anton spoke less and less as they slowly but inexorably headed south. Satisfied with what he had rigged during many nights camping under thousands of stars, Anton announced that the trigger was ready and hid it with the warhead under the potatoes. Boris had no reason to doubt him, though he prayed to find one. Troubled and sad, he watched the passing scenery while Dora's hooves clip-clopped. Stretches of asphalt went missing entirely in places, kicking up clouds of dust when the wagon pulled through them. Mountains rose in the distance, shielding the peninsula's south shore from the northern winds, creating a lush, semi-tropical climate that Boris had only read about and now would never see. His list of nevers had grown in the course of their journey. As had his list of doubts. But any time he tried to express them, Anton burst into rages that grew more violent with time. Boris was afraid of him.

At night, he prayed for strength to accept his destiny, for the Lord to assure him that they pursued a righteous path. But the response was always silence.

"There it is," Anton announced as they approached a military checkpoint. Inkerman was in the jurisdiction of Sevastopol, the last closed city in Ukraine. The others, all former Soviet military industrial centers or sensitive border zone, had opened to the public long ago. But Sevastopol remained closed while Russia and Ukraine battled for custody over the Black Sea Fleet.

"Let me do the talking," said Anton. Neither of them had permits to enter the city. But Anton grew up in Arzamas-16 and knew about checkpoints.

"Do you have your passport?" asked Anton.

"In my pocket." The Kiev Cave Monastery made all the monks take their old internal Soviet passports to the local bureaucrat who put a stamp inside making the passport Ukrainian. He doubted if Anton did the same. What few words his companion said about Ukrainian independence weren't very monkish. That also troubled Boris. Anton didn't act much like a monk but he decided the meaning of the messenger's cryptic words.

"Keep it there," said Anton. "And keep your mouth shut."

Dora twitched her ears when they stopped at the gate. A beefy lieutenant smelling of vodka and sweat approached the wagon, an AK-47 rifle slung over his shoulder.

"*Dokumenty*," he demanded, pushing back his cap with its still-Soviet Black Sea Fleet insignia.

"We don't have any documents," said Anton. "We are monks and have given our lives to God, relinquishing our secular identities."

The blatant lie shocked Boris but he feared Anton as much as he feared the guard. So, he did nothing. *Lord, my fate is in your hands.*

Anton motioned at the load of potatoes in the wagon. "My son, we are taking these to our brethren at the St. Clement monastery in Inkerman."

The lieutenant grunted. "What the devil, monk? There are no fucking monasteries in Inkerman."

Anton winced at the epithet, though he had used it many times. "St. Clement," he said and then repeated the story Boris told him during the earlier part of the journey, when they still talked. "Icon-worshippers fleeing persecution in Byzantium established it in the eighth century. It is a very holy place. The Soviets closed it but a brave group of brothers have reopened the monastery and need the physical and spiritual sustenance we've come to deliver."

"Clement? What the fuck?"

"An early Christian martyr, banished from Rome to Crimea, where they tied him to an anchor and threw him from a boat into the Black Sea as punishment for converting the local pagans. Saints Cyril and Methodius came here to pray, and they found his bones in the sea."

"I don't understand," said the lieutenant. "They prayed and found his bones? How did they find his bones in the sea by praying?"

"The sea ebbed," said Anton authoritatively.

"They prayed and it ebbed?"

Anton raised his head to gaze at the heavens. "Thank the Lord for the miracle. Those bones now rest in the Inkerman monastery."

"The skull is in the Kiev Cave Monastery," Boris added, then kicked himself mentally for helping Anton direct the guard's attention away from their purported lack of documents.

The guard grimaced. "That's disgusting. Scientists proved those relics and mummies were fakes, made out of goat and pig bones."

"Perhaps those Soviet scientists acted under orders from the Communist Party to discredit our holy relics. But one thing is certain,"

Anton said, motioning his head at the mound of potatoes. "Our brethren will go hungry if we do not deliver these."

The lieutenant crossed his arms. "Nice stories, monk. But why the hell should I risk my ass to let you in without documents? I don't give a damn about your church."

Boris tried to hide his elation while Anton twirled the ends of his straggly beard in thought. "Well, I think you should," he said.

"Oh yeah? Why? Because you're sickos that collect skulls?"

"No, because only the Russian Orthodox Church can bring Russia together right now, when it has fragmented and weakened economically and militarily." Anton looked at the guard. "You are in the Black Sea Fleet in Sevastopol, the city of Russian glory. Do you want to be a part of Ukraine?"

"Fuck no," said the guard and Boris's heart sank.

"Well, then, let us in," said Anton. "We must make the Russian Church strong here, in this so-called independent Ukraine, so that it can fulfill its historical destiny to bind Holy Russia during this calamitous time for her."

The lieutenant stepped aside as if in acquiescence. "OK," he said and then stopped. "Hey, I'm hungry, too. Can I have a couple of those potatoes?"

Before responding, Anton leaped out of the wagon to pick them far from the center where their secret lay buried. "Let me select them for you, my son."

The guard cupped his hands for the potatoes. "Great! Our provisions here suck."

His hands full, the guard pointed with his chin for them to pass through the checkpoint.

Clicking to Dora to walk on, Boris's spirits dropped even further and he drove for a time in silence. "That guard sure wanted to talk a lot," he said after a while.

"He's bored," responded Anton. "Checkpoint guards are always bored. They're alone in the middle of nowhere with nothing to do."

It took less than an hour on the Simferopol highway to reach Inkerman but more than two hours to find the monastery, even with the directions they brought from the Protector monastery in Dikanka. But after many wrong turns, they approached the ancient cloister, hewn from sandstone cliffs under the ruins of a medieval Genoese fortress. But the locked gate displayed no signs or instructions for visitors.

Anton climbed from the wagon and knocked at the gate. When no one came out, he disappeared around monastery wall, his footsteps crunching on the gravel. "People are singing inside the cliff," he said when he returned. "There's no way they can hear us knocking."

Boris said nothing. *That's because we're not supposed to do this.*

Suddenly, even Dora spooked when a woman dropped out of the sky with a radio and a red backpack, bouncing down the cliff and safely tethered to a rope.

"Just pull that bell rope above the latch. It'll ring inside and someone will come out," she said with a Moscow twang, pulling her rope and coiling it over her arm. She grinned at the startled monks: "Sorry if I surprised you but the rock climbing around here is excellent."

Crimea was very popular for outdoor recreation, but Boris didn't expect people to appear out of the sky. *Is it a message?*

Anton pulled on the bell rope and soon, a thin, young novice with a sparse black beard and not many teeth opened the gate. Anton explained that they were delivering potatoes from the Protector monastery and the monk raised his arms in celebration when he saw the pile in the wagon. "Praise the Lord," he said. "Come in, come in. I am Brother Ivan. Let us pray to thank the Lord for your safe arrival."

Boris drove the wagon through the gate into a crowded courtyard of low slung stucco buildings.

"Do you have any water and hay for the horse," he asked, after climbing from the wagon and patting Dora on the neck. She snorted as he loosened her harness.

Ivan led them into the courtyard. "We do. But let us pray first," he said, shaking his head with evident anxiety. "There is worrying news."

Boris and Anton followed Ivan to metal stairs leading up into the cliff and then into a chamber lit with tapers that cast shadows against walls of carved rock. An alcove above a wooden door contained dozens of browned skulls.

"In 100 A.D., this was a shrine. One of the first Christian shrines in the lands of Scythia," Ivan explained.

Boris peered into the alcove. "Who were these people?"

"Their names are lost to history."

Ivan led them past the alcove to a tiny church, its whitewashed walls set off with red satin vestments. "This is St. Andrew's Church," he said. "We should pray here. The Apostle also travelled the lands of Scythia and went up the Dnieper to bless the hills that would become Kiev."

"But you spoke of troubling news?" said Anton. They heard nothing during their weeks of travel.

Ivan crossed himself and prepared to kneel. "It was just on the radio. That heretical Ukrainian Patriarch has asked for a meeting with the Ecumenical Patriarch of Constantinople. They are in talks about a date for the visit."

CHAPTER 14:

STING

FAXNEWS-UKRAINE

Quarterly Nuclear Roundup

<u>June 3, 1993 (Kiev)</u>. The New Prime Minister called for using START to dispose of 130 aging SS-19 missiles but keeping the 46 top-of-the-line SS-24s, built by the Ukrainian Missile Factory. The parliament later declared Ukraine the owner of the nuclear weapons on its territory.

<u>June 7, 1993 (Kiev)</u>. The American Secretary of Defense offered Ukraine a 40-million dollar aid package and proposed dismantling the nuclear warheads in Ukraine with monitoring by the United States and Russia. A Russian expert deemed the proposal unacceptable. Because the warheads were designed in Russia, dismantling them would reveal Russia's design secrets to the Americans. "We are no longer enemies," he said. "But we want privacy in this area."

<u>July 3, 1993 (Kiev)</u>. The Ministry of Defense issued a secret decree putting the S-objects under the jurisdiction of the 43rd Rocket Army, thus placing the warhead maintenance facilities under Ukrainian administrative control.

<u>August 2, 1993 (Kiev)</u>. The defense ministry has decommissioned three SS-19 missiles and expects to decommission ten by September. Their warheads have been stored in the S-Objects.
END

Faxnews-Ukraine – Your source of English-language news about Ukraine

---

Date: September 15, 1993
To: K3
From: Deputy Chief of Station Kiev
Subject: SITREP Rasputin

(TS) 1. Request pay increase for Tariq abu Bakr to 6,000 dollars per month for surveillance of suspected North Korean, Iranian and Pakistani agents staying at the Dnipro Hotel.

(TS) 2. Claus Hesse told Tariq that Neil Neilson and Dan Kruger might be planning to smuggle the HEU by concealing it in 500,000 tons of coal they are shipping to Ataturk Imports in Istanbul. He insists that they must obtain the HEU before Rozpad can sell it to the Americans.

(S)   3. Iraq uses a well managed weapons and drug smuggling route that goes through Russia, Georgia and Azerbaijan to smuggle counterfeit US 100 dollar bills using teams of pack horses.

(U)   4. The Presidents of Ukraine and Russia agreed on a maintenance schedule for the nuclear warheads. They also agreed that Ukraine will exchange its share of the Black Sea Fleet for debt forgiveness for Russian gas supplies.

END

Date: October 2, 1993
To: K3
From: Chief of Station Kiev
Subject: SITREP Fertilizer

(S)   1. Today, Neil Neilson and Dan Kruger purchased tickets to Istanbul on October 8 to close their coal contract with Ataturk Imports, Inc. The Minister of Foreign Economic Activity, Viktor Vidkat, is notoriously corrupt and they must have paid a bribe for their export license. But it would be impossible to prove under the Foreign Corrupt Practices Act.

(S)   2. Neilson and Kruger also bought a ticket for the Patriarch of the Independent Ukrainian Orthodox Church (IUOC), who will meet with the Ecumenical Patriarch to seek recognition of his break-away church.

(U)   3. Ukrainian media are providing heavy coverage of the Russian President's decision to dissolve the Russian parliament.

(U)   5. The Ukrainian President announced that Ukraine will not transfer the nuclear weapons to an unstable Russia and called for Western financial aid to dismantle them on Ukrainian territory.

(TS)   6. Purple just called. Claus Hesse has kidnapped Roman Rozpad and is on his way to pick up Tariq abu

---

*W*illiam Kensington III studied the last sentence of the dispatch that his aide, John Petrie, handed him. White never ended reports without completing a sentence or including the customary footers.

"White must be on their tail," he concluded.

"It just came in, K3, but we don't know when White made the drop. It can't have been too long ago. It's still October 2nd here, and Kiev is seven hours ahead of us."

The grandfather's clock chimed. It was five p.m. and October 3rd in Kiev. He tapped his fingers next to an empty crystal ashtray. The New First Lady declared war on smoking in any government buildings, forcing K3 outdoors for humiliating cigarettes with the minions over tin can ashtrays. It was yet another reason for K3 to hate Democrats. They kept cutting his budget, too.

He *did* smoke a lot less, though.

"White knows what to do. That's one damned experienced operative," said Petrie, laying a stack of papers festooned with yellow Post-its on K3's desk. "The other news is not so good."

K3 read the title. "Trends in nuclear crime in Germany," he said and studied the chart. "1992, 59 fraudulent offers of nuclear materials, 99 cases of illegal trafficking and 18 seizures: 1993: 118 fraudulent offers, 123 cases and 21 seizures.

K3 read the paper with excitement. "What do you mean 'not good'? The numbers keep growing!"

"A lot of it's junk and scams, though."

"Junk? What kind of junk?"

"Radioactive junk. Flip to the other chart on the second page."

K3 skimmed it: "Red mercury, depleted uranium, smoke detectors, scrap metal from Chernobyl." He pointed at an offending line. "Smoke detectors?"

"The Russian ones have miniscule amounts of plutonium."

K3 pushed the stack of papers aside. "This is crap," he said. "The Soviet Union collapsed into 15 separate countries. Four of them now have nuclear weapons. All of them probably have enriched uranium, plutonium and other nuclear weapons components that are in big demand for some nasty dictators. AND the only stuff the Germans can find are fucking smoke detectors!?"

"Binoculars, too," Petrie added. "They contain tritium."

"Radioactive binoculars?"

"It's weird stuff." Petrie studied English before going to law school. "Keep in mind, most of these deals involve bumblers, scammers and swindlers. They're not making legitimate sales. The buyers are undercover police and spooks, or journalists trying to generate a scoop."

K3 reached for the papers again and flipped through the pages. "I don't buy it. There must be more going on and we're not seeing it. How much of this stuff is there worldwide anyway?"

Petrie opened his notebook to find the answer. "About 500 tons of plutonium and 1600 tons of highly enriched uranium: Most of it's in Russia."

The aide leaned over K3's broad and mostly empty desk to pull out a photocopy of a newspaper article. "Though there have been serious incidents," he said, sliding the article to K3 who read the typed translation. "German police seize weapons grade plutonium while searching the garage of a German businessman," he read. "Now, that's serious."

"Sort of. He wanted to peddle it to Iraq, but no deal went through."

K3 leaned back in his chair and crossed his legs on the desk. "Who's this German character?"

Petrie snorted with contempt. "A small time trader. He used to import shoes, cigarettes, equipment for making French fries, whatever. The German police were after a counterfeiting ring. They found counterfeits, but they also found the plutonium."

"How much?"

"Six grams."

"Six grams? That's it?" K3 squinted at the grainy newspaper photo of the German's garage.

"It might've been a sample, boss. Besides, there've been other incidents." Petrie picked another article from the pile on the desk. "The Germans caught two Spanish guys and a Colombian on a flight from Moscow to Munich with more than a pound of weapons grade plutonium."

"A pound? Now that's better," said K3, snapping his fingers in satisfaction as he read through the flagged newspapers detailing a rash of nuclear smuggling incidents during four months in Germany.

"Why don't we put out offers on the German market?" he asked. "Plant a rumor that Iran will pay a stupendous sum, three million dollars, for a kilo of plutonium or HEU."

"That might just encourage more of this penny ante business. But we can try," said Petrie. "Still, Neil Neilson might have been telling the truth when he said he knew about a hundred kilos, not a thousand. Should we drop the tail on them?"

"Not yet. Let's first see what White ends up with. They might still try to peddle the stuff if it's available."

K3 perused another newspaper clipping. "What the hell?" he exclaimed and then read aloud: "In July, the Director of the FBI visited Moscow and stressed the risks of proliferation through the efforts of organized crime to steal or buy weapons-grade nuclear material. He called the possibility the greatest long term threat to the security of the United States."

He smacked the desk. "Since when does the FBI have anything to do with counter proliferation? That's our turf."

"He said that the FBI is going to be more active in this, K3."

"The hell they will!" K3 swung his legs off the desk and pulled a cigarette and a lighter out of his top drawer. "Watch for White and don't let *anyone* know – we can't have the FBI trying to nose in on this. If we find enough loose HEU to make just one bomb, the public will scream for bigger budgets to fight nuclear smuggling – and it won't be the FBI's."

"Hang on, K3, there's one more thing," said Petrie, pulling a thin packet of stapled papers out of a manila folder and placing it on the desk. "It's a ten-million dollar sole source bid for Nunn-Lugar money from DSA."

"DSA?" K3 was annoyed by the delay of his nicotine fix.

"DSA is Defense Systems Analysis," said Petrie. "It's the company that Neilson and Kruger used to work for. I told Mike Beedle, our guy there, to have them resubmit their bid for the computerized inventory system for the Ukraine."

"What the hell for?" asked K3. "I thought we'd get sued if we try to give it to anyone except Neilson and Kruger."

"Not Neilson and Kruger," said Petrie with a satisfied smirk. "They worked for DSA when they made the bid. I talked to the lawyers. The company owns it, not them."

K3 approved. "Good work, Petrie. This is perfect. The New President thinks the Ukraine will disarm with carrots rather than sticks. They're idiots but they're the ones spending the money now and we'll look real pretty with the biggest seizure of HEU ever, plus a ten-million dollar carrot for a counter-proliferation inventory system."

*D*ripping saliva, the Dog separated Tariq abu Bakr from the hostage in the backseat of an old black Volga sedan that smelled of grime, old sweat and dog breath. Claus Hesse held a Makarov pistol and leaned over the front seat, his milky blind eye fixed on Roman Rozpad. The red-haired woman drove them to an empty parking lot outside a cinderblock building displaying a grocery sign, but no sign of groceries on its darkened shelves.

"What does this mean to you," asked the German, showing Rozpad a Polaroid and shining a flashlight onto a pretty woman holding that day's *Evening Kiev* newspaper.

The Ukrainian kept his voice even. "What have you done to her?"

Claus rumbled in his guttural Russian. "We have done nothing, and will do nothing. She is safe and will remain so. All we want from you is the highly enriched uranium you plan to sell to the Americans."

"Americans?" Rozpad seemed ready to say more, but stopped.

"The HEU for my client," Claus said, tilting his head towards Tariq, "in exchange for your fiancée's continued well-being."

Tariq's cold expression required using every bit of willpower that he had to conceal his shock over the kidnappings and his terror that Claus might discover he now worked for the Americans. Joe Marchetti swore that another CIA agent would follow them. But Joe didn't know that Claus was armed and, evidently, dangerous.

Claus handed Rozpad the photograph. "It is unfortunate that you refused my initial offer in the park. Your stubbornness has cost you,"

Tariq glanced at the picture. A blond woman sat on a green velour couch. Books lined a wall unit behind her. Her scarf was blue and her eyes, frightened.

Rozpad stared into the German's seeing eye and must have seen little to lose.

"Why don't we try it this way," he said. "I'll sell you 100 kilos of HEU for 100,000 dollars. It's just a fraction of what you first offered me. That way, you can put away the guns, take me to my fiancée and release us both."

Claus's good eye glimmered with respect and then rested on Tariq, who struggled to maintain his frozen expression. *Where'd the Ukrainian get the balls to negotiate?* But maybe the nightmare would end soon and he could return to Sveta.

Claus kept his good eye on Rozpad. *"Ja,"* he finally said, instantly transforming the kidnapping into a business junket.

"It is always preferable to do business with reasonable men, *Nichtwahr*," said Claus, putting his hand out for a handshake. When Rozpad ignored him, he turned around to slip his gun into the leather briefcase on his lap and settle into the front seat. "Your offer is acceptable. But first we must confirm that you indeed have the matériel. You will take us to it."

Rozpad's eyes fixed on the back of Claus's seat, his face stony. "It's two hours away."

"We have all the time in the world."

"I want Tanya released."

"I told you. She is safe."

"She's worried and afraid. I want her released."

"When the deal is done."

"Now!" demanded Rozpad. "And I want to talk to her."

"No, there is no telephone in the apartment." The Ukrainian hesitated – most homes lacked phones – and Claus drove his point. "She is on the other side of Kiev and my client wants to complete this business. The sooner we confirm that you have the HEU, the sooner we can finish this. And for that we need a sample."

Tariq tried to compose his face into that of a ruthless and impatient nuclear smuggler but he sympathized with the Ukrainian. Life with Sveta had softened him. She didn't know that he left their apartment. For fear of the Sultan killing him for his defection, Tariq rarely did except for his meetings with the German. Pursuing her business plan full-time, Sveta was out meeting with former clients in the government to help her through the maze of regulations needed to register her school. After that, she planned to go to the Dnipro Hotel to meet with the whores.

With combined academic credentials to outclass the Dictator's research institutes, they earned more than any women in Kiev. But Sveta had to work on them to plan for their futures. The window of opportunity for prostitutes at the expensive hotels closed quickly. But other windows would open if they invested in themselves and signed on at her school, with classes in management, accounting, office administration and finance. Computer classes held special allure. Back when Tariq pretended to sell modems, he realized he'd go bankrupt if that was his real business. Personal computers were a novelty in Kiev, as were calculators. Most people still used abacuses.

While legitimate, Sveta's visits with her old colleagues also provided the perfect cover for collecting intelligence on their rogue-state clients. One of the North Koreans had a suspicious itinerary that took him to many of the country's military-industrial cities. Sveta reported to Joe Marchetti, who moved from the hotel into an apartment with Irina and her daughter. Irina also quit whoring to develop the accounting curriculum.

Tariq didn't have time to leave Sveta a note when Claus called him. Thankfully, Marchetti answered when he phoned him in a panic. The CIA agent said he needed to tell "the other one" first, and then called Tariq right back. *Play along and wait. The other one will take have your back.*

Rozpad sank back into the seat with resignation. "Take the Odessa highway."

The Patriarch of the Independent Ukrainian Orthodox Church beamed with joy, crossing himself as the engines screamed and the small Boeing took off from the Kiev airport, heading south towards Istanbul. Dan Kruger watched him vaguely, having taken a Xanax for the flight.

Jean went into premature labor soon after he returned from Kiev in July and gave birth to Oksana Beniuk Kruger a month early. After many sleepless nights and anxious days, the baby emerged happy and healthy. Jean had insisted that he travel to Kiev and Istanbul to close the coal deal. "You'll be of more use to us if you do," she told him. But he felt guilty leaving, even with his mother-in-law there to help.

Xanax provided a thick layer of glass separating reality from his senses. He felt very relaxed.

Neil Neilson turned a page of the *International Herald Tribune*. "Listen to this," he said. "The New American Administration has offered to hold talks with North Korea."

"Really?" said Kruger. Just a few weeks earlier, North Korea threatened to drop out of the nuclear Non-Proliferation Treaty. Among other things, the NPT provided for international inspections of civilian nuclear facilities in exchange for countries' promises not to build nuclear bombs. Dropping out of it meant that Pyongyang might have something to hide.

"It's what they wanted all along," he said. "We've never had diplomatic relations with the North. This forced us into direct contacts."

"I'll bet they aren't giving up on nukes," responded Neilson. "Tin pot dictators love big explosions."

"They love attention, too," said Kruger.

"Well, if they're in the market, this place is the Grand Bazaar," Neilson said, watching the rolling countryside far below. "Buy a few underemployed scientists and loose HEU, and you're half-way there. They could have a Bomb in a decade. And what we've seen in Ukraine is just a fraction compared to Russia."

It was quiet during the takeoff but when the seatbelt and no smoking signs went off, the aisles filled with the metallic sounds of belt clasps. Clouds drifted up from the smoking section, carrying female voices and occasional peals of laughter. Stacks of flattened plaid plastic stood next to many of the seats.

The flight attendant barked, pointing at the piles, and two women sporting pastel track suits stopped at Kruger's seat to ask what sounded like a question. He raised his hands mutely and then motioned at Kostya Beniuk, who came to translate for the Patriarch. Zoya wanted to join them but their credit cards were close to maxed out.

The vinyl track suit swished when one of the women stepped aside and pointed down the aisle, repeating what she had asked Kruger. When the translator unclasped his seatbelt to help, the other passengers greeted him with teasing voices.

Confused but unconcerned, thanks to his Xanax, Kruger watched Kostya lift a stack of plastic and push it into the overhead compartment while the two women chatted with the other passengers. When he finished, another female voice called out and he walked over to another stack of plastic to shove it into the overhead. After ten minutes, he stashed all the plastic and returned to his seat.

"What's with the plastic bags, Kostya?" Kruger asked idly.

The translator fastened his seatbelt. "They are shopping tourists, doing business in Turkey," he said. "In Dikanka, I show you cage for Polish people, traders who bring clothes from Turkey? Now, Ukrainians also buy cheap clothes and things in Turkey and sell for big profit in Ukraine."

"They're all women," Kruger observed.

"Most shopping tourists are women. There is very high unemployment for women. They travel in groups. It is more safe."

"The Turks call it the 'suitcase trade'," said Neilson, looking away from his newspaper. "I read up on it when I researched Turkey's regulations for the coal deal. Every year, hundreds of thousands of people from the former Soviet Union shuttle back and forth to Turkey for clothes, shoes, whatever isn't produced at home – which isn't much. There are no regulations, no taxes, no customs duties. No customs inspections either." Neilson turned a page. "It's almost medieval, like caravans. But it's billions of dollars in annual business," he concluded, turning his attention back to his reading.

Kruger confusion failed to penetrate his drug-induced mental fog. "So, what are those stacks of plastic for? Are they going to trade them?"

"No, no. Shopping tourists pay in cash – hard currency. Those plastics are folded luggages. When they open, they make very, very big storages for clothes." The translator held his arms wide to demonstrate their size. "I see them at outdoors markets."

The Patriarch's beatific countenance reflected in the window as he gazed out at the sky and then he turned it to Kostya to say his first words since boarding the plane.

"Patriarch says that if the Ecumenical Patriarch recognizes Independent Ukrainian Orthodox Church, Russian Orthodox Church will lose more than half of its parishes."

Kruger was drowsy. "That's nice," he said.

Though the Patriarch said nothing more, Kostya did. "This is important, Mr. Dan. Russian Orthodox Church is historical channel for Kremlin influence."

"Kremlin influence," Kruger repeated. His mind drifted off into the monotonous hum of the engines. He had nothing to do on the plane anyway. Coco the Greek promised to organize everything in Istanbul.

When the Patriarch spoke again, Kostya continued: "When coal is sold, Patriarch wants to buy Pope-mobile."

But Kruger had fallen asleep.

*T*he weeks passed leisurely at the Inkerman Cave Monastery, in a sunny blur of prayers, chores and evening rides on Dora along empty beaches on the Black Sea coast. The mare was short, almost a pony, and no match for the superb Ukrainian Warmbloods of Boris's youth, but she was a willing and fearless trail horse. They went out for hours, leaving Anton glued to the transistor radio for news of the renegade Ukrainian Patriarch's visit to Constantinople.

Boris decided to take a longer journey on a bright October afternoon, passing the outskirts of Sevastopol, where graffiti on buildings and bridges shouted "Crimea Is Russia!". They cantered along the sea shore and then Boris turned the mare to climb a rocky dune. She picked her way carefully, puffing from the exertion, only to emerge on the northern edge of a sprawling excavation of ancient ruins.

He dismounted and led Dora along the cobblestone streets, her hooves echoing in the emptiness. Helpful museum signs explained that the oldest ruins were from Chersonesos, a vast Greek city state of the Classical Age. More than a millennium later, Prince Vladimir of Kiev went there to be baptized and bring Christianity to his lands.

Foundations of piled stone surrounded mosaic floors sprouting scrubby grass under the open sky. A large bell tower faced the sea from a promontory. Boris learned in school that Crimea had ancient Greek colonies but he never believed they existed until that day he walked Chersonesos' narrow streets.

He rode back to the monastery deep in thought, changed but not sure how. Without speaking to anyone, he went to sleep in the 19th century stucco building that served as the cloister.

Anton watched him during their breakfast of cottage cheese and fresh lavash flatbread sold by a Crimean Tatar woma on a rusty bicycle. When Boris left to go to the caves to pray, Anton followed him, even leaving his radio playing on the rough hewn table in the refectory.

The tall monk opened his mouth to speak when Ivan-the-Novice burst into the cave shouting: "He's going! They just announced it! That cursed Ukrainian Patriarch is going to Constantinople."

Anton's long frame snapped to attention in the cave's candlelit chambers. "He's going? When?"

"He's already left but the meeting is scheduled for Friday," Ivan said with a shaky voice.

"Two days from now," said Anton. "Where?"

"I don't know. I only heard that he's going to Constantinople to meet with the Ecumenical Patriarch.

"Brother Boris," said Anton, his voice sharp. "Isn't Hagia Sophia the Ecumenical Patriarch's seat?"

Boris had no idea. None of the monks at the Kiev Cave Monastery had much education. But his heart sank. The last weeks lulled him into believing that Anton's suicidal terrorist plot wouldn't come to pass.

Terrorist plot. For the first time, Boris said the words, even to himself. He fell to his knees on the cave's smooth stone floor and bent his head over his clasped hands, trying to ignore Anton's agitated questioning of their host. He repeated the Lord's Prayer to bring him spiritual peace. But blood pounded his brain, and cold sweat covered his brow. The cave's earthy smell made him nauseous

"We must go," Anton said, shaking Boris's shoulder and rousing him reluctantly to his feet.

"Go where?" asked Ivan, following Anton as he pushed Boris out of the cave.

"There's no time to explain," said Anton. "You must help us stop this meeting."

"Stop it," Ivan asked with surprise. "How?"

Anton didn't hide his impatience. "We need a boat to get to Constantinople."

The novice opened his mouth wide in disbelief. "Praise God if you can stop that impostor from meeting with the Ecumenical Patriarch. But that's more than 500 kilometers away."

Anton ignored the doubts. "We can do it by Friday."

Ivan held up his palms in acquiescence. "The entire Black Sea Fleet is outside our gate."

Anton swung open the heavy wooden door of the monastery and barked at Boris: "Harness the horse!" He turned back to Ivan. "Is there still a fishing fleet here?"

"No," said Ivan. "They closed it two years ago."

Anton asked more questions but Boris didn't hear the answers as he glumly descended the stairs into the courtyard. Dora muzzled the ground for stray bits of hay, blowing puffs of dust. She lifted her head as he approached and nickered when he laid his cheek on her neck. After a moment's respite, Anton appeared with Ivan in tow.

"What are you doing? We have to go."

Boris turned around. "I haven't given her the morning feeding yet."

"We don't have time."

Boris stood his ground. "We're not going anywhere until I give her water and hay."

Ivan brightened. "I'll help you."

Punching his palms in frustration, Anton paced the courtyard. "Alright," he said.

Boris took Dora's water bucket from the wagon and followed Ivan to a rusty shed made of corrugated metal with a dirt floor. The well was in the back, behind a birch dressed in bright yellow autumn leaves.

Boris walked as slowly as possible, praying for something – anything – to stop Anton's plot. But when he returned with the water, he found Dora munching on a mound of hay that it didn't take her long to finish. After she took a long drink of water, Boris harnessed her and clambered into the wagon. His robe was still dusty after his ride to Chersonesos. *It won't matter when I'm dead.* Sadness permeated his being.

Anton climbed in and Ivan opened the gate, but then Anton told Boris to stop when they passed through. The wagon lurched when Ivan jumped nimbly on top.

"He'll show us the way," Anton explained. "Then he'll drive the wagon back with the potatoes. They'll write to the Protector Monastery to tell them that she's here."

Boris didn't know what Anton told the young novice. But through the dark noise of his despair, he felt a single note of gladness that the mare would have a home.

Ivan pointed to the cracked and dusty road ahead. "We take this to the end."

Boris clucked to the mare and the wagon wheels groaned as she pulled her load past sandstone cliffs and scruffy collective farms, shriveled and dry, their irrigation pipes empty. He gazed at the horizon, where the Black Sea met the sky in a deepening blue and a warship floated motionless in the distance. The sun burned high in the sky.

"Turn right here," said Ivan when they reached a dirt road that took them down a barren hillside surrounded by cement mixers, bulldozers and rolls of mysterious metal. A three storey concrete building with glassed verandas and wood trim displayed a large mural of a tranquil sailboat against a shining sun.

"Stop," said Anton and Boris closed his hands on the reins. The tall monk's eyes searched the site in silence.

"There's no one here," said Ivan, climbing out of the wagon. "One of the officers is building this for his summer cottage, and he's illegally using Black Sea Fleet recruits to do the work for free. They have to return to their base at five o'clock to avoid hazing."

Hazing in the military was brutal and deadly.

Anton climbed out of the wagon. "Where's the pier?" he asked.

Ivan pointed behind the building. "Over there, you can see the trawler. That's what they use to deliver the construction materials. The officer must have taken the boat from the fishing fleet. He uses it as though it belongs to him, just like he uses the draftees. They all do it. He makes the recruits steal gasoline from the fleet, too. A few of them help out at the monastery because they feel guilty about the lying and stealing."

Anton grunted. "Godless thieves," he said, picking his way around the debris on the ground to walk towards the pier. "But if it's stolen, it won't be theft if we take it."

Boris stayed in the wagon, not even trying to hide his misery. He helped Anton steal the nuclear weapon, and now he was helping him steal a boat because he was a coward and too weak to stop him. *I'll end up in hell*, he thought with an existential shudder.

Anton returned after inspecting the trawler's gas and water tanks. "There's more than enough to get us to Istanbul."

"What are you going to do?" asked Ivan.

"We're going to stop them," said Anton, directing his gaze at Boris. "Out of the wagon. We have to go."

Boris didn't move. "But it's almost dark," he protested.

Anton reached for the duffle bag. The round outline of the ZBV3 artillery shell strained against the fabric. "Ivan has to return to the monastery while there is still light. We'll have just enough time to leave the bay and drop anchor before anyone can see us."

Boris clenched his jaw but he climbed out of the wagon.

"Take the water bucket and fill it," Anton commanded pointing at a well near the cement mixer.

Boris took one potato at a time and dropped it into the bucket.

"Hurry up," said Anton, shoving Boris aside and grabbing the bucket. After filling it with potatoes, he carried it towards the pier, the duffle bag heavy in his other hand. "You can go now, Brother Ivan," he called as he climbed into the boat and took the potatoes and duffel bag inside the cabin.

Boris watched Ivan take up the reins with a practiced hand. He could still escape. He could go back to the Inkerman monastery and live out his life, praying in the caves and riding Dora around the Greek ruins in Chersonesos. He thought he cared about the unity of their Orthodox Church, but it couldn't be God's will that they blow up a city with a nuclear bomb. *What kind of cruel God is that?*

"I'm not going," he shouted to Anton when he emerged from the cabin with empty hands.

"What do you mean?" asked Ivan. "You must stop the meeting!"

Boris nervously twisted the tip of his beard when Anton leaped off the boat, his eyes hard. "No," he said, his voice quaking. "Not the way that he wants to stop it." He jerked his chin at the tall monk, trying to muster a challenge.

"Don't you dare," said Anton, raising his fist to strike Boris to the ground with a powerful blow. "Get the hell out of here, now!" he shouted at Ivan, who quickly obeyed, driving the wagon up the road and out of sight.

Anton pulled Boris to his feet and shoved him towards the trawler. "You're going with me."

Boris's heart felt ready to burst from fear. "Why? Why do I have to go? You don't need me to do this."

Anton shoved him so hard that Boris fell on the pier, scraping his hands on the rough wood when the tall monk grabbed his arm and pulled him to his feet, pushing him into the boat. Boris fell again and curled into a corner, covering his head with his cowl.

Anton untied the boat from the dock and climbed back in, glaring at Boris with contempt.

"You know too much," he said and then disappeared into the cabin to start the engine.

CHAPTER 15

MISSING

FAXNEWS-UKRAINE

October 1, 1993 (Kiev, Ukraine). Russian warhead experts in Ukraine at Kiev's invitation identified two warheads that need repairs in Russia because of a dangerous build-up of explosive hydrogen gas.

October 2, 1993 (Chernobyl, Ukraine). Twenty-one nuclear fuel rods are missing from the Chernobyl power plant. Since the evacuation of more than 100,000 people after the 1986 disaster, the Zone is a magnet for vagrants.

October 2-4, 1993 (Moscow, Russia). After the Russian President dissolved the parliament and called new elections, the parliament's supporters put up barricades and blocked traffic. On the morning of October 4, tanks began firing at the building and by evening, the Vice President and leaders of parliament were under arrest.

October 5, 1993 (Chernihiv, Ukraine). Border control detained two nuclear warheads on a train to Russia. "The warhead's custodians said that they needed repairs," said a border agent. "But they will remain here until we receive the proper documentation."

October 7, 1993 (Kiev, Ukraine). Ukraine wants to bid for Nunn-Lugar disarmament money. "We are up to the job and much less expensive than American military contractors."
END

Faxnews-Ukraine – Your source of English-language news about Ukraine

TOP SECRET – PURPLE
Handle via Agent Channels Only
Date: October 8, 1993
To: K3
From: Deputy Chief of Station Kiev
Subject: SITREP Rasputin
(TS) 1. There has been no word from White.
(TS) 2. A North Korean staying in Room 148 of the Dnipro
Hotel, registered as Hong Gil-dong, returned from Kharkiv with
diagrams of ballistic missile guidance systems.
(U) 3. Parliament examined START today without making a
decision on ratification.
END
TOP SECRET PURPLE
Exempt from automatic downgrade

TOP SECRET – GREEN
Handle via Agent Channels Only
Date: October 9, 1993
To: K3
From: Chief of Base Istanbul
Subject: SITREP Fertilizer
(S) 1. Neil Neilson and Dan Kruger arrived in Istanbul with the
Independent Ukrainian Orthodox Church Patriarch and Kostya Beniuk. An
assistant to Greek shipping magnate Pannaioties Kookouvaios, aka Coco,
met them at the airport and took them to the Bosporus Hotel near the Hagia
Sophia Museum. After one hour, Neilson and Kruger left the hotel in a taxi
which took them to the Ataturk Imports building on the Yerebatan Cd.
(S) 2. Kookouvaios was the suspect in a Greek investigation into a
1992 shipment of Serbian weapons to Somalia in violation of two UN
embargoes. But prosecutors found insufficient evidence.
(U) 3. Istanbul police arrested three Russian "shopping tourists" on
their way to Vladivostok and charged them with attempting to smuggle
four kilograms of heroin.
END
TOP SECRET GREEN
Exempt from automatic downgrade

*B*eing next to the Uzin bomber base, with summer cottages for many of the top brass, Dikanka boasted a better main road than most Ukrainian villages. But it didn't have streetlights and the sun was setting by the time their old Volga sedan trundled past the tall fences that barricaded every cottage against the outside world. Roman Rozpad recalled his shock when he went to America, where all the houses looked so open and exposed, with their expanses of green lawns and manicured yards. Ukrainians who didn't live in cities lived in villages, with nothing in between, like those American suburbs. Lucky urbanites had exurban vegetable gardens and *dachas*. But the Soviets prohibited people from making the summer cottages year-round living spaces. They couldn't even be insulated.

In a village, a lawn wasted space needed for orchards, chickens, pigs and the tiny, private gardens that made it possible to survive in the shortage-ridden Soviet economy.

Why am I thinking about gardens? Rozpad was no longer afraid. The German acted innocuously enough and introduced Rozpad to Tariq, the Arab who resembled the Iraqi Dictator; and Helga, the silent red-haired woman who drove the car.

Tanya must be confused and scared. But he had only one way to ensure her safety.

The familiar Dikanka scenery passed by his window. He knew who lived in each cottage. Few people moved. New people were born and old people died. Change came slowly in the village.

No one spoke as Helga drove with Claus in the front seat. The Great Dane spent the entire two-hour drive sitting at attention and dripping saliva, not once taking his eyes off his master and blocking Rozpad's view of the Arab.

"Slow down," he said as they approached his parents' house. He saw their new roof from a distance and swelled with pride at their self-sufficiency. Most of their generation couldn't cope with the disappearance of the old Soviet ways. "It's the house with the blue fence," he said. "Park on the street right in front of it. And leave the dog in the car."

The German tensed and the dog tilted his head, awaiting orders. "But Seggi is very well-trained," he said.

"That's good, but my parents' dogs aren't," said Rozpad, opening the car door. "They'll make an even bigger racket than normal, and that will attract unnecessary attention. This is a small village. Pretend that you are tourists and speak English."

The fence still smelled of its fresh coat of periwinkle blue paint and Rozpad opened the sheet metal gate to find Rosa making happy circles at the unexpected sight of one of her humans, then growling suspiciously when three strangers followed him into the yard. Her yipping prompted Lord, the Alsatian, to launch into his deep warning bark.

"Shut up, Rosa, and stay," he said, shoving the dog aside. She whimpered in offense but stayed, turning her head when Anastasia Rozpad stepped out of the house onto their new concrete steps.

"Romko!" she exclaimed, using his childhood nickname. "What a surprise! Petro!" she called back through the door. "Come outside! Roman is here with his friends!"

"What happened?" asked Petro Rozpad when he emerged from the cottage. "What's wrong?"

"Nothing's wrong," Rozpad said gaily, kissing his mother on the cheek. He and the German planned his cover story on the way. "My new foreign friends and I are returning to Kiev from Odessa."

"Why isn't Tanya with you?" asked his father, who considered the Arab with curiosity. His engagement had thrilled both his parents.

"Tanya has a big project for the committee," Rozpad said. "But my friends have never visited a Ukrainian village and since Dikanka is so close to the Odessa highway, I decided to bring them here for a little visit. We won't take long."

He introduced his companions with the ethnically neutral names of Eva, Peter and Kai. "They speak English," he said, watching them inspect everything as though seeing it for the first time. Tariq acted his part, but Claus fixed his good eye on his host's missing arm and the World War II medal pinned to his chest. Helga lifted one corner of her mouth in a reasonable imitation of curiosity.

His mother wiped her hands on her apron and then opened them in welcome. "Well, you must come in for tea."

"Thank you, momma, but we don't have time," said Rozpad, herding his group on a path through the orchard. "I want to show them around while it's still light. Is the flashlight in the shed?"

"It usually is." Petro had taken off his prosthetic and tucked his empty sweater sleeve into the pocket of his cardigan as he followed his wife behind the visitors.

"We've had a great month, Roman," said Anastasia.

"Have you?" said Rozpad, distracted.

"A big, big sale," said Petro. "Our biggest – to Kazakhstan. Since your uncle started paying the wine company, we can buy a hundred crates at a time – nothing like the small potatoes he took skimming off the top."

Anastasia continued: "We found another Kazakhstan connection at the farmers market. The man imports Caucasian tomatoes but he had an empty truck going to Almaty for watermelons and he bought 150 crates of wine from us. Your uncle sent two trucks to deliver it."

The Rozpads spoke Ukrainian, which the German did not understand, though the Arab seemed to pay attention.

"My parents have a wine business. Transcarpathian Reisling," he explained, leading the group through the yard. Lord lunged at his chain, barking at the strangers but unable to reach them. The chickens and ducks were oblivious but the geese honked and waved their wings menacingly.

"We earned 1600 bucks just on one contract," his mother announced, shooing away the geese. "That will give you a nice bonus after you do the paperwork."

"That's wonderful, Momma." Rozpad said. A bonus sounded good, so good that he felt guilty for agreeing to sell the HEU. The 100,000 dollars he agreed to accept might as well have been a million for all that it did not fit into Rozpad's financial experience the way that a 100 dollar bonus did. *But you're doing this for Tanya.* The reason consoled him but he knew he was doing something very, very wrong.

"And the Hungarian Snickers are selling well, too," added his father. "*Bizness* is good."

"Wonderful," Rozpad repeated, opening the door to go into the shed and leaving his parents to stand awkwardly with their strange guests.

"And where are you from?" Petro asked, directing his question to the group at large but Rozpad emerged just in time to stop anyone from answering. He didn't want his father to find out that he had two Germans in his yard.

"Oh, we can chat later," he said, beckoning for the group to follow him up the gravel path past the pasture where the grey mare swiped at flies with her tail.

Petro watched his son heading for the old root cellar. "What do you need in there?"

Rozpad wondered that himself and stopped at the cellar's battered iron door to wave his hand at Claus. "My friend here has a passion for carriage driving and he wants me to show him our old wagon wheels."

"Whatever for?" asked Anastasia.

Rozpad and Claus discussed this part. "He considers them antiques, from 1956, when Khrushchev made the peasants slaughter their horses."

"That idiot called our horses useless because they gave neither milk nor meat," Petro exclaimed, pointing an angry finger at the injustice. "He said that now that we have tractors, horses should be ground up for sausage. He thought one tractor could replace a hundred horses. What a cretin. What a disaster!"

"I remember, dear," Anastasia said, patting her husband's back. "They made us burn the wagon for firewood."

"But I saved those wheels." It was Petro's political rebellion.

"They don't understand you, *Tato*," said Rozpad, using the old endearment for his father. But he noticed that the Arab's brow was sweating despite the cool autumn air and he kept jerking at the quietest sounds. *He's waiting for someone.*

A sudden shiver passed through him. *Maybe this is a trick, to catch me. Neil Neilson said that the Americans are watching.*

"And? Petro urged him on.

"And what?" Rozpad's thoughts raced. He wasn't breaking the law. The criminal code that Ukraine inherited from the Soviet Union didn't prohibit nuclear smuggling. The possibility never occurred to the code's drafters in their tightly controlled totalitarian state. But if he got caught and the Americans made a stink, he would lose job at the commission. *You have to take the risk for Tanya. You don't know what they're capable of doing to her.*

"What about the wheel?" Petro repeated, jerking Rozpad out of his thoughts.

He opened the squeaky door to the root cellar. "My friend is here to buy horses," he continued. "Our Ukrainian horses are very fine, and very cheap. He wants a wagon wheel from 1956 as a souvenir for his stables to symbolize the rebirth of the Ukrainian breed. I think it's a nice gesture to give him one."

"You want to give him my wheels?" Petro exclaimed. "It was a big risk, taking them. I was almost a dissident."

Anastasia pursed her lips. "That stuff is junk, Petro. I've wanted to throw it our for years."

"It's not junk," the old man insisted. "It's not junk if it has meaning."

"Is there a problem?" the German asked in English, as innocently a scar-faced, half-blind nuclear smuggler could.

"Keep quiet," Rozpad responded in English. "I will handle it." The Arab kept swiveling his head, peering into corners, as though looking for someone.

"He just wants one wheel," Rozpad argued to his father. "Not the whole set."

"Three wheels are no longer a set," Petro said, wagging a finger.

Anastasia disagreed. "Let's get rid of them, Petro, and the other junk in that cellar, too."

"What do you care?" Petro responded. "They're not in your way."

"They are, and you know it."

"You can throw out everything else, but I'm keeping the wheels."

"You haven't given a thought to them years, and now they're so important?"

Rozpad tried very hard not to sound desperate. "I am sure that my friend will pay you for them."

"Pay?" Petro's face transformed from angry peasant to shrewd businessman. "Pay how much?"

Rozpad sighed with relief. "Why don't we show them to him first?" He motioned to the German to follow him down the dirt stairs only to find his father right behind him.

"Where are you going?" he asked.

"Into the cellar," Petro responded.

Rozpad couldn't let his father see the lead bottles of HEU. "But it'll be too crowded with three people," he argued. "Wait up here."

His father insisted. "There's plenty of room."

Claus Hesse blew out an exasperated "*Scheisse*". "This is bullshit," he said in Russian and barked in German at Helga, who leaped behind Rozpad's mother and grabbed her, holding a knife to her throat.

"My God," Anastasia shrieked. "What is going on?"

"Grab the father," Claus ordered Tariq and gave Rozpad a shove: "Now let's do business."

*T*ariq grabbed Petro Rozpad, certain that his prisoner felt him trembling. Terror made his hands slippery but the old man stood still when Helga raised the knife closer to his wife's throat.

"Do what you want," he pleaded. "Just don't hurt her."

Tariq kept an expectant watch while Rozpad and the German disappeared into the root cellar and closed the door. But all he saw was the grey mare grazing in the pasture. Then he heard the slightest whisper and the mare raised her head in attention when Helga grunted and collapsed into a heap on the ground, releasing Anastasia. Tariq let go of the old man in surprise when he saw the familiar woman standing over Helga. She often frequented the Night Bar, with the Americans.

"It's me, Cristina Smythe, the other agent," she whispered in English to Tariq, keeping her attention on Helga, who recovered enough to try to get up. "I don't think so," said Cristina, and pushed the other woman back to the ground with her foot.

The other agent is a woman? Tariq was almost as shocked as when Sveta first displayed her savvy intelligence and so he didn't notice Helga holding the German's Makarov. But Cristina did and shot her with split second timing.

The frightened Rozpads peeked from behind the barn and she held out her palm for them to stay back. "Stay there. It's OK." She turned to Tariq. "Where did they go?"

Tariq saw too many deaths in the Dictator's safe houses to be troubled by Helga's. But the potential consequences of Claus discovering his CIA connection made his knees tremble. "In there," he said, poking his chin at the cellar.

Cristina turned to him. "We have to maintain your cover," she whispered, looking around to spot a length of rope on a wooden bench. She pulled his hands behind his back, wound the rope around his wrists and held a gun to his head. "Pretend you're a hostage," she said, pushing him towards the root cellar.

*W*ith the German following, Rozpad stepped into the darkness, his flashlight weakly illuminating the path before him. He had to reach the corner where he had hidden the HEU. But just as he walked past the old wagon wheels, the door burst open and a beam of daylight streamed into the cellar.

Rozpad turned but the bright light disoriented him and he could only see the dark silhouette of a slim woman with a mane of curls, holding a gun to the Arab's head.

"Go in there," she growled in American-accented Russian and pushed the Arab into the cellar, where he collapsed into a heap. With a gun in each hand, she aimed at Rozpad and the German. "Hand's up for the CIA, gentlemen. You can call me Cristina."

"Roman Petrovich," she said, referring to Rozpad formally, with his name and patronymic. "I know why you're here," she said, staring straight at him. "Show me."

Rozpad pointed at the German. "First, make him tell me where my fiancée is. She's innocent in this."

Cristina motioned at Claus with her gun. "Do it!" The German pointed to his pocket with his raised hand and at her nod, lowered it to pull out a slip of paper with a legitimate address on the outskirts of Kiev, a place where the German never went – unless he wanted to hide a hostage.

"I am cooperating with you," he said to the American. "I am doing nothing that is illegal in my country. This must not affect my job or reputation."

Cristina waved her gun. "We'll discuss that later. Let's move it."

The light from outdoors didn't penetrate the far corners of the root cellar and Rozpad moved cautiously in the poor light, smelling the mildew and soil. Glad that the American woman showed up to stop the deal, he shined the flashlight on the lead bottles of HEU. "Here it is. One hundred kilos."

Cristina exclaimed: "What the hell?" and he looked at the circle of light to see... nothing, nothing but the packed dirt floor.

"What?" he shouted, waving the weak flashlight around the root cellar. But there were no lead bottles of HEU. "I have to find out what happened," he said, with a sincere note of panic that persuaded Cristina to step aside, letting Rozpad race up the steps. She motioned with her gun for the German to follow. "I'll deal with you later," she told the Arab and climbed out of the root cellar.

Rozpad raced ahead, ignoring Helga's motionless body pooled in blood, and called for his parents, who emerged from behind the barn, his mother crying and shaking. "What the devil is going on, son?" demanded Petro, pointing at Cristina. "And what is she doing here?"

"Forget that," he said, feeling sweat bead his back. "When did you clean out the root cellar?"

Anastasia interrupted her crying. "We didn't clean it out."

"But it's empty except for the wagon wheels. Where did everything else go?"

"We didn't see anything else. That's why we put the wines in there," explained Petro.

Rozpad shook his head in confusion. "What wines?"

"The wine shipment to Kazakhstan," said his mother, visibly calmer. "It overflowed the barn, so we stored the extra bottles in the old root cellar until the trucks arrived."

Petro interrupted. "I told the driver to take all the bottles." The old man waved towards the east. "They're all in Kazakhstan."

CHAPTER 16

CONSTANTINOPLE

FAXNEWS-UKRAINE

October 8, 1993 (Kiev, Ukraine). During an impromptu discussion in the halls of parliament, the President of Ukraine said calls to keep the nuclear weapons are "populist slogans". "We can target the weapons. We can launch them. We have that capability – if we want it. We can move warheads around. But we are not able to get at the nuclear package inside them. Without that, we cannot keep them safe or battle ready."

October 9, 1993 (Kiev, Ukraine). The American Secretary of State arrived here today to sign an agreement creating an international scientific center to provide jobs for scientists and engineers who used to work for the military industrial complex. He said that Washington welcomes Ukraine's destruction of SS-19 missiles but its primary focus is on deactivating nuclear warheads. "The missiles are not as important," he said. "But during the Cold War, silo destruction was all that we could verify."
END

Faxnews-Ukraine – Your source of English-language news about Ukraine

TOP SECRET – PURPLE
Handle via Agent Channels Only
Date: **October 10, 1993**
To: **K3**
From: **Deputy Chief of Station Kiev**
Subject: **SITREP Rasputin**
(TS) 1. The 100 kilos of HEU are now in Kazakhstan.
(S) 2. Neither Roman Rozpad nor Claus Hesse can be prosecuted under Ukrainian law. Nuclear smuggling is not a crime.

(S)   3. Take this as my notice. I am quitting as DCS of Kiev as well as my inspector job at Tambrands. I am going to work as the Placement Director of a business school for women here in Kiev. Irina and I married last week. She will head the school's Accounting Department and is designing Ukraine's first curriculum for teaching generally accepted accounting practices.

END

TOP SECRET GREEN
Handle via Agent Channels Only
Date: October 10, 1993
To: K3
From: Chief of Base Istanbul
Subject: SITREP Fertilizer

(S) 1. Neil Neilson and Dan Kruger closed their deal with Ataturk Imports yesterday. Today, they are touring Istanbul with a guide from their hotel. They are leaving tomorrow on Pan Am Fl. 331.

(U) 2. The Independent Ukrainian Orthodox Church Patriarch and translator Kostya Beniuk are at the hotel preparing to meet with the Ecumenical Patriarch.

(TS) 3. This file is closed.

---

*B*oris held up his hand to shield his eyes. Anton dropped anchor for the night near Balaklava, and set out in the morning with the rising sun stabbing Boris's face. He spent a sleepless night crouched in a corner, thankful for his heavy robe in the Black Sea's cool night air. Keeping low to avoid the wind as Anton pushed the trawler into top speed, Boris smelled the old boat's gasoline and an occasional whiff of salty sea air.

Staring miserably at the water, he pulled his robe across his chest and clasped his hands, trying to pray. But he didn't know what to pray for. *Bring down your hand, Lord, to stop this.* Or maybe, instead, pray for the courage to stop it himself?

But he felt even more helpless as the hours passed and he dozed in the sun. When he awoke, his head ached where Anton hit him and his lips were cracked. He stole a glimpse of his companion – now captor – as he busied himself inside the cabin.

Anton unzipped the duffle bag and lifted the artillery shell onto a rusted locker. Its metal casing had a dull shine and the red tip was like a beacon in the sun. Boris couldn't see any buttons or switches but Anton rigged it with mysterious bits of metal and wires that led to the small box he rested on the locker. Boris couldn't see it well and didn't want to attract Anton's attention, so he turned back to staring at the horizon. Sea and sky merged into a blue alloy but the tranquil view couldn't still the churning of his stomach or fill the hollow in his heart. *I am going to hell.*

Anton flipped a switch on the trawler's short-wave radio and it crackled, spitting static. Twisting the dial this way and that, he turned up the volume when he found his target: Ukrainian radio for foreign broadcasting. Once a propaganda arm of the KGB aimed at émigrés, it had become the propaganda arm of the independent government. Anton said he would explode the warhead when the radio announced the meeting of the Patriarchs at the Hagia Sophia.

The announcer had a woman on the phone from Istanbul. "We're staying here at the Bosporus Hotel with a group of shopping tourists," the woman said in Russian. "We saw the Patriarch on our plane and he is also staying here. We're by the Hagia Sophia."

"And what is the atmosphere?" the announcer asked in Ukrainian.

"The atmosphere?" replied the woman.

"What do the people of Istanbul have to say about the Patriarch?"

For a moment, the woman said nothing. "We haven't heard anything. No one knows he's here."

Anton gripped the boat's wheel. "We know he's there."

The radio spit more static before the announcer went on: "You must have seen something at the hotel."

Boris heard a roomful of boisterous female chatter. "My friend saw him at breakfast this morning," the woman reported. "He ate an omelet."

The announcer thanked the woman and then addressed listeners. "Unfortunately, we at Radio Ukraine International lack the resources to send our own reporter to Istanbul for today's historical meeting of the Ecumenical Patriarch with His Holiness the Patriarch of the Independent Ukrainian Orthodox Church. But stay tuned for our next guest, an expert in the history of Ukrainian Orthodoxy."

Anton spat. "How can it have a history if the cursed thing spawned a few months ago?"

Boris said nothing. The radio barely penetrated the dense fog of his despair. He tried to pray but *"You are going to burn in hell for eternity"* repeated in an endless loop in his mind. The radio droned folk songs in the background as seagulls squawked overhead. Anton glanced at them, peered into the distance and announced: "We're close to land."

The gay music pained Boris's ears but mercifully ended. After a short reading of the news, including a disappointing nationwide wheat harvest, the announcer returned with her expert guest, a former dissident poet who started up a Ukrainian Orthodox newspaper.

He had a reedy voice and the perfect pronunciation of the generation for whom speaking Ukrainian had once been a subversive act. He talked for a long time, going back to 988, when Kievan Rus' – the empire of the East Slavs – accepted Christianity of the Eastern Rite from Byzantium. This happened before the Great Schism of 1054, when Christendom split into the Catholics of Rome and the Orthodox of Byzantium.

"No Russian church existed then. The Ecumenical Patriarch of Constantinople appointed a Kiev Metropolitan – which is equivalent to a Catholic cardinal," said the expert, prompting Anton to slam his hand against the cabin wall. "Those cursed bourgeois nationalists want to steal our history. Rus' *was* Russia!" he exclaimed.

Boris roused from his miserable torpor and listened as the expert continued.

"For the next 500 years, the Kiev Metropolitan acted as the center of Orthodoxy in the former lands of Rus even when the seat moved north from Kiev to Vladimir in 1299 and then to the lands of Muscovy in 1325."

"They did that for the Church's safety after the Mongol invasion of Rus' in 1240, right?"

The expert chuckled. "That is what Russian imperial historians want you to believe. Remember, Muscovy was under the Mongols at that time – in fact, the city of Moscow flourished under the Golden Horde."

"I find it interesting that you don't call it Russia."

"That's what it was, damn it. *Russia.*" Anton argued with the radio.

But the expert argued back. "Our modern vocabulary becomes more misleading the further we go into the past. Only in nationalist fantasy can the word 'Russia' stand for a kind of platonic form, immanent even when invisible, constant in essence, though variable in its historic embodiments. Kievan Rus and Muscovy were not "Russia" and it is wrong to call them that. Remember, our northern neighbor didn't start using the name "Russia" until the 18th century."

Anton shouted at the radio, his face red with anger. "This is what we have to put a stop to. This is bullshit!"

But Boris listened, rapt. He never heard of such things, not in the Communist history he learned in school or at the Kievan Cave Monastery. *A Russian Orthodox monastery.*

"But back to the church..." The announcer prompted.

The guest continued. "Now, the Ecumenical Patriarch did not approve the move to Moscow. It violated canon law.

"But by 1439, all that remained of the great Byzantine civilization was the city of Constantinople. The rest had fallen to the Ottoman Turks. So, in the hopes of winning western support, the embattled Ecumenical Patriarch agreed to a reunion with the Roman Catholics. Though the reunion didn't last very long, the Muscovite prince opposed it and in 1448, the bishops of Muscovy elected their own Patriarch – without the permission of the Ecumenical Patriarch and in violation of canon law."

"This happened before the Ottoman Turks captured Constantinople, in 1453?"

"Yes," said the expert. "But in Moscow they saw the union with Rome as a betrayal of Orthodoxy. They considered the Ecumenical Patriarch an apostate and didn't want him appointing the head of their church. After Constantinople fell to the Turks, they saw the Ecumenical Patriarch as a tool of the infidels and started having illusions of greatness as the Third Rome."

The announcer interrupted. "So, this took place in Muscovy. What about Ukraine?"

Boris could hear the expert smiling. "In the same way it's incorrect to call Muscovy "Russia", it's also incorrect to call anything "Ukraine" during this period. But the southwest lands of Rus – most of which are now central and western Ukraine – came under the Grand Duchy of Lithuania. The Lithuanians reestablished an Orthodox Metropolitan in Kiev, subject to the Patriarch of Constantinople. It took more than a century for the Ecumenical Patriarch to recognize the legitimacy of the Russian church."

"So, it is historically ironic for the Russian Orthodox Church to accuse our Ukrainian Patriarch of violating canon law," said the announcer.

The expert murmured agreement.

Anton punched his palm. "Russia became the Third Rome after the fall of Constantinople. How could it have violated canon law if it was the one true church?"

The expert ignored him. "So, for centuries, a separate Orthodox church in what are now Ukrainian lands answered to the Ecumenical Patriarch. In fact, the Ukrainian Kozaks rose in the 16th century in part to defend Orthodoxy from the Catholic Poles and the Muslim Turks. In 1686 – after the Kozaks signed the ill-fated Pereyaslav treaty that put them under Moscow's protection – the Russian Patriarch subordinated the Kiev Metropolitan. It was just one step in the complete absorption of Ukraine into the Russian Empire. "

"Nationalist fairy tales." Anton spat. "They were gathering Rus' lands, reuniting Ukraine with Russia."

"I notice that you used "Ukraine" in this context, even though it had no legal existence in the Empire," said the announcer.

The expert coughed. "The first record of the word comes from Rus times and also in Kozak times. But in the 19ᵗʰ century, our intelligentsia began using the name "Ukraine" more frequently. For most of the previous centuries, we called ourselves Rusyns or Ruthenians – from the word Rus'.""

"We were always told that Ukraine means frontier, on the edge," said the announcer.

"That could be true for people living elsewhere, who saw this land as a frontier to be conquered." The expert audibly sipped and swallowed. "But for the people who lived here, *Ukraiina* meant "in the country", from the word *kraiina* – country."

A certainty began stirring inside Boris as the interview took a musical break. But Anton stopped listening.

"We're here," he announced. "The Bosphorus." He unfolded a map that Ivan-the-Novice found in a bag left by a rock climber making his way from the Black to the Baltic Seas. "We'll find the Hagia Sophia in the Sultanahmet district," he said, steering the boat south into the Sea of Marmara.

For the first time, Boris peered out of his corner to see outside the trawler. A broad expanse of blue sea sparkled in the sunlight, straddled by a suspension bridge. He could see another bridge in the distance. It reminded him of the bridges spanning the Dnieper back in Kiev. Before this nightmare, he could see them every day from the Cave Monastery's perch on the river's hilly banks. It had been a peaceful time for him *until Anton decided himself the arbiter of truth.*

Sundry boats and ships crowded the waters, flying a variety of colorful flags and suddenly Boris noticed that the trawler didn't have one. Anton directed the boat to a secluded spot in a grove not far from the shore and put down anchor. The stone walls of an old fortress peered above the trees and distant minarets pierced the sky.

When Boris returned his attention to the radio, the expert reached the Soviet period of his historical discourse. "After the Russian Empire collapsed, Ukraine declared independence and attempted to re-establish an independent Ukrainian Orthodox Church. But the Communists crushed all religion and the Ukrainian church survived in exile. When Stalin allowed the re-emergence of the Russian Orthodox Church to unify the population during World War II, the Ukrainian S.S.R. had a Kiev Metropolitan subordinate to the Russian Patriarch. Just talking about a separate Ukrainian Orthodox church landed people in the gulag. The Ukrainian Catholic Church suffered even worse persecution, but that is a subject for a different day."

"And the Patriarch of the Independent Ukrainian Orthodox Church used to be the Kiev Metropolitan of the Russian Orthodox Church," said the announcer, "which, after that fascinating historical excursion, brings us back to today and the historical meeting of our Patriarch with the Ecumenical Patriarch of Constantinople. We'll return to that subject after another musical break."

Folk music poured out the radio and Anton grimaced in distaste. "Stupid Ukrainian peasants singing."

His stirring certainty burst out of Boris in a rage. "I am Ukrainian, goddam it!" he exclaimed, leaping to his feet and not caring about Anton's superior height and heft. *I'm going to hell anyway if I don't stop him.* "Have you been listening to the radio? The period of time when Ukrainians' had their own Orthodox church on their territory is much longer than all the time they spent as a part of the Russian church. And now that we have an independent country, we have every right to our own Orthodox Church."

Anton punched his fist. "You dare go against the message from God?"

Boris laughed with contempt, filled with a courage he could finally feel. He had nothing to lose. "God didn't send us a message. Your psychotic head did. You accuse Ukrainians of nationalism when you're preparing to sacrifice an entire city to save your mythical 'Russia'." Boris waved his arms in the air as though beholding a sacred vision as he spoke, and then leaned against the railing.

"You are an insane mass murderer and you will burn in hell."

The tall monk's face reddened with rage but Boris sidestepped his assault and darted towards the warhead, grabbing the makeshift trigger before Anton could reach him. Lunging back to the railing to throw it into the water, he tripped when Anton dove for his feet and when he fell to the floor, the trigger tumbled across the boards. Anton seized it, put it behind him and rose to his feet, eying Boris murderously. But the young monk spun away to leap onto the railing, suspending for just a moment before swiveling to dive into the cold water.

His robe was heavy but he didn't have to swim far to the shore. Perhaps he would have a few hours to pray for forgiveness.

"You'll never find me," yelled Anton. "Don't even try."

*T*he Hagia Sophia swarmed with people, mostly tourists judging by the number of tour guides and the babble of languages. A dome as high as a concrete sky capped the enormous, elaborately decorated interior that smelled of ancient stone and fresh paint. Neil Neilson craned his neck to examine the ceiling. It seemed to float on an arcade of arched windows that flooded the interior with light.

"There are 40 windows under the dome," said their English-speaking tour guide, following Neilson's gaze. "It gives it a sense of lightness."

"Very impressive," said Neilson. He had been in few comparable architectural achievements.

"For over a thousand years, Hagia Sophia was the Church of Holy Wisdom, the largest church in Christendom – until the Spanish completed the cathedral in Seville in 1520," said the guide.

"Emperor Constantine built it?" Neilson asked, recalling his hazy knowledge of Byzantium.

"No," said the guide, a wiry fellow with a British accent. "Emperor Constantine, the first Christian emperor of Rome, founded Constantinople when he moved the capital of the Roman Empire from the West to the East. He rebuilt a Greek trading colony called Byzantium around 330 and renamed it Constantinople, the capitol of the Eastern Roman Empire."

The guide raised his hand towards the dome. "Hagia Sophia – one of the most advanced and ambitious monuments of late antiquity – was built two centuries later, in 537, for the Ecumenical Patriarch, the leader of the Eastern Catholic Church and, after the 1054 schism, leader of the Orthodox Church.

The guide peppered them with facts and dates as he led them past galleries and loges and towering scaffolding used for restoration works. Every surface was adorned with intricate geometric designs or glistening mosaics, reflecting the warm afternoon light streaming into the dome.

"When Constantinople fell in 1453, the Ottoman Turks covered the mosaics of human figures with plaster because of the Muslim prohibition on depictions of people." The guide swept his arm at a mosaic of the Virgin Mary holding the baby Jesus on her lap. "For almost 500 years after that, this was the *Ayasofiya* mosque. Many of the geometric designs represent the Muslim artistic influence."

Neilson glanced at Kruger, who tapped his foot.

"She's fine, Dan. Stop worrying," he whispered, knowing the futility. Kruger had been in a funk since they closed the deal with Ataturk and he called Jean at their designated time to tell her. When he heard the answering machine, he called his mother-in-law, who didn't have one and didn't answer either.

"Yeah," Kruger whispered back. "Jean's mother is a lot of help, too. But I feel guilty leaving her with the baby. Those were rough months."

"At least try to keep your mind off it. That's why we're on this tour." With a dash of bravado, Neilson added: "Think about becoming a millionaire. That money will be in our Lichtenstein bank by the time we get home."

Kruger said little as they followed the guide past mighty stone columns bearing enormous medallions inscribed with Arabic lettering.

"These were hung during the mosque's restoration around 1850," said the guide. "They proclaim the names of Allah, the Prophet Muhammad, the first four caliphs and Mohammad's grandchildren Hassan and Husain."

The guide stopped them in a gallery where a monk kneeled, his cowl covering his face as he prayed below a mosaic of Christ.

"Mosaics became visible for the first time in centuries when restorers cleaned them of plaster. In 1935, the father of modern Turkey Mustafa Kemal Ataturk made *Ayasofya* a museum, but many of the visitors don't know that – especially people from the former Soviet Union. They are badly informed because Soviet society was so closed. Many still think it is the seat of the Ecumenical Patriarch," said the guide.

"Because of its long history as both a church – the Hagia Sophia – and a mosque – the *Ayasofya* – the restoration process must be balanced. In order to uncover Christian mosaics, restorers must destroy important Islamic art. So, they've tried to balance by restoring important mosaics, while leaving the rest of the Islamic art intact. A few of the smaller crosses remain covered."

While the guide lectured them about the difficulties of restoration, Neilson craned his neck to see the ceiling, where a smear of plaster replaced a missing piece in a jigsaw puzzle of colorful lozenges, circles and stylized stars. When he looked back down, the monk roused from his prayers, his sad face stricken with shock.

"Hey Dan," he said, bumping him with his elbow when the monk rose to his feet.

The monk's damp hair and beard hung on his equally damp robe as he approached them warily. "Ahhh," he gasped and tried to speak but stopped, rolling his gaze across the stone sky of the dome in search of something.

"What's with this guy?" said Kruger.

"I can't tell." Neilson saw the monk's hands tremble. "But he looks familiar."

"Not to me."

"We saw him when we visited Kostya's village, Dikanka, and that monastery. He was praying with another monk – a big guy – at that monument to a martyr. I remember him because you don't see that many guys with long blond hair in Kiev."

"All I remember from that morning is wanting to leave," said Kruger.

The guide didn't hear their whispered conversation, and continued his lecture with a history of the four large minarets that surrounded the museum, not caring if anyone listened or not. The monk eyed him suspiciously but entreated Neilson and Kruger with his gaze.

"He's scared," said Kruger, watching the monk.

"Sure is," Neilson agreed and wanted to suggest that they leave when the monk rushed forward and grabbed Kruger's arm, his face pleading. "I," he stammered. "I, uh."

Instinctively recoiling, Kruger brushed the monk's hand off his jacket. "Hey, watch it," he said, pushing the monk away.

"I…uh…I sorry," said the monk, backing away. "I no have words. No English." His eyes darted back and forth from Neilson to Kruger. "Dikanka. I see you."

"At the monastery," said Neilson.

The monk swallowed and clasped his hands to his chest. "You say." He stopped to gulp air. "You say," he repeated.

"What?" said Neilson, more curious than annoyed.

"Nuclear weapons," said the monk, hiccupping in fear. "Destroy Istanbul."

"What?" Neilson asked, incredulous.

Nervously pulling the tip of his beard, the monk repeated: "Nuclear weapons destroy Istanbul."

"That's crazy," said Kruger. "I may not remember much from that day, but I'd have remembered that."

Neilson didn't know what to say. So, he said: "No", shaking his head for emphasis. "No."

The monk gaped in revelation. "No?" he asked.

"No," said Neilson.

"No say 'nuclear weapons destroy Istanbul'?" The monk seemed as incredulous as Neilson.

"No," repeated Neilson.

The monk deflated; his face sagging with fear, despair and regret.

"Nuclear weapons destroy Istanbul," he said sadly and then he left them to go kneel by the mosaic, his clasped hands pressed into his forehead.

Anton Zvezda listened to the short-wave radio playing Ukrainian folk tunes. The cheerful peasant melodies pained his ears but he kept waiting for the regular reports tracking the imposter patriarch's movements. He glanced at the nuclear artillery shell with the complicated bypasses and rested his attention on the trigger. It had been a challenge to build. Luckily, that idiot Boris hadn't interfered.

Zvezda punched his palm at the thought of his traitorous erstwhile companion. *The fool.* He wasn't worried that the coward might try to stop him. Even if his pathetic display of backbone at the end could possibly endure, he wouldn't have enough time. Just minutes earlier, the radio announced that the imposter was preparing to leave his hotel.

Seagulls squawked overhead but he neither heard them, nor saw the afternoon sun glittering on the blue waters of the Golden Horn. He perceived no beauty and the far away minarets of Istanbul jabbed at his eyes. *Corrupt infidels. NATO lackeys.* Back in the Soviet days, when he worked on the nuclear submarines with the Black Sea Fleet, he learned of the plan to capture the Bosporus in case of war with NATO just long enough for the fleet's warships to escape into open seas. A magnificent port, Sevastopol had historically been difficult to defend and fell in both the Crimean and Great Fatherland wars.

Zvezda cleaned his nails with a knife while the folk music crackled on the radio. He felt no fear and did not pray. Power filled him and the vision of that scheming and schismatic imposter patriarch destroyed by the fireball of God's glory hastened his heart. "He deserves it," he said aloud.

They were traitors, weak-willed and corrupt; dismembering the one true canonical Orthodox Church at the time of Russia's greatest weakness. Moscow would once again gather Russian lands and regain her deserved power. Until then, only the Church could preserve her unity.

The radio announcer interrupted the music. "Dear listeners," he said. "We have the receptionist at the Bosporus Hotel on the phone."

His voice was familiar after several hours. He spoke Ukrainian mincingly, divesting it of any similarity to Russian. Despite himself, Anton picked up some of the deranged dialect in his time at Uzin. The peasants spoke it when he went to visit the monastery.

The announcer effortlessly switched to Russian to speak to the Turk. "We have a report that the Patriarch is going to the airport."

The receptionist responded in a heavy accent. "We have a taxi for him."

"This is a surprise," said the announcer. "We thought he was to meet the Ecumenical Patriarch this afternoon. Can you call him to the phone, please?"

Zvezda's heart stopped.

"What the fuck?" He asked the radio for an explanation.

Instead, he heard the receptionist calling out in Russian, followed by a different voice that the announcer recognized but Zvezda didn't.

"Your Holiness," said the announcer, switching back to Ukrainian.

Zvezda spat at the salutation.

"Please, tell our listeners why you are not meeting with Ecumenical Patriarch as planned."

The impostor's voice made him sick. "Oh, but I am," he responded cheerfully. "I am on my way now."

"On your way where?" Zvezda heard the announcer's confusion.

"To Patmos," said the imposter.

"This is a surprise to most of our listeners. And myself, I must admit." The announcer chided the imposter. "Please, can you explain where that is, and why you are going there?"

The radio crackled while the imposter responded, but Zvezda could hear him say that Patmos was a Greek island 400 kilometers from Istanbul in the Aegean Sea. "The Ecumenical Patriarch's residence is in Patmos, not in Istanbul."

"So, why did you go to Istanbul?"

"To get a charter flight."

Zvezda studied the map and calculated. He could never reach Patmos in time. But the artillery shell's kill zone would reach the imposter's hotel by the Hagia Sophia. He had to stop him from going anywhere.

Grabbing the trigger, he saw a speedboat full of Turkish police heading straight for him and shouting on a megaphone.

He held his cross in one hand and the trigger in the other.

Fixing his gaze on the approaching police, he kissed the cross and flipped the trigger with his last thought for eternity.

For Russia.

CHAPTER 17

GROUND ZERO

TOP SECRET – RED
Handle via Agent Channels Only
Date: October 10, 1993
To: K3
From: Chief of Station Almaty
Subject: SITREP Fertilizer

(TS) 1. White checked into Hotel Kazakhstan, room 1204, this morning.

(TS) 2. Six hundred kilos of ninety percent enriched uranium have been identified at a nuclear fuel factory in Ust-Kamenogorsk in a concrete room secured with only a rusty padlock.

(TS) 3. Beryllium, which is used as a neutron deflector in nuclear bombs, was found at the same plant in a crate with "Tehran, Iran" stenciled on the side.

END

TOP SECRET – RED
Exempt from automatic downgrade

*T*he explosion pierced Hagia Sophia's eastern windows with blazing orange and punched the air with a deafening roar that shook the ground, setting off sirens and alarms all around. The ancient monument had endured worse shocks in its history and stood solidly while the tourists and visitors froze in momentary silence before breaking into a polyglot clamor of screams and shouts that rose above the racket outside.

"It's a bomb," shouted an American voice.

"What the hell?" said Neilson, swinging his head in alarm. The shock wave reverberated in his chest the way it used to during the NATO theatre exercises in Germany. "That was no fucking firecracker!"

The translator's eyes searched the cavernous church, where people milled anxiously; craning their heads outside as if that would help them to see what had happened. A woman in a headscarf shouted repeatedly.

"What's she saying?" asked Kruger. Adrenaline raced at his heart.

"She's saying: 'It's an attack by the Kurds'," responded the guide, as if he agreed.

"If that was a bomb, it was one serious piece of artillery," said Kruger, noticing the monk's odd reaction to the explosion. When he raised his head, he gazed at them with wonder. Then he held out his hands, visibly surprised by their existence. Rising from his knees, he leaned against the wall and reached for the mosaic to touch it reverently

The monk turned to the Americans, his face expressing a mix of happiness and excitement. But he quickly turned puzzled. "Anton!" he exclaimed, pushing past them into the museum where babies cried and men shouted. Police sirens approached from all points in the distance.

A passing guard barked at them.

"The building is being evacuated. We must go," said the guide, herding them out of the hall and into the cavernous nave where people streamed towards the exit. The monk went ahead, weaving his way through the crowd.

"We better go back to the hotel, if we can," said Neilson. "There will probably be roadblocks."

They emerged from Hagia Sophia's sumptuous gloom into the bright outdoor light, passing an extraordinary rotunda. Gold embossed the intricate floral motifs on its overhanging roof.

"This is the ablutions fountain," said the guide, still performing, "where people ritually washed themselves before entering the mosque. It is an exquisite example of the Turkish Rococo style."

Across the broad plazas and parks separating Hagia Sophia from the Blue Mosque, built in the cathedral's image by the Ottomans, dozens of police cars and fire engines honked and wailed in the crowded streets.

"They are blocking the road to the Caddesi Kennedy," said the guide, watching the police setting up barricades. "That is the highway a few blocks in that direction, on the sea." The guide pointed to the southeast, where a gantlet of riot police gathered by the barricades. Their shields reflected the faces of curious bystanders discussing the events in a babble of languages. A portly police official sporting a thick black moustache entered their midst, speaking loudly in Turkish.

"He says that a bomb exploded in the sea just below us," said the guide and then stopped to hear more. "Our police identified a suspicious trawler flying no flag right before the explosion but there is no trace of it left. The police are exploring a Kurdish connection."

"Could be," said Neilson, about to leave when he saw the blond monk charge into the crowd, shouting at the police officer in Russian and pointing towards the barricaded street. The crowd grumbled at the interruption and closed in on the monk, who yelled with growing emotion.

"What the…" Neilson exclaimed, watching the crowd ripple from a scuffle around the struggling monk.

"I don't know Russian," said the guide, craning his neck in curiosity.

"He keeps repeating that they have to let him through," said a man next to Neilson. A baseball cap and an NYU t-shirt framed a pleasant face. "He's saying that he knows what happened."

The man lifted his chin at the monk who pushed against the brawny police officer. "He's babbling nonsense about nuclear weapons and patriarchs and potatoes. The guy's nuts," he said and went on his way.

The policeman handcuffed the struggling monk and pulled him to his feet with a forceful shake. Grabbing his shoulder with a beefy hand, he pushed him to a police car.

"I'll bet he knew something," Neilson said, recalling the monk's bizarre behavior. "He didn't seem surprised by the explosion. But he looked really surprised to be alive."

Neilson turned in the direction of the hotel. "And he said 'nuclear weapons destroy Istanbul' right before the explosion. You think there could be anything to that?"

Kruger could only think about the trip home to his wife and daughter. For a while, he said nothing. "If that had been nuclear, we'd be dead," he whispered as they walked through clouds of steam and smoke fragrant with roasted meat, mint and yoghurt. Vendors outside the hotel displayed kebabs and halvah, shouting greetings at them like long lost friends. The four minarets of Hagia Sophia rose above the rooftops.

"I wonder what happened," said Neilson.

"Don't know," said Kruger, staring at the logo of the Bosporus Hotel emblazoned on the glass entry. It was a step closer to home. "But I don't envy a little blond monk that has to do time in a Turkish prison."

CHAPTER 18:

KAZAKHSTAN?

FAXNEWS-UKRAINE

Nuclear Roundup

November 18, 1993 (Kiev, Ukraine). Parliament approved the START treaty, committing the country to destroy 36 percent of its strategic launchers and to decommission 42 percent of its warheads. The remaining weapons' fate is uncertain. Legislators refused to take up the Nuclear Non-proliferation Treaty, which would make Ukraine a non-nuclear state. "How can we declare ourselves non-nuclear if we have nuclear weapons on our territory?" said one lawmaker. "It's logically absurd."

December 16, 1993 (Kiev, Ukraine). The American Envoy secretly visited Kiev for three-way talks with Ukraine and Russia. It is the first time since the USSR's collapse that representatives of Ukraine, Russia and the United States sat down together.

December 18, 1993 (Kiev, Ukraine). The US signed an agreement with the Ukrainian State Committee on Nuclear and Radiation Safety to develop a state system of control, accounting and physical protection of nuclear materials.

December 20, 1993 (Kiev, Ukraine). Ukraine has taken 17 SS-24s off readiness and removed their warheads. It will take 20 off readiness by the end of the year. It will deactivate the remaining 26 in 1994 if Ukraine, Russia and the United States successfully complete their 3-way talks.

January 14, 1994 (Moscow, Russia). The Presidents of Ukraine, Russia and the United States signed a Trilateral Statement committing Ukraine to transfer all of its nuclear warheads to Russia for dismantlement. In exchange, the United States will pay Russia 60 million dollars to provide Ukraine with civilian nuclear fuel. Ukraine will also get security guarantees from the US, Russia and the United Kingdom. The agreement reaffirmed the US commitment to assist Ukraine with the safe dismantlement of the weapons through the Nunn-Lugar program.

March 15, 1994 (Kiev, Ukraine). Ukraine shipped its first trainload of 200 warheads to Russia. They expect to ship a trainload each month. It will take two years to remove all 1,800 warheads.

END

TOP SECRET – WHITE

Handle via Agent Channels Only

Date: April 15, 1994

To: K3

From: Field Agent White in Kazakhstan

Subject: SITREP Fertilizer

(TS)   1. I located the truck that delivered the wines from Dikanka. There is no sign of the HEU. It could be anywhere at this point.

(U)   2. The Turkish Envoy visited Almaty today and expressed his government's concerns about Kurdish terrorism after the bomb explosion in Istanbul last October.

END

TOP SECRET – WHITE

Exempt from automatic downgrade

TOP SECRET – LAVENDER

Handle via Agent Channels Only

Date: April 30, 1994

To: K3

From: Interim Chief of Station Kiev

Subject: SITREP Rasputin

(U)   1. Fred Wexler of Defense Systems Analysis has arrived in Kiev. He complained that the U.S. government is very slow in reviewing Nunn-Lugar projects and still has not approved his company's proposal to introduce a computerized inventory system for nuclear materials.

(S)   2. Stanislav Rozpad has accepted your offer of 2,000 dollars a month for consulting services on non-proliferation. He said there are 165 pounds of unsecured HEU at the Kharkiv Institute of Physics and Technology. He suggested that the United States buy it.

(S)   3. I haven't seen Neilson and Kruger in Kiev since they left last October.

(TS)   4. Take this as my notice. I am quitting to become the Director of Intellectual Property at my wife Sveta's business school for women. If you find yourself in need of excellent administrators and managers in Kiev, we are the place for you!

END

---

*S*ongbirds trilled the distance as the evening sun caressed Dan Kruger's face with a languid touch and he breathed deeply of the salty air. The lagoon reflected the pale blue sky and wispy clouds promised more days of sun. Pleasant days had grown into relaxing weeks on Coco the Greek's private island somewhere on the Aegean Sea. Where didn't matter. Here felt good enough.

Oksana Beniuk Kruger gurgled cheerfully in her bassinet, chewing on her rattle, oblivious to the luxurious surroundings. Every day, Kruger gave thanks for the Turkish coal business. After the first contract, they did two more.

Coco's invitation for them to visit his island for a few weeks of sailing and snorkeling came at a welcome time, when the baby was healthy but still not mobile. Neil Neilson had brought his daughter Susie, who found Oksana a fascinating source for hours of occupation. They shared a well appointed guest cottage with a fully equipped office and a marble terrace furnished with comfortable lounges and urns of flowers. A maid came every day.

Jean emerged from the house in a sky blue sarong carrying a pitcher of margaritas, followed by Neilson holding a tray of salt rimmed glasses and Susie with a bowl of guacamole and chips.

"My mother just called," said Jean, placing the pitcher on the wrought iron table by a potted begonia. "Can you believe it? She's marrying some Ukrainian immigrant that she met at church. It's next month and we're invited."

Jean had blossomed after the painful pregnancy and months of anxiety. Her skin glowed and her hair lightened in the sun.

"Good for her," Kruger said. "Maybe that's why she's eased up on me. She's finally getting some." Slava Beniuk's visits had grown less frequent after the baby grew stronger.

While Jean poured margaritas into the glasses, Neilson pulled a roll of paper from the pocket of his shorts. "We're real popular today," he said. "I found three faxes for us in the office." He unrolled the sheets and flattened them on the table.

"This one's from the Patriarch," he said, squinting through his reading glasses at the broken English. The Ukrainian prelate did not have good translators. "He's thanking us for the joint venture. The Ecumenical Patriarch still hasn't recognized the Independent Ukrainian Orthodox Church. But he is hopeful. With all the money his church got, he wants to buy a Patriarch-mobile, like the Pope's."

"So long as he stays in business with us," said Kruger, sitting up on the lounge with a glance at the baby, who reached happily at a plush yellow bunny that Susie dangled over the basinet. He picked up a margarita and leaned against a stone planter. "What else?" he asked, motioning at the faxes with his drink.

Neilson picked up the second fax. "It's from Annette's lawyer," he said. "Annette has joined a radical feminist commune and has to renounce any dependency on men, including alimony. So, they're dropping all their demands in the divorce."

"Nice," said Kruger. "Happy ending."

"Now it's time for you to find someone else," said Jean.

Neilson thought of Cristina Smythe. She revealed herself to be a woman of many talents and mysteries, and he very much enjoyed their interlude. He wondered what happened to her. "Maybe," he said, ending the personal conversation by picking up the last fax. "This one's from Kostya and Zoya."

Kruger massaged Jean's neck. "What do they have to say?" Kostya and Zoya handled the Ukrainian side of the coal business.

"Well, they got married," said Neilson.

"Good luck with that one," said Kruger.

"From what you told me, though, they treat each other very well," said Jean, scooping some guacamole with a tortilla chip.

"They do," said Neilson, reading the rest of the letter.

Kruger sipped his margarita. "But they're always squabbling about obscure points of history and ideology." At least their linguistic impasse settled into a bilingual truce, with Kostya speaking Ukrainian and Zoya speaking Russian, and both understanding each other perfectly.

"Listen to this," Neilson announced. "They have an offer of 500-million cubic meters of natural gas in Kazakhstan but neither of them can leave the Kiev business to explore it."

He threw the fax on the table and Kruger picked it up.

"Kazakhstan?" he said. "What do you think, Neil? Want to expand your geographic horizons?"

Neilson lifted his eyebrows with interest, his gaze resting affectionately on his daughter as she gamboled in lagoon's shallow waters. "I am ready for something new," he said. "But I don't know about doing business in that part of the world. Who knows if the Kazakh government doesn't have wacko rules that will make us form joint ventures with breakaway churches."

And forge letters, Kruger said to himself. He had told Jean after the first coal deal went smoothly.

"They're mostly Muslims," said Jean.

"There was that terrorist bombing in Istanbul, too," said Kruger.

"Yeah, and that strange monk going on about nuclear weapons destroying Istanbul," said Neilson, leaning back in his chair with his drink. "I guess we'll never know what that was about."

CHAPTER 19:

WHY

*L*ieutenant Ivan Veresen brushed the ashes from his cigarette off the browned pages of the ledger and saw lunchtime fast approaching on his watch. Even the swill and potatoes that passed for rations would quiet his grumbling stomach.

Ignoring the "No Smoking" sign at the entrance to the open air shelter, he walked into the musty gloom where stacked crates of weapons and ammunition reached up to the ceiling. Some of the materiél belonged to Uzin, for defending the strategic nuclear bomber base against a conventional attack. But most of the ordnance came by way of the Eastern Bloc countries' Cold War arsenals, hastily withdrawn when Soviet armies departed during the USSR's final days. When Ukraine became independent, it found itself with mountains of weaponry.

Sweat poured down Lt. Vlad Moroz's pimply skin from opening the heavy crates to identify and count their contents. "Tell me again why we're doing this," he said with exasperation. It was tedious work, visually inspecting each weapon and checking it against the log book.

"Orders from Kiev. They need to know the exact number of conventional weapons on Ukrainian territory to comply with the treaty on conventional weapons in Europe."

"So, we have to count every fucking artillery shell?" Vlad griped. "I thought the treaty only covers delivery systems."

Ivan stamped out his cigarette until not a wisp of smoke remained. Pulling a pen from behind his ear, he lifted the ledger. "Those are our orders, so let's at least get started and then we can go eat."

"Whatever," said Vlad, prying open a crate of artillery. "OF45s," he announced, glancing at the color codes. "These are ours. I remember when we repainted them on Soviet Officer's Day."

"It's your handwriting in the ledger," said Ivan.

"UR660." Vlad read from one of the shells. "UR670," read another. Taking each shell and placing it on the ground to reach for another, Vlad counted all of URs between 660 and 670 – except one.

Ivan scanned the ledger. "We're missing UR666."

"Shit," said Vlad, studying the artillery. "I know what happened. We were all in a rush to go drinking. And one of the dumb recruits accidentally painted one of the shells with nuclear markings. I ordered him to change it but then General Smirnov distracted me." He waved towards the nuclear depots where the strategic warheads still lay while Kiev, Moscow and Washington scheduled their removal. "Someone must've thought it was a ZBV3 shell and put it in nuclear storage."

"Well, it's not here now," said Ivan, closing his ledger. "Russia took out all of the tactical nukes by May 1992."

"So, what do we do? Report it missing? It happened on my watch."

Ivan appreciated the implications. "We'll fix it," he said, turning to leave the depot. "Let's go have lunch."

Vlad balled his fists in the pockets of his camouflage pants and followed. "At least it wasn't *really* a nuclear weapon."

FAXNEWS-UKRAINE

Nuclear Roundup

May 18, 1995 (Kiev, Ukraine). A State System of Material Control and Accounting (MC&A) has been established in Ukraine but no significant improvements in Physical Protection have been made.

January 1, 1996 (Moscow, Russia). There is currently no single, complete and readily accessible repository of records for nuclear weapons in Russia. The whereabouts of Soviet warheads withdrawn from outside Russia and subsequently eliminated or stored remain uncertain.

March 1, 1996 (Washington, D.C.). The United States will spend $330 million over the next six years to finance the installation of monitoring and surveillance equipment at storage areas for fissionable materials in Ukraine, Belarus, Kazakhstan, Georgia, Latvia, Uzbekistan, and Russia. US aid for nuclear security has increased from $2 million in 1994 to $70 million in 1995 and is expected to grow to $100 million in 1996.

March 18, 1996 (Moscow, Russia). Two officers in the 12th Directorate told an investigative reporter about 150 nuclear artillery shells transferred from Ukraine to Russia in 1991. While accounted for on paper, the officers suspect that Ukraine still has the weapons.

May 31, 1996 (Kiev, Ukraine). The last strategic nuclear warhead from Ukraine was delivered to Russia.

November 28, 2002 (Kharkiv, Ukraine). The Kharkiv Institute of Physics and Technology is refusing U.S. offers to buy 165 pounds of highly enriched uranium it has in a lightly guarded storeroom. Ukrainian officials offered to sell the material in 1993, but the United States never responded.

April 12, 2010 (Washington, D.C.). At a 47-nation nuclear summit, the Fourth Ukrainian President agreed to surrender the 165 pounds of highly enriched uranium at the Kharkiv Institute of Physics and Technology.

May 1, 2013 (West Chester, PA). As of this writing, Ukraine still does not have a secure nuclear inventory system. Far fewer than half of the highly enriched uranium and plutonium at various facilities across the former USSR have such systems.

Faxnews-Ukraine - The 1st source of English language news about Ukraine

---

THE END

REVIEW REQUEST

If you enjoyed this book, I'd be grateful if you would write a positive review. In independent publishing, reviews are like currency and really make a difference. All you need to do is go to the *Doing Bizness* Amazon page and scroll down to the reviews where you'll see a big button that says "Write a Customer Review". Click it and you'll be good to go. The URL is http://amzn.to/11xZE2s. Or just search my last name on Amazon to find it. Thank you for your support.

All good things,

Mary Mycio

Turn the page for an excerpt from *Wormwood Forest: A Natural History of Chernobyl*

Wormwood

And the third angel sounded, and there fell a great star from heaven, burning as it were a lamp, and it fell upon the third part of the rivers, and upon the fountains of waters
And the name of the star is called Wormwood; and the third part of the waters became wormwood; and many men died of the waters because they were made bitter.
Revelations 8:10-11

In the years since the 1986 Chernobyl nuclear disaster spewed radiation around the globe and smudged the map of the then- Soviet Union with heavy contamination, the ver y word "Chernobyl" has become a synonym for "horrific disaster," conjuring the frightful radioactive deserts that landscape Atomic Age science fiction and resonate deeply in modern imaginations haunted by the specter of nuclear war.

Surely, whenever I thought about the irradiated lands 50 miles north of Kiev, it was like contemplating a black hole. All I could picture was a dead zone, like a giant parking lot paved with asphalt or a barren desert of dust and ash where nothing could grow and nothing living could survive without protective gear. Only gloomy shades of black and gray colored my mental images.

But when I first visited the Chernobyl region, 10 years after the disaster, I was surprised to find that the dominant color was green. My notes from that trip are filled with emphatically underlined and circled comments like "feral fields," "forests," and "wildlife?!" Contrary to the myths and imagery, Chernobyl's land had become a unique, new eco-system. Defying the gloomiest predictions, it had come back to life as Europe's largest nature sanctuary, teeming with wildlife. Like the forests, fields, and swamps of their unexpectedly inviting habitat, the animals are all radioactive. To the astonishment of just about everyone, they are also thriving.

But to appreciate the land's extraordinary resurrection, you first have to understand its demise.

Pripyat's old wedding registry was not easy to find, even though we had the address. Despite the barbed wire perimeter around this radioactive ghost town less than two miles from the Chernobyl power plant, the hull of an empty high-rise on Friendship of Nations Street had been emptied of anything with the slightest value, including most of the metal signs that announced shops and services. Former residents and looters had stripped apartments and offices down to their faded wallpaper. Only one empty room hinted at its former function, probably because the cardboard sign on the door, reading "School of Communist Labor," was too worthless to steal. But there was no sign of a wedding registry.

A perplexed Rimma Kyselytsia led our little group of explorers outside into a small square surrounded by empty apartment buildings. She studied the number painted on the side of one building and shook her blond curls in confusion. "It's the right address. So, where is it?"

Since Rimma was the guide, my other companion—a botanist named Svitlana Bidna—and I shrugged helplessly.

My dosimeter beeped slowly. The radiation monitor's liquid crystal screen displayed 80 microroentgens an hour. That was several times normal background levels, which range from 15 to 25 in most places. Decontamination, rain, and time have long since washed off much of the radioactive grime that coated the town after Chernobyl's fourth reactor exploded in the wee hours of April 26, 1986. Pripyat was the plant's bedroom community. Heralded as the world's youngest city when it opened its doors in the mid-1970s, Pripyat also turned out to be its shortest lived.

A short flight of concrete stairs sprouting saplings and moss led to the back of the building where Rimma explored a row of what seemed to have once been stores and offices. The glass storefronts were all shattered, exposing the bare rooms to the elements, and she quickly spied a faded red carpet runner, lying dirty and twisted with shards of glass, plaster, and deep piles of yellowed paper.

"This is it!" she exclaimed, vindicated in her guiding skill. Rimma was a Tatar with aquarium eyes and a matter-of-fact but realistic attitude towards her radioactive workplace.

The red carpet runner once led couples to secular Soviet marriage in the Pripyat Registry of Citizens' Civil Status. Known by its Ukrainian acronym as a *ZAHS (ZAGS* in Russian), the office was not merely a marriage registry. *ZAHS*s documented the legal passages in Soviet citizens' personal lives from cradle to grave, issuing birth certificates and death certificates and everything in between.

The deep piles of brittle paper on the floor were *ZAHS* forms and applications. Ivory cards informing brides and grooms of their wedding dates were mixed up with spilled stacks of divorce applications and forms to apply for "compensation in the form of gold wedding rings." Hanging lopsided on the back wall, a red-lettered cardboard sign exhorted newlyweds: "Stand on the threshold of your introduction to the deep familial and social traditions of the Soviet people."

In the neighboring room, two tall bookshelves had toppled over, spilling dozens of pulp folders containing the *ZAHS* archives into a moldy pile. Although the 1986 archives were missing, the records went back to the early 1970s, when the town first opened its doors. Judging by one fat folder, many couples applied to cut to the front of the wedding queue because they had already had a child together.

Sixteen marriage ceremonies took place on the last full day of human life in Pripyat. The only public record of those nuptials, tinged in hindsight with so much sadness, can be viewed in a five-minute film at Kiev's Chernobyl museum. The split-second scene of the bride and groom leaving the storefront wedding registry is too fleeting to see their expressions, but the point of the wedding in the silent and grainy film was to show that April 26, 1986, was an ordinary, if unusually warm, Saturday afternoon in Pripyat. Oblivious to the radioactive cloud invisibly blanketing them, couples wheeled infants in strollers. Toddlers in shorts kicked a ball around a dirt playground. Women in sleeveless summer dresses gathered outdoors under a vendor's umbrella, in the large groups that always signified something (anything) being sold in the shortage-ridden Soviet Union.

But the anonymous KGB cameraman knew that something was wrong. Gamma rays left flashes of light on the scene he filmed of two men in camouflage and gas masks nodding to an unprotected and obviously surprised civilian. Armored personnel carriers drove down Pripyat's boulevards, while uniformed officers checked radiation on a truck's tires. Water trucks washed the streets with foamy detergent, leaving puddles in which sparrows splashed. From the roof of a Pripyat high-rise, the cameraman filmed the Chernobyl plant, shrouded in such a thick cloud of smoke and haze that only its dim outline was visible.

What did not get recorded on film was the nighttime explosion that ripped through the Number 4 reactor complex, spewing flames, sparks, and chunks of burning radioactive material into the air and, subsequently, around the northern hemisphere. Red-hot pieces of nuclear fuel and graphite fell on the roof, starting 30 fires and causing the roof to collapse into the reactor hall. By dawn the roof fires had been put out by 37 fire crews working without protection or dosimeters. Many became ill with acute radiation sickness. Thirty-one died, but at that point no one knew that the explosion had completely exposed the reactor core. The government commission from Moscow didn't arrive until Saturday night, and it wasn't until Sunday morning that its members could helicopter over the cavernous hulk to see that the explosion had ignited an extremely intense graphite fire. The graphite fire was releasing millions of curies of radioactivity that lit the air above the ruined reactor with an eerie glow. The crisis was actually an unprecedented disaster and it was far from over.

That morning, in his apartment not far from the *ZAHS* office, Volodymyr Pasichnyk had been watching his teenaged son playing with the dial on the TV set when the receiver suddenly tuned in on an odd frequency. "There was no picture, just talk, probably by walkie-talkie," he recalled when I talked with him 15 years later. "They were talking about 'people in hospitals' and 'hundreds of buses to Pripyat'." Like most people in Pripyat—all of whose lives were somehow connected with the plant—he had heard rumors about something bad at the fourth reactor block. At that moment he understood the enormity of what had happened. The town was being evacuated.

The official announcement came on Pripyat radios at 10 o'clock Sunday morning. In only four hours, beginning at 2:00 p.m., 1,100 empty buses drove into Pripyat and drove out with nearly all of the town's 45,000 residents in a convoy that was more than 10 miles long.

Officials told them the evacuation would only last three days. Perhaps they really meant it. But that was before anyone knew that the graphite fire would melt the fuel and belch the daily equivalent of several Hiroshima bombs for 10 full days, altogether releasing five times as much radioactivity as the initial explosion.

Pripyat could never be inhabited again. The ritual human cycles of birth and marriage, divorce and death, recorded by *ZAHS* scribes in the thick pulpy ledgers of Soviet bureaucracy, ended on April 26, 1986. And the stacks of cards for secular baptisms, with spaces for the names of new Soviet citizens, will never be filled in.

BIBLICAL BOTANY

Svitlana Bidna, my botanist companion, walked with Rimma and me on the thick moss carpets strewn over Pripyat's crumbling asphalt roads, giving the tangled overgrowth of vegetation names and clarity. The straight rows of poplars lining the streets were planted when the town was built. The asters, still blooming in late October, were once garden flowers that enlivened the cinder-block sterility of the new Soviet town. But poplars are now growing out of storefronts and stairwells. Asters have taken to the wild in large lavender fields. And a diverse profusion of wild species are filling the cracks in the concrete and the voids left by people. Svitlana, who has been studying the town's transmutation to forest after Chernobyl, predicts that the buildings will stand half a century, perhaps. Though, if left to itself, the greenery will consume most of the asphalt roads and concrete plazas in another decade or so.

251

Lichens such as the bright orange *Xanthoria* secrete chemicals that destroy the crystalline structure of minerals in concrete. Acids in the mosses that grow on dead leaves soften asphalt, crumbling it into pebbles. Birch, maple, and pine trees sprout from the cracks, buckling pavements with their roots and exposing more crevices for greenery to grow. Reeds grow in patches where the shallow water table is recreating once-drained swamps. A forest of silver birch, willow, wild pear, and pine fills the former soccer field, and islands of grass covering broad concrete plazas sprout tall bushes of false indigo, its long flower clusters dried into black tassels.

Pripyat was coming to resemble one of those fabled lost cities, devoured by jungle. Abandonment echoed in every corner of the crumbling monument to the disaster. A Ferris wheel and bumper cars rust away in a tiny amusement park, scheduled to open on May 1, 1986, and never used. The town pool's three-story glass facade had completely shattered into deep piles mixed with tiles from the wall mosaics that resembled incomplete jigsaw puzzles, with chalky green lichen replacing the missing pieces and making it impossible to tell what they once depicted. Shrubs and saplings grew in kindergartens scattered with tiny shoes, broken toys, and heartbreakingly small gas masks. We climbed up a high-rise where Svitlana showed us a good-sized birch tree growing from the center of a kitchen emptied of everything but an overturned table.

"Pripyat began returning to nature as soon as the people left, and there was no one to trim and prune and weed," said Svitlana as we started heading back to our car. "It takes a lot of human effort to maintain urban landscapes."

Back near the wedding registry, Rimma crouched down to a short bush that had grown out of a crack between the road and the curb. It was about a foot tall, with small cottony flowers growing directly from purplish stems.

She pulled off one of the leaves and crushed it between her fingers for me to sniff the unpleasant, varnishy aroma, reminiscent of shoe polish.

"What is it?" I asked, wrinkling my nose.

"*Chernobyl,*" she said, using the common—but incorrect—pronunciation. In fact, chernobyl with an "e" is the Russianized version of the Ukrainian word *chornobyl.* You won't find *chernobyl* or *chornobyl* in most Russian dictionaries, except in reference to the disaster, although the word *chernobyl'nyk* is used in some Russian regions in reference to the herb. But because the first version has become the commonly accepted spelling for the disaster and the nuclear station, I will use *Chernobyl,* with an "e," to refer to them. I will use *Chornobyl,* with an "o," to refer to the herb and the town.

"That's wormwood, right?" I asked, hoping to finally clarify the botanical question at the heart of the Chernobyl disaster's putative biblical symbolism. It is often said that the meaning of the Ukrainian word *chornobyl* is "wormwood," and the suggestion that the disaster fulfilled the biblical prophecy of the Wormwood star that augured Armageddon resonated deeply with the fear of nuclear apocalypse. But the botany was actually more complex.

"'*Chornobyl*' is *Artemisia vulgaris.* 'Wormwood' is *Artemisia absinthium.* The Ukrainian common name is *polyn*," Svitlana said, handing me a leaf from a different plant that looked much like *A. vulgaris,* except it was covered with fine silky hairs that gave it a whitish tinge. As I looked around, I noticed that the plants were everywhere.

I crushed it to release the volatile oil, much more pungent than the first plant.

Botanically and chemically, *Artemesia vulgaris* is so similar to *A. absinthium* that *A. vulgaris* is also sometimes called "wormwood," though "mugwort" is a more common English name. In Ukrainian, as well, *polyn* and *chornobyl* are sometimes used synonymously. Both plants are hardy perennials, tolerant of poor soil and thus plentiful in the sandy lands of the Polissia region—where the twelfth-century town of Chornobyl took its name from the plant and, in turn, gave it to the twentieth-century nuclear station seven miles away. Both are bitter medicinal herbs and natural pest repellants, ridding fleas from the home, slugs from the garden, and worms from the body. And both get their pungent fragrance from thujone, an organic toxin thought to be the psychoactive agent in absinthe, the infamous wormwood liqueur banned by most Western countries a century ago. Absinthe was said to produce an unusual intoxication and was highly addictive, although modern skeptics contend that the "high" and the habit most probably came from drinking the 75 percent alcohol absinthe required to dissolve the thujone and prevent it from clouding the emerald solution.

But if the thujone in *Artemisia vulgaris* is dilute, it is concentrated in *A. absinthium.* A crushed leaf of *polyn*-wormwood is much more pungent than a crushed leaf of *chornobyl*-mugwort. It is also more bitter and much more toxic, which is why animals happily nibble mugwort but leave wormwood alone. Even other plants avoid it. *A. absinthium's* extremely bitter chemicals wash off the leaves and into the soil, poisoning it for other plants.

Given its natural repellant properties, many folk believed wormwood to have supernatural banishing powers. Mugwort, too, has magical properties, though none so potent. In Ukrainian folklore, both plants ward off the seductive and dangerous water nymphs called *rusalkas*, who lured victims with beautiful songs and then tickled them to death in crystal underwater lairs.

In Christian legend, when the biblical serpent was expelled from Eden, wormwood sprang in its trail to prevent its return. Indeed, the herb is a frequent biblical symbol for bitterness, calamity, and sorrow; its use to name the third sign of the apocalypse that opened this chapter conjured the desolation that would follow the end of the world.

In the wake of the Chernobyl explosion, few people in the officially atheist Soviet Union had Ukrainian-language Bibles. But some of those who did noted that the word "wormwood" in the Wormwood star of the book of Revelation was translated as *polyn*—and was a very close botanical cousin to *chornobyl*. Suddenly, the biblical prophecy seemed to acquire new meaning: wormwood was radiation, and it presaged the nuclear apocalypse that would end the world. The story spread like wildfire through the notorious Soviet rumor mill and as far as Washington, D.C., where President Ronald Reagan was said to have believed it, too.

I first learned of the apocalyptic connection about a month after the disaster, when a Ukrainian friend in Poland wrote me about it in a letter. I had just moved to Los Angeles from New York City in what was supposed to have been my "American experiment." I didn't want to sever my Ukrainian-American roots entirely. But I did want to try living without the sometimes suffocating support of the ethnic ghetto that was an integral part of my life in Manhattan. Chernobyl put an end to that experiment before it even started. I recall crying on the phone with my best friend in New York and realizing that only someone with Ukrainian roots could share the pain I felt contemplating the swirl of televised speculation about the disaster's calamitous effects on a land that I had been raised to believe was very important to me but one that I had never seen because it was shrouded by an impenetrable Iron Curtain.

Chernobyl's putative apocalyptic connection became so wide-spread, combining fears of radiation with apocalyptic dread, that the state-controlled Soviet media took the highly unusual step of running interviews with leaders of the Russian Orthodox Church (the most tolerated religion in the USSR) to debunk it, largely by arguing that no man could know when the end of time was near.

Perhaps their arguments would have been better served by botany. Aside from the fact that *polyn* and *chornobyl* are different species of *Artemisia*, it is unlikely that the wormwood in Revelation referred to either of them. *Artemisia judaica* is widely cited as the most likely candidate for biblical wormwood.

But judging by a cursory perusal of the 975 results that an Internet search of "chernobyl wormwood" turned up, Armageddon-watchers seem untroubled by such technicalities (though they are troubled by others, such as how anyone can prove that "a third of the waters were made bitter" as predicated by Revelation 8-10). For them, Chernobyl equals wormwood, and the end of the earth as we know it is near. Far be it for me to dismiss biblical prophesy, but as we left the crumbling and *Artemisia*-choked landscape of Pripyat, it seemed that the only end Chernobyl heralded for certain was that of the Soviet Union.

***

This excerpt from *Wormwood Forest: A Natural History of Chernobyl* was reprinted with the permission of Joseph Henry Press. You can read the rest here: http://amzn.to/13AsiGb

www.ingramcontent.com/pod-product-compliance
Lightning Source LLC
Chambersburg PA
CBHW070552130626
46556CB00001B/133